Also by Cornelia Read

A Field of Darkness
The Crazy School
Invisible Boy

valley *of* ashes

by cornelia read

GRAND CENTRAL
PUBLISHING

LARGE PRINT

Grand Central Publishing
Hachette Book Group
237 Park Avenue
New York, NY 10017

www.HachetteBookGroup.com

Printed in the United States of America

RRD-C

First Edition: August 2012

10 9 8 7 6 5 4 3 2 1

Grand Central Publishing is a division of Hachette Book Group, Inc. The Grand Central Publishing name and logo is a trademark of Hachette Book Group, Inc.

The Hachette Speakers Bureau provides a wide range of authors for speaking events. To find out more, go to www.hachettespeakersbureau .com or call (866) 376-6591.

The publisher is not responsible for websites (or their content) that are not owned by the publisher.

Library of Congress Cataloging-in-Publication Data

Read, Cornelia.
   Valley of ashes / by Cornelia Read. — 1st ed.
      p. cm.
   ISBN 978-0-446-51136-0 (hc) — ISBN 978-1-4555-1355-0 (large print ed.)   1. Marital conflict—Fiction.   2. Life change events— Fiction.   3. Psychological fiction.   I. Title.
   PS3618.E22V35 2012
   813'.6—dc23
                                                              2011049675

LARGE TYPE F Rea

For Frederick Harvey Read and Rick Dage
Requiescat in pace et in amore.

valley
of
ashes

PART I

Spring 1995
Boulder, Colorado

[A]fter a child is born the lives of its
mother and father diverge, so that where
before they were living in a state of some
equality, now they exist in a sort of feu-
dal relation to each other. A day spent at
home caring for a child could not be more
different from a day spent working in
an office. Whatever their relative merits,
they are days spent on opposite sides of the
world.

—Rachel Cusk, *A Life's Work:*
On Becoming a Mother

1

When we first moved to Boulder, I was entirely too happy—a state of being so rare in my experience that I found it rather terrifying.

My twin daughters, Parrish and India, were beautiful, precocious, and brimming with good health. My husband, Dean, was happily successful at his new job and my best, most trusted friend. We lived at the eastern feet of the Rocky Mountains in a cozy old house on the loveliest street of a charming university town.

The air was fresh, the sky was blue—our yard a lush and maple-shaded green, our mellow brick front porch banked in the early spring with a cobalt-and-amethyst embarrassment of lilac, iris, and grape hyacinth.

Everything I'd ever wanted, not least the fleeting belief that Boulder might heal the halves of me, split since childhood between New York and California.

Hubris.

Sorrow is always your own, offering no temptation to fickle gods. Fucking joy, on the other hand? You might as well string your heart from the ceiling for use as a frat-party piñata.

We'd lived in Colorado for three months now, and somehow everything about my marriage had shifted. Not in a good way.

Dean traveled a great deal for work, and when he was home he no longer liked me very much.

I didn't know why, exactly, but it was hard for me to blame him: Most days, I didn't like me a whole hell of a lot, either.

I was exhausted. And lonely. And really shitty at the whole housewife thing. And just so fucking *sad*, even though I loved my kids and Dean with great fierceness and should've been overjoyed with my fabulous luck, right?

It was just…well, I had this constant creeping terror that I didn't deserve any of the good parts, that I wasn't holding up my end of the bargain. That fear wafted across the bottom of everything, like dry-ice mist rippling along the floor of some cheesy horror-movie set.

And also I should've been eating nothing but salads and taking up jogging or something. Plus washing my hair more often.

But mostly I really, really wanted to be able to sleep for three straight days.

I often found myself thinking of this French kid, Pascal. We'd met one college summer while I was crashing in Eliot House at Harvard with some pals who were actually attending classes there.

Pascal gave himself an odd punky haircut in his dorm room one day with a razor trimmer before wandering around Boston Common for an afternoon, thereby enduring catcalls of derision from every last roving gang of blue-collar youth.

He used to be cool, Pascal said of himself that night in dining hall, *but now they call him "Maggot Head."*

Lately, those words had echoed in my brain every time I looked in the mirror.

Snotty Parisian accent and all.

The Flatirons jut up at the western end of Colorado's high plains. Boulder's bookend: a crooked row of five-hundred-foot shark's teeth, tipped vertical eighty million years ago by the cataclysmic upthrusts that had whelped the Rockies.

You really couldn't miss them, from any vantage point in town.

I'd only ever lived away from the ocean once before, but this time I was determined not to bitch about it.

I pulled my daughters toward Pearl Street in their little red covered wagon, my throat dry in the thin mile-high air.

We were buffeted, as usual, by random clots of joggers, bikers, and Rollerbladers—obsessive jocks with an o'erweening sense of entitlement being as ubiquitous on the sidewalks of Boulder as those pompous blowhard leveraged-buyout guys and their calcium-deprived blond wives had been in the better restaurants of Manhattan.

I'd let my driver's license lapse while we lived in New York, but hadn't been in any great hurry to set up a DMV appointment out here to regain one. Joggers aside, Boulder had a terrific pedestrian culture, and we were only a couple of blocks' walk from nearly everything one could want downtown. Plus it was sunny 330 days a year here, on average, and I figured having to walk instead of ride most of the time wasn't going to do my ass any aesthetic harm.

Dean and I usually did big grocery runs on the

weekend, and me not driving also meant that he had to pitch in on that front.

The only time it sucked was when he was out of town and I needed supplies in a hurry. I was fighting my way toward Pearl Street just then because my husband was at a sales conference in New Orleans and I'd ripped a giant hole in my very last extant vacuum bag while trying to empty it into the kitchen garbage so I could use it over again.

Not that I was addicted to vacuuming or anything, but my mother was due to arrive around lunchtime in the camper she was driving across the country and my house looked like a complete shithole.

Well, okay, my house *usually* looked like a complete shithole. I just wanted my mother to think I'd made some progress, on that front at least.

Mom Lewis-and-Clarking from sea to shining sea at the wheel of her little beige secondhand Chinook meant that she and my father were both currently members of what Dad had long ago christened "the In-Car Nation." As far as I knew, this was the first thing they'd had in common since their 1967 divorce.

For her it was a lark. Dad, meanwhile, *lived* in his VW van. He was probably the only homeless guy in America to have voted for Reagan. Twice.

It was two days before Parrish and India's first birthday, hence Mom's imminence, and I also was expecting my bestest pal Ellis to show up with her own two children the following day.

I was kind of hoping the pair of them could help me figure out what the hell had gone wrong with my marriage. Or, better yet, tell me everything was totally fine and I was just being weird and paranoid for no reason at all, and then maybe let me nap a lot.

The Radio Flyer's metal handle bit into my palm. I peeked under its little white hooped-canvas roof to make sure the girls remained happily engrossed in their respective fistfuls of soggy Cheese Nips. They grinned up at me, laughing, rosy little cheeks bedizened with orange crumbs.

I had dressed them that morning in brightly contrasting turtlenecks, cotton jumpers, and striped tights—with blue jean jackets and miniature biker boots.

"Sweetness and light," I said, reaching into the wagon to stroke India's glossy dark hair and Parrish's skimpy blond fuzz, then soldiered on across Spruce at Sixteenth.

The sky was a saturated Easter-egg turquoise and it was seventy degrees out even though the sidewalks were edged with snow.

Up here, the sunlight packed a wallop you never found at sea level. Everything looked sharper, cleaner, because there wasn't as much atmosphere to buffer the rays.

I muscled the wagon up an awkwardly angled curb cut, past a row of newspaper racks. The *Daily Camera*'s headline praised local firefighters for their quick response when someone torched two cars out on Arapahoe.

I kind of hated the *Camera*, since I'd sent them my clips and résumé when we first moved here and got a curt and badly xeroxed form-rejection postcard in reply—not even the simple courtesy of "You suck so profoundly we wouldn't employ your illiterate lack-talent ass if you were the lone hack to survive a pan-galactic nuclear apocalypse, *neener neener*," on actual letterhead.

Pompous fuckers.

I reached into the next box and grabbed the *Boulder New Times*, a free weekly that hadn't yet ruled me out.

Something to live for.

On the off chance I'd ever find employment with these guys, I'd taken to stockpiling issues in a downstairs broom closet.

Ten feet past the bollards demarcating Pearl Street's pedestrianized stretch, a brand-new red

Saab convertible's tires squealed slowly against the curb: stoner parking. It still had paper dealer plates on, but there was already a MEAN PEOPLE SUCK sticker affixed to the custom ski rack.

The car's front doors popped open and two dreadlocked, PataGucci-fleeced white boys tumbled onto the sidewalk in a Lilith Fair billow of clove cigarette and patchouli.

The tall kid began torturing passersby with tuneless moans on a nose flute.

His diminutive Trustafarian friend shoved a limp crocheted rainbow skullcap in my face. "Spare change."

A demand, not a question.

"Dividend checks late again?" I asked, dragging my wagon in a wide arc around his expensively sneakered feet.

"We're *hungry*, man," said the nose flautist.

Parrish squealed with glee and threw two drool-sodden little orange squares onto the sidewalk.

"Cheese Nips," I said, pointing down. "Enjoy."

Yeah, so much for that whole not-being-a-bitch thing.

2

When the girls had first figured out how to crawl in our Manhattan apartment, Dean built them a giant, beautifully constructed playpen "fence" out of dowels and two-by-fours. Out here we put it up around the dining room table and filled it with toys to keep them occupied so I could occasionally try to get grown-up stuff done, like cleaning the rest of the house before Mom arrived.

It was about eight feet square, a nice space for them to toddle around in, not least since the landlord must have gotten a deal on orange-shag wall-to-wall carpeting so there was a cushy landing whenever they wobbled and fell over.

I changed both their diapers, scrubbed off my hands and forearms, made two quesadillas and chopped up some raw broccoli, strapped the girls into their primary-colored plastic booster seats, filled two sippy cups with milk, and started on the piles of dishes in the sink.

When they were done eating, smearing each other with melted cheese, and shot-putting various bits of lunch around the kitchen, I gently sponged their faces, hosed off their drool-and-cheddar-and-banana-slice-decked bibs, picked chunks of greasy tortilla out of their hair, and set them loose in the playpen so I could start sweeping leftover chunks off the kitchen floor (also a disgusting "antique" shade of orange, to match the shag rug and rancid-rust Formica countertops).

I yearned to win some giant Powerball jackpot just so I could buy the place and rip out every speck of orange in it, then pile it up in the dirt-road alley behind our backyard and set it all on fire.

Because the house itself was beautiful—probably built sometime in the teens. It had high ceilings and tall graceful windows and doorways.

There was a solidity to it, as well. This was a house built by people who wanted to stick around. People who'd headed west, maybe, thinking about California, but got to the foot of the Rockies and said to themselves, "You know, this is really pretty damn great right here. Let's plant a whole lot of graceful shade trees and lay out some generously Euclidean streets and make a life. We'll have wide porches and deep backyards, and we'll plant gardens and talk to our neighbors over the side fence. Take our time with things. Maybe start a university."

I looked through the door to the dining room to check on the girls. They'd both climbed into an empty Pampers carton and were grinning at each other, convulsed with laughter.

The sun was streaming in through the front windows, and as exhausted as I was, I had a sudden gut-shot of pure joy, watching them play together. I grabbed our video camera and recorded a minute of them giggling in the box.

After putting the camera back on its high shelf, I started hosing down the girls' booster-chair trays in the kitchen sink, the drain of which then backed up and spilled over onto the floor when the washing machine's rinse cycle emptied.

By the time I'd mopped that up and joined my children in the dining room, lugging the country-blue vacuum cleaner my mother-in-law gave me for Christmas some years earlier, Parrish had taken another massive dump in her diapers, removed them, crawled smack-dab through the middle of the steaming pile of crap, and left a serpentine fecal Hansel-and-Gretel trail crisscrossing the carpet under and around the table.

I dropped the vacuum and ran to grab the kitchen garbage can, a clean diaper, a box of butt-wipes, a roll of paper towels, and the dish soap, then climbed into the playpen.

By this point, Parrish had liberated a fistful of bowel product from the back of her diaper and mashed it against the table's edge.

"Dude," I said, snaking an arm around her chubby little waist to pull her away from the bur-geoning shit-mural, "contrary to popular opinion, your butt does *not* make Play-Doh."

Parrish laughed up at me and tried to grab my hair with her *merde*-encrusted fists. I captured her wrists in one hand and started the haz-mat reme-diation with a thick wad of wipes.

Ten minutes later, I had her swabbed down, re-diapered, re-dressed, and sweetly reeking of *Eau de* Johnson's-Baby-Whatever, plus all the crap scraped up, the carpet and table sudsed and lath-ered and rinsed.

I plopped her back down in the playpen, kissed the top of her downy blond head, said, "Good thing you're cute, sweetness," and grabbed the vacuum cleaner.

I plugged the damn thing in and got down on my hands and knees to begin assaulting the rest of the ugly rug fronds.

This posture was necessary because our vacuum had about as much sucking power as a pair of asthmatic elves armed with defective crazy straws, so the only way to make it actually pick up dirt and detritus was to remove all accoutrements from the hose-end before scraping it rapidly back and forth across the orange fronds of shag.

The mind-numbing number of hours I'd devoted to this activity had worn down the hose's plastic tip to a slanty point, like a giant black lipstick.

My mother-in-law vacuumed her entire house every day. And did all the accounting for the family farm. And was generally cheerful, but witty. Which is kind of tough to measure up to.

Especially since I was now lying stomach-down on the floor with both arms shoved on a blind mission into the murky depths beneath our sofa—having already raked out six desiccated baby carrots, two Popsicle sticks, half a sesame bagel, and our missing copy of *Velveteen Rabbit* (the pages of which appeared to be cemented shut with a thick mortar of hummus). I was just wondering how long it had actually been since I'd *last* vacuumed, considering the thick ruff of velveteen-ish furry stuff growing along the edges of the petrified hummus, when the doorbell rang.

I caught sight of myself in the front-hall mirror as I stood up to answer it. My skin was gray, my dark blond hair was stringy, and there was a spit-lacquered floret of broccoli affixed to the center of my right eyebrow. Also, I was fatter than I'd ever been in my life by about twenty pounds—and I hadn't exactly started out as a rail.

Awesome.

I had a second of wistfulness for my misspent youth, the years when all I worried about was scraping up a few bucks to go bar-hopping with my pal Ellis, and there were always drunk old guys mumbling about how I looked like Ingrid Bergman.

"Get a load of you now," I said to the mirror. "You'd be lucky if they said Ing*mar*."

She used to be cool, but now...

The living room behind me still resembled Bourbon Street at dawn on Ash Wednesday—minus the confetti and vomit, at least.

I took a halfhearted swipe at my verdantly cruciferous eyebrow and reached for the doorknob.

My beautiful dark-haired mother danced in off the porch and threw her arms around me. "Oh, Madeline, it's so good to *see* you!"

I hugged back with gusto, burbling my gratitude that she was visiting against the side of her neck.

Mom pulled back half a step from our embrace. "Hold still a sec."

She plucked something from my hair with her fingertips, then threw whatever it was back over her left shoulder toward the lawn.

"That was a lump of shit, I think," she said. "Did you just change the girls' diapers?"

Whereupon I nodded and burst into tears.

3

Do you miss Dean when he's away, or do you like having your own space?" asked Mom.

We were on our way to the pediatrician's office with her at the wheel of Dean's beat-up Mitsubishi Galant.

"It's hard sometimes," I said. "But then it always feels like we have new stuff to talk about when he gets home. We're happy to see each other, you know?"

She nodded. "I think the hardest thing for me when you kids were little was never feeling like I could *finish* anything...everything was always interrupted. And then your father would come home from the stock exchange and I was so hungry for what was going on in the *world*, and I wanted to be told I was doing things right after singing 'Itsy Bitsy Spider' all day. Just, 'Goodness, you've painted the dining room table—how wonderful!' But he wouldn't say anything at all, he'd just read the paper and have a cocktail and grumble through dinner."

"You guys were so young," I said. "I mean, *babies*. No wonder your entire generation got divorced. I can't imagine what it would have been like to marry the first guy I slept with, just presuming it would all work out."

"It never occurred to me that it wouldn't. Mummie and Daddy always seemed fine. I thought all you had to do was get married and then that was it."

"And cloth diapers," I said. "I remember you rinsing them out in the toilet, when Trace was a baby."

"Well, on Long Island we had a diaper man, at least. He took the dirty dipes away and delivered a pile of clean ones every week."

"I don't care," I said. "No Pampers, no Prozac? No fucking way."

She nodded. "*And* no birth control. You and Pagan were both products of the rhythm method."

"Jesus, Mom. I'd've had myself committed, just to catch up on sleep."

She laughed and turned left, into the doctor's

office parking lot. As she looked for a spot, I thought about the end of her marriage to my father.

In 1967, Mom discovered that she was pregnant a third time, and wept, and told Dad she didn't know how they could handle having another child. There wasn't enough money, and they were both so exhausted already.

He asked around on the floor of the New York Stock Exchange, where he was an ill-paid fledgling broker at the time. Someone knew someone who knew where a woman could get an abortion—from a doctor in San Juan, Puerto Rico, for four hundred dollars cash.

So Mom drove herself to Kennedy airport in the dark one morning, racked with such bad morning sickness it took her the entire drive *and* four-hour flight to finish one jelly doughnut. She ate it in little tiny pieces, trying to keep something in her stomach, some sugar in her system, so she wouldn't throw up.

When she arrived at the doctor's office, the nurse told her the price had gone up to five hundred.

Mom put her four bills on the doctor's desk. "This is all I have. Please help me."

She drove herself from the airport back to our tiny rented house in Jericho, New York, arriving home around midnight—bleeding profusely, doubled over with cramps.

She got into bed carefully, not wanting to wake up my father.

He turned toward her in the darkness as she drew the covers up to her chin.

"I've changed my mind," he said. "If you don't want to have my child, I don't want to stay married to you. I've packed my bags and I'll be leaving in the morning."

I was four years old, my sister two and a half.

In my pediatrician's parking lot, a gigantic Range Rover finally pulled out of a space.

"No, Mom, really," I said. "I couldn't have handled the shit you dealt with when we were little. You're fucking amazing."

We sat in the waiting room for twenty-five minutes, then the examining room for another ten before the doctor came in. Mom took the chair and settled Parrish in her lap. I sat up on the crinkly-papered exam table with India.

"Do the girls need shots this time?" she asked.

"Probably. It seems like they have to get a few more every time we come in. Hep B, DTaP, meningitis… endless."

Mom shivered. "Poor little things."

The doctor bustled in, clipboard in hand. "Mrs. Bauer?"

Dare, I thought to myself, having kept my maiden name. But it seemed needlessly strident to correct her so I just nodded.

"We're behind on the girls' vaccination schedule," she said. "I'd like to get them caught up today."

Mom raised an eyebrow at me, having always been a proponent of the "I don't think that really *needs* stitches" school of parenting.

"Okay, I guess." I mean, I didn't want to leave my children vulnerable to typhoid, or whatever, right?

Parrish wailed in my lap as she got an injection in each arm. I closed my eyes and stroked her hair, whispering *shhhh* in her ear. "It's okay, sweetie… It's okay. All done now."

India screamed next, struggling in Mom's lap.

I was just so damn tired. The pitiful sound of both children's sobs made tears well up in my eyes.

"Now, we find these shots are usually tolerated really well," said the doctor, "but if the girls have any discomfort tonight, it's all right to give them a little liquid Tylenol."

"Okay," I said. "Thank you."

The woman grabbed her clipboard and race-walked out of the room.

"What a *bitch*," said Mom in a stage whisper the moment the exam room door had clicked shut.

I snickered despite myself and turned to look at her.

"Oh, Mom...you cried, too?" I said, handing her a wad of Kleenex from the doctor's stash. "Your mascara's running."

"I couldn't stand it," she said, sniffling and dabbing at her eyes. "Getting a shot in each arm? Horrible."

We carried the girls back out to the parking lot. India was asleep before Mom had finished fastening the straps on her car seat.

"Why don't you go up and take a nap when we get home, Madeline?" said Mom. "You look exhausted."

"That would be my idea of Nirvana," I said, right before Parrish projectile-vomited all over me.

I was looking for clean clothes for Parrish once we'd gotten back to the house.

"I'll do all that," said Mom. "Don't be silly."

"But you shouldn't have to—"

She took me gently by the shoulders and turned me toward the staircase.

"Go upstairs," said my mother. "Wash your face. Put on a clean shirt."

I just stood there for a minute, then glanced back over my shoulder.

Mom had already somehow stripped Parrish down to just a diaper and laid her gently on the sofa. "I think she's finished throwing up, poor little thing."

Even so, the cushions beneath her were now miraculously, tautly sheeted with several clean towels.

I shook my head. "How did you get—"

"Go upstairs," said Mom, shaking a crook'd finger at me. "I'm the mother, and I say so."

When I reached the landing, I heard her call my name from below.

"Yeah?" I said, peering back down over the banister.

"Turn your dirty clothes inside out and throw them down here once you've got them off. I'll start a load of laundry."

"Thank you."

"And then I think you should run yourself a bath."

"Okay."

She stepped into sight beneath me. "After that you can go to sleep."

I bowed to her in gratitude, knocking my forehead three times against the banister.

*   *   *

I'd just gotten out of the bathtub and wrapped myself in a big towel when Mom came upstairs.

"Is Parrish okay?" I asked, reaching back into the tepid water to yank out the plug by its chain.

"I gave her some apple juice and she kept it down. She might go to sleep for a while."

"Do you think I should take her temperature?"

"I think you should take a *nap*."

I padded down the hallway toward Dean's and my bedroom, my skin not even damp anymore.

"It's so weird," I said. "You barely even *need* towels at this altitude. It's like going through the dryers at a car wash."

I put on a bra and pulled a clean T-shirt over my head.

"The clasp broke on these pearls you got from Mummie?" asked Mom, lifting the string of cultured orbs from the jewelry box atop my bureau, my third of what had been her mother's triple-strand necklace.

"The clasp is fine," I said, rubbing my wet hair roughly with a towel. "The thread snapped, right near the end where it attaches."

She nodded. "I'll take the girls out for a walk later and let you nap. We'll have a little adventure and find a jewelry store to fix these."

"You sure Parrish is okay?"

"Just go to sleep for a while."

I felt so refreshed after the bath I didn't think I'd drift off, but I blinked my eyes a couple of times and the next time I opened them the bedroom walls were tinted blood orange, reflecting the sunset.

Downstairs, Mom had made dinner for all four of us.

Parrish woke up around three that night, weeping and screaming. She was hot and sweaty and crying as though she were in great pain—or being chased by rabid wolves.

I gave her liquid Tylenol and carried her downstairs and held her as I walked slowly back and forth across the moonlit living room floor. I buried my nose in her sweet, alfalfa-smelling hair as she shrieked in my ear, humming softly until she exhausted herself back to sleep once more.

Sitting with her cradled across my lap for another ten minutes, I gazed at her dear little face in the blue moonlight.

She made a fist and raised her thumb to her mouth, dark lashes grazing her cheeks—so beautiful it made me ache.

Lucky, lucky, lucky. Yes I am.

4

Most days I woke up brimming with a sudden terror—that I'd forgotten to do essential things, that I'd never make friends in Colorado, that my appearance as an adult in the world was only a thin candy shell hiding a tiny, rattling center of incompetent thirteen-year-old or, worse yet, nothing at all.

That morning I was too tired to care. I came downstairs in my underwear and my favorite black EAT THE RICH skull-and-crossbones T-shirt, toting a just-awakened child on each hip.

Mom was in the kitchen drinking Postum, having already put away last night's dishes and started a second load of laundry for me.

"Does it bother you if I clean when I'm here?" she asked.

"Are you fucking kidding?" I said, buckling the girls into their seats. "You are the goddess of the world."

"Daddy used to always straighten the pictures when he and Mummie came to visit. Then he'd polish the silver. Drove me crazy."

"Well, *I* kiss the hem of your garment." I shook my head, starting to slice bananas for Parrish and India. "Besides which, your father was the most anal-retentive man who ever lived."

Mom smiled.

I scooped up the bananas. "Whereas I am anal-*intentive*...I always mean to clean up, but never quite get around to it."

I knelt down to pile bananas on the girls' respective little yellow plastic trays along with sturdy dry helpings of Life cereal, then tied on their bibs and let them have at it.

By the time I'd filled two sippy cups with milk, Parrish had half a slice of banana up her nose and was busy mashing the remainder against India's chubby left cheek.

"Another fine day, my beauties," I said, patting their silky heads.

Mom put a yellow receipt into my hand. "I forgot to give you this last night. Your pearls should be ready Tuesday. The people in the store were very sweet."

"Didn't your mother used to say that you should always make a jeweler restring them while you watch, so they can't switch any of them out?"

"Only for natural pearls. Doesn't really matter with cultured," she said.

I boggled yet again at all the useless knowledge we'd accrued as a family since my four great-grandfathers left their childhood farms for robber-baron ascendancy in textiles, banking, bonds, and shipping, respectively.

We could arrange flowers, navigate deb-party receiving lines, replace divots in polo fields between chukkers, and write charming thank-you notes on good stationery. Fat lot of good any of that did us now, three generations down the pike with everyone broke as shit.

I mean, my poor mother got shoved into the 1960s wearing a hat and gloves and seamed stockings and a Bendel frock, having been educated to gracefully oversee a husband's household's staff. Preferably during the reign of Edward VII.

She'd ended up on the outskirts of Big Sur

smoking dope in our living room with a lot of Black Panthers—gracefully.

So, okay, I *also* knew how to get food for striking AFL-CIO farmworkers through a Salinas police line, tie-dye T-shirts, wring every last dime out of any educational institution's financial-aid office, sing the word-perfect entirety of "Alice's Restaurant," and fire off a deeply authentic, heartfelt black-power salute.

But I'd married an alpha farmboy with a fine head for business.

Go figure.

Does that make it sound as though I wanted to be rich again, ride on Dean's coattails, put a yoke around his neck?

Wrong. I wanted to reboot everything back to scratch, start over, tabula rasa—yes, abso-goddamn-lutely. But the point was to shoot for kindness instead of glory and power and bloodthirsty bullshit this time around. Teamwork. Good talk and sharing books and time to laugh. Long fine dinners around a big table with all the people we loved. Maybe a little safety, comfort, and education for our children. Just enough to go around, to share, to live without being dogged by fear. Give peace a chance.

"What time does Ellis get in?" asked Mom.

"Noon, I think." I tucked the pearls receipt into

my shorts' pocket and staggered toward my hideously orange kitchen counter to stoke the espresso machine for my own much-needed sustenance.

"Are we picking her up at the airport?" she asked.

"Too many car seats to fit in the Galant, with Hadley and Peregrine. Ellis is renting a mini-van or something."

A mini-van. Jesus. What the fuck happened to us?

"I can't *imagine* her married," said Mom.

"Yeah," I said, laughing. "Neither can she."

"Do you straighten up the house before Dean gets home?" asked Mom, taking another sip of Postum as she surveyed the five overflowing baskets of laundry still listing to starboard alongside the washing machine.

"Sure," I lied. "Right before I greet him at the door in a freshly starched French maid's costume and patent-leather thigh boots, bearing a monogrammed sterling shaker of chilled martinis."

Mom tsk-tsked.

I yawned so hard that tears started leaking down my cheeks, then crossed my arms on the heinous autumnal Formica and slumped down to glare at the trickle of rocket-nectar leaking all too slowly from the espresso machine's steel teat.

India squealed with glee and threw a piece of banana in my general direction. I left it stuck to the side of my thigh, intent on pouring adequate sugar and milk into a pint glass with my now-finished double espresso.

The washing machine buzzed and Mom started moving wet clothes to the dryer.

"Thank you, dearest Mummie," I said, toasting her with my flagon of Light Sweet Crude. "You are indeed the bestest ever."

When Mom had shoved the dryer door closed and hit START, she glanced at my bombed-out living room.

"Madeline," she said, head shaking slowly, "*promise* me you'll never have pets."

"*Wilkommen*," I said some hours later, skipping down the porch steps as Ellis rolled her rented vanlet's side door open. "*Bienvenue. Céad míle fáilte.*"

My svelte gamine pal flashed me a wide wicked grin. "How's tricks?"

"I'm fat, my marriage is tanking, and I want to run away with the circus," I said. "Which is remarkable because I've always *despised* circuses. You?"

She rolled her green eyes skyward. "I just want to be a widow. Is that so wrong?"

"Scorpio's in the House of Suckbag again at your place, too?"

Our husbands had been born on the exact same

day in 1962, and we'd long since discovered that their sine waves of biorhythmic testiness were perfectly synced.

She unlocked the straps on towheaded little Hadley's car seat. "We married beneath us."

"All women do," I replied, making my way around to the car's street-side door to release Peregrine.

He was four years old, the spitting image of Ellis, and immediately sank his teeth into the meatiest part of my forearm.

I yanked all appendages beyond reach of the kid's fangs to check for blood and gore. He'd broken the skin, but only just.

"No worries," said Ellis. "He's had his shots for distemper."

"Imagine my relief."

She pointed at the back of Mom's little Chinook camper. "Nice bumper sticker."

The slogan was affixed beneath a window box brimming with road-weary plastic geraniums: POSSUM, it read, THE OTHER OTHER WHITE MEAT.

"Perfect," I said.

Hadley laughed, smacking her mother audibly upside the head with a Cookie Monster sippy cup.

Ellis sighed. "Now I know why tigers eat their young."

5

We spent the morning of my daughters' birthday driving north in the mini-van to Rocky Mountain National Park, an expedition cut short when Ellis reached into her diaper bag for a camera and Peregrine took the opportunity to bolt away across thin ice toward the thawed center of a pond.

The surface gave way when he was fifteen feet from shore, Ellis already sprinting toward him, smashing through the frozen surface up to her knees with each frantic stride.

The frigid water only came up to his waist, thank God.

"That child is a *menace*," said Mom once we'd exhaled our panic-stilled breath.

"No shit," I replied, thankful once again that I'd had girls.

Ellis threw Perry over her shoulder in a fireman's carry and slogged back toward shore.

"If we'd brought the camper," said Mom, "I could have wrapped them both up in blankets."

"The camper has nothing to hook the car seats to, though," I said. "So we would of course have driven off a cliff on the way home."

Mom shook her head. "A little time airborne might be just what that boy needs."

Ellis stepped back onto dry land, Perry already blue-lipped and shaking in her arms.

She looked at me.

My eyes must have mirrored everything so plain in hers: exhaustion, self-recrimination, and the profound gratitude one always feels in the aftermath of sheer-adrenaline maternal terror.

"I *have* considered calling the child-abuse hotline," she said. "For tips."

I gripped her shoulder. "On the bright side, he can't drive yet."

"Try telling *him* that. We're on our third garage door."

I opened the van and she bundled Perry into a spare set of warm clothes—claiming not to be a bit cold herself—then posed us all beside the shore for photos with the cracked ice clearly visible behind us.

"Say *fromage*," she said, focusing in.

Mom and I smiled and the kids tried to pull away from us.

Ellis said, "Parrish, look at the camera, honey!"

I knelt down.

"Parrish, over here, pretty girl!" said Ellis.

"Pretty!" said India.

Ellis started waving her free hand. "Parrish, sweetie. Look look look."

I put my arm around my little blond child, gently cupping her cheek with my hand to turn her face forward.

"Got it!" Ellis said, then set the timer and raced over to stand next to me for a full-cast shot.

She pressed her arm against mine, shivering.

"*Your* lips are blue now," I said, having a sudden flashback to Mom telling me that same thing when I was little and she thought it was time to come out of the water.

"I don't mean to be a wuss, but would you guys mind if we went home?" Ellis asked.

"Not at all," said Mom. "Want me to drive?"

Ellis shook her head. "Actually, I'd love to be up front. Closer to the heater."

When the kids were locked down in the car, Ellis leaned in toward my ear. "Don't tell Seamus, okay? I'm so sick of getting yelled at."

The last time I'd stayed at the monstrous junior-executive house he'd insisted they have built in a soulless cookie-cutter development outside Cincinnati ("great rooms," granite countertops, sad little fledgling trees held upright by guy wires), Ellis's flabby, assless, nepotism-anointed corporate-cog lizard-princeling of a husband had spent twenty minutes shrieking at her for buying a bottle of Elmer's Glue.

"You bought *glue*?" he'd said, shaking his head. "Jesus Christ, Ellis, what kind of idiot *are* you? The kids'll have that smeared into each other's hair and all over our furniture in a heartbeat."

She didn't say a word as he continued berating her. Neither did I.

I'd endured enough spousal tantrums in my own household to know full well that if Ellis hadn't bought glue, he would've attacked her for buying Brussels sprouts, or vitamins, or Scotch tape.

Seamus took my silence as complicity.

"Madeline, you gotta admit the bitch is *incredibly* stupid," the shithead said, lipless grin fueled with certainty that I'd consider his scathing, entirely baseless abuse of my dearest friend proof of swoon-inducing virility on his part.

Then he'd fucking winked at me.

I turned my back on the shattered Colorado pond and hooked elbows with Ellis. "Seamus *who*?"

I made tortellini with a side of hummus for the kids' lunch and peeled some apples to slice.

When Ellis had changed into dry clothes, she and I washed all four pairs of sticky little hands and got our offspring strapped into their respective mealtime restraint devices.

Mom had gone out to her camper to lie down for a bit, saying she'd be happy to take second shift.

As the kids dug in, Ellis and I leaned back against the orange Formica, winded.

"What would the grown-ups like for lunch?" I asked.

"Tequila."

"I'd lapse into a coma."

"You say that like it's a bad thing."

"*After* crying for an hour."

Ellis punched me in the shoulder. "Pussy."

I shrugged. "Could be worse."

"How?"

"Could be Mormons."

"Twenty kids, no booze?" Ellis shuddered with horror.

"*Or* caffeine," I said, handing her a cold can of

Diet Coke and opening one for myself. "Plus they'd make us refer to Jell-O as 'salad.'"

"Fuck me gently with a chain saw," she whispered, voice pitched only the slightest hair above inaudibility.

"Chain saw!" chortled India.

I raised my eyes heavenward. "Do we really have to give up *swearing*, on top of everything else? It's the only vice I have left."

"You forgot sloth," said Ellis, eyeing my laundry pile.

Peregrine upended his tortellini bowl over Hadley's head.

His sister took a deep breath and held it, her face amping brighter and brighter crimson as lukewarm butter-and-Parmesan trickled down toward her pale eyebrows.

Ellis gestured balletically toward this tableau with her soda can. "You ever notice how the longer they don't breathe, the louder they end up screaming?"

"Daily," I replied.

We knocked back bracing slugs of beverage.

Hadley's blue eyes went wider, and then she shrieked like an entire mill-town's worth of lunchhour steam whistles—all playing at 78 rpm.

"That girl's got a future in Chinese opera," I said, when she paused to inhale.

"You'd think the asthma would slow her down."

Hadley screamed again, louder this time. I figured the neighbors would be trying to remember whether Boulder had fallout shelters.

I swallowed more Diet Coke. "Please tell me your son still naps."

"Of course he does. I brought duct tape."

I clinked her soda can with my own. "There *is* a God."

"Yeah." Ellis laughed. "Too bad he's such a vindictive asshole."

We ran the kids around the backyard for another half hour so they'd be exhausted enough to sleep—worked like a charm.

Back down in the kitchen with Ellis, I held up two tablespoons and pointed them at the half-Cuisinart-ful of leftover hummus. "Sloppy seconds?"

"Perfect."

"They always say we're supposed to sleep when the kids do." I said, handing her a spoon.

"Fuck that. My brain's already atrophied beyond repair."

"Yeah, me neither."

We were scraping the sides of the bowl when Mom breezed in.

"I went for a little walk," she said. "They're having a graduation fair at the psychic academy. Ten bucks for fifteen minutes. Why don't I watch the kids while you two go, my treat?"

"Constance," said Ellis, hugging my mother, "have I told you lately that I love you?"

6

"Free at last, free at last," said Ellis, as we escaped at a lope toward Pearl Street.

I chimed in with a "Thank God Almighty."

We were so goofy with liberty that we grabbed hands and started skipping down the sidewalk.

"Have you met anyone cool here yet?" she asked when we'd run out of breath and lapsed back into a walk.

"I'm pretty certain I will never have friends again," I said. "I'll just die alone, unknelled, uncoffined, and surrounded by twenty-seven cats."

"Oh, please," she said. "Our problem has never been *making* friends. The hard part's *liking* them."

"You know, I actually enjoy moving—finding

the new drugstore, figuring out where to get a decent baguette. But I kind of freeze up about people. It's like the abyss opens up and I don't know whether I'm going to be a complete reject geek like I was as a kid in California—"

"Or queen of the universe like you've been *every* fucking place you've lived since?"

"Thank you."

"So, join a mothers' group or something. Tiny children—the great equalizer. You're never short of small talk."

"Tried it," I said.

"So what happened?"

"Well, I went in the first week—it was at this community center—and they had a facilitator chick. The kids are all bonking each other over the heads with plastic shovels and shit, and meanwhile she wants us to sit in a circle on the floor and have a 'sharing' session about some parenting question of the week, or whatever."

"Not liking the sound of this so far…"

"No shit," I said. "And the question that first week was, 'What is your bedtime ritual,' which, you know, right away—"

"Gag."

"Exactly, right? So they start going around the

circle, and all these women are talking about how the kid picks out three storybooks, and then they have a warmed mug of soy milk, and then they sing lullabies in French and Mandarin, and then they all sleep 'in the family bed' and shit—on and fucking *on*—and I'm starting to freak out."

"And then they get to *you*," she said.

"And then they get to me."

"So what'd you say?"

"I told the truth: I take my kids upstairs, tuck them into their cribs, say good night, and then shut the door most of the way and drink a goddamn beer in my kitchen."

"Bet that went over like a lead balloon," said Ellis.

"Plutonium, more like." I hopped over a crack in the sidewalk. "I mean, there are some nice people here, but I don't even know who *I* am anymore. I know who I used to be—a writer, a survivor, this chick who could think on her feet and stand up for people. I mean, shit…*you* know, better than anyone."

"You saved my life," she said.

"You saved mine."

We weren't speaking figuratively.

"So what the hell am I now?" I asked. "A failing housewife? A crappy mother? And we're the fucking lucky ones—I *know* this is a life of goddamn privilege. I mean, we have health insurance, I don't have to waitress at some all-night truckstop diner to feed my kids—"

"Good thing, too, because you were the suckiest waitress who ever lived."

"Don't I know it," I said.

"You're still you."

"God help us all."

"You're going to make friends here, we're both going to survive the toddler years. Hey, our marriages might even improve. And someday, we'll get to become ourselves again."

I closed my eyes. "That is just so hard for me to believe, right now."

"You *know* it's true," she said. "I mean, you're smart, you're funny, and you're a total babe."

"I'm fucking fat."

"Which has *never* mattered," she was kindly quick to say.

"Says the bitch with the body of a Parisian cheerleader. You're like a twelve-year-old boy with a Mighty Rack, dude."

"And you're the only woman I know who still looks hot even when she's twenty pounds over."

"Thirty," I said. "Probably. I'm too scared to get on a scale."

"I fucking hate you. You could still crook your little finger in any bar in America and have three guys clamoring to fuck you—in a heartbeat."

"Sure, right after the full-frontal plastic surgery."

"So you're a quart low on mojo. You need to get laid."

I jumped into the air, tapping my hand against a high overhead branch, the way I used to when I was out walking in the woods as a kid. "I imagine that will happen when my Intrepid Spouse gets home. Not that our fucking's been entirely mojo-building of late."

"At least your husband doesn't look like a lizard. Swear to God, I'm tempted to put a bag over my *own* head just so I don't have to see Seamus's reptilian countenance pulling closer at night."

"So? Screw in the dark."

"Doesn't help his technique."

"Technique," I said. "I have vague memories of that . . . lost somewhere back in the mists of prehistory, along with any pretense of foreplay."

"That bad?" She shook her head in sympathy.

"We're talking thirty seconds of ass-pawing on his part, max. The rest of it might as well be drive-through. I'm completely on my own in the getting-off department."

"At least Dean knew how at *some* point. Swear to God, Lizard Boy is unteachable—not to mention he thinks cunnilingus is an Irish airline."

"You need a nice thick Lanz nightie."

"I need a *pool* boy," she said.

"Oh, come on, sturdy ramparts of flannel, rendered in a sickeningly twee calico? Nothing puts a man off like preppy sleepwear."

"Yeah, that'd work. With a *Taser.*"

"She's holding out for the pool boy," I said. "I *know* that look."

"Preferably a well-hung seventeen-year-old to give me a good solid thrashing every afternoon, before I have to go cook dinner while watching my husband snatch flies from midair with the otherwise-useless tip of his tongue."

"Remind me why you married Seamus, again?"

Ellis shrugged. "Health insurance. And dental."

I burst out laughing.

She cracked up, too. "Thank God the kids look like me, right?"

"Yea," I said, "verily."

She threw her arm across my shoulder. "Why couldn't God have made us dykes, instead of this bullshit?"

"Because he's a vindictive asshole, remember?"

*   *   *

We were standing in the entryway of the local psychic academy, which resembled the cheapest available Holiday Inn banquet room somewhere outside Indianapolis: bad "fruitwood" paneling, wagon-wheel ceiling fixtures, and giant versions of those plastic chairs we'd had in California grade school—the kind with splayed aluminum Jetson legs and three parallel slots cut down the middle of their injection-molded backs.

"Are we *sure* we want to do this?" asked Ellis.

I shrugged. "It's Boulder. You can't really escape: Every fucking day's the dawning of the Age of Aquarius, *ad aeternum*."

"I'd prefer the Age of Scorpio," she replied. "Suckbags and all."

There were pairs of people scattered around the room, seated to face each other.

A woman with a mass of Pre-Raphaelite red-blond curls approached, wearing a tie-dyed caftan.

"Five bucks she's wearing pentacle earrings," whispered Ellis.

"We are *so* evil. And I have nothing against Wiccans, per se."

"Not even that bitch in your dorm senior year?" whispered Ellis. "The one who kept leaving bloody feathers outside your room, after you snaked the hot Irish dude right out from under her at the Spinning Wheel on kamikaze night?"

"Not my fault. You're the one who pulled him over to the table and told me, 'I brought you a present.'"

"Welcome, ladies," said She-of-the-Caftan, raising her slender arms as she drew nigh. "Blessed be."

"Back atcha," said Ellis.

"I'm Becca Tay." The Caftan Lady smiled. "Are you here for readings?"

Ellis shot me a *"psychic" my ass* eyebrow.

I kicked her in the ankle. Discreetly.

Not like I didn't think it was complete horseshit, too, but just for courtesy.

"We are indeed, Becca," I told the woman. "Thank you."

She turned to survey the room. "Anthony and Willow are just finishing up. Let me get you squared away," she said, turning to lead us toward the cashier.

I wanted to make fun of it all, but there was something calming about this lady's presence. Plus she had amazing hair.

Okay, I really *didn't* want to make fun of it. I wanted it to work—all of it.

I was so tired, so bereft, so hungry for comfort

that I wanted to believe: in the New Age, in wheat-grass, in *something*. Pick a card, any card...Kali, Vishnu, Batman-and-Robin.

Was there anything that could relax me enough so I could let go of the wheel for thirty seconds?

No. Of course not. I had long since become utterly fucking incapable of trusting anything beyond the confines of my own tiny black heart.

Too much risk out there. Too much downside. Too much certainty of pain.

I pulled Mom's twenty from my pocket and fell in line behind Becca Tay as she started across the room, dragging Ellis by the wrist in my wake.

Ellis was placed with Anthony, well across the room from me.

Willow turned out to be a guy—young, with black curly hair and a twitchy Adam's apple. I sat down on my highly inorganic chair and surveyed the fields and pastures of wrinkled hemp in which he was arrayed.

He lifted his wrists toward me, palms up. "*Your* hands atop mine, please."

German. Which explains the black socks and sandals. Which are not really helping me with the whole willing-suspension-of-disbelief thing here.

I laid my palms lightly across his, and he closed his eyes.

Let me just say here that I don't dismiss all fortune-telling out of hand.

A very kind old man once did a reading of my face, peering into my future and reporting back some deeply scary auguries, all of which proved true in the end. But he'd been taught the knack for it by an old Gypsy woman in the cattle car bearing them both toward Auschwitz—her dying gift, as it shortly turned out.

I'd always figured you couldn't tap into this stuff without having survived a plunge so deep into the magma of the world's black depths that everything else was burned away.

But young Herr Willow, no doubt named Helmut or Rolf at birth and now holding my hands in his, looked pretty damn unscathed. Like maybe the worst tragedy he'd ever endured was discovering that his midmorning soy latte had been tainted with an actual dairy product.

I glanced over at Ellis.

Anthony was checking out her tits and she was trying not to smirk. Well, *sort* of trying.

Willow swallowed audibly, his Adam's apple bobbing like a cork in winter surf.

I felt a wave of compassion for him. He couldn't have been more than nineteen, and no one would ever mistake him for a well-endowed pool boy.

He yanked his hands out from under mine and shot to his feet, knocking his chair backward to the floor.

"I need *grounding*! I need *grounding*!" he screamed, the whites of his eyes showing all the way around each iris.

With that he sprinted for the door, sandals flapping.

Becca the Caftan Lady blocked his egress and gathered him in her arms, pillowing his head against her shoulder.

"Shhh, Willow...shhhhh...it's all right," she said, leading him from the room. "Let's get you some water. You've had a long day."

Jesus, now he was *crying*. I guess I still had enough Manhattan snark to short out a psychic. Or maybe he'd just sensed my inborn fondness for bacon cheeseburgers.

Oh fucking well.

A tall, thinly bearded brunette guy came in moments later, heading directly for me.

"I'm Jesse," he said, sitting down in the vacated chair. "I'll be finishing up for Willow."

"Okay."

No hand-holding this time. Jesse let his eyes go unfocused, then muttered a few adenoidal niceties about how my life was like a rose, and the earth was our mother, and blah-blah-tofu-flaxseed-blah that I basically tuned out, being still not-a-little freaked by the shrill bedside manner of Karnak Numero Uno, frankly. Other than that, it was stultifying.

"Thanks a lot," I said, when he'd finally droned to a close. "That was very, um, helpful."

Jesse nodded, smug. "Go in peace, sister."

"Jesus," said Ellis, once we'd escaped the building. "What were you thinking about, the Spanish Inquisition?"

"Pool boys, actually."

Ellis's hand popped up for a high-five slap.

I didn't disappoint her.

But I sure as hell should've kept my fingers crossed for a very long time afterward, because the universe was about to chuck a veritable barge-load of shit, sidelong, into the whirling blur of a rather enormous fan.

The blades of which were angled directly toward still-oblivious me.

7

My front porch pillars were still twined with spiraling green Christmas garlands and strings of unlit-by-day white lights.

"You know," said Ellis, "it being March, you might want to think about taking down the holiday crap."

I shook my head. "Fuck that. I'd only have to put it all up again come Thanksgiving."

"You guys're going to be here that long?"

"Probably," I said, kicking a small rock down the sidewalk. "It's not like I exactly have a choice."

"Well, it looks like you're in mourning for Martha Stewart."

"You say that like it's a bad thing." I kicked

the little rock again, sending it skittering into the snowy grass of my lawn.

A pair of fire engines caterwauled south along Twentieth, belching low plumes of diesel exhaust.

Ellis shook her head. "I can't believe Dean isn't here for the girls' birthday."

"*But Bunny, it's Pittcon,*" I said, quoting my absent spouse, "*the premier annual sales event of the global scientific-instrument industry.*"

"Sounds like a giant fucking drag."

"No doubt," I said, "But they have it this time every year so he's probably going to miss all our birthdays forever, barring employment catastrophe."

I peeked into the living room window before we mounted the front porch—no sign of children. "They're not up yet. Want to sit out here for a while?"

We settled back into the bouncy old metal chairs that had come with the house.

"When should we open the girls' presents?" asked Ellis.

"After dinner, probably. Once we bring out the cake."

"When do you want to open *your* presents?"

"I don't officially turn thirty-two until Sunday—trying not to think about it."

"So Dean's going to miss that, too?"

I stretched out my legs, crossing them at the ankle. "Reply hazy. Ask again later."

"Shitheel," she said. "He better come home with a deeply excellent present."

"T-shirt from the airport, probably. New Orleans if I'm lucky, Denver if I'm not."

"What'd he get you last year?"

"Sushi delivery and a gold bangle from Tiffany. But I was just back from the hospital, having successfully whelped dual offspring."

Ellis nodded at that. "Raw fish and good jewelry . . . commendable."

"Except for the part about me having called in both orders myself with Dean's Amex. Which started out as a subsidiary card to mine, by the way."

"And did you ask his permission first?"

"Of course."

She shook her head, smirking. "Amateur."

"*Dude.* I am acquisitive, not floridly delusional."

A high, thin screech rattled the upstairs windows.

"Hadley," we sighed in unison, rising slow and weary from our chairs.

Mom produced the candle that had graced my own first-birthday cake: a ladybug-strewn white stub she'd kept in the bottom drawer of her jewelry box for nigh on thirty-one years.

She sank it into a yellow-frosting rosette on Parrish and India's cake, added a tiny pink grocery-store taper "to grow on," then lit both wicks with a stout kitchen match while I doused the living room lights.

I looked at my mother's face in the flickering glow, and pictured the old white-edged snapshot of myself in a high chair with a paper hat on my head as she leaned forward into the frame, slender-armed and laughing, touching another match flame to that ladybug candle's wick for the first time.

The eighth of March, 1964: my mother not yet turned twenty-five and me in a little blue smocked dress with a white Peter Pan collar, my swinging feet in tiny red socks. The colors have faded long since, but on that square of glossy paper I gaze upward with awe, drinking her in.

And now I watched Mom lift up my daughters' cake and start walking toward the living room, the door frame briefly illuminated as she stepped through it.

Ellis started snapping pictures, the two of us singing "Happy *birth*-day Parrish and India" along with Mom before we grown-ups blew out the little teardrops of flame in their honor.

I'd made party hats the week before, tall medieval princess cones of gem-toned poster board.

This was the type of project I got up to during the girls' naps, basically *stuff I do when I have enough energy not to fall asleep on my feet, drooling, but am still goddamned if I'm going to waste a single rare moment of clarity on cleaning the fucking house.* Ditto the extensive front-porch Christmas decor.

These things weren't earth-shattering, by any means, but even the tiniest modicum of creativity made me feel like a human being again. Albeit briefly.

Maybe that's why I'd left all the crap up on the porch: as testament to even my smallest actual accomplishment in the world above and beyond pushing a vacuum hose back and forth across the orange shag on my hands and knees. Again.

I mean, you vacuum the rug, and it looks like shit again by the next morning. But first-birthday pictures stick around, and I wanted my kids to know full well that they had been adored when they were little.

Parrish's birthday hat was emerald green with a fat striped bee glued on, its waxed-paper wings glitter-veined. Perry's was dark sapphire with tinfoil stars, comets, and moons. Ellis's read GLAMOUR BUNNY in tiny pearls on lavender, Mom's EMPRESS OF ALL SHE SURVEYS in rhinestones across a faux-ermine-trimmed field of scarlet. Hadley's was hot pink with leafy vines of lemon-lime sequins, India's saffron with a jade-colored Buddha seated atop a garnet lotus, the words OM MANE PADME HUM written beneath him in Sanskrit.

After the cake, the girls started opening their presents, a project that required heavy guidance from the rest of us. Parrish kept sticking the bows in her mouth, Perry wept when he tipped his ice cream and cake onto the floor and stepped in it, and Hadley and India pretty much shellacked each other's hair with frosting while the grown-ups were scraping Perry's sticky mess out of the shag fronds.

At that point, of course, the phone rang.

"Go ahead, we've got this," said Ellis, shooing me toward the kitchen. "If it's Dean tell him everything's under control."

I got it by the fifth ring.

"Hey Bunny," said my husband, "how're the girls?"

"Very happy and slathered with melting ice cream and crumbs," I replied. "How are you? How's New Orleans?"

"Exhausting. Sorry I haven't called before this, but they've been running me ragged. I'm just back up in the room for a quick shower and then we've got another dinner with clients."

"Anywhere good?"

"Some Cajun place. Which doesn't exactly narrow it down."

Perry knocked Hadley over and she started to wail, so I stretched the cord of the kitchen phone as far as it could go out onto the back porch and shut the door behind me.

"I miss you, Intrepid Spouse," I said.

"Listen, the car's gonna be downstairs in a second. Did the girls like their presents? What'd we get them, anyway?"

"We" my ass.

"Parrish shoved *Where the Wild Things Are* into the middle of the birthday cake. I think that's a thumbs-up."

He laughed. "I have something great for you. Saw it in the airport and knew you had to have it."

"Can't wait."

"I gotta run, kiss the girls for me?"

"Sure thing," I said. "Have a great time tonight. Knock 'em dead."

I was talking to the dial tone.

Just as I was walking back into the living room, our doorbell chimed.

I went to answer it, discovering a colleague of

Dean's on our front porch. Nice guy called Cary. We'd had him over to dinner a few times—our first pal in town, really. He and this chick Setsuko, the receptionist, were the only people at Jim's office I dealt with at all regularly.

Cary and my husband had quickly become biking partners, on the commute to work most days and often recreationally on weekends. Maybe because they were both six-five, evenly matched for racing each other up and down the canyons.

"Hey there," I said, stepping back from the doorway and waving him inside.

He shook his head, the motion making a hank of dark hair fall across his left eye. "I gotta run home in a minute, just wanted to stop by and wish the girls happy birthday."

"How come you're not in New Orleans with the rest of the gang?"

"Someone had to keep the home fires burning."

"By which you mean Bittler's being a vindictive asshole again?"

Bittler was Cary's boss but not, thank God, Dean's. Nasty little man.

"Exactly," he said, laughing. "Left me behind with stacks of bullshit paperwork."

"He's just jealous...And for chrissake, Cary, it's

cold with this door open. Come inside and meet my mom and my best pal from college. Have a slice of birthday cake."

"Well, if there's *cake*," he said, stepping into the front hall.

I closed the door. "Let me take your coat."

"Take these, instead," he said, producing two presents from behind his back.

They were wrapped in tinfoil, bachelor-style, but he'd sketched a pretty decent Elmo on one package and Big Bird on the other with a black Sharpie.

I took them out of his hands, complimented his artwork, and then stood on tiptoe to give him a peck on the cheek. "You are an *awesome* friend. Thank you."

"And you told me you didn't know *anyone* here yet," said Ellis, waving good-bye to Cary from the front porch after he'd wolfed down both his slice of cake and the beer she'd insisted he split with her after that, paperwork or no paperwork.

I laughed. "Fold your tongue back into your mouth, you unrepentant slut."

"Oh, like *you* don't think he's a hottie."

"I don't, actually."

"Well then," she said, nodding, "no wonder you're friends."

"Mostly he goes biking with Dean."

"Biking: the new golf," she said. "Our generation's excuse to leave your wife alone with the children all weekend."

"Exactly."

8

Mom and I stood on the front porch the next morning, kissing Ellis and brood good-bye before they headed out for the airport.

"*Ciao*, my darling—keep those cards and letters coming!" I said as we all broke free and Ellis started down the steps.

She paused, looking back up at me. "Speaking of, madwoman, I think you should try figuring out how to use email. You guys have an account, right?"

"Dean does, I think."

"I mean, it's great that you've finally started writing letters, but if you upgrade to the cutting-edge technology available to us in the late twentieth century, we could alleviate each other's suburban angst and alienation without having to buy stamps."

"I'll try," I said.

She blew me a kiss. "That's all I ask."

Mom and I kept up our farewell waving until she'd lurched away from the curb in her rented mini-van, homeward-bound.

"That one won't stay married," said Mom.

"Oh, come on. Not even for the health insurance?"

Mom laughed. "No way in hell. She's too much like me."

Parrish made a strange little noise and I was suddenly enveloped in a rather foul diaper-centric miasma.

"Good God," said Mom. "What *have* you been feeding that poor child…liver and kimchee?"

Breathing through my mouth, I swung Parrish up onto the changing table's squishy white-vinyl-sheathed mat, cooing "pop-pop-pop *pop*" as I tugged open the inseam snaps on her overalls.

"Pop!" she agreed.

I peeled back her diaper's tape squares, gripping her crossed ankles in my left hand. "Bottoms up."

Her Pamper brimmed with khaki-avocado gruel, rank as a Tangiers latrine.

"We may need to go ix-nay on the occoli-bray, *ma petite*."

I'd just flipped said offending diaper into the

step-bucket and grabbed a thick wad of butt-wipes when the goddamn phone rang.

Doing an expert swab of my daughter's lower decks, I re-toed the garbage open while yanking the receiver up off the hook, then held it pressed between my left ear and shoulder. "Hello?"

"Is Madeline Dare available?" A man's voice, Midwestern.

"This is she," I said, keeping Parrish's ass aloft as I groped blind for a fresh diaper.

"We want your eyeteeth," said the guy.

"I beg your pardon?"

"Your eyeteeth," he said. "We want them."

"What're you, like, a fetishist? Jesus, I'm changing my kid's *diaper* here, trying not to goddamn inhale."

The guy laughed. "This is Jon McNally at the *Boulder New Times*. Your cover letter claimed you'd give your eyeteeth to write for us?"

Fuck me.

With a chain saw. Not gently.

I'd written that four months ago. But still . . .

"Wow," I said, sliding the fresh dipe under Parrish's ass. "I am now hugely deluged with an abject dump-truck-load of embarrassment."

"Your writing clips are stellar, though." He sounded amused.

"Um. Thank you."

"We need a restaurant critic, maybe some local art coverage. Any way you could swing by this afternoon?"

Thank God for Mom. "You bet."

"Threeish?"

"Awesome," I said, before hanging up.

I snapped Parrish's overalls shut and swooped her off the changing table, twirling us both around three times with a giant grin on my face before plopping her down in the playpen.

The paper's small gray building was flat-topped and rectilinear as soot-besmirched sugar cubes, precisely stacked. Things were sparser, this far south of downtown: My neighborhood's stately trees were testimony to the nineteenth-century East Coast diaspora's arboreal homesickness.

Someone panted "on your right!" and a fish-school of stringy marathon types jostled me hard on the sidewalk, tropical in their Day-Glo Lycra.

I checked myself for errant chunks of toddler spoodge in the *New Times*'s shiny glass front doors and hustled inside.

"I'm here to meet with Jon McNally?" I said to the chick behind the bullpen desk nearest the top of the entry stairs.

She was a bit older than me, whole-grain buxom with thick dark braids wrapped around her head.

"He's in that corner cubicle, over by the windows." She smiled, pointing. "I think he's still on the phone, but if he's expecting you just go in and grab a chair."

"Cool. Thank you so much."

I felt ridiculous in my Manhattan-interview pearl earrings and black blazer. The indigenous dress code was grunge flannel and high-tech hiking sneakers, like they were all just back from a group-bonding rappel off the roof of the Hotel Boulderado. I pictured GORP-and-Gatorade office parties, with Secret Santas exchanging pitons, carabiners, and foil hiking-trip packets of freeze-dried beef Stroganoff.

I poked my head around the corner cubicle's doorway. McNally had his feet up on the desk, a phone to his ear, and his beat-to-crap leather chair tilted as far back as it could conceivably go.

Any self-respecting wife or girlfriend would've long since barbered the man's loose gray curls while he slept, with poultry shears.

"Benny, come *on*," he was saying.

His was face sun-browned as oiled teak except around the eyes: the old reverse-panda ski tan. He caught sight of me and smiled, palm across the receiver's mouthpiece as he silently mouthed *Madeline?*

I nodded and he held up an index finger to say he'd be just another minute, then pointed toward two chairs alongside his desk.

I took the one near the window, checking out a picture of him hanging by an all-too-thin rope off this crazy-vertical rock formation south of Boulder: the Devil's Thumb.

Death-wish mountain-climber dude. Perfect.

"*Three* fires last week and you're telling me there's no connection?" He shook his head, raggedy locks bouncing. "Don't fuck with me here, Benny. You never could lie for shit."

I laughed, McNally smiled at me, and the voice on the other end of the line got a whole lot louder.

He tilted his chair farther back, eliciting a creak of protest. "Of course I wouldn't jeopardize any ongoing investigation. You know me better than that, for chrissake."

He leaned forward, grasping for a notepad and pen that were just out of reach.

I pushed them closer, and he smiled his thanks.

"*Fine*, Benny . . . off the record. But you're gonna tell me everything in the end. You always do."

I stifled a second laugh and McNally shot me a conspiratorial smirk.

He covered the mouthpiece again, looked at me. "You want coffee or anything?"

I shook my head. "I'd rather just listen, if that's cool."

That got me a wink.

He bit the cap off his felt-tip, spiral pad flipped open against one raised knee. "So you've got a garage, two cars out on Baseline, and now the gas station."

He started jotting. "Right…right…Any link to those brush fires last month?"

A squeal of protest from the other end of the line.

"Don't get your panties in a knot, Benjamin…"

Rapid chatter in response to that.

"Come on, it's the classic pattern—start with a couple of fields…shove burning cardboard under a few doors, see if anything catches…but we both know he's fucking with you."

Benny sighed, loud and clear from wherever he was in real life.

"What do you have on accelerants?"

Silence.

"Benny," said McNally, "the goddamn cars were serious escalation. And that gas station would've been a nightmare if you hadn't caught it so fast. Kudos by the way, seriously."

Another sigh as he looked up at me, his expression telegraphing gratitude for my patience.

"Look," he told Benny, "you and me both know where this train's headed. We're not talking about some teenage stoner playing Ring-Around-the-Dumpster with a fistful of matchbooks."

His pal's Charlie-Brown-grown-up *wah-wah* grew stentorian at that. Downright affronted.

"*Benny*... He's already tipped his hand, this guy. There's gonna be a history. Not here, but somewhere. This isn't after-school fledgling angst, it's a grown-up getting the lay of the land, checking to see who's paying attention."

More phone noise.

"Right... right..."

A question.

"Of *course* not. Come on, how long we known each other?"

McNally tilted back again, tucking the pen behind his ear. "But I find out you gave those smug *Daily Camera* pricks a damn thing before me, you're blackballed straight out of poker night."

That got him a good laugh from Benny.

"Yeah, yeah... kiss Ellen for me. Tell her I'm still waiting to sweep her off into the sunset the minute she realizes how little you deserve her."

He sat up straight and dropped the phone in its cradle. "Sorry about that, Madeline."

I shrugged. "Hey, permission to eavesdrop on talent is always a treat."

I could tell he liked me for that.

"You've known this guy awhile," I said.

"Benny? We were smoke-jumpers together, summers back in college."

"Leaping out of a plane when the ground's on fire? Now, there's a job requiring *serious* balls."

"Benny stuck with it, went through the academy. Now he's a muckety-muck here. Just made chief."

"While you opted for the big-money glories of journalism?"

He snorted, hooking a thumb over one shoulder, southward toward Golden. "School of Mines. Geology."

"How'd you end up here?"

"Got tired of fucking people over for the benefit of petroleum companies, couple years back."

I watched him ruffle through one of the stacks of papers on his desk. He located a sheet of stiff ivory woven and pulled it out: my résumé.

McNally ran his eyes down the thing, lips pursed.

I cleared my throat. "What'd Benny tell you

about accelerants, speaking of petroleum? It doesn't sound like this guy's dabbling in explosives yet."

He looked up and cocked an eyebrow at me, curious.

This was probably not the time to bring up the guy who'd tried offing me in a fire, back in upstate New York.

I shrugged again, eliding over that with a sideways head-tilt. "I used to teach high school. One of my kids was into arson. Eventually he started blowing shit up."

" 'Shit' like what?"

I looked out the window. "His grand finale was a helicopter."

"Anyone in it?"

I turned back toward him, nodded, dropped my eyes. "One guy. Not exactly the world's foremost humanitarian."

McNally whistled through his teeth, tilting the chair back. "What'd the kid use?"

"A big wad of C-4, remotely detonated with a soldered-together fistful of crap shoplifted from Radio Shack."

He smiled, waiting for more.

I shrugged. "Allegedly."

9

C-4," said McNally. "*Allegedly.*"

I crossed my arms, still looking him dead in the eye. "I'd resigned from the school by then. Being a teacher...well, let's just say secondary school education wasn't exactly my calling."

"Uh-huh." He smiled, tapping the upper-right corner of my résumé slowly with the side of his index fingertip. "And you want to be a *restaurant* critic?"

"Damn straight," I said, thinking of Parrish and India.

No crime beats, nothing stupid or dangerous. I was a *mother*, for chrissake.

"You have someplace in mind, to start?" he asked.

"Daddy Bruce's Bar-B-Que, out on Arapahoe."

He liked that. "These pieces go about seven hundred and fifty words."

"Great."

"By Tuesday?"

I nodded.

He leaned back again, fingers steepled in front of his mouth.

I waited.

"On spec," he said.

"Oh joy, oh rapture unforeseen."

"You don't sound surprised."

I shrugged again. "This isn't the first time I've worked for an erstwhile hippie free weekly."

McNally cackled.

Yeah, dude, you like me already.

I crossed my arms. "And what do you pay if you actually have the wit to appreciate my deathless prose?"

"Forty bucks. And we'll reimburse for the meal."

"Look at me," I replied, "living the goddamn dream."

I woke up the next morning to sunshine, birdsong, and my mother bringing me breakfast in bed.

"Happy birthday, dear Madeline," she said, carrying in a tray on which she'd arranged a croissant, a linen napkin, a butter plate, and a bud vase filled with sprigs of forsythia that I was pretty sure our neighbors wouldn't begrudge me, considering.

"Oh, Mom, how glorious!"

"I would've made you coffee, but I have no idea how to work that ridiculous contraption in your kitchen."

She brought in a box of presents and then the girls, so they could cavort on the duvet next to me while I opened everything.

For lunch, I pitched the idea of barbecue.

It was so warm and sunny out that we decided to put Parrish and India in their little red wagon and walk to Daddy Bruce's, before Mom hit the road again for California.

The sky overhead was pristine and deep and cloudless, its hue so rich I pointed up and said to Mom, "If egg yolks were blue instead of yellow, that's what they'd look like."

We smelled the place blocks before we could see it, the dry mountain air perfumed with meat-rich smoke. Daddy Bruce's tiny white shack was banked with cords of split hardwood and set in the middle of a parking lot beside one tree that was just starting to leaf out.

Squint and this was rural-route backwoods: Carolina, Alabama, East Texas. Some green crossroads place where the first drops of afternoon rain sizzled to steamy nothing on hot metal roofs and pairs of old hounds drowsed in the shade of every sagging roadside porch.

I parked the red wagon and hoisted Parrish to my hip as Mom reached down for India.

There were two four-top tables, two bar stools, and a battered upright piano crowded inside, all four walls fluttering with thumbtacked-up Bible verses and newspaper clippings in the front door's draft.

The man himself smiled from behind the back counter at all of us—grease-spattered white sleeves rolled to his elbows, baggy trousers belted with packing twine. I perused the menu and then asked for a pair of three-meat plates with coleslaw and beans.

"Now, aren't those the two *prettiest* little girls," said Daddy Bruce, grinning at Parrish and India in turn. "Are they twins?"

I nodded, smiling back at him. "We just celebrated their first birthday."

"You have your hands full, young lady," he said. "I'll bring everything over when it's ready, all right?"

I thanked him profusely, shifting Parrish to my other hip as she crowed "Meow!" and grabbed at my hair.

"And whatever you'd care to drink, please just help yourself from that there," he said, laughing, as he pointed toward a grimy Styrofoam cooler on the floor beside the piano.

Then he picked up a cleaver and went to work on ribs and chicken and a big hunk of brisket.

I walked back toward the table Mom had chosen, stopping off at the drinks cooler. "Do you want anything?"

"I'm fine," she said.

I grabbed a couple of Sprites anyway. "Hey, live large. I'm getting reimbursed."

When I'd settled into a chair with Parrish on my lap, I opened both sodas and handed one to Mom.

"To the revolution," I said, raising mine in the air.

"Wherever it may be," my mother replied, clinking my Sprite with hers.

As we each took a sip, Daddy B came out from behind the counter with our meat-laden paper plates held high.

"I hope you all enjoy your meal," he said, depositing them on the table before us.

"Oh, this looks *wonderful*," said Mom, smiling up at him.

I thanked him, too, as Parrish reached out to grab a slice of Wonder Bread, toppling a rib off my groaning plate.

Mom sampled a bite of brisket, then put her fork down and looked at me, suddenly serious. "Madeline, there's something I've been meaning to tell you."

She cleared her throat.

I pulled Parrish tighter against my belly, the rib I was about to take a bite out of paused in midair. "Is everything okay?"

"Well," she said, "I got married. Three months ago."

India slapped her hands into Mom's baked beans and started paddling around in them. Neither of us moved to stop her.

"Um," I said. "Wow."

Mom's fourth marriage, commenced on a Valentine's Day, had lasted all of ten months. Considering it was to this straight preppy Republican guy who lived in the most uptight and schmancy part of Maine, we offspring had been stunned the union endured through the subsequent Fourth of July.

After that divorce she'd often joked that she should found Marriage Anonymous, so that if she ever again felt a wedding coming on she could call a friend to talk her out of it.

But she'd never gotten married secretly before. And her waiting three months for the big reveal didn't exactly make me want to know who Bachelor Number Five was.

I put the rib down, untouched. "To whom?"

"Bill Garrison."

Bill Garrison: my mother's death-row pen pal, currently residing at San Quentin. He'd spent the last twelve years appealing his conviction for the murder of two pawnbrokers in Joshua Tree, California—an event the biker friend who'd testified against him at trial claimed had been inspired by Garrison's lack of funds to cover the eight hundred bucks he owed some local meth wholesalers.

On the bright side, my siblings and I wouldn't have to worry about generating the usual awkward new-stepdad small talk, come Thanksgiving or Christmas.

But an appropriate response for my mother here and now wasn't exactly something Emily Post could help me with.

I wondered why Mom never seemed to marry anyone cool.

Like, say, Daddy Bruce, who'd just plopped himself down at the piano and started in on the keys with some serious boogie-woogie chops.

Sure, the man's wardrobe could use an upgrade, Mom had never dated anyone black, *and* he had to be closing in on eighty—but he was charming, gainfully employed, probably not a predicate felon, and God knows he could *cook*.

"*Mazel tov*," I said anyway, toasting her with my bottle of Sprite and all the enthusiasm I could fake. "And may you both enjoy every happiness."

"We've already had two conjugal visits," she confided, giggling. "And since he's been in jail for twelve years, I *know* he doesn't have AIDS."

I bit my tongue, literally, at that sheer departure from logic—then scootched my plastic fork under the coleslaw, circumventing a sudden and over-whelming desire to stab its tines into my right eye-ball, repeatedly.

But then I looked up at her, and realized how relieved she was to have let me in on her secret.

My mother was *beaming*, damn it—as truly happy as I'd seen her since the death three years earlier of her greatest love, Bonwit.

And, okay, Bonwit had been a *total* asshole, but still...Who the hell was I to take potshots at my mother's joy?

I reached across the table to squeeze her hand. "Good for you, Mom."

Admittedly, I was still a teensy bit bummed that her *first* après-Bonwit marriage—to the guy from Maine, who always urged us to order shrimp cock-tails when he took us out for dinner—had lasted a mere ten months.

Mom walked out without taking a dime from

this man. She'd even given the chunky-sapphire engagement ring back.

When the guy's mother died several months later, his cut of the familial chemical-dynasty inheritance had been $187 million. After taxes.

Oh fucking well.

I pulled a notepad and pencil out of the diaper bag by my feet and stood up. "You got the girls for a minute, Mom? I need to get a couple of quotes from Mr. Bruce."

Just after I'd hugged Mom good-bye on our front porch, she reached into her bag and pulled out a check.

"When you guys were little," she said, handing it to me, "Mummie and Daddy started giving me an allowance of a hundred dollars a month. I'd like to do the same for you. Maybe you can use it for a little babysitting while you're doing this newspaper job, or so you and Dean can go out for dinner."

I kissed her cheek and hugged her again. "You're amazing, Mom. Thank you."

"I remember how it was," she said. "Having a little something of your own really matters."

Before I tucked the girls into their cribs that night, I gave them each an extra kiss. "That's from your dad," I said. "He is apparently having too much fun partying in expense-account New Orleans to remember his wife's birthday, *and* that, as such, it might have been a good idea to call home."

India murmured and shifted onto her side, her eyes already closed.

I was officially an ancient thirty-two-year-old with an AWOL husband and a brand-new step-father on death row, but my little daughters *totally* fucking rocked.

And I figured I might as well write up the Daddy Bruce piece, since there was nothing decent on TV and the girls were asleep.

My friend Melissa, back in New York, insisted that placentas were composed pretty much entirely of maternal brain cells, "which is why we've all gotten so goddamn stupid now that we've given birth."

Her point was borne home to me once more when I sat down in front of the computer in our laundry room closet and tried to start writing about lunch.

I had vestigial inklings of how to write an article, don't get me wrong. It was just that all the little gobbets of quotable triviana orbited my head like some Elmer Fudd halo of stars and bluebirds, chirping and whirling in the wake of Bugs Bunny's sledgehammer.

I stared at the blinky cursor, thinking about how Carolina-style barbecue was vinegar- rather than tomato-based...how Daddy Bruce helped his father (Daddy-Daddy?) dish up several thousand free meals in Denver, every Thanksgiving...how I'd found his culinary artistry more uplifting than a truckload of Prozac...

And then I just started typing and free-associating: Melville's Ishmael blathering about his "hypos," Robert Johnson's rosy-crossroads fixation (hat tip to Henry Miller best left only implied), nation sacks and John-the-Conqueror root, hard-wood smoke and blue-tick hounds, Delta diasporas and the Great Migration, alienation and Angola and Alan Lomax and our collective yearning for authenticity...I mean, fuck it, why let a good liberal-arts education go to waste?

By the time I was ready for bed, I had my word count—and at least a hint of my mojo back.

10

"This has voice in *spades*," said McNally, suede cow-boy boots slung across his desk as he read through my draft the next day. "A little over the top, but I'd sure as shit rather rein you in than crowbar style into the usual flat blather."

He looked up at me, tapping the page ends square against his thighs. "Job's yours if you want it."

"Excellent," I said. "Thank you."

"You have little kids, right?"

I nodded. "Twin girls."

He squinted at his watch. "Any way you might have a couple of hours free this afternoon?"

Parrish and India were already at a drop-in day care center, run out of the same building that hosted the mother-and-toddler meetings I'd blown off for the last three weeks.

The allowance check would cover at least a few more hours of babysitting there.

Thank you, Mom.

"I might be able to swing that," I finally answered McNally. "What've you got in mind?"

"Another fire. My pal Benny's meeting me over there in twenty minutes, and I need a wingman to write the sidebar."

"About?"

"Q and A with the arson investigator."

"What's it pay?"

"Twenty bucks."

"Babysitting's gonna cost me more than that, McNally."

"Thirty," he said, extending his hand.

I shook it. "Can I borrow your phone?"

McNally's old Land Cruiser was splotchy-primer gray, cabbage roses of rust blooming through at the doorsills.

The thing about SUVs in Boulder is that people actually *need* four-wheel drive, especially up in the canyons. I mean, navigating Fourmile or Sunshine or Lefthand in your Camry, September-to-June?

Might as well RSVP "delighted" for the Donner Party, God help you.

"Sweet ride," I said, hauling myself up into the passenger seat.

There was a VISUALIZE WHIRLED PEAS bumper sticker across the cracked door of his glove compartment and serious guy-smell: wet dog and neat's-foot oil, maybe a hint of roll-your-own Bugler tobacco.

"I need to get the lowdown from my old pal Benny," said McNally, belting himself in beside me. "Probably take him for coffee. He's been on-site since the wee darks this morning. Okay if I drop you off? Mimi Neff's going to let you shadow her at the scene."

"She's the investigator?"

He cranked the ignition, nodding. "She's good. Some of these guys, you'll get a line of crap about how the forensic aspect is 'more art than science,' but Mimi's the real deal. You'll have to glove up and stay out of her way, though."

"No problem," I said, as he panzered out of the parking lot.

The car's suspension was for shit and the engine was loud enough that McNally had to yell over it. "I'll be going for the big picture from Benny— overview of the earlier fires, whether this one fits in as a serial thing. Your sidebar is tight focus on Mimi. Concrete stuff about her process. Give me a feel for how she decodes *this* scene, detail by detail."

"I can do that," I said, crossing my fingers and hiding them under my thigh.

Lucky for me, Mimi was low-key but chatty.

McNally parked in front of a big old brown-shingled Craftsman place, ten blocks and just as many tax brackets up Mapleton from Dean's and my funky rental.

Mimi was probably Mom's age, slim-hipped and tall with thick blond hair falling dead-straight to her shoulders. She spotted McNally and waved us forward from her perch on the building's scorched-stone front porch.

There was a very expensive camera slung around her neck, its worn leather strap studded with little silver conchas.

"You *again*, Jon?" she called out, as we ducked under the crime-scene tape at the sidewalk's edge.

Her diction was preppy "ladies sailing" New York, and she had a smoker's laugh.

"You know me, Mimi," McNally replied, "I always want to hang out with the cool kids."

He introduced the two of us, then jogged around

to the backyard once she'd told him where to find his pal Benny.

I climbed up three stairs to the porch. Somebody'd axed the front door open, and everything smelled of wet soot and char with a chemical undertone—sour and astringent. I was glad I had on my boots. The porch floor was littered with broken glass.

"We need to get into some haz-mat gear," she said. "Never know what you're going to run into at a scene."

We went out to her truck, and she got out a pair of crinkly beige jumpsuits and booties, then two hoods for us to put on.

"What's this stuff made of?" I asked, fingering the material.

"Nomex," she said. "Like Tyvek, only it's flame-retardant. Your hair and clothes will still stink, but there'll be less crap to scrape off when you get home."

I put everything on and Mimi opened the lid of what looked like a giant tackle box.

"Your hands look about the same size as mine," she said. "You can wear my spares."

She handed me two pairs of gloves—one thin, one chunky leather.

"Thin ones are liners. Those go on first," she said, demonstrating.

Even with the liners, the leather gloves were tough to get on, pinching a little against the skin on the backs of my hands. "Tight fit."

"You need 'em tight for finger dexterity. Picking stuff up. And palm dexterity for grip—liners help. Always a trade-off with the gloves, and when they fit right they're a bitch to get on and off, but you never know what's still going to be hot, inside."

"How 'bout I just try not to touch anything?"

She nodded, then handed me a respirator.

I must've looked like I was balking at the idea of putting it on, although I had total respect for her expertise.

"I worked with a guy several years ago," she said. "Battalion chief. He went into a house the day after a fire to check out a canister someone found in a back closet."

"I have a feeling this is not going to be a really *happy* story."

Mimi shook her head. "He got a lungful of whatever was in the thing. Came back outside to talk to the chief and passed out. Life support for a month, dialysis after that. Early retirement and he's still waiting for a kidney transplant."

I took the respirator. "Poor guy, that's awful."

"We call it off-gassing. A lot of times it's worse after the fire's out. More toxic."

"Good to know," I said.

"I've documented the structure's exterior, so we're good to go inside, all right?"

I nodded.

"I'll need you to keep behind me," she continued, "and I'm going to be moving pretty slowly—collecting samples and taking a lot of photographs."

"Slow is fine. I'll do my best to keep out of your way. But you can work a camera with these gloves on?"

"It's not great, but I've had a lot of practice."

"I'm impressed," I said.

"Just make sure you step pretty much where I do, all righty?" she continued. "The place looks pretty decent structurally or I wouldn't let you in there, but there may still be hot spots. We don't need either of us falling though to the basement."

I shifted my weight and crunched some glass underfoot. "McNally told me the owners were away skiing?"

"Thank God. A neighbor called this in around three A.M. They would've been upstairs, asleep."

I shivered.

"This fire moved fast and burned *hot*, too," she said. "Flashover up front, here—very high temperatures."

"How can you tell?"

She picked up a triangular blade of glass from the ground and handed it to me. "Hold that up to the light."

The gloves were good, but it still felt weird to hold the piece of glass in my thickened fingers.

I turned toward the west, squinting as I raised the little shard up against the afternoon sun. It glistened, shot through with tiny spiderweb cracks that caught the yellowing light. "Crazing from the temperature?"

"You see that when superheated glass gets hit with cold water."

"The fire hoses?"

"Exactly," she said.

"But wouldn't the water pressure have pushed the glass *inward*?"

"I talked to the crew. They'd just swept a hose across this façade once when the front windows blew. Lucky no one had gotten in closer than the sidewalk."

"Jesus," I said. "No kidding."

"And look at that…"

I followed the trajectory of her pointed finger to the front door's threshold.

"That sill's aluminum," she said. "It melted, so the fire was burning at twelve hundred twenty degrees Celsius at least—and the wood *under* it is charred."

"So, what, the fire started in the basement?" I asked, squatting down beside her. "I mean, flames burn *up*, don't they?"

She shook her head. "I've seen investigators claiming arson because of exactly that. They think the wood can only burn if there was accelerant running under the sill. Which is total horseshit, frankly."

"What makes it char, then?"

"The heat of the aluminum itself."

"Jesus."

"But from the exterior damage, I can tell this front room is where the fire originated. The hallway door was closed..."

She motioned me over to the blackened window frames, pulling a Maglite from a front pocket and clicking it on. The room was on the eastern side of the house—and the sun was sinking westward, not to mention shaded by the deep wraparound porch.

Mimi moved the light's beam across the far wall inside, across the remains of a sofa. Not like we had to worry about it reflecting off the window glass anymore.

She brought the beam to rest. "See that vee-mark scorched on the paint, above the couch?"

I peered in at the charred hulk of something, resting against the far wall.

Could've started out as a sofa, I guess, though at that point it looked more like something you'd find smoldering in a cornfield after a 747 crash.

She was right—the vee-scorch was easy to pick out, even by flashlight.

"Okay," I said, "I see it."

"You get those above objects that burned intensely."

"Why the vee? What makes that shape?"

"Flames and hot gases angle outward when they hit a horizontal surface. The ceiling, a tabletop. Often indicates a point of origin, but there can be multiple marks like that throughout a structure."

"If someone touched off different starter fires?"

"Not necessarily. You find them above pieces of furniture, anything substantial that burns hot."

She lowered the beam to the burn-crater centered in what was left of the sofa's seat cushions—which was nothing, basically. Springs stuck up out of the hole, tilted every which way like a bed of robotic ferns.

"The heat's intensity turned that metal white," she said.

"So this *isn't* arson?"

"Might find out when we go inside," she said. "If we're lucky."

She put her respirator on, then helped me with mine.

"You kind of have to yell when you're wearing these," she yelled.

"Okay," I yelled back.

Very Darth Vader, the pair of us.

11

We'd stepped inside the front hallway of the burned house.

Mimi played her Maglite along the walls of the room we'd just been peering into from the porch. "Fire started here, probably *in* that sofa."

I nodded.

"Hallway door and windows were shut," she continued, "and it burned hot enough to hit flashover."

"What?"

"FLASHOVER." She yelled louder, and kept the volume up. "Superheated gases gather at the ceiling. The cloud thickens and starts banking down the walls, hotter and hotter as it gets closer to the floor. At a certain point, that cloud *becomes* fire. The whole room does."

I caught most of that. It was weird, not seeing her lips move, but I was getting better at deciphering with every word she spoke.

"And that's when the windows blew out?" I said.

"WHAT?"

I tried again, louder.

She nodded. "Blew the glass out, blew the door wide open, and now you've got a fireball with more oxygen suddenly available, so it roars into the hallway—*still* so hot it melts that aluminum sill."

"So what do you look for next?" I yelled.

"Traces of accelerant. I'll need samples from this front room, to start with. Carpet, flooring, anything left of the sofa cushions..."

She walked back to grab her tackle box from the porch floor, snapping its latches shut and hoisting it up to her hip. It looked damn heavy.

I reached for it. "Why don't I carry that?"

"Great." She let me take it. "Okay?"

The thing must have weighed fifty pounds, but I nodded assent.

"Ready?"

Another nod from me.

She stepped over the front room's threshold, and I was all set to follow when she looked back over her shoulder at me. "Let me go in alone first. I'm worried about the floor."

"No problem," I yelled, stopping at the doorway.

Jesus, my throat was already sore. How did these guys do this all the time?

Her giant tackle box was digging into the side of my thigh and I thought my right hand was about to fall off, so I wrestled with the damn thing until I had it in both arms instead.

Mimi walked toward the center of the room, slowly and carefully.

"Okay," she said, waving me in.

I humped the tackle box forward and lowered it beside her, with a bit of an unbecoming groan near the end of that effort.

"What's in this," I asked, "anvils and bowling balls?"

She chuckled, the flash on her Pentax charging up with an ascending whine.

I kept quiet while she took photographs.

Only when she'd documented every aspect of what the room looked like untouched did she start taking actual samples.

The tackle box had those stacking trays inside that accordioned up and out until it was the size of a small desk. Mimi knew the contents blind— X-Acto knives, chisels, needle-nose pliers, a box cutter, tweezers…zippered plastic bags in a bazil- lion sizes, with an equivalent number of manila envelopes. Glass slides that looked like they were for a microscope. Little tiny jars. Wide transparent tape and squares of card stock to stick it to.

"*A Thousand Clowns*," I said, thinking of the miniature circus car filled with same that Jason Robards referred to, during the course of my favorite early-1960s anti-establishment flick.

"Great movie," yelled Mimi, scissoring a chunk of singed foam rubber from the arm of the ruined sofa. "'Good morning, campers, I'm disappointed in the *very* sorry turnout for last night's volleyball game—'"

I understood every word of that, and laughed.

She turned around and looked across the floor of the room again. "The problem with flashover... wipes out evidence. You lose the 'pour pattern.'"

"Yeah?"

"Splash accelerant around and light it, burn pattern's uneven. Flooring, carpeting..."

"Okay," I yelled back.

"Usually fire burns *up*, pattern's intact. Not with flashover."

I nodded for her to continue.

"Extreme temperatures down low in a room? Pour pattern's obliterated. No differentiation."

"Bummer," I yelled, looking at the evenly scorched flooring. "So how do you check?"

"Gimme that hammer," said Mimi, pointing to an upper tray of her tackle box.

I picked it up and held it out toward her.

"Chisel," she yelled, so I gave her that, too.

She walked over to the corner of the room closest to the sofa. "See? Floor dips down?"

I nodded. "Sure."

"Liquid accelerant runs downhill and pools. So if it's near a *wall*..."

She knelt. I watched her angle the chisel's tip to rest against what looked like a join in the baseboard, about eight inches away from the corner of the room.

Mimi gave the handle a good whack and the chisel bit into this seam. She pulled the tool free, then brought the narrow tip to rest at the topmost juncture of baseboard and wall.

One more hard tap popped the entire piece of wood free. She picked this up, twisting at the waist so I could see it.

"Accelerant pools next to a wall," she yelled, "the baseboard gets charred up the *back*."

She turned the wood over.

Goddamn if that side wasn't charred to shit.

I gave her a thumbs-up and watched her eyes crinkle into a smile, above the respirator.

I checked my watch. We'd been here over an hour.

"Babysitter?" she asked.

"Half an hour left."

"I'll show you the big room at the back."

"You are a total goddess," I yelled.

"What?"

I gave up. "*Thank* you."

"Need to check one more thing," said Mimi.

"Sure."

She moved back over to the sofa, shining her flashlight down into the oddly white springs, angling it toward the arm of the thing.

"Ha!" yelled Mimi, plunging her gloved hand down into the furniture guts.

"What?"

She raised her hand so I could see the little yellowy tube of fluff pincered between her thumb and index finger.

"Cigarette filter," she said. "Simplest fuse going—Marlboro stuck in a matchbook. Light it, stick it between the cushions, leave…"

She bagged it up for evidence, then got to her feet, waving a thumb toward the back of the house.

I nodded and followed her out of the room.

We moved down the hallway, slowly.

When she passed an open door on the left, Mimi stopped and played her flashlight slowly over the small room beyond its threshold.

"See that?" she asked, as the beam of light came to rest on a scorched metal cup resting on a waist-high countertop.

Downward-pointing spikes of multicolored plastic were hanging from all around the cup's lip. It looked like a houseplant from Mars, but I nodded anyway.

"Toothbrushes," she yelled.

I watched the light swing to the left, down a blackened rod a little higher than my head, draped with more plastic stalactites at regular intervals. "Shower-curtain rings?"

She nodded at me.

The curtain itself had joined the choir eternal, leaving not so much as a grommet in the wake of its cindery demise.

Mimi dropped the tip of the flashlight lower, playing its beam across the tub surround. "Flame-retardant eats into marble, see that?"

"Okay."

She turned away from the door frame, walking carefully toward the rear of the house.

Stopping between some half-opened pocket doors at the end of the hall, Mimi whistled softly, a descending note of dismay. "I feel sorry for the claims adjustor..."

She stepped into the room and I followed.

"From the insurance company?" I asked.

She nodded. "What I used to do. Horrible—you have to count up *everything* for depreciation. Down to the number of Q-tips and tampons."

I shook my head.

We were in a west-facing large room at the back of the house, and Mimi turned off her flashlight. The place was filled with golden late-afternoon sunlight, and the sour chemical smell was much stronger.

There were scummy puddles of water on the Saltillo-tile floor.

The fire hadn't been as intense in this part of the house—even I could tell that.

There were more shards of glass everywhere. I wondered whether the windows had been bashed manually by firefighters, or just blown inward by the intense pressure of hose-water.

Mimi had knelt down to take a sample of the oily water. "The worst part, you've gotta quantify personal things. Like those..."

I turned toward where she was pointing, at a row of five antique quilts hanging along the wall behind us.

Two were scorched, but even the ones still somewhat intact were sooty, waterlogged, and ruined.

A sixth quilt had slid to the floor in a sorry heap after the pole that'd held it up pulled free of the wall.

"Can I walk closer?" I yelled, pointing.

Mimi nodded.

I moved in, then crouched down next to the wet lump of fallen quilt.

My pal Sophia had taken me to a domestic-textile exhibition back east the year before, so I knew what it was: a log-cabin pattern pieced from hundreds of "cigar silks"—narrow embroidered ribbons that various tobacco companies included with their premium brands as a come-on collectible, back in the teens.

Someone must've hit this one with an arc of chemical foam, melting the fabric away in ragged splotches, revealing batting that was filthy and wet.

I wondered how many hours of work had gone into the quilt, how many years invested in collecting the silks themselves. A quiet testament to some long-ago women's communal work, ruined in one angry flash.

I smoothed out a bunched flap of fabric tenderly with my gloved hands. The stitches were so tiny, so regular. All made by hand.

When my thighs started to prickle, I got to my feet.

"Oh, God, the books...," I said, looking at a floor-to-ceiling shelf of old volumes to my right, their leather spines swollen and bent.

Mimi stepped up beside me.

She squatted down, pointing toward a lower shelf. "See those?"

The shelf housed a row of matching albums, bound in different colors of leather with names and dates embossed in gold on the spines.

Rivulets of sooty water dripped to the floor when Mimi pulled two of these volumes out. The empty shelf had been painted white, the row of books' scalloped footprint now outlined in greasy black from the smoke.

"Scrapbooks," she said, peeling each one open in turn. "Good..."

I looked over her shoulder. The pages were gummed together, the handwritten captions illegible.

"Good?" I yelled. "Sad!"

"Both. If the owners had set the fire, they'd probably have tried to sneak these out first."

"Oh! Good, then."

Mimi glanced at her own watch. "Babysitter?"

We both stood up, and I followed her back down the hallway to the front door.

"Want me to get you a ride?" she asked, when we were back out on the street and respirator-free.

"I'm okay, thanks. My house is right down the hill and the child care place is on the way."

"You're sure?"

"We could throw the wagon in the back of a truck, but I don't have car seats."

"Right," she said, nodding. "It's been a long time since I had to deal with all that. Forgot about the car seats."

"Thank you so much for letting me follow you around today," I said, when we'd reached her truck. "What you do is really fascinating, and it's a rare pleasure for me these days to hang out with grown-ups."

I meant that sincerely, wishing I had time to keep talking.

I took off her gloves, then the suit, hood, and booties.

"You can just throw everything in the bed, there," she said. "I'll deal with it later."

Mimi took her own gloves off and grabbed a business card and pen out of her glove compartment. She jotted her home number on the card's back, then handed it to me. "If you have any other questions, feel free to call."

I decided to do what my mother does whenever

she meets someone interesting: ask her to come by for a glass of wine when she'd finished up.

"That'd be great," she said. "Long day, 'and miles to go before I sleep.'"

"Nineteen thirteen Mapleton." I wrote that out with my phone number on the end of her card, then ripped it off and gave it to her. "It's the house with totally lame Christmas lights still wrapped around the porch columns."

12

I picked up Parrish and India at the community center, handing over my last forty bucks to the child care boss-lady, who then got all snippy with me about not having left them with enough diapers, just as I'd finished loading the girls into our little wagon.

She was tall and stern with a prissy little mouth. "It isn't our responsibility to provide supplies for *your* children."

"I'm sorry," I said. "I got asked at the last minute to work for another two hours."

She stepped closer to me and wrinkled her nose.

I took a step backward. "Sorry. I was following an arson investigator around the scene of a recent fire. The smoke is kind of cloying."

"And *that's* why you were late?" she asked, pinching her tiny mouth even more tightly around the words.

"I'm not late. I'm actually five minutes early," I said, pointing at the wall clock above her head. "I mean, early for the readjusted pickup time."

"So you just presumed we could fill in for you, at the last minute?"

"I beg your pardon, but where exactly does presumption come into this? I reserved a block of time through your office yesterday, and called to request more time today when it became apparent I needed it. I don't drive, I just got hired at the *Boulder New Times*, my husband is away on business, and I was given a last-minute extra assignment by my editor. Which will almost but not quite cover the money I just *paid* you."

So lighten the fuck up and show me a little feminist solidarity here, bitch.

She crossed her arms, nostrils wrinkling again.

"I mean, look," I continued, "taking my one-year-old twins to a crime scene didn't seem like a really splendid parenting move. And this place is called a *drop*-in child care center—not to mention one that claims to be 'dedicated to supporting the families of Boulder,' right on the front door."

"One of your children ate a great deal of sand on

our playground," she sniffed, turning on her heel to dismiss me. "It's developmentally inappropriate."

"As is your attitude," I muttered, watching her goose-step primly away down the hall, "and I feel sorry as hell for that poor two-by-four you've got shoved up your fascist butt, you haggity sphincter-mouth cow."

"Moo!" chortled one of the girls, from beneath the wagon's canvas roof.

At home, I changed the girls' diapers and then plopped them into the playpen so I could wash my hands before attempting to scrape together some reasonable facsimile of dinner.

"Oh, *crap*," I said, catching sight of myself in the medicine-cabinet mirror.

Where the respirator had been was still relatively flesh-toned, but the rest of my face and neck were so soot-encrusted I didn't know whether to belt out "Chim Chim Cher-ee" or clutch a plaid shawl around my head and go sell matches on Pearl Street.

I lathered up my hands with a bar of Dean's Ivory soap instead, watching the blue-black runoff swirl drainward. Once I'd scrubbed my face clean with the moistened corner of a towel, I used it to scrape grime off the now-filthy bar of soap.

I'd just dumped my clothes on the kitchen floor,

grabbing a quasi-clean high school football jersey of Dean's out of the laundry pile, when Parrish got weepy in the dining room. I pulled on the shirt, hoisted her up onto my hip, and threw a frozen pizza into the toaster oven before slicing up two bananas and a crown of broccoli one-handed.

"Your mother," I observed, as I nuke-steamed the broccoli bits soft in the microwave, "is a goddamn genius."

She rested her head against my shoulder, popping a thumb in her mouth.

I kissed her fuzzy scalp and rocked her gently. Out beyond the kitchen window, the sky above Boulder's steeply pitched rooftops deepened to purple.

The toaster oven dinged at the exact second the phone rang, of course. I strapped Parrish in her booster seat and yanked out the pizza before grabbing the receiver.

"Hello?" I tucked the phone between my shoulder and cheek, stretching the cord as far as it would go into the dining room so I could scoop India up out of the playpen.

"Hi, Bunny," said my husband. "They overbooked my flight out of New Orleans."

"That sucks, I'm so sorry. Any chance of catching another one?"

"One more U.S. Scare plane through Pittsburgh, but it's full. I have to stay here another night."

"That *really* sucks." I fastened India's booster belt and started slicing the pizza, hissing when I singed my fingers. "Ow. *Shit*."

"You okay?"

"Hot cheese," I said. "I'm getting the girls' dinner ready."

"How are they?" His voice got all soft and I could hear echoey background noises.

"They're gorgeous. They're hungry."

I filled their yellow plastic trays with foodstuffs and snapped them into the booster armrests.

"I miss them so much," said Dean. "It just kills me when I'm on the road."

"I know."

"Kiss them good night for me, okay?"

"Of course," I said. "I always do."

It was too dark to see out past our kitchen window anymore.

My reflection looked old and tired: Queen Victoria in an East Syracuse–Minoa varsity football schmatte.

"I should get in tomorrow about noon," said Dean, "but I have to go straight to the office. Bittler's got some conference-call thing set up for one thirty."

I wove the phone cord through my fingers. "Okay."

And how've you been, Bunny?

Just great, thanks for asking. Hey, guess what? I even got a job.

"Listen," he said, "the hotel shuttle's pulling up to the curb. Gotta run."

"Call me back when you get—" I said.

I heard the pay phone's receiver click to rest, all the way from Louisiana.

Perfect.

I sat on the kitchen floor next to my girls, Indian-style.

They were happily slathered in pizza sauce, head-to-toe and ear-to-ear.

Parrish had cheese strung through her fuzzy hair like Christmas-tree tinsel, and India smiled, pressing a mushy sprig of broccoli to my lips.

"Eat!" she said. "Yum!"

Parrish patted my cheek with a well-sauced little hand. "Mummie!"

Even though I was solo-parenting for yet another night, I had a great time doing it.

Sure, I hadn't slept more than six hours at a stretch all month, Dean had been away for three of the last four weeks, and I still wanted to bitch-slap that day care lady, but giving the girls a bubble bath in the old clawfoot tub upstairs just felt fun for a change.

I gave India a kewpie-doll spike 'do once I'd lathered up their heads with baby shampoo, and Parrish kept looking at her and giggling.

They pounded the water's surface with their little fists and scootched around a lot, sloshing fresh-smelling sudsy breakers over the tub's curled lip and onto the floor.

The knees of my pants got soaking wet, as did the entire front of Dean's jersey, but I figured I'd take a bath myself once I'd put them to bed so it was a head start, what the hell, and anyway it was terrific, hanging out with my kids and being ridiculous.

Most nights when I was on my own, I was totally exhausted by this point—dragging ass through the last couple of hours until the girls were asleep and I could crash on the sofa to bond vicariously with Sipowicz on *NYPD Blue*.

I knew exactly what had made tonight feel better than that. It was having gotten to go out and do something on my own during the course of the day, something I was *good* at, for a change.

I also knew exactly how I was going to write up my afternoon with Mimi: the sour-thick smell of that house, the blackened walls and heat-alligatored paint, the drooping horsetail points of each melted toothbrush and shower-curtain ring, the soupy puddles of hose-water delineating Mercator-projection oceans and continents across the floors . . .

I reached my arm into the lukewarm bathwater and popped out the old white rubber drain plug, then bundled up both my kids in fluffy clean towels.

"Life is good," I told them. "Your mom has her chops back. And also she put the laundry away for once so we actually *have* fluffy clean towels, all folded up in the linen closet."

I had a fleeting flashback to the ruined scrapbooks in that house. Baby pictures. Wedding. The travesty of the quilts . . .

Not now.

Right now it's all good. Now is the best.

Enjoy this. Be here. Revel in it.

I blew a raspberry on India's belly and made her laugh, then it was Parrish's turn.

Ten minutes later they were diapered and pajamaed and tucked into their cribs.

"And tomorrow your dad will be home," I whispered, standing at the threshold of their room.

I eased the door almost closed, leaving a yellow band of hallway-light reassurance across the wooden floor between them.

*　　*　　*

Colorado was the first place I'd ever lived where the grown-up shows came on at nine instead of ten, via that whole "Central Time" scheduling loophole. Kind of great, actually.

When the phone rang, I was kicked back on the sofa with a towel around my head and Sipowicz had just explained that some perp was *a rage-aholic, which means he's often pissed off—unlike the vast majority of us gliding along devil-may-care.*

I jogged to the kitchen, picking up on the third ring. "You got back to the hotel okay?"

Mimi Neff said, "Actually, I'm still down at the station."

"Hey there, sorry. Thought you'd be my husband."

"Not in this lifetime," she laughed, "but is that glass of wine still on offer, or am I too late?"

"Your timing is exquisite. I gave you the address, right? I'll turn on the porch light."

"Need anything from the outside world?"

"All set, thanks. Just bring your most excellent self."

I said *ciao* to New York's fictional finest and jammed several truckloads of living room detritus into a handy nearby closet.

13

I've got Zinfandel, Liebfraumilch, or Anchor Steam," I said to Mimi as I stared into the icebox. "And the Liebfraumilch is my mom's, so I'd recommend giving that a pass."

"Beer sounds perfect."

I grabbed one for each of us. "You want a glass?"

"Bottle's fine."

"A woman after my own butch heart," I said, handing her one. "Pretty sure they're twist-offs."

She trailed me back to the living room and we sank into the sofa with happy sighs.

"Any recommendations on getting rid of the smoke smell?" I asked. "I did the lather-rinse-repeat thing three times and my hair still reeks."

She sniffed the air. "Not so bad. At the scene

today, there weren't any—" Mimi stopped mid-word, eyes to the floor as she took a sip of beer.

"Any what?"

"It's just, you know, *worse* if there's been a fatality. The, uh, composition of the smoke being different."

I grimaced, sucking a little air inward through my teeth. "Yeah, that makes sense."

"Sorry," she said.

"That's okay. I mean, I admire you guys for dealing, you know? I don't think I could handle it."

"Well, that part's rough," she said. "Otherwise, I kind of dig it. I like how exacting I have to be, figuring out what happened, piece by piece."

"You must be *incredibly* organized."

"Yeah." She looked around the still-rather-chaotic room and smiled, then patted the edge of the sofa: the front panel of fabric just under the floral-chintz seat cushions had lots of large holes in it, with cotton batting poking out.

Mimi tried poking it back in. "Interesting, um, decor."

"Funny story about that," I said, taking another swallow of beer.

She took one herself. "Hmmm?"

"Well, there was soy sauce and stuff spilled down the front of the sofa, and I thought it looked kind of crappy so I bought this foaming upholstery-cleaner spray, back in New York…"

She nodded.

"Unfortunately," I continued, "the stuff turned out to be made for *car* upholstery. The sofa got really clean for about fifteen seconds. Before it melted."

Mimi started laughing.

"Yeah, go ahead," I said, "rub it in. Made me cry at the time. First piece of furniture I ever bought new, and I turned it to shit."

"Look at the bright side," she said. "It wasn't on fire."

"Excellent point," I replied toasting her with my beer bottle. "Speaking of which, do you have a verdict yet on the place today?"

"Definitely arson."

"You figure it was set by the same person?"

"I'd say a ninety percent likelihood, but I'm still waiting on lab results."

"About the accelerant?"

"Exactly," she said.

"What kind of analysis do you do?" I asked.

"Mostly, we seal activated charcoal into a glass container with whatever sample we've got. Then you desorb the charcoal and—"

"Run a little gas chromatography on the sample?"

Mimi squinted at me. "I had you figured for an English major."

"We didn't actually *have* majors, at my college. Or, you know, tests. Or grades."

She snickered. "Sarah Lawrence or Bennington?"

"Sarah Lawrence," I said.

"Me too."

"Dude!" I crowed. "No fucking way!"

"Way," said Mimi, pleased.

"And here you are, all technologically savvy and shit...what was your concentration?"

"The nineteenth-century French symbolist poets."

"Perfect. Bet that comes in really handy at crime scenes."

Another snicker. "You?"

"Fiction writing. Useful for doing my taxes."

"And yet you're conversant in gas chromatography?"

I shrugged. "My husband sells scientific instruments. I pretend to know the lingo."

"Spousal business-dinner osmosis...I know it well."

"*Exactement*," I said. "So if the accelerant matches up, you think this fits as part of the recent serial stuff?"

"The guy's used cigarette fuses before. And—off the record?"

I nodded, crossing my heart. "Scout's honor."

"He's doused his sites with acetone, exclusively."

"So arsonists are usually male, I take it?"

"Statistically? White male, aged twenty to forty, with low self-esteem, poor communication skills, probably unemployed. Given the places he's targeted, he might be motivated by a need for change, or an expression of anger, or possibly revenge. Almost all these guys have a problem with alcohol. And there's a good chance he lives within a two-mile radius of the fires."

"Smart?"

"The vast majority of profiled arsonists have low IQs. Then again, if they're profiled, that means we caught them. Maybe the ones who get away with it are all mad geniuses—hate to say. We only clear about seventeen percent of arson cases."

"Holy shit," I said.

"Yeah. And if this guy's graduating to structure fires . . . He's going to end up hurting people."

"That's got to be stressful for *you* guys," I said, thinking about McNally's end of the phone conversation with his friend, back at the paper.

"Some days it's awful," she agreed. "Mostly, I've been lucky. And on a good day, it's the best work there is."

"What's the worst thing, on a bad day?" I asked.

She looked down at her beer bottle, picking at one corner of its label. "The 'pugilistic position.'"

14

What's the 'pugilistic position'?" I asked Mimi. I knew pugilism was boxing, but I still wasn't following.

She looked up at me, somber. "Intense heat causes the muscles in a victim's body to contract, but the flexor muscles are stronger than the extensor muscles."

"Wait, which ones are the extensors?"

"You use extensors to straighten out your limbs and digits."

"Okay."

"Flexors make you do this." She raised her arms so her fists were in front of her face and lifted her knees a little, bringing the soles of her feet off the floor. "Almost always, when you find someone who burned to death, their knees are bent, their arms are raised, and their hands are making fists."

I shivered.

She lowered her arms, relaxed her legs.

I closed my eyes for a long moment.

"Yeah," said Mimi. "When you have to see that, it's a bad day. A soul-wrenching day."

Eyes open again, I said, "I can't begin to imagine."

I placed my empty bottle on the coffee table, standing up to shake off the specter of that image. "May I grab you another beer?"

"Thank you," she said, "but I should get home. My dogs—and your kids—will probably wake up early."

"Most assuredly."

Mimi stood, grabbing our empties and toting them into the kitchen.

"Thank you," I said, trailing after her.

"I appreciate the beer. And the conversation. Perfect antidote for today's work."

"I appreciate *you* letting me tag along, and thank you for coming by the house, too. When Dean's away it's always nice to have someone to talk to after the girls are asleep."

"You mentioned New York, earlier," she said as we walked back toward the front door. "What part?"

"West Sixteenth between Sixth and Seventh when the girls were born, but Oyster Bay off and on when I was a kid."

"Ah ha," she said. "I grew up in Locust Valley."

"Jesus," I said, "no *wonder* you lit out for the Wild West."

That made her laugh. "I'll keep you up to date on the investigation, and let's get together for lunch at some point, talk about civilian stuff—see if we know anyone in common from the old stomping ground."

I walked her out to the porch. "That would be terrific. Dean's away quite a bit and I don't know a lot of people here yet."

Even outside in the crisp winter air, I could still smell the smoke in my own hair. "So how long *does* it take to get rid of this, um, fragrance?" I asked, holding up a lock of it.

"Depends," she said. "I got to see an archive of documents in San Francisco last year that had been rescued after the earthquake in 1906, when half the city burned down. They still reek of smoke—made my eyes sting."

"So I'm basically going to smell like refried shit for the next ninety-nine years?"

"Try rubbing your hair with a couple of those

dryer sheets. Always works for me. Baby wipes are pretty good, too."

"Cool. I've got major stockpiles of both, as it happens."

"If all else fails, white vinegar."

"I value your expertise."

"And don't worry," she said, heading toward the sidewalk, "you'll have *loads* of friends by the Fourth of July—that's what I love about Boulder."

"From your lips to God's multitude of ears, Mimi," I replied, lifting my palms like a plaster front-lawn saint as I gazed up beseechingly at the porch light.

"Call me if you need anything else for your article?"

"Will do."

I waved good-bye as she climbed up into her pickup truck, its cab's illumination making her blond hair shine, a beacon in the night.

Before I went to bed, I dragged our old red-vinyl kitchen stool around the house, putting fresh batteries in every smoke detector. Then I got the box of dryer sheets down from the laundry-closet shelf.

The girls were restless all night. Parrish woke up shrieking around two. I opened the hallway door into their room and found her standing up in her crib, wide-eyed and sobbing.

"Shhh, sweetie, it's okay," I said, lifting her up and out over the wooden sidebars. "Did you have a bad dream?"

She wrapped her arms around my neck, clinging tight. I rubbed her back, swaying gently until her body relaxed and she quieted down.

Her forehead was cool and her diaper was still dry. I could hear the steady rhythm of her sucking her thumb and tried to lower her back into the crib, but that made her start crying again, which woke up India.

Now they were both cranky and red-faced and sobbing. I moved back and forth between the cribs, trying to soothe each of them in turn. After ten minutes of this with no diminuendo in the stereo crying jag, I was sorely tempted to just bring them into bed with me, but knew that would set a precedent sure to bite me in the ass for many long nights to follow.

"I need you guys to hang on for a sec, okay?" I said. "I'll be right back. I promise."

The wails cranked up the moment I crossed their threshold, the girls' cries echoing down the hallway behind me as I jogged groggily back to the master bedroom. I grabbed up two pillows and my duvet from the marital futon, bashing my shoulder against the door frame as I hurried back out.

"Shhhh," I said softly, tossing my bedding against the baseboard between their cribs. "I'm back now. It's okay. It's okay."

I got them both to lie down, tucking little quilts around their bodies, stroking their hair.

"I'm going to stay right in here with you guys, until you go back to sleep. Nothing to worry about."

I propped my pillows up against the wall's cool plaster and sat down, drawing the duvet over my raised knees.

"Once upon a time," I began, "there was a little girl named Goldilocks, who went for a walk in the woods. The trees were very tall, and it was cool in their shade, but every once in a while the breeze would come up, rushing through the leaves on their branches and making little spangles of sunlight dance across the path before her..."

Parrish's eyes fluttered closed just as Goldilocks sampled the third bowl of porridge. India followed suit when our discerning heroine had finally tucked herself into Baby Bear's bed.

By that point, I couldn't be bothered to go back to my own room, so I just curled up on the rug and settled in for the night.

Mimi's advice on getting the smoke out of my

hair had worked like a charm. Now I smelled liked I'd spritzed myself with the kind of drugstore perfume hopeful eighth-grade wallflowers wear to dances in twilit gymnasiums: half cotton candy, half Holiday Inn bar soap.

I didn't want to think of flashover temperatures, or the comparative weakness of flexor muscles under infernal duress, or flame-ravaged houses whose sodden contents would off-gas lethal fumes.

So instead I pictured Goldilocks's Nellie Oleson ringlets scattered across a plump little pillow, a tiny cigar-silk quilt pulled up under her dimpled chin. She lay dreaming beneath the dark wooden eaves of the forest cottage, breath sweet as honeyed milk.

Mama Bear raised the silky finger of one paw to her lips for quiet when she found the sleeping girl, then she and her ursine family padded softly back downstairs to the warmth of their kitchen.

15

Parrish and India were wide awake by seven the next morning, standing up in their cribs and babbling happily at each other. Sodden diapers sagged down between their knees, not a visual anyone sane relishes waking up to.

After my short night with nothing but thin rug between me and the hardwood floor, I could've used a forklift's help to get vertical.

"Your mother is old and creaky, my darlings," I croaked, rising slowly to my feet. "She no longer springs back with the meadow flower's dewy freshness, of a morning—undoubtedly because she drank far too much beer in college, though she only had one last night."

India laughed and performed three bouncy

pliés, gripping the side of her crib as a barre while her pendulous diaper swayed lower with each dip.

"So let that be a lesson to you," I concluded, "O my tiny wonders."

I lifted them up, positioning Parrish on my left hip, India on my right.

"Ah, just what I've always yearned for . . . ," I said, feeling the sides of the sweatshirt I'd slept in grow instantly hot and wet against my skin, "leakage."

On the bright side, their crib sheets were still dry.

Twenty minutes later, the three of us were clean, dry, freshly clothed, and—God willing—no longer hotbeds of urinary microbial splendor. The girls gave each other scalp massages with their maple syrup–drenched strips of French toast while I put the finishing touches on a pint of coffee I hoped would be strong enough to eat through several dozen marble tub surrounds.

"Ah," I said, raising the glass in my daughters' honor when I'd knocked back the first gorgeous, life-giving swallow, "more powerful than a locomotive. Just the way I like it."

Parrish drained her sippy cup and threw it at my feet. "More?"

"That's *good* asking, sweetie," I said, groaning as

I bent down to retrieve the damn thing from the autumn-hued linoleum. Sleeping on the floor had been sheer idiocy.

When I'd hosed down the kitchen and de-syruped the offspring, I decided this morning was the perfect occasion for a Disney-video double feature. I plopped the three of us down on our decrepit, sorry-ass sofa as the previews I'd long since memorized started rolling.

A basket of fresh laundry sat in front of me, yearning to be folded, but by the time Scatman Crothers was jazzing around fin-de-siècle Paris with Phil Harris and Eva Gabor in twee feline drag, my eyeballs felt like I'd dunked my face repeatedly into a sandy beach bucket brimming with soy sauce.

The girls were so entranced with the story I figured it was safe to put them on the floor for a minute and hit replay on the espresso machine.

"Kitty!" said Parrish. "Kitty kitty kitty kitty!"

"Kitty says 'meow,'" added India.

"Cheese Nip!" agreed her sister.

Thank you, Sainted Uncle Walt, for your blessed succor in this, the hour of my starkest need.

After *101 Dalmatians*, an extended family jaunt around the sunny backyard, and second kiddie-luncheon helpings of steamed carrot slices and

ravioli, I finally got the girls back upstairs and napping. I would've given my right arm and sore eyeballs to join them, even curled up on their bedroom
floor again with no pillows, but I figured it would
be my last chance all day to get my article written
before Dean came home from work.

I'd had so much coffee by this point that my
stomach felt like the English Channel on a rough
day, complete with lanolin-slathered Gertrude
Ederle doing the Australian crawl.

Once I got the computer booted up and my
opening paragraph written, however, I started feeling okay. I was in the zone, constructing a little
diction-fueled movie of everything I'd seen the day
before.

There was no chaos on the screen—unlike
pretty much every room in the house around me.
I knew the rules; all that mattered was exactitude.

Heaven.

When I was closing in on the allowed word
count, I realized I wanted to explain a little more
about what would happen in the aftermath of
Mimi's investigation, at the hands of the claims
adjustor.

What else did these people do, besides tabulat-
ing the household Q-tips and tampons? How long

would it be before buildings with that kind of damage were habitable again, if ever?

I scrabbled through the laundry pile until I found Mimi's card, then dialed her at home.

I typed as she spoke, describing how everything electronic in the house would probably be "TL'd," chalked up as a total loss: stereos and speakers, microwaves, telephones and answering machines, videotapes, televisions, computers, mini-fridges, hair dryers, and clock radios.

It didn't matter whether these items had been anywhere near actual flames or the slightest heat: The smoke would insinuate itself into the deepest recesses of any mechanism at all, ensuring the utter obsolescence of, say, a curling iron.

"Jesus," I said, typing faster to catch up when she paused for breath.

"The cabinetry will have to be ripped out," she continued, "and those bookshelves. Even if they're not damaged, there's no way to get the smell out, or the chemical residue. And the smoke leaves stencils around everything. Inside closets and cupboards, you'll see outlines of what was on the shelves— toilet paper, shoes. You can't get those marks out, either. All their clothing will have to go to a dry cleaner, but they'll still have to throw most of it out afterward because of the smell. Same thing with bedding, towels, mattresses...all Dumpster fodder. And that's not getting into Sheetrock, flooring, subfloor, structural damage."

"And how long before they can move back in?"

"Hard to say. With good insurance, you get two years of ALE—additional living expenses. That's a whole other story, pretty corrupt sometimes. And then there are the contractors who pack everything up and move it out of the house. A thousand and one details."

"Endless nightmare?"

"Yeah," she said. "All around. Most houses, you might as well torch them again and finish the job, start over from scratch."

I thought about that, quiet for a moment.

"But they're alive, Madeline. Five people in that family," said Mimi. "That's the only thing that matters, in the end. You can always buy more scrapbooks, take new pictures to fill them with. When I can go through a scene without the medical examiner, I count all of us damn lucky."

"Amen."

PART II

None of her friends thought she was the better for the surrender of her fine free spirit to the control of a man, I am ready to believe, of strong intelligence and ability—but also, I certainly know, of a dry and narrow and supercilious temper.

—Percy Lubbock describing Edith Wharton's relationship with Walter Berry, quoted in Louis Auchincloss's introduction to Wharton's *The Reef*

16

Nobody will care," said my husband when I asked him whether I should dress up a little for the Sunday-afternoon barbecue to which we'd invited a couple of his pals from work.

He'd been home for several days now. Hadn't mentioned my birthday again, or the fabulously great present he'd promised me on the phone from New Orleans.

"I'm a total hag," I said. "And also my hair is stupid."

"Don't be ridiculous," he said, his back to me as he rooted through his sock drawer.

I felt about as sexy as Queen Elizabeth trudging through gorse in the Scottish rain: imaginary corgi under each arm, body thick with tweed under my

Barbour coat, damp Hermès scarf tied over my lac-
quered blue-white hair.

Yeah, me and Liz Windsor: sex on wheels.

"You look perfectly all right," said Dean, still
with his back to me.

"The endearment every woman longs to hear."

That got me a put-upon sigh. "You know what I
mean, Bunny."

I stepped up behind him and twined my arms
around his waist, standing on tiptoe to press my
cheek between his shoulder blades.

"I'm sorry," I said. "I just feel like a Betty Friedan
cypher-eunuch, plummeting disenfranchised into
the black bourgeois abyss of toddler muck and Dis-
ney vids."

Dean grunted, shoulders tensing.

"I started whistling in the grocery store the other
day," I said, "and realized five bars in that I was
musically regurgitating the goddamn theme song
from *The Lion King*. What next, Andrew Lloyd
fucking Webber?"

"I can't believe I don't have a single pair of goddamn socks that match," said Dean, slamming the
drawer shut. "What the hell do you *do* with them?"

He pushed free of my arms.

"Airlift them to Romania," I said, repulsed by

my actual reflection in the mirror over our bureau, now that he wasn't blocking my view. "UN volunteers stitch them into fluffy monkeys for all those poor little orphans to play with."

Dean sat down on the edge of the bed and yanked on two socks that looked pretty damn similar, if you asked me.

He stood up. "Let's get the goddamn grocery run over with. I need at least a couple of hours for a decent bike ride."

"Sure," I said. "And hey, here's a thought...you can buy me a birthday present. A cantaloupe or a lemon zester or something. King Soopers has pretty much everything."

He sank down to the bed again, eyes downcast.

I crossed my arms. "Because I guess you left that super-fabulous gift you bought me in New Orleans on the plane or something, right?"

"It was a T-shirt," he said quietly. "Turquoise, with LADIES SEWING CIRCLE AND TERRORIST SOCIETY printed across the chest in white script. I thought it would make you laugh. And I left it either on the plane or in my hotel room."

"Huh."

"*I* thought it was funny," he said.

"We first met in what, March 1986?" I asked.

"David Goldsmith's birthday party. Central Park West."

His tone of voice was way more "as you perfectly well know" than "aw, honey, remember how romantic?"

Dick.

"It's now March 1995, Dean. Which means we've been together how long?"

He cleared his throat. "Nine years."

"And in that period of time, have you *ever* seen me wear a single item of turquoise clothing?"

He looked at the floor.

I kicked one of his shoes at him, making it skitter across the hardwood into his ankle. "Buy yourself some fucking socks for my birthday. I'd *cherish* the gift of not having to hear you whine about how they've all gone missing every time you open that stupid goddamn drawer."

By the time Dean walked back into the house that afternoon, sweaty and red-cheeked with his bike helmet tucked under one arm, I'd finished making three salads (orzo-feta-kalamata, buckwheat tabouleh, and hominy with diced Granny Smith apples and roasted sweet potatoes—in a lemon-thyme vinaigrette), a platter of marinated hamburger patties plumped for the grill, another of romaine lettuce with sliced onions and tomatoes, and a flourless chocolate-whiskey torte with a bowl of fresh mint–spiked whipped cream on the side.

The girls were bathed and dressed in their playpen, and I was just stacking whole wheat kaiser rolls and burger-ready chunks of sourdough baguette in an alternating pyramid.

"The house still looks like shit," said my husband. "They're going to be here in half an hour."

"I wanted to get the food prepped first, so I can relax a little later on. It's been forever since I talked with actual grown-ups."

Except for Mimi, but what business is that of yours? I mean, if you're going to be such an asshole, generally.

He yanked his sweat-soaked T-shirt up over his head and threw it on the floor, about a foot away from the laundry pile. "I'm sick of running around to shove all your crap in random closets at the last possible moment, every single time we have people over. It's ridiculous."

I glanced into the living room. The girls' toys were everywhere, but other than that there were only the two buckets of clean laundry I'd actually folded already, and a pile of dry-cleaned suits Dean had left draped across the sofa.

Well, along with a couple of coffee mugs here

and there. And several sections of last Sunday's *New York Times* spread across and around the coffee table.

"Just take your shower," I said. "I'll handle it."

"I mean, I work my ass off, day after day," he said, timbre of his voice shifting from pissy to shrill, "and I have to come *home* to this shit after a week on the road? We live like goddamn *animals*."

I gritted my teeth.

For this I went to college. Excellent.

"What the hell is *wrong* with you, Madeline? Jesus, you're the lightning rod for entropy in the universe, and you obviously have no respect for me whatsoever."

I dropped my eyes to the kitchen floor, which, admittedly, could have used a little sweeping-and-mopping action.

His voice ratcheted up another key. "You expect me to entertain my professional colleagues in this pigsty?"

Fuck you . . .

"It's goddamn embarrassing."

Fuck you . . .

"I'm ashamed to have people know I put *up* with this. To know I allow my children to be *raised* in this *filth*."

Drop dead, you petulant sack of rapidly bald-

ing shit. You and the glad-handing fancy-fucking-restaurants-every-night expense report you rode in on.

Arguing back just prolonged his tirades. So did crying.

"I'm sorry," I said, eyes squeezed shut as I bit the inside of my lip, relieved my hair had fallen forward to veil my face.

I'd gotten the last lick in about the socks and *that* was now his excuse to come back at me over something else.

It was never about anything, or it was about *everything*. I couldn't tell anymore.

The litany varied: If the house was clean, I was spending so much money we were "doomed to end up living in some refrigerator box over a heating vent in the sidewalk." If our expenses were in order, I was letting the girls watch videos all day instead of taking them out for "fresh air and healthy activities, like any sane woman would considering we live in such a beautiful place."

Lately it had been like being married to a brown paper bag full of Africanized bees. The tantrums were random as summer thunderstorms—squalls of pique during which he fumed and yelled and found fault with everything I did.

And then the storm front would pass and he'd joke around like nothing had happened.

I couldn't remember anymore whether he'd always been like this, or whether he'd morphed into a wife-berating shithead gradually, over time.

He never did it when we had an audience, and he was always unfailingly kind and patient with Parrish and India.

Maybe it was the pressure of being low-on-the-totem-pole middle management. Maybe it was unmedicated depression.

Or maybe my childhood damage had programmed me to seek out a man who'd treat me as badly as the majority of my stepfathers had—once he'd gotten me geographically isolated and financially dependent, saddled with kids.

Dean took off his socks, shorts, and boxers, tossing them all vaguely in the direction of the laundry pile. He stalked naked out of the kitchen and toward the shower, slack white-boy ass jiggling.

I scraped his clothes off the floor and shoved them into the washing machine, not bothering to turn the damn thing on.

Or, worst of all, maybe I deserve it.

I half wanted to hit him over the head with a cast-iron skillet for being such an asshole, half cowered with nauseating certainty that his rants were my fault and entirely justified. Mostly I was too tired to string together any kind of cohesive rebuttal.

Plus which, for all I knew, this shit was what *all* husbands did—by definition, if you stuck it out in any marriage long enough.

It might be just another thing the sitcoms of my childhood had glossed over, right up there with the prime-time pretense that all persons of the married persuasion slept solo and fully clothed in well-spaced twin beds.

I jogged toward the living room, willing the tears that pricked at the corners of my lashes not to fall. People were due to arrive in twenty minutes— not enough time to rub ice cubes across my eyelids, erasing the evidence of a good cry.

We'd been married seven years—two longer than my mother's personal best in her four times at the nuptial bat.

We had health insurance. We had two gorgeous children. And life with Dean was pretty decent at least 80 percent of the time.

I hoped this was a rough patch, that maybe we just needed a couple of solid naps to restore the best aspects of our couple-hood.

This guy called Fassett (my favorite stepfather-type person when I was fifteen) had once remarked that it was pointless both spiritually and practically to spend your time in a relationship bitching about what the other person should be doing for *you,* because the only thing you ever have control over is what you're doing for them—how much you give and forgive, how generous you are—without worrying about what you should be getting in return for the effort.

Maybe that was terrible advice, and, okay, Fassett *had* been married to someone else the entire time he was hanging out with Mom, but how the hell would I know? It's not like I had a whole bunch of other marital paradigms to hold up for comparison so what the hell.

When all else failed, I figured it couldn't hurt to try kindness or some vague kind of Gandhi thing. I mean, it's not like I was going to win any awards for vacuuming prowess anytime soon.

My husband was smart, and a charming host. He was solicitous of my friends. He was on his way up in the corporate game, and our daughters wouldn't be laughed at for wearing poor-relation castoffs and Goodwill rags when they were old enough for school, the way I had been after my father took off.

I didn't have to serve up cheese-with-the-mold-pared-off or powdered milk or dented cans of generic chili that always turned out to be made from shredded beef hearts, if you were dumb enough to read the ingredient list on the "No Frills" label.

I wouldn't have to explain to Parrish and India

why their father lived in a VW van behind the Chevron station in Malibu, buying weed and Volkswagen tools from the Snap-on truck guy who showed up once a week in lieu of paying child support—while worrying that the KGB was reading his mail.

With Dean's help I had washed up safe once more on the shores of the lower middle class, despite my parents' headlong sprint away from all remaining vestiges of their childhood wealth and privilege.

And he and I were a team, right? It's just that we were tired, and overwhelmed, and doing our best to keep it together most of the time. The bad cranky shit would probably pass: Scorpio would move out of the House of Suckbag. Life would go on.

Besides which, it wasn't like I was a pregnant single truckstop waitress in Fresno, or undergoing chemo. Nor, for that matter, was I currently being bombed by the Luftwaffe in Guernica.

Hey—in the grand scheme of things, I had very little to complain about.

And for that I was fucking well grateful.

17

You did a nice job with the food, Bunny," Dean said, casting an approving eye over the culinary handiwork I'd arrayed across the kitchen table. As though none of it had been there before his shower.

His wet hair was neatly combed back, his pink Brooks Brothers shirt crisply starched and pressed by the cleaners on Pearl Street. Even his boxers were from The Brothers—my Valentine's present to him the previous month.

I thought of Edith Wharton's once having described a character's husband as being blond and well dressed, with "the physical distinction that comes from having a straight figure, a thin nose, and the habit of looking slightly disgusted."

He walked behind me, smelling of shampoo and

peppermint, then sat down to slide his feet into a pair of Belgian shoes, brown with black piping and topped with discreetly tiny black bows (my Christmas present).

These were pretty much the WASPiest footwear in the history of the universe, and I had a momentary flashback to what Dean had been wearing the night we'd met: green garbage-man pants, white poly-blend Sears dress shirt through which you could see the outline of his undershirt (a pack of Viceroys rolled up in one of its short sleeves), thick-soled black cop shoes. Not to mention ugly glasses and a bad haircut.

None of which had mattered to me. We stayed up talking about FDR's policy of farm parity until four in the morning after a party at my pal Sophia's parents' apartment, and then he'd carried me up the stairs to an empty bedroom with a view of Central Park.

I apologized the moment we were naked in bed for not having shaved.

"That's perfectly all right," Dean replied. "I've dated English majors before."

At which point I realized he might well be a keeper.

Since then, I had taught a Syracuse farmboy to look carelessly effete.

Perhaps that explained at least part of his bad mood. I'd become the man behind the curtain to whom one was supposed to pay no attention.

I rubbed at the smear of cake-batter craquelure on my sweatshirt's cuff. "Could you watch the girls for a minute while I go change?"

It was only Setsuko and Cary coming over, but I felt like a fat lumpen mudhen compared with my minty-fresh spouse.

He glanced at his watch, lips pressed thin.

I hustled back upstairs to our room, throwing on a longish red skirt from Target and this dumpy black Goodwill sweater Mom had found me, then scraped my hair back into a ponytail.

I spent money on the girls' clothes, or Dean's. There never seemed to be enough for mine, too.

I looked myself up and down in the closet-door mirror: Ellis Island, fresh out of steerage—minus only the kerchief and hobnail boots.

Fuck that.

I yanked the skirt off, dumped it on our floor, and changed into my last pair of jeans and a pair of black Converse sneakers.

Low-tops, no socks.

Because I didn't actually own any socks, either.

I'd never been a big sock person. And in a

pinch—snowstorms, et cetera—I could always wear my husband's.

Back downstairs, I found Dean with his pink sleeves crisply rolled back to each elbow, talking cheerful nonsense to make Parrish laugh as he replaced her diaper.

He looked up at me, smiling. "The food really does look amazing, Bunny. I can't believe you pulled all that together in one morning."

"Thank you for changing her," I said, stepping up close behind him to wrap my arms again around his waist. "I'm sorry the house was such a pit."

I squeezed my arms tighter, planting a kiss on his back.

He leaned forward over Parrish.

"Darling petunia," he cooed, "your dad missed you so much."

Through the living room window, I watched Cary's truck pull up to the curb.

Setsuko swung her long legs gracefully out from its passenger door when he'd walked around to open it for her, extending a hand to help her down.

She was willowy—tall for a woman who'd grown up in Tokyo. A breeze fluttered the silky hem of her blossom-pink dress, tossing the artfully curled ends of her long black hair.

I liked her well enough. She was the receptionist at Dean's office, unfailingly sweet to me when I called him at work—but our small talk always ground to a painful halt right around "I'm well, thanks, how are you?"

"They're here," I said.

Cary said something that made Setsuko giggle, and she lowered her lashes, raising a demure hand to hide perfect teeth.

The woman was so indelibly feminine she might as well have worn a powder-blue T-shirt that read I AM THE ANTI-MADELINE across the front, in swirly girly paste–hued script.

I'd read once that the Japanese language has gender-specific first-person pronouns, which I immediately took to mean that women weren't *allowed* to use the same "I" and "me" as men were. Perhaps because I also knew it was still perfectly legal to fire a woman there for having gotten married—or just having reached, say, her mid-twenties, should the male bosses decide they were in need of a fresher "office flower."

Granted, this prickly attitude may well have been pure cultural chauvinism on my part, or the result of having read far too many smugly misogynistic stroke-lit James Clavell novels, but I did try to cut Setsuko a little slack and at least think of her as *involuntarily* insipid.

If I'd been raised female in her milieu, I suspected I'd've long since stormed a bell tower brandishing twin AK-47s, my belt strung with grenades.

Setsuko reached back into the truck's bed for two bags of groceries, waving Cary away when he offered to help.

Dean pushed past me to open the front door for them. I followed him out onto our front porch, fighting a sudden urge to plant my foot firmly in the exact center of his ass and shove him down the stairs.

18

Dean and Cary had taken the girls out into the backyard, intent on firing up our barbecue.

Setsuko, meanwhile, had started unloading her grocery bags on the kitchen counter.

I figured she'd brought a salad or something, maybe a pie—the usual sort of adjunct foodstuffs one totes to an informal lunch at someone else's house—but she kept reaching into the bags and pulling out piles of items. (I counted three packages of hamburger, two bags of buns, catsup, mustard, relish, tomatoes, lettuce, a tub of store-bought potato salad...and she *still* wasn't done.)

I realized she'd virtually replicated my entire menu for the afternoon.

Well, okay, mine was way better—not least

since I wouldn't be caught dead serving French's yellow mustard, iceberg lettuce, or Wonder Bread anything—but it was bizarre.

"That's really nice of you," I said, "but, um, we kind of already *have* food?"

She turned around to smile at me and I gestured toward the kitchen table, loaded down with my jam-packed trays and platters and bowls, not to mention a large jar of Grey Poupon, poppy- *and* sesame-seed-garnished kaiser rolls, and mixed baby field greens.

"Yes," she said, beaming. "And I brought things, too."

I wondered whether all females were Stepfordized at birth in her home country, and how quickly I could get her the hell out of my kitchen.

I looked out the window and watched Dean and Cary fiddle with the Weber on our backyard's lawn.

Parrish and India were in their little sandbox a few feet away, brandishing plastic shovels with glee.

My husband filled a foot-tall metal chimney with charcoal, then wadded up half a sheet of newspaper and shoved it into the bottom of the thing, no doubt lecturing Cary on the efficacy of this lighting method as he lowered it into the barbecue's kettle.

Our pal nodded, handing Dean the box of

matches that had been sitting on the grass at their feet.

"Shall I start making the hamburger patties now?" asked Setsuko, from behind me.

"I'm so sorry, Setsuko, I'm a *terrible* hostess... would you care for something to drink?" I turned to smile at her, pointing pointedly toward the kitchen window and the great outdoors beyond it. "We have wine and beer on the picnic table. Or juice. I'm sure Dean and Cary would enjoy some company."

"A glass of wine would be lovely, Mrs. Bauer, thank you."

"Please call me Madeline," I said, for possibly the hundredth time.

"I'll *try* to remember," she said.

"For one thing, 'Mrs. Bauer' isn't my name."

I hadn't ever told her that before. Perhaps the information would act as a mnemonic device.

"No?" she said.

I was about to say it was what Dean's *mother* was called, but instead found myself telling her, "I kept my own surname: Dare."

"That's interesting."

Funny how much crisper her English got the minute there weren't any men in the room.

Setsuko returned my smile and began picking

her way toward the back door, pink skirt swaying with each tiny, ever-so-slightly-pigeon-toed step she took in her kitten-heeled sandals.

Yeah, good luck keeping those *from sinking into the lawn.*

The sandals were white. A good two months, I might add, before the advent of Memorial Day.

Just as I was about to forearm-sweep her three individually wrapped *pounds* of hamburger off my kitchen counter and into the brown-paper grocery bags on the floor, Setsuko turned back toward me.

"Would you like me to leave this door open," she asked, "or closed?"

"Open, please," I said.

We smiled at each other *again* and I fought the urge to sprint across the room and hip-check her down the back-porch steps, just so she'd finally fucking leave.

The moment she was out of sight, I tossed all her crap into the bags and shoved them under the kitchen table with my foot.

A billow of smoke rolled past our kitchen porch like ghostly surf, and I caught a sharp hit of charcoal at the back of my throat.

The muted trill of a giggle made me look out the window.

Setsuko held Parrish on one hip and was pushing

India gently back and forth in the little plastic toddler swing that hung from our tallest maple tree.

"The man *hates* me," said Cary. "He relishes any opportunity to humiliate me. He lives to crush my spirit and render my life a film-noir nightmare. And I don't mean ordinary cruelty, I mean 'lie awake all night thinking of hideous new ways to torture my pathetically defenseless underling, *mwa ha ha*, today-Cary-tomorrow-the-world' sadistic glee."

"Bittler?" I asked, putting the bowl of hominy salad down on the picnic table before I slid into its last open bench seat, beside Cary.

Bittler was the head of marketing and the spitting image of my dickwad middle school vice principal—right down to the disturbingly ginormous seventies mustache, though thankfully not sharing his predilection for beige vinyl leisure suits.

Setsuko leaned across the table to refill Cary's beer glass, cradling the bottle in both hands as she poured.

Dean reached for some Grey Poupon to spread on his burger. "Bittler's an asshole. You can't let him get to you."

Cary shook his head. "Easy for you to say, you're not the guy's direct-report. I can't *work* for him anymore. It's killing me."

"I'm doing my best to get you over to sales," said Dean.

Cary held the back of one hand up to his forehead—a gesture brimming with Mary Pickford melodrama.

"Hurry!" he cried, in a piping falsetto. "I fear that the uncouth cur will succeed in tying me to the railroad tracks at any moment!"

"That bad?" I asked, laughing. "Really?"

"*Really*, Maddie," said Cary, his voice dropped several octaves back to normal. "I shit you not."

Dean looked at me. "Last week, Cary was xeroxing his résumé when his phone rang. He grabbed all the copies from the out-tray, but forgot the original."

Cary gave me a sheepish grin. "—For thirty *seconds*."

"—But it was still there a minute later, so he figured he got away with it," continued Dean. "Until more copies started appearing around the office."

"*Fifty* of them fanned out next to the break room coffee machine, twenty minutes later," said Cary. "Then I get back from lunch and I find ten more taped all the way around the edge of my desk, folded into points like a string of flags at a car dealership."

"Dude," I said, "sucks *ahoy*."

Setsuko refilled Dean's glass.

Cary closed his eyes, pinching the bridge of his nose. "It gets worse."

"How?" I asked.

He looked at me. "The asshole puts copies into every single person's mailbox. The *entire* office."

"—Eight times last week," said Dean, "at random hours of the day."

Cary shivered. "I'm on constant red-alert, trying to gather them up before anyone else sees them. He's going to give me a freaking *heart* attack."

"Envy," I said. "I mean, you're a foot taller with shoulders to die for and Bittler looks like a hard-boiled egg jammed onto a golf pencil. Nancy Reagan with a smaller dick."

Setsuko looked confused by my use of idiom.

I patted Cary's forearm. "Look, the guy probably can't decide whether he wants to burst into tears or blow you, every time you walk past his desk."

Setsuko looked even more confused, then said, "Bittler is *not* a nice man."

"Exactly," I replied, looking her in the eye.

"Confused" my ass.

She took a tiny sip of white wine as I killed my bottle of beer.

I looked down at the ice bucket on the grass

beside me, but the only thing left in it was a bottle of Chardonnay.

"Can I get you another of those, Maddie?" asked Cary, standing up.

"I'd love that," I said. "I think there's another six-pack in the icebox."

Dean rose from the table with him. "Anything for you, Setsuko?"

"Oh, no, I'm very happy."

We watched them walk toward the house.

"Your daughters are so pretty," she said to me. "Playing with them makes me miss being a teacher."

"You were a teacher?" I asked.

"In Tokyo, at a preschool. The kids were adorable."

"I taught high school for a year," I said. "'My students were interesting, but I wouldn't go as far as 'adorable.'"

Especially the one who'd blown up the helicopter.

Setsuko laughed. "If you ever need a babysitter, Madeline, I hope you'll call me. I really do love children."

"That's very sweet of you, Setsuko."

"No, really, it would be my pleasure. Anytime I can help, okay?"

"Okay, I'll do that. Thank you."

In the sandbox, India hit Parrish over the head with her plastic shovel. They began to wail in stereo.

"Naptime," I said, rising from the table to tote them both upstairs.

By the time I came back down, most of the lunch equipment had been ferried inside to the kitchen counter. I covered the salads with tinfoil and stuck them in the icebox, then loaded the dishwasher with plates and utensils.

Cary came in with two more empty platters. "Want these rinsed?"

"That'd be great," I said. "Thank you."

He moved to the sink and started running some water. "This was all really delicious, Madeline. I love coming over here."

"We love having you. And you were sweet to give Setsuko a ride."

"Her place is on my way." Cary turned the water off and put the platters in the dishwasher.

I glanced out the window.

Dean battened down the Weber while Setsuko shook out the tablecloth. He said something that made her smile as she floated the blue-checked fabric back aloft over the picnic table.

Once it had fluttered to rest, she began to fold the thing with completely anal precision.

"Dude, wad it the hell *up*," I said, under my breath.

"Huh?" asked Cary.

"Setsuko's folding the tablecloth. I'm just going to throw it in the washing machine."

"Well, she's like that. Everything's got to be very precise and color-coded."

"Which would pretty much make her the Anti-Madeline," I said, thinking of the T-shirt I'd envisioned for her. "I mean, Dean called me 'the lightning rod for entropy in the universe' this morning. Not without cause."

"You're a woman of many other talents, and he knows he's lucky to have you."

Yeah, right.

I gave him an affectionate mock shoulder punch. "You're a magnificent friend, sweet Cary, and I hope all the work bullshit gets way better for you ASAP."

"Can I tell you something, in confidence?"

"Of course," I said.

"I don't want to sound like a total pussy, but I really *don't* think I can handle the Bittler situation much longer."

"I promise to kick Dean's ass about it, okay? This too shall pass."

"Hey, he's being great, your husband—totally

above and beyond. I know he's got my back, but this whole thing is fucking with my head."

There was a note of anxiety in his voice he hadn't allowed himself at the picnic table. No bravado now, no kidding around.

Well, hey—sometimes that's why men like talking with women. They can just tell us shit straight without having to wave their dicks around and pretend everything's fine.

Especially if the man and woman in question didn't happen to be fucking each other, or have designs on doing so at some future point.

Cary had a reputation as a cocksman—Dean once told me the guy had slept with something north of two hundred women.

And, okay, since I've already all but confessed that Dean and I did the nasty the first night we met, obviously I hadn't exactly been a virgin on my wedding night. (Nor would my husband have been interested in marrying one. Yay, Dean.)

In fact, a group of louche older guys in college had nicknamed me "the underrated middleweight" during the fall of my freshman year. Apparently it amused them to think I was duking it out for some sort of promiscuity-championship title.

I'd known right away Cary was hip to that. Not that I'd racked up anywhere near his numbers, just that we, well, *recognized* each other. Which somehow allowed for a strong, immediate foundation of respect.

Probably because even gussied up I wouldn't have been his type. Nor he mine. Not in a million years.

But him opening up like this was new.

He sighed, kind of a strangled noise.

I suppose Cary's anxiety shouldn't have surprised me. Those of us who take up sport-fucking aren't usually, after all, the most well-adjusted, *happiest* creatures on the planet.

"You sound really freaked out," I said.

"I just feel like I'm on the verge of disappointing everyone in such a major way...Dean, my family."

"I feel like that pretty much every *day*, dude. And you're way more together than I am."

"Oh, come on," he said. "That's ridiculous."

"Cary, you totally pass as a competent grown-up, no matter what it feels like in your head. You're doing incredibly well at your job—Bittler or no Bittler. I mean, Dean's not offering to help you get into sales because he pities you, he thinks you'd be *good* at it."

He turned toward me, all big-eyed.

"Cary, you look like someone just ran over your dog. On purpose. Dean has *total* faith in you, okay?

As do I. Just trust me on that. This is all going to be okay. And Bittler's a fucking asshole. You can't take his opinion seriously. It has nothing to do with you."

He closed his eyes, still looking gut-shot.

I put my arm around his shoulder. "Look, I have something for you upstairs, okay? Just hang out for a minute."

I left him there, jogging upstairs without a clue what I could give him, but he seemed like a guy in serious need of some kind of mojo talisman.

I threw open the lid of my jewelry box, on top of our bureau. There was the dented lid from a can of betel-nut chaw I'd found years before on a sidewalk in New Delhi, a string of fake pearls, and some really ugly brushed-gold animal pins I'd inherited from my father's mother—a fish with a pearl in its mouth, a grinning midcentury-Modigliani cat, and a truly heinous Scottie in an enameled-plaid tam-o'-shanter. (Funny how the *good* jewelry always gets left to the cousins with money enough to buy their own . . .)

But beside those was a chainless pendant. This was equally ugly but it seemed suited to the task at hand: a two-inch-wide gold four-leaf clover with a tiny emerald-bodied frog in the middle.

Perfect.

I raced back downstairs and pressed it into Cary's hand.

"This thing is tacky as shit," I said, "but it's always been incredibly lucky for me. Why don't you hang on to it until things turn around, okay?"

He was dumbstruck, looking down at the stupid thing in his great paw of a hand.

"This means so much to me...thank you."

"Eminently deserved," I said. "And everything really is going to turn out just fine. I promise. Dean will make sure of it."

"Thank you."

"Hey, you were our first friend here. And still the best. It's the least I can do."

"Aw shucks," he said. "I just want to be you guys when I grow up."

"Pshaw, *mon chevalier du* Ohio. Let us drink more beer while the offspring sleep."

I opened the back door to find Setsuko halfway up the porch steps, bearing the tablecloth before her like a military-funeral presentation flag.

"I would be happy to launder this for you," she said, smiling at me.

I reached for it. "You're lovely, but let me put it in the washing machine."

She avoided me, gracefully. "Please tell me where it is, then."

Fine. Whatever.

"First door on your left in the dining room," I said. "And thank you."

"Oh!" She looked around the kitchen, crestfallen. "You have finished the dishes. I wanted to help."

I shook my head. "You've been a *wonderful* help already, Setsuko. I wouldn't dream of letting you do a single thing more."

She dropped her eyes. "Well, thank you for such a beautiful meal in your home."

"Which is just my way of thanking *you* for all your hard work at the office. I'm grateful that you make Dean's hours there so much more pleasant, and I always enjoy talking to you. You're very gracious on the phone, and in person."

Jesus, we might as well have been snorting fat rails of Sweet'N Low through a Hello Kitty straw.

I wondered how many weeks I'd have to devote to cleaning the house beforehand, if I ever actually took her up on her babysitting offer.

I tried moving things along. "Won't you please come outside with us, perhaps have another glass of wine?"

Or some tequila shots, preferably.

"I would love to, in just a moment," she said,

ducking her head at me as she minced/glided past toward the laundry room.

"She kind of gives me the willies," I said to Cary.

"Nah...Setsuko's okay."

He slid the charm into his pocket and we walked outside.

I went back into the kitchen five minutes later when she still hadn't come out. She was standing at the sink, washing the contents of our recycling bin in soapy hot water.

"Setsuko, dude—cease and desist already. Come sit down with us. You're making me feel hugely guilty here. I should be giving you a foot rub or something."

She looked embarrassed. "I am so sorry—"

"Just come have some wine, okay? This is meant to be your day of rest. Please."

"One more glass."

We walked out.

"I feel so bad for Cary," I said, as Dean and I lay side by side in bed that night. "He looks like such a giant bear, and then you get to know him a little and find out he's got the tenderest heart in the world. I just want to pat him on the head and cocoon him in Kevlar, you know?"

"He's a lot like you, Bunny," said Dean.

"How so?"

"He *wants* to be tough…thinks it's expected of him, but he's pure empathy instead. And he never had any interest in corporate crap."

"So why's he in the salt mines with you guys?"

"His dad. Ultimatum."

"Jesus—"

"Did Cary ever tell you he played trumpet, as a kid?"

"Nope," I said, reaching my arm across his belly.

"Classical, mostly. Got hired by the Cincinnati Symphony when he was fifteen. Then his father refused to pay for college unless he majored in business, so he gave it up."

"And now the poor guy's getting his teeth kicked in on a daily basis by Bittler, the rice grain–dicked Napoleon? Horrible."

Dean yawned, shuddering. "Exactly."

"Help him out, okay? He's an amazing friend to both of us."

"Mmmm," he said.

"And can I just say that Setsuko gives me the creeps? Nice and everything, don't get me wrong, but—"

In answer to that I felt Dean's leg twitch, and then he inhaled with a bit of snore.

Sigh.

"Sweet dreams, Intrepid Spouse," I said.

He muttered something and twitched again, fully out.

I turned onto my other side, yearning for maximum sleep before one of the girls woke up.

Just as I finally drifted off, a fire truck's siren echoed in the distance.

19

About the last thing I expected the following afternoon—entertaining the girls on our sun-drenched back lawn while Dean was off on yet *another* hours-long siphon-off-the-final-ounce-of-my-wifely/parental-will-to-live biking excursion—was that my Intrepid Spouse would return through the yard's side gate practically carrying a battered and bloody Bittler.

"Found him on the creek trail," said Dean, crouched and breathless, arms cinched around the smaller man's waist to hold him upright. "Didn't think we could get all the way to his place...six more blocks."

They were still wearing bike helmets. Bittler's looked like a rottweiler's chew toy: chunks of Styrofoam missing all along the right side, tufts of his blood-darkened hair poking through the gaps.

There was even blood soaked into his mustache.

"What'd you do there, Mr. Bittler, stick your head in a wood chipper?" I said, to jolly him through the long wince of pain that hissed through his teeth while I drew his free arm across my shoulders.

"M'okay," he insisted, but he leaned on me hard all the same.

Dean and I piloted him gingerly toward the picnic table, taking tiny steps while he hopped right-footed between us.

I glanced at the girls. They were fine. Toddling happily around in T-shirts and diapers—it was that hot out.

Bittler kept asking where his bike was, over and over, until we'd maneuvered him gently down onto the wood-plank bench.

"In the creek," Dean told him each time. "In a lot of pieces."

I crouched down in the grass the second we had him settled. "Look at me, okay?"

Bittler blinked, then slowly raised his head.

His left pupil was twice the size of his right.

"Call nine-one-one," I said to Dean. "*Now.*"

He took off at a sprint. Three leggy strides and he'd cleared the back porch steps, barreling into the kitchen—screen door yanked wide so fast and hard it slapped the wall's brick face with a *crack* before rebounding twice off the door frame.

Bittler fidgeted like he was trying to stand up. Well, not "fidgeted," exactly—unless you could stretch the use of that word to include the movements of someone just waking up on the bottom of a swimming pool, after a long winter. But "trying to stand up" was definitely being telegraphed, all the same.

"Stay on the bench," I said. "You have a concussion."

"Do *not*." He gripped the bench plank's front edge with both hands, knuckles paling on either side of his bloodied knees.

To our left Parrish shoved India, who toppled backward onto her diapered butt and started wailing.

I stood up. "Mr. Bittler, do I look like a woman who needs a *third* one-year-old here?"

He glowered at that, all pissy, while I scooped India off the grass and onto my hip.

Her crying ratcheted up to full aria mode.

Bittler squinted up at me, slurring "Where's my bike?" through the racket.

"In the creek," I said.

"D'you do that for? Creek."

"*I* didn't…"

India hiccuped, gave one more whimper, and then dragged her face back and forth across the front of my right boob, grinding snot into my shirt.

I was about to raise my left hand to wipe it off, but Bittler looked groggier all of a sudden and started listing to port. "You took my bike?"

I whipped my left arm across my stomach and India's chubby calf, gripping his shoulder to steady him, willing Dean to come back outside.

How the fuck long could it take, dialing three digits on a goddamn Touch-Tone phone and telling whomever-the-hell picked up, "send an ambulance to Nineteen thirteen Mapleton"?

"Where's Setsuko?" mumbled Bittler.

"Mr. Bittler, you're at Dean Bauer's house, remember? You had an accident at the creek."

"Fine piece of tail," he said, leering.

Well, not like a concussion *stops* someone from being an asshole.

Bittler leaned harder against my hand. "Lost my bike."

He was getting heavy. I tried moving my feet farther apart for leverage.

That worked for all of five seconds.

I slid my right foot toward my left, trying to lean back into him.

"Want to lie down," he said, pushing against my arm with his torso's full weight. "Tired."

"Mr. Bittler, you have to stay awake now. You've got a concussion, okay?"

I needed to get my body wedged between him and the bench before he knocked all three of us over—which meant moving India to my other hip so she wouldn't get crushed between us.

"Dean!" I yelled, trying to pivot in the other direction, but I was already canted at too weird an angle, India weighing on me like a downhill anchor.

I couldn't put her down—she'd dug her knees into me, front and back, and I was afraid of dropping her.

Like a bad game of Twister, with a bucket of blood and snot thrown in.

My arms started quaking. "Dean? Get back out here!"

No answer.

"Look, can you just...," I said, but then Bittler coughed up scary-red phlegm all over his chin and his eyes rolled back.

I got one knee up on the bench next to him.

Then he got all floppy on me, India's foot now

wedged between his shoulder and my knee. Along with my left hand.

I said, "Mother*fuck*," clenched my right arm tighter around India's waist, and just yanked her across my stomach, which thankfully popped both her foot and my hand free of the man's slack weight.

But it also started him toppling forward.

I don't know how the hell I did it, but somehow I twisted and kind of ducked simultaneously—without letting go of my daughter—and managed to get under him before he did a face-plant into the lawn.

I ended up down on one knee with my back to the guy—crouched forward with his head lolling over one of my shoulders and his arm dangled over the other.

He was hot and sticky-wet and he weighed a gazillion pounds.

I gripped poor India, meanwhile, diagonally across my hunched chest like she was a Kalashnikov and I was Che fucking Guevara.

Bittler moaned, drooling into my neck.

I yelled Dean's name at the top of my lungs, telling him to get his sorry ass back out into the yard.

I must have arched my back with the effort or something, because Bittler's other arm flopped down, crashing into the outside of my thigh.

"Mummie," said India, "want down now."

"Want down now *please*," I muttered automatically, letting go of her legs.

She got her feet under her and wriggled free.

I dropped my hands to the dirt, elbows locked to brace myself against Bittler's deadweight. I took the deepest breath I could and started yelling, again, for Dean.

A siren started up in the distance—drowning me out just as my husband walked back onto the porch, phone still in hand, his head craned away from us toward Mapleton Street.

I realized he was waiting to flag the ambulance, probably still talking to the dispatcher, but the siren sounded entirely too far away.

Bittler felt like a dump truck, parked across my back.

And where is Parrish?

I tried to turn my head toward where I'd last seen her, but Bittler's weight shifted ominously.

Then I couldn't catch my breath, and dark spots started crowding the edges of my vision.

"Daddy!" piped India, toddling toward her father with both arms up in the air, "Look!"

The paramedics burst into our backyard just as Dean was lifting Bittler off me, which meant the three of us were covered in blood and must have looked like a particularly scary tableau of domestic threesome what-the-fuck scary shit, right off the bat.

I dropped my other knee to the ground and then slid over onto a hip, straightening my legs out.

"Sir!" said the first guy hauling a stretcher. "Please step back!"

"I don't want to drop him," said Dean. "He's out cold."

My legs prickled with a rush of blood, but I got to my feet as quickly as I could. "The guy crashed his bike—this isn't a fight or anything."

They looked unconvinced.

"Really," I said. "He has a concussion. My husband went inside to call you guys and he kind of fell on me when he passed out..."

Bittler groaned in Dean's arms.

"For God's sake," I said, "they *work* together. Bittler crashed his bike by the creek and Dean *carried* him here. Get him onto that stretcher."

And then it was like everything sped up again, all crowded.

Dean handed off Bittler and reached for me but I told him to make sure Parrish was okay first, because suddenly I was so exhausted I didn't think I could make my legs move again, but I could see

India sitting right on the porch steps in her diaper so I knew *she* was all right.

Dean said, "She's right here behind the table, sucking her thumb. She's fine."

And then I kind of slumped over and he got me onto the bloody bench, his arm behind my back, and the ambulance guys shined a penlight in my eyes and wanted to know if any of the blood on me was mine, and they put a blanket around me even though I kept saying I was fine.

Dean was holding my hand and I told him to just get the girls inside, and safe.

They had Bittler in a neck-brace thing by then, strapped to the stretcher all snug.

One of the guys said, "Miss? We'd like to take you down to the hospital, make sure you're all right."

"Look, nothing *happened* to me," I said. "I mean, the guy fell over and I caught him, but the whole thing probably lasted three minutes or something, okay? Bittler's the one who's hurt. I just need a bath."

And then suddenly I was really, really tired... like all the adrenaline had galloped off at once, with the dregs of my iron-poor blood riding along into the sunset on the back of its horse.

I yawned, and right then it seemed like holding

my eyes open was the hardest thing I'd ever had to do.

"You're sure?" the guy asked.

I nodded, yawning again.

"Let me just take your pulse, okay?" he said.

His hand was gentle on my wrist.

I eyed the ground, aching to lie down on the grass.

"You're fine," he said.

"Told you. I just need a bath. And maybe a nice long nap."

He smiled. "Your little girls are twins, right? How old?"

"Just turned one," I said.

"In that case, I'll tell your husband that you *not* getting a nap for the rest of the afternoon would constitute a life-threatening emergency. How's that?"

"Dude," I said, humbled with gratitude, "I would so hug you right now, but I don't want to get Bittler's blood on your shirt."

He laughed at that.

"Should I ever lose my mind and decide to have more children, however," I continued, "I'm naming them *all* after you."

PART III

No really provident woman lunches regularly with her husband if she wishes to burst upon him as a revelation at dinner. He must have time to forget; an afternoon is not enough.

—Saki, "Reginald on Besetting Sins"

20

Dean and I were upstairs in our bedroom several days later, getting ready for a business dinner now that the babysitter had finally arrived. Well, *I* was getting ready. Dean had already been primping for an hour while I fed the girls their dinner.

"Who else is coming tonight?" I asked.

"Lots of visiting Japanese, Renfrew, most of the VPs, Bittler," he said.

"Bittler couldn't be out for a *few* more days with that concussion?"

He didn't answer, busy rifling through his ties.

"Who else?" I asked.

He selected a tie, draped it around his neck. "Cary's driving Setsuko."

"Again?"

"What's *that* supposed to mean?" He leaned in front of me, commandeering the mirror to deal with his tie.

"Let me do that," I said, turning toward him. "I mean twice in one week? Doesn't Setsuko have a car?"

"I think so."

I knotted the tie. "So, what're they, dating?"

"That's ridiculous."

Now that I'd perfected his tie's dimple, Dean looked over my head at the mirror again and started smoothing his hair back with both palms, then raised his chin and waggled his face side-to-side to check the closeness of his shave.

I turned back toward the bureau to reach for my freshly re-strung pearls. "*Why* is that ridiculous?"

I watched him roll his eyes in the mirror.

"Nice tie by the way," I said, trying to hook the clasp on my pearls at the back of my neck. "You get that in New Orleans?"

Dean leaned down to pick up his loafers off the bedroom floor. "Where's the shoe polish?"

"Linen closet," I said. "Third shelf from the top."

Where it always fucking is. But don't worry about me, I can fasten these by myself.

I pulled the pearls around, the clasp's ends to the front.

Everything felt hollow, slipping away from me.

Had I changed, somehow? Was this discomfort with Dean my fault?

Maybe I was just so exhausted I was imagining all of it. Maybe we were fine.

I tried to remember the last time he'd seemed truly happy in my company, and all I could think of was the way he'd grinned at me the morning after our girls had been born, walking toward me across my crowded maternity-ward room at New York Hospital.

I leaned forward until my forehead rested on the edge of the old white bureau.

Don't fucking cry, you don't have time to do your makeup all over again.

Well, hey. At least I'd finally remembered to pick up my pearls from the jeweler.

I looked like shit, but they were real.

So I had *that* going for me.

"You look great," I said, after Dean and I had given our last instructions to the babysitter.

"Thanks," he said, pushing past me through the front door and across our porch, out toward the car.

I stood on the threshold transfixed, one hand raised to my throat.

Really? "You look nice yourself, dear," was too much to fucking ask?

"For God's sake, we're already late picking the guy up at the Boulderado," said my husband, scowling back at me across our car's roof.

"What guy?"

"Mr. Tanaka. From Tokyo. What the hell's *wrong* with you?"

Okay then: As a couple, we were officially, totally, utterly fucked.

Dean always drove like some ancient cranky elderly lady in a vicious girdle: constipated velocity with a perpetual smolder of road rage. He'd only brake at the last possible moment, as though any obstacle with the goddamn gall to thwart his progress deserved the squealed-rubber threat of imminent retribution.

I smiled at the visiting business dignitary in the rearview mirror. Mr. Tanaka was directly behind Dean—the seat I'd've paid good money for, especially winding up Boulder Canyon's switchbacks with my petulant spouse at the wheel—but Japanese politesse supposedly dictated that only the *untermensch* rode shotgun. A category that of course included wives.

"We will see beers, in this mountain?" asked Mr. Tanaka.

"*So* many beers," I reassured him, smiling. "Microbrews, Budweiser…Kirin and Ichiban…"

Dean downshifted as the incline of Boulder Canyon grew steeper. Swear to God, he could've made a Bentley drive like a tractor.

Mr. Tanaka shook his head and said, "*Beers*," raising his hands up like claws and growling at me.

"Oh. *Bears*."

He growled again, nodding. "Many bears?"

"Maybe," I said. "Also elk, and moose."

The skin between his eyebrows crinkled. "Moose?"

"Antlers?" I said. "Very big animal?"

The poor guy looked really confused.

I turned toward the backseat and raised my hands to either side of my head, thumbs touching just above each ear with my fingers splayed out wide as they could go.

Chin raised, I bellowed "*Mooooose*," in the lowest range I could manage.

"Ah!" said our passenger, making finger-antlers himself. "Bullwinkle!"

"Bullwinkle!" Dean agreed, raising a hand of his own to the side of his head, while I grinned and nodded at our passenger like an overmedicated psychotic clown.

"This is going to be the longest business dinner *ever*," I confided to my husband, through clenched teeth.

"Alcohol will help," said Dean, waggling his one-handed antler once more before dropping it to regrip the steering wheel. "Preferably several martinis."

Our passenger was busy peering out the window now, searching the canyon for Moose and Squirrel.

"I think that sounds like a really bad idea," I said, for Dean's ears only. "I mean, the poor guy just flew into Denver from Tokyo yesterday, and we're driving him up *another* four thousand feet to this restaurant, right?"

Dean punched the brakes halfway through a particularly tight turn in the darkening canyon.

Idiot. You accelerate out *of a curve.*

I gripped the dashboard. "It would be highly irresponsible to let him have half a wine cooler, much less pound straight gin."

"He's a prospective *client*. Basic Asian business etiquette requires that we encourage him to puke repeatedly."

I figured it would be lousy for business were said honored guest to check out permanently, à la high-altitude Hendrix, but I kept that observation to myself.

And martinis would help *me*, as long as I didn't get hammered enough to trot out the only Japanese phrase I knew: *Tayo agay detekoy*.

My first stepfather had been ordered to memorize that circa February 1945, during his third Pacific tour with the United States Marine Corps.

It meant, "Come out of the cave with your hands up."

We hooked a right at Nederland—8,233 feet above sea level—and barreled along the spine of the Front Range for a few more miles. The engine sputtered, trying to gain purchase on the high thin air, and our passenger chuffed and panted like the Little Engine That Could in Lamaze class.

Dean turned into a narrow dirt lane still banked with waist-high snow. I caught Mr. Tanaka's eyes in the rearview, white showing all the way around his irises as he ratcheted up toward sheer stranded-goldfish panic.

"Look," I said, pointing out the right-side corner of the windshield, "baby beers!"

Two fat little furry cubs lolloped and tumbled through fresh powder, crossing a pine-ringed glade.

"So wonderful," said Mr. Tanaka, grinning as Dean slowed the car to a crawl.

The sun was low behind us, tipping the snow's

meringue peaks pink and gold amidst long pools of cobalt shadow.

The mother bear padded into view behind her furry twins, glancing our way before she loped ahead to chase them toward invisibility, beyond the trees. When her children were safely away she stood on her hind feet and stared at us.

Dean took my hand.

"A good mother," he said. "Like you, Bunny."

He squeezed my fingers and then let go, the car doing a little shimmy beneath us when he stomped on the gas.

Maybe we're okay, after all.

21

After another mile or so of jouncing along the dirt road, we pulled up in front of a low-slung wooden lodge. Dean set the emergency brake and pulled the keys from the ignition.

I swung my door open and got out.

There was a small rounded lake to our right, its shore hemmed all the way around with the last few yards of winter ice, inner edges thin and clear as windowpane glass.

Dean and Mr. Tanaka trudged toward the lodge's front doors, their dress shoes sinking into powdery snow, making it squeak with each step's compression.

I followed along behind them, tipping my ex–hippie kid's spiritual hat to Arlo Guthrie when

I saw the ALICE'S RESTAURANT sign just inside the vestibule.

The dining room was all gray stone and golden wood, dimly lit by a tall fireplace and antler chandeliers. My husband's colleagues raised a jolly forest of arms and cocktail glasses in welcome, around a long table across the room. Dean and our passenger were cajoled toward two empty seats at its far end.

Setsuko helped Mr. Tanaka's silver-haired boss rise from his chair at the table's head as they approached, inaugurating a quadrille of bows, handshakes, and ceremonial business card exchanges and appreciation.

I'd been stranded mid-carpet like the Farmer-in-the-dell's cheese, hi-ho the fucking derry-o.

When the backslapping salesfellow-well-met rampart of blue serge and gray flannel finally simmered down a little, Cary caught my eye and pointed out the unoccupied seat beside him.

This would put me between him and Bittler, whose little moon of a face was already brick red with Scotch and resentment, behind his stupid mustache.

Cary pulled the empty chair out for me.

I gave him the usual cheek-peck hello, whispering, "What crawled up your boss's ass *this* time?"

"His chair's closest to the door," he whispered back, "huge Japanese seating-order diss."

I cocked him a *Dude, you are so going to owe me for this* eyebrow.

"Absolutely," said Cary at regular volume. "And what can I get you to drink?"

"A great big martini glass of ice-cold gin," I said, tucking my skirt smooth as he slid the chair in beneath me. "One olive. Have the vermouth send it a brief poignant telegram of regret. From Havana. Or possibly Gstaad."

Bittler didn't register my presence, just continued glowering down into a glass of something expensively single malt–looking, his sense of ignominy distending that fat scarlet lower lip into a budgie's-perch pout.

Yeah, nice to see you, too, asshole. Took me all night Sunday to get your blood out of my shirt.

Cary resumed his seat beside me. He raised one finger, and a waiter appeared instantaneously.

"Didn't think I'd see *you* here tonight, Margaret," said Bittler, raising his cocktail glass vaguely in my direction.

I really, really wanted to open my response with the word "*Heil.*"

"Mr. *Butler*," I replied instead. "Always a pleasure."

Yeah, and it's too bad I didn't kick you in the balls while you were unconscious on my lawn, you skeevy little dick.

Setsuko had been deployed to the guest of honor's left at the power end of the table, her translation skills no doubt making her functional as well as decorative.

I watched her pour beer into Mr. Tanaka's boss's glass, then Dean's. She used two hands, as though the bottle were far too heavy for her.

Dean raised his glass in a toast and Mr. Boss clinked his own against it, saying something that made Setsuko lift a hand to her mouth to hide her teeth while she giggled.

The gesture struck me as far less coy, in this setting.

She was essential to the proceedings but nobody looked her in the eye, especially not the visiting dignitaries. Sure, they looked *at* her, but in an offhand, sniggering way, as though she were some sort of party favor.

Hey, I was no stranger to gender power-game bullshit, but I'd played mere checkers, by comparison. This was chess. Setsuko earned her place at the table by pretending—exquisitely, convincingly—to know full well she didn't, being female, deserve one.

I couldn't imagine having to be that *on* all the time, not least at work.

And the woman's offered to babysit for you, Madeline. Show a little solidarity.

Bittler, meanwhile, glared at Dean while fingering the NRA "Golden Eagle" pin piercing his lapel.

The waiter rematerialized, depositing my blessed martini before me in the nick of time.

Bittler dropped his chair back down, planted his elbows firmly on the tablecloth, and cleared his throat so loudly that all heads around the table swiveled toward him.

"So," he said, tapping a fingernail against his glass, "Bill Clinton's walking around the White House lawn with a new puppy under his arm."

The underling straight across from me egged him on with a fawningly anticipatory chuckle.

Bittler smirked at him, pleased. "One of the Marine Corps guards says, 'Nice dog, Mr. President. Is he new?'"

I took a nice, long, deep sip of cold gin.

"'Why, he sure is,' says Bill..."

Bittler's "Clinton" was half asthma, half Gomer Pyle.

He gave the imaginary dog a pat on the head. "'In fact,' says Bill, 'I got the little fella for Hillary.'"

Well, this martini wasn't going to drink itself. I took another gulp.

"The marine smiles and salutes," said Bittler, right hand now snapping crisply to his forehead. " 'Congratulations, Mr. President. *Excellent* trade.' "

This was greeted by a Stooge-ian *Nyuk-nyuk* chorus of appreciation from around the table, with a second wave of reprise guffaws from the visiting dignitaries once Setsuko had finished translating.

Bittler, meanwhile, was getting loudly high-fived by his frat-boy lackey.

"Another drink?" asked Cary.

"Please *God*," I said.

He raised two fingers in a Churchillian vee and I swear our waiter rematerialized within a nano-second.

The guy was ostensibly gifting the important end of the table with a full fifth of Johnnie Walker Blue, but even so he gave Cary a nod and shortly bustled backward toward the bar on our behalf.

Bittler lurched to his feet beside me, fixated on that bottle of Johnnie Walker.

I figured he'd be shunned by the heavies down there, but they thought he was a regular laugh riot—their very own Dean Martin, deserving of a very full glass and lots of hearty *Kanpai!*s to ensure he drank it down quickly.

Bittler didn't disappoint.

The big boss raised his own bottle to offer him a refill, laughing his ass off.

Bittler shoved between Dean and Setsuko, reaching across the table until his glass rattled against the boss's bottle.

He wobbled badly, pawing at Dean's shoulder with his free hand until he got a decent grip.

Mr. Boss uncapped the bottle, grinning, then slyly pulled it out of reach when Bittler pushed forward with his glass.

"Someone should feed these people before things get *ugly*," I said.

Bittler swayed forward...back...forward...the crowd's volume of encouragement swelling/fading/swelling as he arced through each gyration.

"Oh!" said Mr. Boss, snatching the bottle away once more. "So *close* that time!"

Frat puppy was up on his feet, applauding.

Everyone else was red-faced with laughter, some pounding the table.

Well, not Setsuko, of course, but even Dean was trying to look wildly amused, despite Bittler's death grip on his shoulder.

I sucked down more gin and glanced at Cary, who was looking about as enthralled as I felt.

"Dude," I said, "you need to be *laughing*. Serious

bad employment juju if you don't join in, right? Not to mention Bittler will probably shank you at the Xerox machine."

"Say something funny."

I gave him a little elbow nudge to the ribs. "Ten bucks Bittler cops a Setsuko-boob feel at the very *moment* Mr. Boss finally pours him a drink."

"Sucker bet," said Cary, lifting his beer, teeth bared in a totally lame smile.

"*Totally* lame smile, my friend. Like, transparent."

"Be funnier."

"How many Dada-Surrealists does it take to change a lightbulb?"

"I don't know."

"The *fish*."

"Not helping," said Cary, gulping beer as camouflage.

"Oh! Poor Setsuko!" I said, wincing.

"What?"

"Bittler just nailed her with a full-on groin grind to the shoulder, right as he was getting his Scotch poured."

"*Harsh*," said Cary, wincing right along with me.

"They should give her a huge fucking bonus for this. She totally deserves it." I raised my martini glass in her honor, then drained it.

"You, Madeline," Cary said, looking at me very seriously, "are a very nice person."

"I just hate seeing people treated like shit, is all."

"They want to send her home."

"Setsuko?"

He nodded.

"Why the hell would they do that?" I asked. "She's really good at all this crap."

"She's almost twenty-five. Time to trade her in for a dewier model."

"The whole 'office flower' thing? Are you fucking kidding me?"

"Not at all," he said.

"Isn't that illegal, here?"

"Well, all they have to do is not back her up on the visa extension, make some excuse."

"Does she want to go?"

"She thinks she's a freak in Japan. She's so tall, you know?"

"Oh, come on, she's hardly ripe for the WNBA."

"Over there, she's huge."

"So we need to keep her here."

The woman bored the shit out of me, but still.

Cary did the Churchill thing again, garnering two more drinks for us without even having to ask me.

"Your appetizers will be out momentarily," said the waiter, before vanishing again.

I looked down at the small hand-lettered menu on my butter plate, announcing which non-optional delicacies had been ordained for us as this evening clanked painfully onward.

Pâté de lapin au campagne was first up. With fucking organic whole-grain toast points and a tarragon-mango coulis.

"Culinary fascism," I said. "First time I get to eat with grown-ups in, like, *forever*, and some VP back at you guys' office dictates what we get served? And who the hell puts tarragon with *mangoes*?"

"O ye of little faith," said Cary, rubbing his hands together as waiters appeared bearing little white first-course plates. "Our God is a merciful God."

"In what tiny, begrudging way?"

"The Lord hath given us catsup. And the miracle of A.1. Sauce, I sayeth unto you."

I winced.

"What's *lapin*, anyway?" Cary asked as our waiter deposited the tidbits before us, with a flourish.

"Wabbit," I said, Fudd-like.

Cary took over in the wincing department.

Everyone at the other end of the table started pounding their fists in unison, egging Bittler on as he chugged the boss's bottle of Johnnie Blue.

"Fuck it," said Cary, reaching for his beer. "You and me need to drink up and *be* somebody."

"*Kanpai.*"

"Here's to your new journalism career," he said, tapping my glass with his bottle.

"You read the *New Times*? I thought I was the lone member of their audience."

"I'm a huge fan," he said. "And I had Daddy Bruce ribs last night for dinner. Your article was pretty convincing."

"Well, shit. Thank you. I haven't even told Dean yet."

"Why not?"

"Um…" I looked down at the tablecloth. "…hasn't really been a good moment? I don't know."

"Want me to leave a copy on his desk?"

"Let me think about it."

"So what are you going to review next?" asked Cary. "This place?"

"Why write about a meal that was already free?" I asked.

"Hey, we work *hard* for the bunny," he said, waving a forkful of wascally wabbit in my direction. "You and me both."

I smiled. "Even so. I'm big into the whole reimbursement thing. Few enough perks in this life. Maybe that Thai place out by you guys' office, next."

"Why don't you come out with the girls tomorrow and we can all go for lunch?"

"That'd be great, actually."

"Want me to soften Dean up for you?"

"Sure," I said. "What the hell."

Figuring that halfway through my third martini, I'd better sponge up a little gin with some carbs, I loaded a toast point and dragged it through the mango goop.

Cary doused his forkful of rabbit with A.1. and swallowed it nearly whole, with his eyes shut.

"I'm also working on a bigger piece," I said. "Less fluffy, more hard-ass."

"About?"

"The fires around town."

"They're definitely arson?"

I nodded.

He put his fork down. "What's the matter?"

"That's really the part I'm not sure how to explain."

"To Dean?"

I nodded again.

"Why?" he asked.

"I suspect he might not be too excited about me

doing a crime-beat story. Given, you know, motherhood and all that."

"It's not like you're chasing ambulances, right? Or serial killers."

"Well...not just at the *moment*."

He raised an eyebrow. I cleared my throat.

"I mean, these things can snowball," I said. "I've worked at papers before."

"It's Boulder, Madeline," he said. "Not Polanski-town."

Exactly what I myself would once have said of Syracuse, or Stockbridge, Massachusetts, or—well, okay, perhaps *not* Manhattan and Queens—but still, I had made rather a habit of inadvertently churning up dark scary shitstorms in climes of heretofore pastoral serenity. Shitstorms Dean had been forced to weather. My husband's "lightning rod for entropy" comment referenced a *Titanic* iceberg's worth of subtext juju, not just my deficiencies as a housekeeper.

"Sure," I said to Cary. "Nice little town, Boulder. Except for the arsons, which are, you know, sort of..." My voice trailed off.

He leaned toward me, more serious. "What were you going to say?"

"Just...fire. Kind of central to my family's mythology, actually."

"What's *your* family fire story?" he asked.

And then I realized he'd pursued this line of conversation because he had a fire connection of his own. I could tell just by looking at him: sad and pale and suddenly exhausted. Some bad, bad memory weighing him down.

"Tell me yours," I said. "You look like you might need to."

Cary nodded. "I will. But ladies first."

22

Bittler had rejoined us. I glanced at him to see if it'd be kosher to talk about something this dark and personal out loud, but we might as well have been invisible to Boss-man and his frat minion.

Bittler stood there swaying awhile, then stuck his hands in his pants pockets and tried to sit down at the same time. Not a great plan: He managed to knock over his chair, simultaneously dropping his keys and a bunch of change to the floor.

Frat puppy kept him from falling.

I knelt down, scooped the contents of his pockets off the floor, and put everything on the table next to his pâté.

Bittler had a Playboy Bunny key ring. Ewwww.

The shrimpy little bastard didn't thank me, either. Again.

I turned back toward Cary.

"My father was the youngest of nine children," I began, "and this happened when he was seven years old, sometime in 1945. His father and the six older brothers who'd served were just home from the war, I guess."

"Where did they live?" asked Cary.

"Purchase, New York. About an hour north of Manhattan. Dad went to school in the city—a place called Buckley—so he probably didn't have a lot of friends to play with when he got home. The kid he hung out with most was called Hazy."

"Your grandparents drove him an hour each way to school?"

"Not exactly," I said, taking the last sip of my third martini.

"How'd he get there, then, train?"

"Chauffeur."

Cary looked skeptical.

"And Hazy was the son of one of the gardeners," I said.

"So you're *totally* fucking rich," he said.

"Actually, no. I'm what you'd call nouveau broke."

"Seriously?"

"Have you ever heard the expression 'shirtsleeves to shirtsleeves in three'?"

"No."

I sighed. "Okay, it means that you can pretty much guarantee that a family will go through a fortune in three generations, no matter how big it was."

"So that's, like, by the third generation they're not wearing suits and ties anymore?"

"Exactly."

"And you're the third generation?"

"Fourth. My generation mostly sits on the front stoops of Section Eight apartment buildings in our undershirts with a pack of Kools and a scratch ticket. When we're not screaming at our feral offspring in Laundromats."

"Wearing real pearls, though, I notice," he said.

"Damn right. I'm trying to claw my way back into the middle class."

"Sure," he said, chuckling, "like *that* would be a huge leap."

I sighed anew. "My father's lived in a VW van since 1976, and my mother just married her death-row pen pal. That would be husband number five."

Cary stopped chuckling, his eyes gentle again. "That's pretty, um. . . . Wow."

The waiter arrived with our elk medallions in

port-wine-shiitake reduction with roasted balsamic baby root vegetables. Somehow, both these foodstuffs had been teased into utterly phallic twinned towers: cockstand comestibles, Leggo-My-Lingams, a priapic *plat du jour*.

Cary was still mulling over what I'd said.

This is always kind of the tricky point of opening up to anyone I hope will become a bona-fide friend.

We get to the actual personal-history stuff and some just decide I'm a pathological liar, or otherwise nuts—at which point they move right the fuck along.

And maybe those were the healthy people.

I mean, hey, there was a ton of crap in my personal record that required a willing suspension of disbelief—right up until you saw more of it raining down on my head in real time.

Let's just say I've never bonded with anyone over a shared love of sparkly unicorns or anything. It's virtually always the dark shit. The damage.

A more accomplished conversationalist might be able to tap-dance around all that. Or maybe I'd just never seen the point of trying. I figure land mines have a habit of making themselves known, no matter how many hours you invest in blathering about needlepoint or curtains or housebreaking new puppies beforehand.

I just cross my fingers and come out of the cave with my hands up. Life is short and shallow sparkly-unicorn people have always bored the shit out of me, so why prolong the agony?

I started in on my elk, which was actually pretty damn good.

"Madeline...," Cary began.

But Bittler interrupted, guffawing at something beside me with his mouth full before snapping his fingers at the waiter for more Scotch.

"Hey you," he yelled, "*Pedro!*"

Frat boy chimed in with, "How 'bout some damn refills over here?"

I turned to Cary. "You were about to say something?"

"Your father and Hazy," he said. "Tell me the rest."

"We should probably eat first."

I toppled both food phalli with the edge of my fork, then mashed them into vulva-shapes for good measure.

Fuck Freud. Georgia O'Keeffe rides again.

"Granddaddy Dare bought an autogyro before the war," I began, once we'd plowed through the rest of the elk. "He'd had a hangar built for it on the property—big steel warehouse kind of thing on a concrete pad. Dad always called it a 'Butler Building.'"

"What's an autogyro?" asked Cary.

"Kind of a helicopter-airplane hybrid, before helicopters were invented. It had stubby wings with a propeller and a big overhead rotor, so you didn't need a lot of ground run to take off and land."

He nodded.

It was nearing the end of the school year, I explained, and Grandmama and Granddaddy had planned a trip to Canada to fish for salmon on the Restigouche River, taking Dad's twelve-year-old sister with them.

My father was to have stayed home with his nurse, in order to finish out the academic year. I don't know whether my aunt's vacation at Spence started earlier, or whether their parents just didn't think it was problematic to interrupt a daughter's education.

My mother presumes this all took place on a Friday afternoon, when Dad had finished his week of school in the city.

It would've been a day lengthening into summer, the fine old trees on the family place lush and verdant, the acres of close-napped lawn sweet with clover.

"Hazy and Dad sneaked into the hangar, one day after school," I continued. Something they'd done before.

The boys were armed with slingshots, their pockets crammed with wooden matches.

"Not the safety kind," I said. "The strike-anywhere kind."

Cary blanched, hearing that part, knowing this wouldn't end well.

My stories tend not to.

Somehow they'd learned the trick of shooting a match at the concrete floor sulfured head down so it'd burst into flame on contact before bouncing back into the air, like a stone that skipped once when skimmed across the surface of a pond.

Maybe Hazy's older brother had passed along this trick, maybe Dad had learned it from a fellow student at Buckley. Hard to say.

"One of those lit matches bounced into a forty-gallon barrel of varnish," I said. "I don't know if the thing was just open at the top, or there was a little cap or something that had been left off, but the shit ignited and blew up. All over Hazy."

Cary grabbed my wrist.

"You okay?" I asked.

He nodded.

"So," I continued, "Dad told him to roll on the ground to extinguish the flames, but Hazy's older sister—"

"*Jesus*," said Cary. "His sister?"

"It's never been clear to me when she arrived at the scene—she's just suddenly there in every rendition of this I've ever been told—but anyway, she screamed at Hazy to get up and run to the brook, a hundred yards away."

Cary gripped my wrist tighter, but he didn't ask me to stop.

"Yeah, so . . . Hazy didn't make it to the brook."

Dad's parents took him away to the Restigouche the following afternoon. They didn't talk to him about what had happened—or even mention it, ever again. They just told him he'd be coming with them for the salmon fishing.

"That's appalling," said Cary.

"No shit. My mother says that for months afterward, whenever my father heard a siren he presumed it was the police, coming to put him in jail for killing his best friend."

"But at least he talked to her about it. That must have helped."

"Right before they got married. He took her to visit Hazy's grave."

I think that loss was the basis for everything,

really. As though Hazy's death were the first black rectangle tipped in an elaborate paisley arrangement of dominoes—if dominoes could somehow be made of anti-matter.

My family is defined by the absences, the negative space.

There'd been a dad-shaped void in my life for as long as I could remember, always bleeding just a little bit, around the edges.

"Anyway," I said. "I don't know how you could come out of something like that undamaged. Especially to be left alone with it, as a seven-year-old kid."

"I'm terrified of fire," said Cary. "Always have been."

"Me too."

He gave me one of those wonderful crinkly-eyed empathy smiles.

Tribal identification.

"Your turn," I said.

Cary took his hand off my wrist, drew in a deep breath. "This kid on my street—his house burned down when we were ten."

"I'm so sorry."

"Everyone else made it out, the whole rest of his family. He died."

"You guys were close?"

"Best friends. We were born a week apart. I still have pictures of us in a playpen together."

I put my hand on *his* wrist.

"The worst part was..." He hesitated.

"What?"

"Well, you could smell it for weeks afterward. The whole neighborhood—even upwind. Rain didn't help. I couldn't sleep."

I shuddered.

"I kept badgering my parents to buy rope ladders for all the windows, in case it happened to us. My father thought it was pretty funny. Teased me about it mercilessly."

"No offense," I said, "but I think that's a total dick move on your father's part."

"He had a point."

"You were a little kid, Cary. *And* you'd just lost your best friend...?"

"Yeah, but Madeline." Cary shook his head, grinning at me. "We lived in a one-story house."

I smiled at that. "Well..."

Before I could finish the thought, Bittler passed out. Face-first into his plate of elk.

"*Kanpai*," whispered Cary, whereupon I had to pretend I'd been overtaken by a sudden coughing fit to cover my laughter.

23

Cary showed up on our porch bright and early the next morning, mountain bike tucked under his arm.

Dean was still in the shower so I answered the door. "He's running a little late today."

"That's fine," said Cary. "Gives me more time for coffee."

"Espresso or cappuccino?" I asked as he yanked off his Styrofoam helmet.

"If you're offering to foam some milk, cappuccino would be a dream come true."

"I'd be honored." I started back toward the kitchen, waving him along behind me.

He carried the bike inside, as always. It was a serious machine: carbon fiber and way too kuh-razy expensive to leave on a porch. My husband drooled with lust every time he saw the damn thing.

The girls had finished their French toast, so I sponged off their faces and hands and lifted Parrish up out of her booster seat.

"Hey there, little beauty," Cary said, unlatching India so he could carry her to the playpen in my wake.

I refilled the coffee machine and started it up.

"So," said Cary, "are we on for lunch at the Thai place?"

I shrugged, a little embarrassed.

"Madeline, you haven't told Dean yet?"

"Not exactly."

"Why not? I would think he'd be happy about it, you getting a job."

"Well..."

The machine started chugging in earnest, and it was time to get the foamer-nozzle into my glass of milk.

I twisted the dial open and didn't bother trying to finish my thought over the onslaught of noise, keeping the nozzle's tip at the perfect depth so the froth burgeoned satiny and uniform, its bubbles too tiny for even Don Ho to detect.

When I'd handed Cary his coffee, I crossed my arms. "I have another fire story."

"About these arsons?"

"No," I said. "This was when Dean and I lived in Syracuse. Right after we got married."

"The plot thickens."

"I had to watch someone getting prepared to light a house on fire, once. Scary as hell."

"Given our mutual history with flame, I can see why someone even thinking about doing that would've freaked the hell out of you."

"Well, it wasn't so much the idea of him *lighting* it that scared me—more the fact that he planned to chain me to a fireplace inside it, first."

"Did he actually do it? I mean, not chain you to a fireplace in a burning house…you wouldn't be here."

"He got as far as pouring a bunch of gasoline around. And then a lot of other stuff happened…"

He shook his head. "Jesus. That's just…I can't begin to imagine."

"Yeah," I said. "We're not exactly designed to imagine shit like that."

"And you still have the guts to walk through a place that burned down *here*?"

"That wasn't guts," I said, "it was morbid curiosity. I mean, it's not like the house here was still *on* fire at the time. It was just the aftermath."

He nodded, unconvinced.

"But the people who show up first and deal with the actual flames," I continued, "they have major balls. Running *into* a burning building to get people out? I can't imagine."

Cary shuddered. "No fucking way I could do that. I don't even like yanking burned Pop-Tarts out of the toaster oven."

I smiled at that image.

"What?" he asked.

"I'm picturing you with your eyes clenched shut, subduing your breakfast pastries with a fire extinguisher."

He laughed. "I'd be cowering outside in the parking lot, curled up on the asphalt and making little mewling noises."

That made me crack up entirely.

"Yeah, big tough old Cary," he said, smiling, "total pansy. But I've learned to live with my utter wussitude. And who knows, maybe this will help..." He shoved a hand into the right front pocket of his shorts and pulled it out again, my grandmother's four-leaf-clover charm now centered in the valley of his meaty palm.

"Hey, I hope so," I said.

"I'll break the news of your employment to your husband at the first opportunity this morning. I've been craving pad Thai since we talked about this yesterday."

Dean breezed into the kitchen, briefcase in hand. "Somebody mention Thai food?"

"Your lovely wife has some *really* great news," said Cary.

Dean looked at me, tense. "What kind of great news?"

Thanks, Cary . . .

"Um," I said. "I got a job. As the restaurant critic at the *New Times*."

"Oh, thank *God*, Bunny." Dean's face flooded with relief and he slumped back against the kitchen counter, letting the strap slide through his fingers until his briefcase rested on the floor. "I thought you were going to tell me you were *pregnant*."

My husband and I looked at each other and both started laughing, somewhat hysterically.

"Triplets . . . ," I said, almost choking.

"Quadruplets . . . ," Dean replied, tears streaming down his face.

"*Boys* . . . ," we said to each other at exactly the same moment.

Which made us both laugh so hard that Cary started looking seriously concerned.

Dean slid down the base cabinet until he was

cross-legged on the kitchen floor, and I couldn't breathe—had to lean over, put my hands on my knees.

Cary whacked me on the back.

Which helped, a little.

But just when I was calming down enough to inhale, I heard him say, "So I guess this means you're okay with the newspaper thing, then?"

Which totally set me and Dean off again.

I sank to the floor, then flopped onto my back, kicking my sneakered heels against the orange linoleum.

Cary cleared his throat. "I told Madeline we'd go with her to that Thai place out by the office. For lunch."

I banged my fist against his ankle. "Stop *talking* . . . you're going to make me puke."

When we finally, *finally* stopped laughing, Dean wiped his eyes on his sleeve and said, "Sounds great, Bunny. Can you bring the girls in the wagon?"

"I'd love to."

He turned to Cary. "I'm sorry to be a pain in the ass, but would you mind throwing your bike in the back of my car? I have to haul a pile of shit out to the office. Or you could ride and I'll drive. Sorry I didn't call this morning, let you know you could've gone direct."

"Free excellent coffee and a nice chat with Madeline," said Cary, raising his glass. "Not to mention getting to watch the pair of you lose your shit like that? *Totally* worth it."

Dean stood up, kissed the top of my head, and ducked his head under his briefcase strap. "We should hit it. Sorry to run so late, Cary."

He walked out to the dining room, stepped over the playpen fence, and hoisted the first of two cardboard cartons up off the table.

Cary put his helmet back on, hooked his bike over one shoulder, and reached for the second box. "I'll get this one."

Dean shifted his own, exhaling. "Watch your back, they're heavy."

I pulled a corner peg out of the playpen and pulled it open so they wouldn't have to haul themselves over the railing, thus encumbered.

While they duck-walked single file toward the living room, torsos tilted back to counter the weight of their respective burdens, I jogged ahead to open the front door.

"Great to see you, Madeline," said Cary, breathless. "Thanks again for the fortifying beverage."

"Dude," I said. "Thanks for being so *subtle*."

I heard him cackle as he started down the porch steps.

24

I always took what the girls wore pretty seriously, opting that day for contrasting OshKosh overall jumpers, shiny black lug-soled mary janes, striped tights and turtlenecks, and little knit hats that looked like a strawberry and an eggplant, respectively.

This wasn't some grown-up reversion to playing with dolls; I'd preferred fort-building and Hot Wheels as a kid.

It was more because I still felt the sting of my own childhood wardrobe: half raggedy Salvation Army crap, half outlandishly expensive castoffs from older and wealthier cousins back east.

If you would like to make a small child morbidly self-conscious for life, equip her with a large vocabulary and send her to public elementary school in early-seventies Stevie Nicks California wearing knee-socks, penny loafers, kilts, and moth-eaten shocking-pink/acid-green cable-knit Shetland sweaters that have been monogrammed with other people's initials.

Trust me, she will be contemplating the abyss by third grade and quoting Kafka under her breath well before she ever attends a middle school dance.

It was gorgeous out, surprise surprise. Sparkling sunshine, fluffy clouds, trees just budding out into pale leaf or fluffy blossom.

Three generations' worth of blooms from the local iris farm, Long's Gardens, nodded from virtually every yard and swale like orchidy daffodils: salmon, cobalt, amethyst, Burmese-ruby fuchsia, yellows from butter to egg yolk to topaz, nursery-pastel pinks and powder blues.

I pulled the wagon onto the Boulder Creek Path and a slight breeze picked up, making new aspen leaves quake and shiver along white boughs so they all winked in the light like a thousand buckets of loose change tossed in the air at once.

Dean's office was situated in one of those eastward industrial parks out where Boulder started getting really high-plains-y and treeless.

I'd figured it would be a thirty-minute walk, and that I could use the exercise, but the creek path was hilly enough to slow me down with the girls' wagon in tow.

Then I got out onto the flats and had a moment of vertigo when it struck me once again how very broad the high plains were.

Okay, maybe it's not vertigo when you aren't standing on top of something tall and looking down. It was all sideways.

The whole Big Sky Heartland thing made me itchily paranoid, like I was about to get strafed by some Hitchcockian crop-duster biplane, or burned at the stake for being pro-choice and anti–Jell-O salad.

There was just something about the sheer numbing expanse and tonnage of those amber waves of grain, once you'd turned your back on purple mountains' majesty.

This was Dean's line of country, not mine. It must have reminded him of the corn-rowed acreage of his boyhood: that overcast upstate New York landscape in which things botanical were planted for income, not decoration.

I wanted to be near water, preferably an ocean. Somehow it always felt like then I'd be able to escape if things got really bad. Which was crazy...

I mean, what would I have done if there'd been a nuclear holocaust while we were living in New York City, stolen a canoe and paddled up the Hudson with the girls in their car seats at my feet? Not bloody likely.

I trudged onward, wondering if my new pal Mimi had gotten any farther with the arson investigations. I decided to call her that afternoon once I'd gotten home and seen the lab results were in . . . *after* I called McNally at the paper and asked whether it'd be okay to review Alice's Restaurant for next week.

Despite what I'd said to Cary about not wanting to review a place I'd already gotten a free meal from, I realized Dean might take off at any time on another business trip, and I'd already spent this month's hundred bucks from mom on babysitters.

Or maybe I'd get a check from the paper, for the first three articles? Kind of ridiculous, really, to realize I'd have to spend it on child care so I could keep writing.

Then again, I figured having even a semblance of a job was an investment in sanity—mine *and* Dean's—whether or not I broke even at the end of the month.

Thank God I could bring the kiddos along to the Thai place for lunch. That was at least twenty bucks I wouldn't have to blow on getting someone to watch out for them while I took notes on the quality of satay and green-papaya salad.

I'd loaded the wagon with boxes of apple juice and ziplock bags of Cheese Nips, but Parrish and India were sacked out for their morning nap beneath the white hooped-canvas roof. Perfect timing—they'd be bright and cheery at the office.

I stopped for a minute to catch my breath, tucking a bright patchwork quilt under their dear little chins.

And smiled to myself. *Jesus* but it had been a long time since Dean and I'd shared a good laugh.

The girls were just coming around by the time I entered the corporate park, murmuring and chirping drowsily as I tried to remember in which of the several dozen identically stark, flat-roofed beige buildings I would find my Intrepid Spouse.

The lawns looked as if they'd been spray-painted green, the parking lot asphalt was freshly smooth and black, and not one of the randomly capitalized company names emblazoned across each corporate barracks revealed a thing about what the persons employed within actually did: VanaTel, AccenTron, Tacti-Tek, Micro*Next*.

I wandered right, left, and right again, squinting now and really wanting to get out of the sun, which had reached the blinding acme of its mile-high noonday glare.

No one outside but we mad dogs and English majors...

I turned one more corner and saw our beat-up Mitsubishi wedged into a row of shiny white and ice-blue LeSabres and SUVs.

Here was Dean's building, at long last—the company name etched in early-eighties-hair-salon sans-serif gold across a squat pink-granite head-stone slab: IONIX, LLC.

I checked my reflection in a spotless car window before heading toward the glass-doored entrance. Bonus: There was no actual dirt on my face, and I only looked half as tired as I felt.

I hauled the red wagon inside, blinking while my eyes adjusted to the lobby's dimmer interior light.

Setsuko smiled at me—cool and prim and per-fectly coiffed behind the reception counter's speck-led gray Formica.

"Would it be okay if I parked this in here," I asked, "or should I tuck it away somewhere out-side?"

She smiled again. "You can bring it right back here next to me, okay? I'll watch it."

I thanked her and pulled the wagon around. She knelt down to help me pull India free, as I reached inside for Parrish.

"Very, very pretty, your little girls," she said, holding her hands out so India could grab on with chubby fists to steady herself. "Such *cute* dresses."

"Thank you," I said again. "And thank you for looking after the wagon, Setsuko. You're always so thoughtful."

"My pleasure. I'll buzz your husband and let him know you've arrived. But you have to promise you'll let me babysit, sometime?"

"You're wonderful," I said. "And I *will* call you."

Dean and Cary and the girls and I were finally settled around a faux-walnut six-top in the Thai place, having secured a pair of booster seats once I'd taken each kid in turn to the ladies' room for a quick diaper change.

We plopped Parrish's chair between Cary and Dean, with India and me ensconced directly across from them.

I'd broken out the Cheese Nips and boxes of apple juice, tied the girls' bibs around their necks, and finally settled down myself to peruse the menu.

All I really wanted at this point was a personal

gallon of Thai iced coffee—extra heavy on the caffeine—but I ran a list of appetizers and entrées past my dining companions that seemed like a reasonably varied overview of the place's culinary aptitude.

Cary and Dean were discussing some new technical developments at work. I'd gotten a D- for the year in high school chemistry, so they might as well have been reciting toaster-oven instruction booklets in Lithuanian.

Our young waitress returned with a round of ice waters and my blessed gigantic vessel of high-octane caffeine, whereupon I proceeded to order a yellow curry and a green, a beef salad, the requisite pad Thai and chicken satay, and a handful of other house specialties I'd have to remember to write down and rate in my trusty notebook the minute we were back out the door.

India started tossing back Cheese Nips as Parrish drained her juice box.

"Look," said Cary, "I think Bittler's embezzling."

I looked up, suddenly interested. "What?"

"You're getting paranoid," Dean said soothingly. "I mean, the guy's an asshole, but—"

Cary shook his head. "When was the last time you got reimbursed for expenses? He's late again, right? Used to take him a month, then six weeks.

Now we're talking two months, minimum. Sometimes more."

Dean nodded, his face sour. "Not for the VPs, of course."

Cary ran the tip of his index finger along the rim of his water glass. "Just for the underlings. The people who can't really complain, am I right?"

Dean nodded again.

"That's *totally* shitty," I said.

"I had to hit up my father for the entire rent check this month," said Cary. "I promised I'd pay him back as soon as I got reimbursed, but still..."

Parrish got a Cheese Nip wedged in one nostril. I reached across the table and pulled it out.

Dean leaned back in his chair. "It's not like we're lagging in receivables. P and L's looking damn solid. We outdid ourselves on sales this quarter— and most accounts are paying early."

"That's my point," said Cary. "There's no cash lag. Just Bittler, fucking around. But there's some weird shit going on with shipping spares, too. Fulfillment's all backed up."

"Well, that's not good," said Dean. "But really, man. I mean, I hate to say it, but you're sounding a little paranoid."

India chortled and shrieked with joy beside me. I looked over to check the level on her Cheese

Nip cache only to realize that she'd managed to drink my entire liter of iced coffee while I'd been distracted with adult conversation.

Oh fucking well, so much for the afternoon nap.

"Look," Dean was saying, when I tuned back in to the grown-up channel, "you get that kind of wrinkle occasionally, with this whole just-in-time business model. Somebody forgets to replace one little belt on a drill press in Malaysia, and the global supply chain gets tweaked for a month. Shit happens. Just another downside of the old Japanese Management Style."

"You guys heard about the four international CEOs who got abducted by a Marxist revolutionary front?" I asked.

They shook their heads.

"French, British, Japanese, and American. Marxists have them up in a plane, tell them they're going to push them out one by one, so do they have any last words..."

Parrish threw a Cheese Nip.

"Brit says he wants to sing 'Rule, Britannia,' French dude asks if he can do the Marseillaise, and the Japanese guy pipes up that he'd like to deliver the lecture on management techniques he was going to present at the conference they're never going to get to attend now."

"And the American?" asked Cary.

"He says, 'Just shoot me first, before I have to listen to another fucking lecture on Japanese management techniques.'"

They liked that.

But Cary got serious again quickly.

"Look, Dean," he said. "Have you been out to the warehouse lately? I'm telling you, something's fucked up."

25

I haven't had any reason to go out to the warehouse for a while," said Dean. "Not for a couple of months, anyway."

"Well, I needed to check over some shit this morning," said Cary.

Dean nodded. "What kind of shit?"

"Invoices that were misnumbered. A spares order for that new Pemex facility. Same problem we had with Bangalore last month, remember?"

"Of course," said Dean. "Rajiv wanted to beat the hell out of me."

"Well, different client, same clusterfuck. I'm telling you, Bittler's doing some weird shit."

"All appears yellow to the jaundiced eye," said Dean.

"Jaundice didn't re-key all the warehouse locks without telling anyone," retorted Cary.

That got Dean's attention. "*What?*"

"I went out there this morning," Cary said. "Couldn't get in the damn place. Setsuko says Bittler's got the only set of new keys. And he's conveniently in Houston all week. What the fuck, right?"

Dean thought this over.

"Come on," said Cary. "Your wife should do some investigative reporting, here… *60 Minutes* the guy a little. Right after she figures out who this arsonist is—"

"*What* arsonist?" asked my husband, turning toward me.

"Um," I said, swallowing audibly. "The guy in my second article."

Dean started shredding little bits off the edge of his napkin. "I thought you were writing about *restaurants*."

I looked down at the table. "I got an extra assignment."

"That you conveniently neglected to mention this morning?"

"Yeah, I was *totally* hiding it from you, Dean," I said, crossing my arms.

Well, technically I *had* been, of course, but this

whole cranky-husband-bullshit thing was starting to piss me off.

He looked up at me, having now destroyed his entire napkin.

I stared right back. I mean, when had he decided our marriage was a dictatorship, for fuck's sake?

"Madeline's really talented," said Cary, smiling at me. "You have to read her stuff. It's outstanding."

"No," said Dean. "*Not* outstanding. By any stretch of the imagination."

Cary's eyes widened and he turned toward Dean, but my husband was focused on me.

"Not even *acceptable*," Dean continued, frostier with each syllable.

"Acceptable to whom?" I asked, looking him straight in the eye.

He leaned forward, nostrils flared just a bit. "Jesus Christ, Bunny, what the hell were you *thinking*?"

"What the hell do you *think* I was thinking? I've finally got a job again, doing what I'm good at. I'm making a little money, trying to do my bit for the familial finances."

Okay, so not exactly in any big fat profitable way, *yet*, but still . . .

"Goddamn it," said Dean. "You're a *mother* now.

Haven't you put us both through enough of this shit already?"

Both my hands were clenched into fists now. "Enough of *what* shit, specifically?"

"Your morbid fascination with violence and mayhem. Your goddamn death wish."

"I do *not* have a death wish."

"Really?" He pursed his lips into an annoying smirk that made me want to kick him, under the table. "Let's see...there's the guy who was going to light *you* on fire, the woman who tried to push you off the fourth-story roof, oh...and the gang boys in Queens who were planning to *shoot* you, after they'd managed to run you over with a car and break your arm during a *homicide* investigation. None of that qualifies as a flirtation with your own mortality?"

"None of which I sought *out*," I said. "Or even instigated. I mean, if anything, I have a *life* wish. Otherwise I wouldn't still be here—"

Cary's head swiveled back and forth between us, following these volleys.

"And now you're jumping *right* back into it," said Dean. "Putting yourself at risk. Putting our *children* at risk. Our *daughters*."

"I am not," I said, starting to tear up. "I am *not*."

But my gut went cold with fear at what he was

suggesting, like I'd just choked down an entire tray of ice, *and* the tray—the old aluminum kind with a ratchet-lever on one end to tilt the cubes out of their tinny rectangular partitions.

Hadn't I thought the *exact* same thing myself, when I assured McNally the first day we met that I had no interest in anything other than restaurant pieces?

Yes. Of course I had.

"You need to give up this *writing* shit," said my husband.

Cary blanched, turning toward me with such a tenderly crinkle-browed faceful of sympathy that I couldn't decide whether I wanted to hug him or crawl out of the restaurant in shame.

Yes, Dean had been tantrummy for the last couple of months. But this was different. He'd never bullied me in front of a friend before, never in public.

I surveyed him through narrowed eyes: the pompous jut of his chin, the moue of entitlement twisting the corners of his mouth.

And suddenly I felt like I'd x-rayed through to what this was really about.

Not about danger for me, not even concern for the girls' safety . . . at least not at the root of it all.

My father would've laughed, summarizing with

the Marine Corps's unofficial motto: *Shit flows downhill.*

Dean was at other people's beck and call all day, every day. Bittler and the rest of them.

"Working for wages," *his* father said, every time we visited the family farm—a mere three words to dismiss his son's every achievement, out in the world.

Damn right it all comes downhill, and here I am, up to my waist.

"You need to give up this writing shit, Madeline," Dean said again. "You've never made any money at it, and I want a *homemaker.*"

I was just about to tell him to get royally fucked and rot in hell when India knocked his water all over the table and the waitress arrived with our lunch.

26

Dean was petulantly silent with me for the rest of the meal, not to mention the entire drive back to Ionix after lunch.

Yet he chatted with Cary as though nothing had happened, while I sat in the backseat between the girls.

And the whole time my confidence receded, the way the tide does before a hurricane hits. Maybe Dean was right, maybe I was putting the girls in danger, and I sure as shit wasn't making any money. In fact I had to rely on being subsidized by my mother even to attempt this job, this *hobby*.

"Listen," I said, reaching forward to put my hand on Dean's shoulder, when he'd pulled into a parking spot back at work.

He flinched my hand off and yanked up the emergency brake. Pocketing the keys without a word, he got out, slamming the door shut behind him, and stalked back into the lobby.

Cary and I took a minute, just sitting there with our seat belts still on.

"You okay?" he asked at last, turning around to give me a tentative smile.

"Sure," I said, from my perch between the girls' car seats. "I'll be fine. Eventually."

I didn't feel fine. I felt like a small dog that had gotten its ribs kicked in by the very human it most wanted to serve and protect.

Cary was still doing sympathy-face. "That was total bullshit, everything he said in the restaurant."

I looked away. "It's complicated."

"Your husband is being an utter dickhead. What's complicated about that?"

"I mean, from a certain perspective, I can see his point. He's got a right to be concerned..."

"'Concern' my ass, Madeline. There is *no* excuse for spewing vitriol at your wife in a restaurant. Or anywhere else, for that matter."

"Granted, Dean's mode of expression was appalling. And I'm sorry you had to be there..."

"Does he speak to you that way at home? When you guys are alone?"

I didn't answer.

"Madeline, that was not a rhetorical question."

"Cary... look, Dean and I, we're both exhausted."

"Answer me."

"Oh, great. Now *you're* going to start ordering me around?" I looked out the window.

"I'm sorry," he said. "Please. Talk to me about this. I'm your friend. I think it's important."

"Does Dean do this at home, when we're alone?" I said. "Yes. Often. He's been an asshole since we moved here. Intermittently, but still... huge gobs of assholish-ness."

"Madeline," he said, putting his hand on my knee.

"Look, do *you* think I'm endangering myself, or the girls?"

Cary thought about that. "Do *you* feel like you might be?"

"Well, I'm not investigating an ax murderer or anything," I said. "This is just some guy who likes to light shit on fire. Junior-varsity crap."

"Compared with that other stuff Dean was talking about?"

"Yeah."

Stupid, dangerous, lethal "stuff"... and my fault for getting caught up in it, every damn time.

"People have really tried to kill you?" asked

Cary. "Not just the guy who wanted to chain you in the fireplace?"

I sighed. "Several people."

"Seriously? Jesus..."

"You got a few minutes? I'll flesh it out for you."

"Sure," he said. "Bittler can go fuck himself. I'm not in any hurry."

So I proceeded to tell him the story of the Madeline Dare Misspent-Youth Massacre, with full orchestration and five-part harmony.

At the end of it, Cary didn't speak for a good thirty seconds—just stared at me with this look of tremendous sadness on his face.

"You think Dean's right," I said.

Cary shook his head but still didn't say a word.

I dropped my eyes, whispered, "*What*, then?"

"I think you're a goddamn *hero*," he said, his voice hoarse, "and I'm going to tell your husband it's about time to get his head out of his ass and start *appreciating* you for it."

I closed my eyes. "Please, don't."

"Why the hell not?"

"Look, you aren't married. It's like a dance after a while. You hit a rough patch, and there's stuff on both sides, and it's not about taking sides or who's winning. It's never about that. But anybody external joins into the fray, it just bends things more out of whack."

"I don't believe that."

"I'm not kidding. Dean's been through a ton of shit lately. And everything's resting on his shoulders. He's on the road at least two weeks a month, he's worried about supporting all three of us. He's worried about what Bittler's doing to *you*, and this job, and whether or not he's going to make it all work out—and he knows his father and brother would love to see him fail, come back to the farm with his tail between his legs. And it's *exhausting*, having little kids. Just generally. He gets home from getting beaten to shit on the road and I'm exhausted and the house looks like a bomb site and all I want to do is order a fucking pizza and have him take the wheel for a while, you know?"

"Maddie, that's not—"

"I'm serious, Cary."

"If you can't treat the person you're married to as your friend, what's the goddamn point?"

I shrugged. "Hell if I know. My mom's on her fifth husband. I figure the best bet is you just suck it up, play it as it lays."

"You deserve better. And Dean can goddamn well *treat* you better, starting today."

"Cary, we're okay. We're going to be okay. We've got a good solid base and we'll get through this bit. It's just toughing it out a little longer, just getting a little more sleep. And he's right, I haven't been pulling my weight, not as well as I could be. I'm just so fucking *tired*. But this too shall pass. The only thing I want to explain to him is that for me, having something going on outside, in real life—that's only going to help me be *better* at the homemaking shit. We all need perspective. You have to leave the fucking house every once in a while so you notice it needs vacuuming or whatever when you get back. That's all."

"I still don't see where he gets off—"

"Cary," I said, "don't fuck with this, okay? Promise me."

"You're sure?"

"Yeah. I really am."

"Okay. Cross my heart and hope to die, stick a needle in my eye: I will not berate your husband for giving you crap for wanting to balance a career with being a mother. Much as I want to, and much as he deserves it."

"Thank you," I said. "And look, I'm not, like, the abused wife in a movie of the week here. I'm just married to a guy who gets cranky-pants with the occasional bit of stress overload. In real life, he's got my back. And I have his."

"I still—" But then he stopped.

"What?" I asked.

He looked away. "Nothing."

"Cary," I said, leaning forward to touch his arm. "You're an incredible friend. To both of us. And that's totally huge."

He blushed a little, then helped me get the girls out of their car seats and carry them inside.

Setsuko must have taken off on her own lunch break, but the little red wagon was still safely stowed behind the reception counter.

I wrote a thank-you note on one of her pink Post-its, fixing it firmly to the desk's prairie of speckled Formica.

I bumped a hip against her wheelie chair as I stood up, making it roll about ten inches to the right. Stowed neatly in front of its former position was a tote bag filled with ball after ball of pink and pale blue angora wool, edged by a stripy fringed triangle she was apparently constructing out of the yarn.

Good God, she's crocheting a poncho. Or knitting it. Or something.

Now, here was a woman who'd make the *perfect* home, down to the last insipid hand-loomed fuzzy toilet seat cover.

I shivered, the chill of claustrophobia trickling

down the nape of my neck, drawing my shoulders tight.

Poor oppressed bitch.

I thought about what Cary had told me concerning Setsuko's predicament for the entire walk home, wondering if there might be some way Dean could help her stay in the country.

Probably because I didn't want to think about my marriage. Or what an asshole Dean was being. Or what the hell I should do about it if he didn't get the fuck over himself in a big fat hurry.

Well, to be honest I was thinking about *that* at the same time. It was just all mashed up together in my head.

Because Cary's response was identical to what I'd felt when I'd had to watch Seamus tear Ellis a new asshole over the bottle of Elmer's Glue. And I wondered at myself for being able to be more pissed off on my friend's behalf than my own.

Not to mention angrier on Setsuko's behalf, during that complete turd-fest of a business dinner. And I didn't even really *like* her.

Yeah, solidarity. Even though I had to admit I'd spent that evening distracting myself from Dean's having been a jerk with the idea that some other chick had it worse than I did.

Same shit, different hill.

I mean, not like Setsuko was facing suttee or genital mutilation or whatever back in Tokyo—I wasn't that naive and ignorant a cultural chauvinist—and God knows I would've given my eyeteeth for the kind of subsidized health insurance and day care available in Japan. It was just…okay, yes…solidarity on the gender front mattered.

Sisters in arms.

Glass houses.

And like Arlo used to say, "You want to end the war and stuff, you gotta sing loud."

I should ask Dean if there was any way he could help her out.

That would be the right thing to do.

Fuck me, though, what the hell was *I* supposed to do? Start giving my husband ultimatums? Dump his ass if he didn't shape up?

Follow in Mom's footsteps?

I'd already lost my father, did I really have to lose my best friend, too? Not just temporarily, but forever.

I wished I could shine a flashlight into Dean's eye sockets and send up a couple of flares to see if my real husband was still *inside* there somewhere.

27

I was back home with the girls and on the phone with McNally.

It didn't look like I'd be getting down to the paper in person anytime soon—Parrish was sound asleep in her crib upstairs but India was careening around the giant playpen like a one-toddler roller derby, still totally jacked up on my iced coffee and laughing her head off.

I'd called him about the Alice's Restaurant review. But then he started talking arson.

There'd been two more fires. Stores near Pearl Street this time.

"Check with Mimi," McNally said. "They're holding a community meeting tomorrow night at some church. It would be great if you covered it for us. Write up what the fire department recommends people do to stay safe. You know the drill."

"Listen, I have to—" and then I couldn't figure out what to tell him.

I have to check with my husband, make sure I have his permission to write about anything but food?

"Have to what?" asked McNally, sounding testy. "Find a babysitter?"

"Something like that."

"You *do* have a husband lying around somewhere, don't you?"

I laughed. "Are you even allowed to ask me that, as my employer?"

"I didn't mean…"

"Relax, McNally. Yes, I have a husband. He just travels a lot for work."

"Look, all I wanted to say is that I understand perfectly well that men can be selfish shitheads—especially husbands. I should know, I am one."

"A husband?"

"A *guy.*"

"I was actually aware of your gender, McNally."

"Smart woman. No wonder you went into journalism."

"Smart women go into advertising."

"Is he traveling right now?"

"Who?"

"Your husband."

"No."

"So, can't *he* watch your kids for a couple of hours?"

"Have you ever been a husband?"

"Once. Briefly. She wanted me to go into advertising."

"I thought you used to be in petroleum."

"This was later. And briefer."

"Well, McNally, here's the thing... my husband would like me to avoid the crime beat. Something about how I'm the mother of small children and dangerous assignments should therefore be verboten, considering. Stuff like that."

"Did you tell him to get his head out of his ass?"

"Not exactly."

"Madeline, I'm asking you to cover a *community* meeting."

"Which happens to be about a string of arsons."

"If you want to be all *exact* about it."

"So, basically," I said, "you're suggesting I leave the whole string-of-arsons deal out of the discussion, when I ask him to babysit."

"What are the chances he'll actually *read* the article? Husbands are notoriously crappy at that kind of thing. Especially when their wives write about community meetings."

"Or he might be, you know, *traveling*. When it actually gets published."

"See, I knew you were smart."

"And you, McNally, are a terrible influence."

"That's why they pay me the big bucks."

"Yeah, whatever. Did Mimi get the Mapleton-fire lab results back yet?"

"You'd be wasted in advertising," he said.

"So would you. Answer the question."

"You want to know what the accelerant was, I take it?"

"Obviously."

"Find a babysitter and call me back."

"Or I could call Mimi."

"You could, if she weren't in Denver today."

India took her shirt off and started swinging it around her head, shrieking.

"What *is* that?" asked McNally. "A car alarm, or did they have another nuke spill up at Rocky Flats?"

"Um. That would be one of my daughters. The one who drank a liter of Thai iced coffee at lunch today while I was trying to review the restaurant."

"Tell that husband of yours that you *deserve* a babysitter," he said. "Then call me back."

I took the phone into the bathroom and tried calling Mimi, just to see whether he'd been bullshitting me.

She didn't pick up at home or at work so I left her messages on both machines, asking her whether she'd gotten the lab results, and when and where this meeting was to be held, and to please call me back whenever she had a minute.

India was no longer shrieking so I edged back out of the bathroom and sat down beside the playpen.

She waddled over and patted me on the head.

"Hey there, my cutie," I said.

"Mummie Mummie Mummie. Hey," she said back, then sat down and started piling up some wooden blocks.

I briefly considered calling Dean at work. Like, for a nanosecond. Or possibly less.

I leaned back against the wall and dialed Ellis, instead.

28

The asshole actually *said* 'homemaker'?" asked Ellis. "You're fucking with me, right?"

"Direct quote," I said.

"Hold on a second..." I heard the palm of her hand smush over the phone's mouthpiece, then her slightly muffled voice. "Perry, give me those scissors *right now*. You are *not* giving your sister another haircut..."

I laughed.

"Jesus," she said, voice clear again. "Where were we?"

"Homemaker."

"Exactly. What is *wrong* with him? Why's he being such a dick?"

"Well, it's not like I'm the greatest roommate in the world. I mean, you've lived with me..."

"And this comes to him as a fucking *surprise*? You guys lived together for a solid chunk of time before you got married. I'd say his *caveat* was entirely *emptored*."

"I guess it's wearing thin."

"Let me call the rat bastard at his goddamn office, tell him to hire a goddamn *maid* already..."

"Then it will be my fault he has to spend money on a maid, and it will be worse."

"Okay, then I'll just fly out there and slap him around a little. He's lucky to have you. I think he needs a little reminding."

"He basically rescued me from being homeless," I said. "Who the hell else would've married me?"

"*I* shouldn't have to remind you of this: Dean got a gorgeous woman who's brilliant and funny and an amazing cook and who likes to fuck. *Plus* you did three years' hard time in Syracuse for him. More than he deserves. All of it."

"Thank you for hating my husband for me."

"Anytime," she said, and we agreed to hang up.

Upstairs, Parrish resurfaced from her nap and started weeping—just as India was finally winding down in the playpen, eyelids already at half-mast.

I reached across the little wooden fence to pick

up India and started for the staircase, relishing the warmth of her sweet weight in my arms as she drifted fully off to sleep.

When I'd tucked India into her crib and carried Parrish downstairs, I got walloped by my daily midafternoon wave of exhaustion.

It came on hard as a Jones Beach breaker, the kind that smacks the wind out of your chest and then scours you, tumbling, across the green-lit underwater sand.

I tucked Parrish into her booster seat and started slicing up a small red apple, sleep deprivation's bone-deep illogic making me wonder yet again why I always had to stay awake with the conscious twin when at that moment I ached with such visceral longing to abscond into the luxuriant bliss of her sister's nap, right there on the kitchen floor.

While I was arranging the apple slices into a happy face on the chrome-yellow plastic of Parrish's chair tray, the phone rang.

I shoved the last slice into my mouth on the way to the phone.

So it was a one-eyed happy face, who'd know? And if my child remembered this when she grew up and felt deprived, I'd tell her Mr. Happy Apple had been winking.

"Yo," I said into the phone, hoping that might be a quasi-intelligible salutation through my juicy mouthful of Red Delicious chunks.

"Acetone," said Mimi. "That and using a cigarette for a fuse, I'd say it was definitely the same guy."

29

My love for you is untrammeled and pure, *chère* Mimi. Among all the world's questioners of things *flambé*, you are and shall remain my one and only heart's forensic desire, *ma petite chou-fleur*."

"It's *petite chou*."

"Oh, come on."

"Why would you call someone 'my little cauliflower'?"

"Like *cabbage* is somehow more deeply romantic? At least cauliflower has 'flower' in it."

"Granted," she said.

"So when is this neighborhood meeting thing supposed to be?"

She told me and I wrote it down.

"I have to wrangle a babysitter," I said, sighing.

"And avoid getting myself further into the spousal shithouse."

"For what?" she asked.

"For masquerading as a cub reporter when I should be mopping and vacuuming, apparently."

"In your calico dress and prairie bonnet?"

Happy Parrish waved a spit-shiny apple slice at me, current mouthful giving her cheeks the hemispheric breadth of a nut-hoarding squirrel's.

You, my darling, are the twin most likely to be Heimliched.

"Hey, I get it," said Mimi. "I've been married."

"Kids?" I asked, sliding down against the kitchen door frame until I was sitting Indian-style on its threshold, straddling the shag-linoleum border.

I wanted to ask her what her husband had thought about the kind of work she did—whether she'd waited until their kids were grown to get serious about it.

"Terry, Chris, and Stewart from his first marriage," she said. "Then we had Michael and Laura."

"*Five* children? Mimi…wow. I am *so* going to stop whining now."

"*I* never had twins, which is a project of an entirely different order—Everest without oxygen tanks. And whining, by the way, is how we all survive this part: diapers and no sleep and striving husbands who can't understand why we didn't pick up the dry cleaning."

Another exhalation from me, on that point.

"No, I take it back," she said. "'Whining' is the wrong word, and it's not what you're doing. *Talking* is how we survive."

"Everyone?"

"Women."

I closed my eyes, letting my head loll back against the door frame.

"We narrate the truth to one another," said Mimi. "Only way you can maintain perspective on all the thousand petty little crap details we're supposed to keep raking into piles day after day, make sense of, weave into goddamn afghans, cook for dinner..."

I sighed.

"Fevers and vomit and we're-out-of-milk and what-the-hell-did-you-do-with-all-my-clean-socks—"

"Wait a second, *you* got the sock lecture?"

"Constantly," she said.

"You're really making me feel better, here, Mimi. Just hang up when I start sobbing uncontrollably over the Moebius hamster wheel of endless, thankless shit that is my life: insurmountable, with laundry pile and juice box for all."

"That's why you have to talk about it," she said.

"I'll keep it in mind."

I pinched the phone between my ear and shoulder so I could spring Parrish from booster jail, then swung her up into the air before settling her on my cocked hip.

"Want to switch back to arson now?" asked Mimi.

Parrish patted me on the boob with a sticky little fist, then stuck her thumb in her mouth.

It was getting dark out, and I had no doubt India was going to wake up any minute.

"Come over," I said. "I have beer. And you can help me convince Intrepid Spouse that my bush-league journalistic endeavors pose no threat of disharmony to our bower of familial bliss."

"You make the invitation sound so tempting," she said.

"No hard sell, I promise. Just, you know… you're interesting and cool with a meaty job that actually *matters*, and you've raised kids and it turned out okay."

"This may require cheese and crackers."

"Brie," I said. "Nice and runny, with fig paste and Stoned Wheat Thins."

"Give me ten minutes," she said, laughing.

30

By the time Mimi pulled up out front, I had the living room in reasonable shape, both kids in the playpen—pink-cheeked and freshly diapered—the offspring *and* grown-up dinners well under way, and my promised appetizer-bribe attractively arrayed on a sterling Tiffany plate engraved with my great-grandmother's initials.

Oh, and three pilsner glasses chilling in the freezer, because hey, when you're trying to smooth troubled marital waters, why fuck around?

I led Mimi into the kitchen and opened us a couple of IPAs.

She thanked me, leaning against the counter with her frosty glass in hand while I strapped the girls in for their steamed broccoli and chicken nuggets.

"So this guy's used acetone before?" I asked, doling out the meal components once their bibs were secured.

"Yeah. Except for the car fires. Looks like he's developing a bona-fide MO for himself now."

"McNally thinks he's done all this before, somewhere else."

"Yeah, he talked to Benny about it. They're on the same page."

"You agree?"

"I wouldn't rule it out."

I turned on the kitchen tap to rinse off my hands. "So do arsonists get ritualistic about method?"

"The pros or the fetishists?"

I cranked off the faucet and reached for a dish towel. "Either, I guess."

"I suppose they both do, but the reasoning's a little different."

"Want to go sit down in the living room?" I asked.

"Love to," she said as I picked up the cheese plate. "Can I help you carry anything?"

"All set." I bowed her through the doorway ahead of me.

A car pulled up as I was setting the Brie on the coffee table.

Lamplight had transformed the windowpanes

to mirrors now that it was full dark outside, so I couldn't tell whether it was Dean until I heard his footsteps climbing the front-porch stairs.

"Hail the conquering hero," said Mimi, smiling at me as she raised her glass toward the sound of the twisting doorknob.

I raised an eyebrow in return, then walked toward the front hall.

"Hi honey, you're home," I said, as Dean stepped inside.

"Hey, Bunny," he said, leaning down to plant a kiss on my forehead. "I'm sorry I was so pissy at lunch…"

Had Cary given him shit, after all?

He pulled me in for a hug, tender.

I felt something in my chest unclench. Loneliness, or whatever sour fist of apprehension had been wrapped around my heart.

"All is forgiven, kind of," I said. "But we have a guest."

He shrugged off his coat and hung it on one of the hooks under the staircase. "For dinner? I don't want to be rude, but I might need to bail. Early flight tomorrow."

"You're leaving *tomorrow*? For where?"

"Japan."

"Japan?"

"I told you about it."

"No, you didn't."

"Really?"

"Dean, I think I'd remember that you were planning to leave for, like, *Asia* in the morning, had you mentioned it at any point."

"Wow," he said. "I *really* forgot to tell you?"

"Yeah."

"Dude," he said, "your husband is *such* an asshole."

"Apparently."

"Unfortunately, he is an asshole who has to pack for a trip to Japan in the morning."

"No worries. We're just having cheese and crackers. And a couple of beers."

He rested a hand on my shoulder and followed me back into the light.

"Dean, this is Mimi Neff," I said. "She's the arson investigator who's been kind enough to let me tag along lately. Another ex–New Yorker."

They exchanged pleasantries and shook hands. I told Dean I'd grab him a beer and check on the girls.

Parrish and India had plowed through round one of dinner, so I dished out a few more mushy broccoli florets and mushier chicken nuggets.

"Applesauce for dessert," I confided, opening the freezer to retrieve Dean's glass.

"So Mimi was just going to tell me about the difference between the ritualism of professional versus fetishist arsonists, when you came home," I said, walking back into the living room.

I gave Dean his beer and knelt down next to the coffee table to pre-load some crackers before passing the plate around. "I'd imagine that the pros just rely on what works, what they're comfortable with. Less ritual than acquired competency?"

Mimi accepted a cracker, but kept it balanced it in her hand. "Well, of course the pros don't want anyone to know they had a hand in instigating a fire, for the most part. If they've developed a ritual, it's more to do with enhancing the appearance of accidental combustion. Sometimes that can mean changing it up, method-wise—taking advantage of existing circumstances."

Dean was enjoying his own Brie-laden Stoned Wheat Thin, but looked intrigued by what she was saying.

As well you should be, Mr. Oh-by-the-way-I'm-off-to-Japan.

I moved up into a chair. "So, for instance, messing with wiring that already looks a little wonky?"

"Or enhancing the look of wonkiness to begin with," she said, nodding.

"Makes sense," said Dean, "making it seem 'natural' if you're after insurance money. And why else would you hire someone to set a fire, right?"

"For the most part, it's for the money," said Mimi. "Sometimes it's to cover up another crime. Occasionally it's a warning, or to take out a rival business, but that's usually an urban thing. Organized crime."

"Remember that house on the next street in Syracuse, Bunny?" asked Dean. He looked at Mimi. "The landlord set it on fire two nights in a row—didn't get enough damage the first time. Idiot."

Mimi laughed, took a sip of her beer.

"I can understand that kind of stuff," I said. "I mean, I wouldn't ever *do* it, I don't think. But the people who are just in it for kicks—I can't get my head around the attraction. Just, glorying in destruction, or whatever kind of passion it quenches, for the person? Fire's too intense. Scares the shit out of me."

"Is it a power trip?" Dean asked Mimi. "Being in control of something? It's always struck me as the grown-up version of aiming sunlight at dry leaves with a magnifying glass, when you're a kid—messing around with something scary to feel powerful."

Mimi looked thoughtful. "I have to confess I

haven't dealt directly with that many arsonists like the guy we're investigating now. Besides the pros, it's usually kids lighting a grass fire, just to see what happens. Stupid crap."

"Do you guys have to study up on the psychology of it, though?" I asked.

"Absolutely," she said. "And to get back to what you were asking, Dean, I think that's more of an impetus for people who get involved with firefighting—wanting to pit themselves against a force of nature."

"You guys must really have to be rock-solid on the science of it," he said. "So many factors to consider: chemicals involved, structural integrity, potential electrical hazards...whether you're fighting a fire or trying to figure out what caused it."

"For starters," said Mimi, flattered.

"I used to do construction with my father," Dean continued, "so I've got a good, hands-on sense of all the factors you have to keep in mind just *building* a house..."

Mimi smiled.

So did I. *Good* Dean was back...for the night at least.

And I wouldn't exactly have to ask his permission about the community meeting...not if he was off to Japan in the morning.

Dean was shaking his head, thinking about what Mimi had said. "But running into a burning building, staking your life on your own split-second comprehension of the sequence in which it will most likely *deconstruct* around you... That takes an astonishing level of courage."

"Damn satisfying when you do it right," said Mimi.

"I bet," I said.

I still needed a babysitter, of course...

Mimi took another sip of beer. "I miss it. Well, the part of me that's a little crazy misses it. But even going through the aftermath of a fire, in my line of work—you're struck by the devastation, the randomness, the magnitude of damage fire's capable of, reflected in even the smallest detail at a scene."

"Those melted toothbrushes," I said.

And what that level of heat would do to flesh.

Mimi looked me in the eye, acknowledging the thought I'd left unspoken.

"It's awful," she said, "in the oldest sense: awe-filled. Even after the fact, my heart rate picks up on behalf of our crew—every time."

She took another cracker.

"I'm really grateful to you for letting me tag along on your job," I told her. "It was fascinating, and so generous of you to take the time to explain everything."

"Well," she said, looking from me to Dean, "I'm sure you both know how gratifying it is to talk to someone about your work. And Madeline's article was one of the best I've read by someone outside our field."

Dean reached for his beer.

"Your wife is quite a talent," Mimi told him. "You're a lucky man."

"Thank you," I said.

"Listen," she continued, looking at him. "We really need Madeline covering this for the paper. There's a community meeting tomorrow night..."

I tried giving her an *ix-nay on telling him about the eporting-ray* look, now that Dean was leaving the country, but she ignored me.

"It's important that what we say gets reported accurately, compellingly. I trust her to do that," she continued.

"I'd be happy to spring for a babysitter," said Dean. "I'll be away for a few days."

Mimi looked at her watch and stood up, smiling at us both. "I should hit it, let you guys have your dinner."

When he went ahead of her to open the door, she gave me a big fat wink.

Dean went upstairs to pack. I called McNally, who was still at the office. Lucky for me since I didn't have his home number.

"Acetone," I said, when he picked up. "And I have money for a babysitter."

"Yeah, I figured."

"That I'd get the money, or that it was acetone?"

"That it was acetone," he said.

"Why?"

"It's miscible with water."

"Meaning what?" I asked.

"If someone uses most petroleum distillates as an accelerant—kerosene, gasoline—they don't mix with water. So sometimes you might see a rainbow sheen on any water left at the scene. And you'll continue to get an odor, too, especially if you hit the fire with water early. The water keeps non-miscible liquids from evaporating for a while, so the scent lingers. Acetone mixes with water, so it evaporates more quickly. Doesn't leave any smell by that point, doesn't rainbow."

"Huh."

"You were there. What do you remember?"

"The water in that back room wasn't rainbowed, and the house didn't smell like gasoline or kerosene."

"Exactly," he said.

"*Arson* Guy had been using acetone, so you

all kind of already figured that's what had been used this time, right? Before Mimi got the gas-chromatography results back."

"Pretty much, yeah," he said.

"Glad I didn't have any money riding on this, then."

He laughed. "And we won't be mentioning *any* of these details in any articles we write, either."

"Of course not. Why give a primer to wannabes?"

"You've been trained well."

"I like to think so. Some might beg to differ."

"So," McNally said, "you said you have a babysitter?"

"I have *money*. Finding someone willing to take it is step two."

The chick I'd used for the business dinner always wanted a week's notice, at the very least. So she was out.

"Anybody in mind?"

"Yeah, actually."

"Good," he said.

31

Cary made me read your article this afternoon," said Dean, as we were lying in bed a couple of hours later. "Mimi's right. You did good pieces for the paper in Syracuse, but you've learned a lot since then. You're even better at it now."

"So is that your way of saying I don't need to give up this writing shit because you want a home-maker?"

Even in the room's moonlit half dark, I could see him wince.

"I *said* that?" he asked, contrite.

"Today. At lunch."

He laughed at himself. "Jesus, your husband is such a prick, Bunny. I don't know how you put up with him."

"He's mostly patient with my absolute lack of homemaking skills. But yeah, he can occasionally be a total pain in the ass. Especially lately."

"He better start flying right then, appreciate how good he has it at home."

"Ya think?"

"Definitely," he said. "And this is my official apology, *mea maxima culpa*. You need to take advantage of work that makes you happy, and I need to shut up about it and help out more, okay?"

I turned toward him, sliding my arm across his chest, pulling his head close to kiss him. "Okay."

"Let's have Mimi over for dinner when I get back," he said, turning toward me, his breath sweet and warm on my cheek. "She was fascinating."

"She's damn good at her job."

"No doubt."

"Raised five kids, too."

"Wonder Woman. Like you." He snaked his arm under my ribs, started stroking my back.

A galleon of cloud sailed across the moon outside, leaving us in shadow.

When it reappeared I could see Dean's face more clearly, my vision sharpened by the interlude of darkness. Blue light played along his cheekbones, the stripe of fair hair that had fallen across his brow.

He looked about ten years old, and I told him so.

"You're my best friend," I said. "You know that?"

He kissed my forehead, then my mouth, whispering, "I'll try not to fuck it up. Any more than I have already."

"Hey," I whispered, "the two of us? Navigating all this grown-up shit? I *feel* like a ten-year-old, most days. At least in terms of general competence."

Dean tucked a wisp of hair behind my ear. "You're doing a great job. You're an amazing mother."

"Dude, come on—we both know I'm barely domestic enough to housekeep a fucking *tree* fort, with someone else's mom providing snacks."

He pulled me closer, resting his chin on the top of my head. "That's not how I see you at all."

I turned my ear to his chest, looking up at the light-dappled ceiling. "What do you see?"

"The woman I'd want with me in a wagon train."

I could hear the words rumble, behind his ribs.

"Calico dress and a prairie bonnet?" I kissed his collarbone, amused.

"I'm serious," he said. "That's the first thing I knew for sure, when I came to see you in Williamstown for our second date."

I trailed a fingertip down his waist, slowing along the crest of his hip. "Probably because I hadn't shaved, the first time we slept together."

"No, Bunny, I mean the way you *look* it didn't matter. Most chicks, Jesus … three months on the Oregon Trail, no access to waxing?" He shivered. "But you, you'd just get tanner and blonder. And you'd think it was an adventure. You'd make it more fun, instead of whining."

"Oh, please," I said, "I'd've been bitching about the lack of Szechuan before we crossed the Missouri."

"And meanwhile would've shot an elk, skinned it out, and stir-fried that sucker over the campfire in a little hot oil and black bean paste."

"Huh," I said, quite pleased with us both.

"You know I'm right."

"Okay, but if we ever fall through a rent in the fabric of the space-time continuum and have to actually *do* this?"

"Mmm?"

"We're bringing paper plates."

He laughed, yawning.

I brought my hand up to his cheek. "Are you leaving really early, tomorrow?"

"No." Dean yawned again, voice fading. "Couple of hours at work. I'll catch the Airporter from there."

"How long will you be away this time?"

He didn't answer, already asleep.

I closed my eyes, happy the evening had borne out all those strident parking-lot marital pronouncements I'd made to Cary, after lunch.

Admittedly, I was even happier that he'd forced Dean to finally read my article.

True friends are the ones who totally see through your bullshit façade of humility and self-sacrifice whenever you protest too much.

I raised myself up on one elbow, peering over Dean's shoulder at the glow of the digital clock.

"Ten P.M.," I whispered, "and all's well."

Famous last words.

32

Dean got off without a hitch the next morning, and I called Setsuko as soon as the office opened.

I apologized for asking her whether she could babysit at the last minute, but she was really great about it—telling me she was glad I needed her that night, as she was taking a couple of vacation days to go skiing the next morning.

And then I asked her if she could connect me to Cary, who practically begged me to bring him to the arson meeting.

"Are you sure?" I asked. "I mean, it's going to be listening to people talk about fires and shit. I thought you didn't like fires and shit."

"Madeline, I *hate* fires and shit. Which is why I want to avoid having an arsonist wandering around in my neighborhood. This seems like a good way to find out how, you know?"

"Well, okay then. And I'd love company."

He offered to drive me there, but I figured I'd rather walk, relishing the relative freedom of not having to drag the wagon behind me for once.

After that I tried to clean the house, *thoroughly*, over the course of the day—not wanting to scare poor Setsuko.

She arrived early and got settled in with the girls before shooing me out the door for the meeting.

"Go," she said, smiling at me. "Enjoy yourself, Madeline. It's beautiful out and we'll be fine."

And it *was* beautiful out—the light only just going softly gold.

The mountain peaks above me looked ancient and wise and close enough to touch. The spring air was dew-soft to breathe, fragrant with green promise. The houses sat companionably close on their modest lots. There were porch swings and knee-high picket fences and tabby cats sunning themselves and irises everywhere, begging to be picked by the armful.

Approaching strangers wished me "good evening," as I did them, and we all really meant it.

I felt suffused with this fizzy, feathery luminosity of gratitude. Poignant, ephemeral.

If there'd been a pay phone, Information would, I'm certain, have magically parted with Spalding Gray's home number in Manhattan to my perfect-stranger self just so I could call him up and say, "Dude, you totally don't know me, but I'm having a Perfect Moment right goddamn *now* and I wouldn't even have known that's what it was if you hadn't made *Swimming to Cambodia*. So thank you."

Cary was waiting for me outside the church. We were both a little early. Me because hey, I actually had an excuse to leave my house unencumbered with offspring for once, tra la, at Setsuko's behest, and him for no good reason I could think of.

"Want to go inside, get a front-row seat while they last?" he asked, when I'd come within reasonable hailing distance.

"It's so gorgeous out," I said. "I just want to marinate in all this outdoorsy freedom for a little longer, you know?"

"It's Boulder," he said, amused. "Isn't outdoorsy freedom kind of a given?"

A pack of Rollerbladers whizzed down the street past us, as if to underscore his point.

"It feels so *different* when I'm not pulling a wagonload of children, though." I spread my arms wide, tempted to break into a little dance step on the sidewalk. "Like, all the way here, I kept having this odd sensation that I was breaking the law or something. It felt *too* good, walking through the neighborhood. And then I realized it was just being alone. This is like . . . *recess*."

Cary laughed. "Four-square and monkey bars?"

"Exactly. And I should probably wait for my pal Mimi. I want to introduce you guys before things get officially under way."

People started drifting into the church in twos and threes as we stood there, chatting.

A big red official Boulder FD car pulled up. Its driver put on his dress-uniform hat before he got out.

I didn't catch his full name from the tag on his chest, but it was prefaced with the word Capt.

Mimi backed her truck into a spot across the street. I raised my arm in greeting.

She waved back and jogged across to us, once a couple of cars had passed.

"The best way you can help us right now is to be aware of who's in your neighborhood, and to check the perimeters of your houses and places of business regularly," the captain was saying.

Cary, Mimi, and I had gotten seats together, third pew from the front.

"Captain's name is Buzz Rainer," she whispered. "Good guy."

"Clear away any brush that you can," Rainer continued. "And keep trash to a minimum. Especially in the alleyways, and around outbuildings like garages or sheds."

I'd had a notebook open on my knee for ten minutes, but that was the first thing I wrote down.

"Arson can be a crime of opportunity," he continued. "We'll be passing out padlocks for residential garbage cans and commercial Dumpsters to anyone who wants them, following the meeting tonight. I know that might sound like a hassle, having to unlock something every time you take out a bag of trash, but you don't want to provide this guy with the tools of the trade. A number of recent fires were started with bits of burning cardboard, shoved under a rear door. A pizza box, in one instance."

I jotted down *locks, pizza box, door.* Then *opportunity*, underlined.

"Yes, sir." Rainer pointed to someone behind us. "You have a question?"

I swiveled my head. A youngish man with a goatee was on his feet, near the rear pews.

"I've been camping out in my store for the past week, just in case," he said. "It's…well, my stock seems so *flammable*. Antique furniture. Do you have specific recommendations for fire extinguishers?"

"Of course fire extinguishers are a great idea, and

the more the better," answered Rainer. "But I want to urge business owners *not* to take up residence in their establishments. If you're in a commercial building outside normal hours of operation, my people aren't going to know you're there. We've been tremendously lucky so far that the damage has been limited to property—I'd like us all to do everything we can to keep it that way. We'd be happy to help you set up a neighborhood-watch rotation instead. You'll be a lot more effective as a deterrent *outside* your store, and we'll both sleep better."

Mimi said "damn right" under her breath, beside me.

The goatee-antiques guy thanked Rainer and took his seat.

When everyone started swiveling their heads back toward the dais, I caught sight of Bittler's face about ten rows back.

Awesome. My lucky night.

"Fucking Bittler's here," I whispered to Cary. "Let's make sure we duck out the back way when this is over."

"Or just demand sanctuary," he whispered back.

Mimi gave me a gentle nudge in the ribs. "Am I going to have to separate you two?"

She was kidding, but I concentrated on my note-taking thereafter.

Most of the questions were low-key until this ponytailed Baby Boomer in a Jah Guide T-shirt interrupted Rainer's explanation of sprinkler-system regulations.

"All well and good," the guy whined, "you trying to put the onus of this crap on *us*. Why can't you people take some responsibility here? If you were doing your damn *job*, we wouldn't be in this mess. I don't see how padlocks and citizen patrols can make up for your department's professional incompetence."

I heard clapping and turned to look: two more graying hippies with AARP cards and an outsized sense of entitlement.

"Sir," said Rainer, "I agree with you. I could tell you about limitations of our manpower or equipment or funding, but the fact is that we're failing to catch this person. All I can do is ask my teams to do their best, and ask all of you for your help—we need your eyes and ears, your attention to detail."

"Well what the hell have you found out about this creep?" Jah Guide dude yelled. *"Anything? What are we supposed to be looking for, while you're asleep at the wheel?"*

Oh for fuck's sake, would my parents' generation *never* grow the fuck up?

"There are some details of the investigation that we don't want to make public, of course," said Rainer. "But here's what I'd like you to know: The fires have been set at all different hours, so we're probably looking for someone who doesn't have a regular job. While we can say with some certainty that the arsons have been the work of one individual, to date—based on evidence I can't get into in a public forum—there has been some variation in his method. He's employed sophisticated techniques on several occasions that lead us to believe he's not a first-time offender, though he may be new to this area."

"Pretty damn vague," the heckler shot back.

I thought I heard Mimi's teeth gnashing.

"Sir," said Rainer, getting a little pissed now, "would you prefer that I give everyone in this *room* a tutorial on the specifics of do-it-yourself arson, step by step?"

"Of course not," the man harrumphed, "but isn't it true that most of these people turn out to be firefighters themselves, in the end? Firebugs who get into the business to play with what obsesses them in the first place, and then make themselves out to be heroes?"

Rainer took that shot head-on. "There have been cases of that, I'm very sorry to say."

"That man in California...wasn't he a chief or something?"

"Sir," said Rainer, "let's stick with the case at hand. We're doing everything we can to stop these crimes—interagency cooperation, investigative work, you name it, using all the resources we have. But we need to work together as a community. Stop this guy before he does more damage, before anyone gets hurt. I wish we could do it alone. I wish *I* could do it alone—"

"Well, damn it, then why don't you—"

"*Please* let me finish, sir. Please. I'm willing to admit to you that I'm failing at my job right now. Failing you, failing myself, failing everyone in this room by not performing as well as I *want* to be performing, on behalf of our community. But we—myself and every firefighter in this county—are *not* asleep at the wheel. It's just an overwhelmingly large wheel."

Rainer got some enthusiastic applause for that. Much deserved.

"Look," he continued, "arson is a *huge* problem in this country. Anybody have any idea what it costs us nationally, over the course of a year?"

He looked around the audience, side to side. "Anyone?"

Silence.

"Let's start with property," said Rainer. "Last year alone, our communities sustained roughly three point six billion dollars in property damage—during the course of an estimated *five hundred eighty-four thousand, five hundred* separate instances of arson."

Heckler dude didn't have a comeback to that.

The captain's hands were clenched now. "But the property damage isn't what keeps me up nights, sir. What keeps me up at night is that five hundred sixty people *died* in those fires. And I'm doing my damnedest to make sure we don't have any fatalities in Boulder."

Someone called out "hear, hear!" from the back of the room.

Rainer leaned forward, over his podium. "And let me tell you that my damnedest means asking *all* of you for help. Yourself included, sir."

"Well," said the heckler, "if you put it that way—"

"I'll put it any way I *have* to, to get you on board."

"Sign me up," the man responded, before sitting heavily down amidst general applause.

"What, you think I'm taking advantage?" I asked Cary.

He, Mimi, and I had adjourned to a microbrewery on Pearl Street: Sunshine, Rainbow, whatever.

"Not exactly," he said.

I squinted at him. "Then what? I mean, she offered to babysit, and I needed a babysitter. But if you think it's inappropriate...Like, what, she feels pressured because my husband is kind of her boss...?"

"Maddie," said Cary, "look, it's just that—"

"Oh, my God, that *is* what you think!" I said, suddenly horrified with myself.

"Who are we talking about?" asked Mimi.

"This really nice chick Dean and Cary work with," I said. "Setsuko. Cary, seriously, am I a total asshole? It didn't occur to me that she...I mean, *shit*. I figured she could use the money."

"She's not going to let you pay her," he said.

"That's even worse. Like I think she's a serf or something. Cary...help me. Should we leave right now?"

"Finish your beer," said Mimi. "And then have another. Make a night of it."

"It's fine, Maddie," added Cary. "Just, Setsuko's got a lot on her plate right now."

"Anything I should know other than that they want to deport her and stuff?"

Cary sighed.

"It's not Bittler, is it?" I asked. "Oh, God. I mean, he's hard enough on *you*—I'd hate to have to deal with him as a chick."

"Bittler?" said Mimi.

"The butthead guy we wanted to duck out of the church quickly to avoid," I said. "And thank you for sneaking us out the back door, by the way."

She looked at Cary. "So 'the butthead guy' is harassing this Set-Sue person?"

"No," he said. "Not like that . . . it's just that she's been working her ass off, and she's supposed to be leaving on vacation tomorrow, and . . ."

He stopped and looked away. Exhaled.

"And what?" I asked, touching his wrist.

"Nothing. Really." He still wouldn't look at me.

"*And* I'm totally exploiting her, on top of that, but you're too nice to say so?" I said. "Excellent."

Cary shook his head. "It's fine, Maddie. You didn't take advantage. Setsuko just has a hard time not feeling obligated. She's always on the verge of volunteering herself beyond the capacity of any single person. She needs a break."

"Dude," I said. "You're not helping me in the guilt department, here. At all."

"Drink your damn beer," said Mimi. "And then I'm going to go get you *both* another pint."

So we did. And she got up to keep her end of the bargain.

But I still felt like there was something more Cary wanted to say to me.

"Dude," I said, "I'm totally feeling like there's something more you want to say to me. *Spill*."

"I'm sorry, I'm just really distracted."

"By what?"

"Everything I was talking about with you and Dean, before. Bittler, and the warehouse crap. The whole situation is getting under my skin, worse and worse."

"Look, if he *is* embezzling, or whatever, he's only going to fuck himself up in the end, right? Come on...could be the best possible way to get rid of him."

"I have this crazy feeling that he's going to set me up."

"Oh, come on...Bittler? He's a pompous little low-rent petty-Napoleon shitbag, not a criminal mastermind."

He just looked at me, and I swear to God I thought he was going to burst into tears or something.

"Cary, you're really scared of him, aren't you?"

He took the last sip of his beer.

"Dude, come on—big tough guy like you? You could, like, break that pathetic windbag in half over your knee without increasing your *heart* rate by a single rpm. And here you are, acting like he's Vlad the fucking Impaler and you're fresh out of garlic. Don't be such a pussy. *I* could kick his ass."

"I need to get into that warehouse," he said.

"Crazy talk."

"I need to know what's going on before he fucks me completely. I don't want to just stand around waiting for the goddamn anvil to drop on my head, you know?"

"So, what, you're Wile E. Coyote and he's going to launch you off a cliff with some Rube Goldberg Acme rocket? Pshaw. Take a fucking Ativan."

"Madeline, I am absolutely serious."

"Pussy," I said. "You are absolutely, seriously *pussified*."

"Madeline, for chrissake."

"Big, fat, pink—"

"Damn it—"

"Hairy—"

"Fuck *off*."

"*Genitalia*," I said. "Of the female persuasion."

"You're not funny."

"Bullshit. I am hysterically funny."

"Which is why I'm laughing. So hard."

I poked him in the solar plexus. "You are *totally* laughing. In here."

He crossed his arms.

"And *blushing*."

Okay, that part was true.

"Like a little girl," I said.

"What the hell is *wrong* with you?"

"I'm trying to distract you."

"From what?"

"See? It worked."

"Oh, for God's sake…"

"Okay, look… as your friend, I feel it is my duty to distract you from breaking into a fucking warehouse that belongs to your employers, you idiot. Because that's the stupidest idea I've ever heard. And I happen to be the queen of stupid ideas, most days: the imam. The hierophant. The *empress* of stupid. So I'll have you know I speak with some authority, because me and dumb-assery," I held up two fingers, pressed tightly together, "we're like *this*."

"How the hell is it stupid to want to figure out what the fuck my corrupt sadist of a boss is up to, before he pins whatever it is on me?"

"He's got the only set of keys to the place?"

"Yes."

"So how are you getting in?"

"I don't know. Crowbar."

"You planning to wear gloves?"

"I guess… even though I've been in the place

before and my fingerprints are probably on stuff already."

"They have an alarm system?"

He didn't answer.

"Security cameras?"

Silence.

"So for all you know," I said, "there's going to be *video* of you breaking into a warehouse with a fucking crowbar, while wearing latex gloves. Whereupon whatever alarm system they have is probably going to, like, light up a goddamn jukebox-slash-calliope's worth of bells and whistles down at the nearest cop station."

Cary's mouth had contracted to the size of a sesame seed.

"And Bittler's been keeping tabs on you for how long, now? Your résumés, your general dissatisfaction with the company...Got any cover letters to potential employers saved on your hard drive at work?"

Poppy seed.

"Not to mention you've been a little hard up for cash lately. Because they'll look at your bank records, too. Been carrying much of a balance in your checking account, these past few months? Oh, that's right...you're basically flatlined, except for the money you had to borrow from your father to make last month's rent."

I rattled my fingernails along the side of my beer glass in four-four time. Sounded like a very tiny horse, galloping away.

"Yup, I gotta hand it to you," I said, looking up at the ceiling. "That's a genius plan—start to finish. You might as well wear a Hamburgler costume and a fuchsia T-shirt that reads, I YEARN TO BE ASS-RAPED IN THE STATE PEN FOR THE REST OF MY NATURAL-BORN DAYS across the back, in sparkly six-inch-high letters."

"'Made it, Ma. Top o' the world,'" said Cary, utterly deflated.

"Hey, at least you know enough not to misquote Cagney."

"Fat lot of good that's doing me."

"Exactly," I said. "So let's come up with a different plan, shall we?"

"Like what?"

"Damned if I know. I'm the empress of stupid ideas, remember?"

"I am so fucked, Madeline," said Cary, looking ready to weep. "So so *so* fucked."

Mimi came sauntering back, juggling three pints of Fat Tire. "What the hell happened? I leave you alone for five minutes, and the pair of you look like you just got out of chemo."

"Madeline," said Cary, grim about the mouth, "has just explained to me the multitude of ways in which I am utterly fucking irredeemably *fucked*, right now."

"Join the club," she said, slopping two fat paisleys of beer across the table as she brought our glasses to rest.

33

Figuring I'd successfully yanked Cary away from jail time, at least for the rest of the evening, I primed Mimi for a distracting treatise on my own current obsession.

"Who was that heckler guy talking about, earlier?" I asked. "When he was trying to paint all firefighters as crazed arsonists?"

Mimi looked up at me. "Hm?"

"Some chief from California? Rainer sure didn't seem like he wanted to elaborate."

"Oh, Jesus," she said. "That would be John Orr: arson investigator, fire captain, shithead."

"Somebody you guys worked with?" asked Cary.

"No, thank God. He was strictly West Coast. Got started in Glendale, outside LA."

I reached for my new beer. "What'd he do?"

"Serial arsonist," she said. "They called him 'the Pillow Pyro.'"

She took a sip of Fat Tire. "He had a habit of starting fires in stores that had a lot of pillows. Furniture places, et cetera. That kind of foam burns fast and hot—off-gases some nasty toxic stuff, too. Lethal."

"And he must have known how to cover it up," I said.

"You bet. He'd have places mapped out—easy access off highway exit ramps. Start seven or eight fires in quick succession, then show up at one of the scenes and act like a hero, knowing perfectly well that there were too many simultaneous fires for his department to handle."

"That's horrible," said Cary.

"Worst one was a hardware store," Mimi continued. "One of those big places, like a Home Depot. Four people died. A toddler..."

My stomach flipped.

"Yeah," she said. "Evil, evil man. And then he even wrote a 'novel' about it. Only it turned out he'd actually done most of the stuff in the book."

"Is that how they got him?" asked Cary.

"No. He left one fingerprint on a piece of paper

he'd wrapped around a homemade delay fuse—a cigarette and a bunch of matches."

"Like Mapleton," I said.

She nodded. "Somehow, that shred of paper didn't burn. Goddamn miracle. Still took them eight years to nail him, though."

"His fingerprints weren't on file?" I asked.

"Nope. But he did something really, really stupid...set serial fires around two cities in California during arson-investigator conventions. Bakersfield and Pacific Grove. Bakersfield is where they got the print. Someone started setting fires all over LA with the same MO a few years later. Only ten people had been at both conferences. Word got around, someone knew about Bakersfield, then they connected it to Pacific Grove, then they got Orr's prints."

"Jesus," said Cary.

"Yeah," Mimi replied. "Tell me about it. Creepy, frustrating, and tremendously embarrassing to the profession as a whole."

"What'd he call the novel?" I asked.

"*Points of Origin.* The main character was named Aaron. Orr said something like, 'He was, after all, the only one who knew how the fire had started. To Aaron, the smoke was beautiful.'"

I shivered. So did Cary.

"But he was convicted?" I asked.

Mimi nodded. "Life without parole, plus twenty years."

The three of us finished our pints in silence.

Cary offered to drive me home.

Which turned out to be a really, *really* stupid idea. On both our parts.

34

I was riding along in Cary's truck, feeling mellow from the beers I'd had with him and Mimi, and just riffing in my head on what little knowledge anyone had about this arsonist guy, presuming it was a guy of course.

"I should really map the locations," I said, suddenly musing out loud.

"Of the arsons?" asked Cary, as he slowed for a stop sign.

All the houses around us were battened down for the night, a few upstairs windows cozily yellow as people prepared to turn in.

"Yeah," I said, feeling warm and lazy. "I remember Mimi saying at one point that if they profiled the guy, it would probably turn out that he lived within two miles of where they'd been set. Hadn't thought about that before. I mean, one of them was down on Arapahoe, which I was thinking meant way *out* on Arapahoe, but don't you think her saying that has to mean they've kind of clustered?"

"Madeline, as much as I think you've been a hero and everything, Dean did have a bit of a point—"

"Like," I went on, "the house that burned right up Mapleton? I mean, that's really *my* neighborhood. I could totally keep an eye out for—"

"*Madeline*," said Cary, his tone sharper than I'd ever heard it—as though I were a little kid about to chase my errant kickball onto some busy street without looking both ways first.

"What?" I said, as he turned off Nineteenth and onto my block.

Cary pulled into a spot right in front of the house. Turned off the engine.

He was quiet for a moment. Not looking at me, just staring straight ahead through his windshield.

I glanced toward the house.

Through our big living room windows, I could see blue light dancing across the ceiling's white plaster.

Setsuko's probably watching some sappy Hallmark movie.

"What, Cary?" I asked again.

He took a deep breath, then said, "You're scaring me."

"*Scaring* you?"

Now he turned toward me. "Dean's away—several thousand *miles* away—and you want to start nosing around these fires?"

"Dude, I just want to look at a *map*. Dial in the geography a little."

"That's not exactly all you said. You mentioned 'keeping an eye out.' For what?"

"Just...stuff," I replied. "You know."

"I don't know. But even though I don't want to see Dean harassing you about all this, I want you to be careful, okay?"

I thought about that. And he was right.

"Make you a deal," I said.

"What kind of deal?"

"You stay away from that damn Ionix warehouse, I stick to plotting things out on a map. At least until Dean gets home."

We shook on it—each convinced we were saving the other from a flight of sheer, delusional idiocy.

"Can you give Setsuko a ride home?" I asked. "She took a bus here from the office."

"Of course," he said. "Her car's been in the

shop for a week. If I'd known she was coming here tonight I'd've driven her over, too."

Cary and I opened our respective truck doors and climbed down from its cab, into the neighborly demi-darkness of Mapleton Street.

My house smelled suspiciously of lemon Pledge when I preceded Cary over the living room's threshold.

I couldn't exactly tell in the dim light of the television, but the place looked way crisper than it had when I'd left Setsuko in charge of the girls a few hours earlier.

Jesus, this poor woman straightened up for me—after doing a full day's work at the office. I should've known better, should've cleaned more before she got here.

I felt a deep roiling pang of domestic guilt, what with Cary's having told me how she always worked herself to the bone on everyone else's behalf.

"Setsuko?" I said.

She looked up at me and Cary, smiling. "Did you have a good time?"

"It was lovely," I said. "And you're so kind to have watched the girls for me. Thank you."

I reached my hand toward her, fifty bucks already folded up in my palm. "Here."

She looked confused but held her hand out.

Then said, "Oh, no, you don't have to do this," when she realized I'd given her money.

"Please," I said.

She shook her head, hand still extended toward me. "It was my pleasure, really. Your girls are so sweet."

I crossed my arms. "Setsuko, you absolutely saved me tonight. Please let me do this."

"Why don't I drive you home?" said Cary.

"Are you sure?"

"*You* know it's on my way, and *I* know your car isn't back from the shop yet. And we should let Madeline get to sleep."

There's that insistent tone again. Cary seems less wussy with every passing hour. Good for him.

Setsuko dropped her eyes. "Yes. You are right. Thank you."

She gathered up her wool and stuff, packing it carefully into the tote bag at her feet.

I said good-bye and offered profuse thanks to both of them until they were well out the door.

I kept my hand on the switch for the porch light, turning it off once they'd reached Cary's truck.

Its dome light came on when he opened the driver's-side door. His face looked strained.

The pair of them hadn't said a word to each other as they'd walked away from my house, but the minute the truck doors slammed shut behind them I could hear their voices rising inside the re-darkened cab: his a dull rumble, hers a little shrill.

An argument? Maybe they were dating, after all.

None of your business, Madeline.

The engine rumbled to life and Cary pulled away from the curb, my whole sleeping block momentarily bathed in taillight red when he tapped the brakes turning onto Nineteenth.

I told myself I'd call him in the morning, remind him of our mutual promises not to do anything stupid over the weekend.

Then I went inside to find a map of Boulder. And some straight pins I could stick in the damn thing, once I'd tacked it up on the corkboard tiles some previous tenant had left glued to the laundry room wall.

It took me until midnight to plot the fire locations. I'd been saving copies of the *New Times* for a while, tucking them away in a broom closet so Dean wouldn't be tempted to start the barbecue with them. Or bitch me out for creating more mess.

I suppose it was also a juju thing on my part: I'd secretly hoped that if I saved all the back issues, they might eventually hire me. Which I guess had worked.

Prescience. Heh.

I sat cross-legged on the laundry room floor and read through my pile of newsprint, trying to locate anything written about each of the arsons over the last nine months.

I probably could've just saved time by calling Mimi, but it was more satisfying to do this on my own.

And I suppose I figured I might find something else useful in the old articles, reading through them all in a row like that.

At ten past the witching hour, I had eight pins in the map and a nasty crick in my neck.

I'd been right—the fires had all taken place within fifteen blocks of my house. The first grass fires up near Mount Sanitas, the cars, the gas station—even the one on Arapahoe wasn't really far away.

And now, of course, the fire at the house actually *on* my street, albeit up where the money lived.

Not like our place was the epicenter, or anything, but I was still on the edge of the exact neighborhood Rainer wanted rallied to attention.

So I'll only be doing my civic duty here, right? Paying a little extra notice to the local comings and goings. Who could possibly find fault with that?

And hey, maybe I could swing by his station in

the morning, tell him I figured it wouldn't hurt to grab a couple of free padlocks for our garbage cans. See if I could catch him in a chatty mood.

I pulled the length of chain-and-string dangling from the laundry room's bare ceiling bulb, then padded upstairs in the dark.

My daughters were tucked up all snug in their beds, while visions of crime-fighting danced in my head.

35

Parrish and India didn't wake up until nine the following morning, God bless them.

I strapped both girls into their booster seats for breakfast, feeling more rested than I had in weeks. Or months, probably. Sleep deprivation tended to blur my retrospective time lines. And everything else.

Dean still hadn't called home from Japan, but even *that* couldn't piss me off. It was Saturday, it was gorgeous out, and I had something concrete with which to occupy myself over the course of the day to come.

Fucking awesome. All around.

I dialed Cary while the girls chowed down on their whole wheat toaster waffles, leaning against the laundry room door frame so I could check out last night's map work.

The phone rang eight times before his machine picked up.

"This is Cary. I'm not at home right now, so please leave a message and I'll get back to you as soon as possible. Have a great day!"

I asked him if he maybe felt like going for a walk later, and hung up.

Probably out biking or jogging or whatever already. Typical Boulderite.

"Well, my darlings," I said to my children, "how would you like to join your mother on a wagon tour of arson sites around our fair city?"

I figured I could type up my notes on Rainer's talk later on. The article wasn't due until Monday, and I had the whole weekend to myself.

The girls had finished breakfast. I cleaned them up and gave them each a fresh diaper, realizing I only had four more left in the Pampers package—which meant I'd have to buy more sometime today. Like, soon.

I packed two into my kid-care travel kit along with the usual complement of sippy cups, butt-wipes, and Cheese Nips.

The fifty bucks to Setsuko had put a serious

dent into my cash liquidity, so I grabbed my Amex card before loading the girls into the wagon. Fuck it, Dean could hardly give me shit for buying diapers—even on credit.

But then I figured I should check that month's bill before we headed out. I remembered having put it in the pile of mail on Dean's desk.

I didn't usually read through the monthly statement, but I wanted to make sure I could charge the Pampers—and a couple of gallons of milk—without leaving him stranded somewhere in the Western Pacific with no money for a bowl of ramen or whatever.

The bill was addressed to me, since his card had started out as a subsidiary of mine once upon a time back in Syracuse.

As far as I remembered we had a monthly limit of a thousand bucks or something—or maybe it was up to twelve hundred between the two of us?

I tried not to be crazy with the plastic, but it wasn't like Dean gave me a formal household allowance or anything so sometimes I'd buy the girls a couple of dresses at Target. Or, hey, treat myself to a burrito—with tip for delivery—when he'd been on the road for a tiresome stretch and I was sick of toddler-food remnants for my own makeshift dinner.

Remarkable how tempting the latter option became on the nights when he'd call home from wherever to regale me with details about some fabulous expense-account dinner with clients. He knew I loved hearing about the foodie shit, especially from Asia. In the old days he'd amuse me with scathing descriptions of Midwestern-airport-layover pizza ("catsup on a matzoh") or *Poulet Frit de Kentucky* in the rural paper-mill hamlets of French Canada.

When home was an apartment in Manhattan before the girls were born, I'd delighted in teasing him over the phone with lavish riffs about how I couldn't decide between Korean barbecue or Shanghainese soup dumplings, West Indian curried-goat roti from our corner deli or chunks of Cuban roast pork basted with garlic-spiked lemon juice and browned to a crisp.

Culinary foreplay was something at which we both excelled.

He'd come up in the world since then, and relished getting to pay me back at long last with food-porn of his own from hotel rooms in Bangkok or Taipei, Bangalore or Seoul.

Even his description, once, of getting taken out to this Beijing restaurant specializing in snake-meat cuisine had been exquisite torture, not least since

I'd just eaten cold leathery mac-and-cheese scraps out of the pot with a wooden spoon.

"Twelve courses," he'd said, describing each one.

"You are such an asshole," I'd replied.

"But wait, Bunny...I haven't told you about the deer-penis liqueur they brought out with dessert."

"I hope it was hideous."

"Surprisingly smooth," he said.

"This sounds like a major case of *Hey dudes, let's fuck with the giant blond* gweilo*!*"

He laughed. "Obviously."

"Over which you of course totally prevailed, twisting circumstances to your own nefarious anthropology-major advantage."

"Doesn't pay to fuck with this particular *gweilo*," he said. "I may not be able to spit snake bones on the floor with suave native rapidity, but I'm bigger and I can drink *way* more."

"I just hope you weren't expected to eat the deer penis. Like the worm in the tequila bottle or whatever."

"No," he'd replied. "And thank God, because I would've been an utter pussy had it come to that."

"Probably one of those things where you're actually *expected* to refuse, insisting it's an honor you couldn't possibly deprive your host of, being yourself so pathetically unworthy."

I heard him snort in agreement, laughing.

And I knew Dean was still grateful to me for what had undoubtedly been my finest moment as a junior-corporate wife: insisting he read Ian Fleming's *You Only Live Twice* before his first business trip to Japan.

I figured a quick run-through of Tiger Tanaka's training regimen to help Bond pass as a deaf coal miner from Hokkaido couldn't hurt, considering. And I'd been right.

When Dean's host the first night asked him to please squeeze some lemon juice over the platter of lobster sashimi (served sliced in situ, with only the upper half of the shell removed), my Intrepid Spouse hadn't batted an eye.

Poor Bond, of course, lost major face by leaping to his feet and shouting a British obscenity when his own unfortunate crustacean scuttled rapidly off the platter and across the table, desperate to escape the acidic juice.

Because a lobster served as sashimi is, of course, still very much alive.

Dean had been well prepared for this eventuality, thanks to me and Ian Fleming.

I grinned to myself, remembering that as I slit open the Amex bill with a paring knife at the kitchen table.

The total was just under seven hundred bucks: charges from Dean's trips to Texas and Louisiana, mostly.

I'd had two rolls of film developed and bought the girls some really cheap sneakers. Granted, those purchases weren't exactly necessities, but I figured I was still well under the limit of spousal chastisement, whenever Dean finally came home and read through these pages himself.

I packed the girls into the wagon after writing STOP AT 7-11 on my hand, hoping they'd have a pack of age-appropriate Pampers in stock so I wouldn't have to slog all the way out to King Soopers by way of the Creek Path. Especially since King Soopers was nowhere near the crime scenes I wanted to check out in the meantime.

Twenty minutes later I was standing at the 7-Eleven checkout counter, royally pissed.

"What do you *mean*, my card's been declined?" I said.

The dude behind the register wasn't exactly sympathetic. He pushed my Amex back toward me with the tip of his index finger, one corner of his lip curled up like he was all worried I'd infect him with food-stamp cooties.

"Dude," I said, "I just read through the bill for

this month. I should have at *least* five hundred more bucks on that thing."

He stared at me, unimpressed.

"Run it again," I said.

"I'm sure you have some other form of payment?"

"No I do *not* have some other form of payment. Besides which I'm only trying to buy diapers and milk. Run it again."

"I'm sorry, ma'am, but it won't change anything. The card's been declined. And there are customers behind you."

I leaned toward him, my hands flat on the countertop between the big jar of Slim Jims and the seriously tacky vase filled with long-stemmed artificial roses, the buds of which were apparently wadded-up pairs of women's underwear in various insipid pastel shades.

"Dude," I said, "give me a break. It's a fucking *Gold* Card, for chrissake."

He winced and turned red, Adam's apple bobbing wildly in his long pale throat, fat as a baby's fist. "Please, ma'am. *Language.*"

I'd missed the clip-on tie attached to the thick polyester collar of his uniform.

Oh, great, a Mormon.

I snatched my card back up. "Fine. *Whatever.*"

He crossed his pale weaselly arms, lip curled farther up.

"And when my kids are reduced to shitting on the kitchen floor," I said, "I'll be sure to thank you *personally* in my prayers to our heavenly father, you candy-ass little schmuck."

With that, I stormed back out into the parking lot.

Okay, not that one can actually "storm" through a swinging glass 7-Eleven exit door with a four-foot-long Radio Flyer wagon in tow. But I sure as fuck stormed in spirit, despite the dopy little automatic bell chiming in my wake.

Thirty-seven bucks in cash to last me until Dean gets home...I should've let Setsuko give me that money back.

Madeline, you are so royally hosed.

And Setsuko was probably on a chairlift in Aspen right now, wearing some fluffy angora ski suit while she crocheted a goddamn overcoat or bassinet or whatever, for whomever.

I called the Amex 800-number the minute we got home. I'd considered dialing from the pay phone on the 7-Eleven's exterior wall, but feared my flouncingly irate exit had been flawed enough as it was.

Or that I might burst into tears, which would've

been a deeply hideous and unbearable indignity at that point.

The corporate voice-over-robot lady gave me ridiculously placid guidance through the usual customer-service bullshit: Press "one," press something else, and then "something-something *nueve, para continuar en Español*," which always seemed ridiculous because how would I have gotten that far already, if I didn't speak English? But it's not like there was anyone to point this out to.

I punched in the card number and the expiration date. Then it wanted the last four digits of my Social Security number.

After five minutes of dreadful Muzak, a live person finally picked up: Tanya, who wanted to know how she could be of service today—but only after I told her my card number, expiration date, security code, and last four digits of my Social.

"Now, how may I help you today, Ms. Dare?" she asked.

"I'm hoping you might tell me why my card was just declined for a fourteen-dollar-and-thirty-two-cent purchase at my local 7-Eleven here in Boulder, Tanya, when it appears that the current charges on this account are under seven hundred dollars, so we should still have plenty of available credit."

"I'm so sorry, ma'am," she said.

"Thank you for your concern, Tanya. My children need diapers and milk and my husband is currently in Tokyo, along with his wallet. This is rather a bummer."

"Let me just check on that current balance for you, all right, Ms. Dare?"

"Thank you very much. I appreciate your help with this."

Hey, I'd worked as a customer-service phone chick at a book catalog in New York. Customers who'd gotten pissy about screwups not-of-my-making hadn't ever inspired me to go the extra mile.

"Just another moment, ma'am. Our system is slow today."

"That's fine. Please take all the time you need."

She didn't say anything for a minute or so. I could hear the hum of other voices in the room around her, wherever she was.

"All right, Ms. Dare. I think I can explain what happened..."

"I hope we can get it cleared up?"

"Well, I'm afraid that there are some new charges on the account. Made in Tokyo over the last day or so on your husband's card."

"And?"

"And the credit limit for the card has been reached, until the existing balance is paid in full."

"What exactly did he charge?" I knew his hotel room might've been expensive, but it was booked through the company travel agent so he shouldn't have had to pay for that part of the trip.

"Well, ma'am, I'm not supposed to disclose the details of specific charges to the subsidiary card member."

"Tanya, my *husband* is the subsidiary card member. This account is in my name."

"I'm not sure that I can—"

"I'm sure that you can, Tanya. I'm not only asking about this as his spouse, legally, but as the person to whom the account belongs. Please tell me what the new charges are."

"Well, I don't know what the charges are actually *referring* to, ma'am."

"Well, what exactly is he supposed to have spent five hundred bucks on, Tanya—gold-plated sushi?"

"No, ma'am," she said. "I mean, it's not just one charge."

"And you can't tell me what the charges are?"

"I could tell you the names of the establishments, but they're not in English. I mean, they're *spelled* in English, but I don't know if they're restaurants, or hotels..."

"Oh. All right. I understand."

Jesus, I had maybe forty bucks cash left, to last until the following week. Maybe I could get McNally to front me some money?

Yeah, great career move...

"Tell you what," she said. "I think I may be able to add another twenty dollars of credit here, so you can go back to 7-Eleven."

"Tanya, really? You have no idea how much that would help."

She laughed. "Hey, I've been married. And maybe he bought you a really nice present."

"Wouldn't that be wonderful? You're a total goddess. Thank you."

She laughed again. "Nobody's ever called me *that* before, in seven years at this job. You have a good afternoon now, you hear?"

"Thank you, Tanya. Same to you."

I decided I'd give Cary another call, see if he was home and up for a walk with me.

I didn't want to ask him for money, either. Not if he'd had to hit up his father for rent money because Bittler was fucking him over.

And we had plenty of food in the house, it was just milk and diapers we were short on.

I dialed Cary's home phone but he still didn't pick up. I left another message, packed up the girls again, and headed for the 7-Eleven out by his apartment. If Cary wasn't home by then, at least I could leave him a note.

No way I was going to give Mormon boy any satisfaction by shopping again at *his* establishment. Although if I'd had a deer penis handy, I totally would've swung back through the place so I could make him eat the damn thing and then apologize.

Patronizing little petty-bureaucrat fuck.

36

Cary still wasn't home when I got to his apartment complex.

I'd only been there once before: an end-unit apartment in this seventies-Bauhaus complex up toward Table Mesa.

I remembered thinking it was the kind of place where graduate-student marriages would die loudly and often—neighbor kids no doubt adept at sleeping right through slammed doors, squealing tires, and the answering chatter of cheap bedroom windows rattling shut within their aluminum tracks.

I just stood there for a minute, trying to remember how many rows back his apartment was—fourth building out of six?

The sun was really hot now. I was glad I'd remembered a hat.

I pulled the girls' wagon up a crappily poured curb cut and onto the sidewalk. Had to nip around the sun-bleached Big Wheel some preschooler had abandoned upside down on his front walk, one black plastic tire spinning slowly on its axle.

Cary's truck was parked out in front of the fourth building back, but he didn't come to the door when I knocked.

He kept his bike hanging from a big hook in the entryway ceiling, I remembered. I leaned out from the little front stoop and peered into the closest window, hands scooped around my face to block out the noonday glare.

No bike, and for all I knew he was out on some crazy daylong endurance ride.

I grabbed my notepad out of the diaper bag, then realized I hadn't remembered to bring a pen along with it.

Goddamn genius, Madeline. Brain like steel wool that's been sitting wet on the edge of a sink for about three weeks, rusting into slime-bits.

Oh, well, so I'd have to do the arson tour on my own. I could get in at least a couple of stops before I had to swing home and make lunch for the kids, anyway.

*   *   *

By the time I got back to my house, I felt like even more of an idiot. I was hot and thirsty and had to pee really badly, plus which the girls were cranky and starving.

What the hell had I expected to find, anyway? I'd checked the gas station, the open fields, and the block where the cars had burned. All of which had happened months earlier, of course.

There wasn't an iota of indication that anything at all had happened in these locations. Except that the gas station was still abandoned.

And I'd figured it would be a shortcut if I walked part of the circuit on the Creek Path—avoiding traffic and having to wait at intersections.

Got myself nearly run down by a bunch of haggard marathon trainees for that bit of brilliant forethought.

Perfect.

Diapers and two gallons of milk had come to $19.47 at Cary's 7-Eleven.

I should've gone to King Soopers.

The answering machine's message light was blinking, but I got the girls fed and upstairs for their naps before I sat down to check the actual voice mails.

First was Ellis, just checking in: "Still hating your husband for you. Call me."

Then Mimi, asking if I needed any follow-up info for my article about the neighborhood meeting.

The little digital-LED readout thing on the machine clicked from two to one—last message. I was expecting Cary, but it was my husband.

"Hey, Bunny," he said.

My slightly inebriated husband.

I could hear lots of background chatter, wherever he was calling from. The chink of china and glassware.

A bar? Some fancy restaurant?

"Sorry I haven't checked in sooner," he said. "Things have been crazy busy here. Good, though. Think I have that chem-plant order sewn up."

My forearms were stinging. I looked down and realized I'd gotten myself a nasty sunburn.

"Taking the bullet train back up to . . ." There was some drunken group shouting in the background, drowning him out. ". . . tomorrow morning. Good thing I read up on my Mishima, flying over here. Made some cultured chitchat with the locals."

The sound got squishy, like he'd covered the mouthpiece with his hand. I thought I heard him say, "Be right there."

Then everything was loud again.

"Anyway, Kobe beef tonight. You'd have totally dug it. Everything it's cracked up to be."

Yeah, great.

"I should take off," he said. "Guys are waiting on me here. Love to the girls. Hope everything's going great on the home front, okay? I'll try to get you again when I'm back in Tokyo. If not, see you Tuesday."

He rang off and I smiled to myself, heartened that he'd thought of me in the midst of everything else he was juggling, so far away.

And the girls and I had plenty of organic mac-and-cheese, diapers, milk, and cheddar and tortillas here. Plus three packages of frozen tortellini and two more boxes of waffles. Even broccoli and apples.

Supplies enough to last through Tuesday, at the very least.

I pushed down the little plastic button to disconnect, then tried calling Cary again.

Still no answer.

Mimi wasn't home, either.

"Well, fuck all y'all anyway," I said aloud to the empty room. "I'm taking a nap on the sofa."

I didn't sleep, though.

I was plenty tired enough, and it felt great to be

horizontal with my eyes closed, but even so it was like the cogs of the conscious-mind machinery in my head refused to disengage.

And of course thinking to myself that the girls were going to wake up any minute—so this was my last chance to get any meaningful rest before nightfall—didn't help the situation at all.

My sunburned arms felt all pinchy and weird, and I couldn't get comfortable on the old decrepit sofa cushions. Not to mention the fact that their foam inserts were off-gassing a distinct miasma of petrified hummus and Cheese Nips.

I tried rolling over onto my other hip, but that meant I was facing the back pillows—only a six-inch gap between my nostrils and a wall of the sofa's tired chintz.

Oh, gag: Cheese Nip *farts*. Seriously. Mixed with *Eau de* Dean's socks and something else I didn't even want to attempt identifying, though diapers came swimming to mind. Not the kind that were fresh out of the plastic Pampers packaging sleeve, either.

No wonder Setsuko had misted the place with lemon Pledge the other night. She'd been forced to it, in self-defense.

I twisted back onto my original hip, eyes still shut but facing out toward the living room again.

Better, but Mimi's respirator would still come in handy right about now.

I thought about calling Cary again, but the fact that I couldn't settle into sleep didn't make me any less tired. Now it felt as though some really nasty rotten dwarfs had Super Glued my eyes shut. After packing sand behind my lashes and lids with their little tiny evil-dwarf shovels.

Hi-ho.

And my arms really hurt. I tried to remember if we had any Solarcaine in the first-aid kit upstairs. Or, you know, laudanum.

Good thing I'd been wearing a hat, anyway. But why the hell had I walked all the way to Cary's?

Idiot.

Think about something else. Get some goddamn sleep while you can.

I tried retracing my steps around the three fire scenes I'd visited, mentally. Brought up each in as much detail as I could muster.

The field up by Sanitas was full of grass and weeds again, like it had never burned. Tons of joggers and hikers on the trail through it, moving uphill and down.

Had the fire happened during the day? Hard to believe someone could have started one there without anyone seeing him. Not a lot of tree cover.

Have to ask Mimi about that.

There wasn't anything at all to see on the blocks where the cars had burned. Just more cars parked along the same sidewalks. Nothing underneath—no scorch marks or whatever I'd thought I'd find there.

Old quasi-industrial-looking buildings that hadn't seemed open for business. Nobody on the street, either.

So at least the guy had picked someplace where he hadn't been likely to run into witnesses. And he hadn't had to bring along any acetone that time, as Mimi had pointed out. Just matches and some rags to shove in the fuel tanks of the cars themselves.

Had it been a weekend when he did it? Would there be more pedestrian traffic around those blocks, come Monday?

I could always swing back by and check, though it didn't seem like that would really tell me anything useful.

Same thing when I thought about the gas station: nothing at all useful.

I might as well have patrolled the streets of Boulder randomly, towing my red wagon. I could have eyed wandering vagrants with great suspicion to see if it made them act twitchy, or just cruised by them all nonchalant while sniffing for stray whiffs of accelerant.

Not like you could tell an actual vagrant from the vast majority of the CU student body, anyway. Or from the psychics who'd been in that banquet-hall place with me and Ellis.

A car schussed by, outside. Then the wind came up.

The trees were leafy enough that their boughs made a watery sound, instead of clattering the way they did when winter-bare.

Cary should have called me back by now.

I told myself again that I should get up and phone him.

But then I must have gone to sleep, because I started having a really, really bad dream.

And he was in it.

37

Bittler was in my dream, too. And the warehouse, even though in real life I'd never actually seen the damn place.

Cary was inside. And I couldn't get to him, even though I knew he was hurt.

Bittler told me not to bother, that it was Cary's own damn fault. "You tried to tell him, but would he listen?"

"He's *crying*," I said, banging on these giant metal doors. "Help me!"

I could hear Bittler laughing behind me, and I turned around to tell him what an asshole he was, but he wasn't there anymore.

And then I woke up—thrashing up to the surface

of sleep like a drowning woman desperate to secure one last breath.

It hadn't been Cary crying, it had been Parrish.

I hauled my ass off the sofa and jogged upstairs, pit of my stomach still clenched in cold knuckles of dream-fear, dream-helplessness.

I scooped Parrish up into my arms, whispering "shhhhh" in her ear, rocking her back and forth gently to quiet her.

"Winnie," she said. "Pooh."

"I can play you *Winnie-the-Pooh* downstairs," I said. "Absolutely."

I slid the video into our VCR and got the TV turned on, once Parrish was in the playpen.

Then India cranked up, weepy herself as she woke up alone in their room.

"Time to go get your sister," I said, but Parrish was fully entranced with the antics of her favorite bear.

I hadn't rewound the tape, so he was already singing, "I'm just a little black rain cloud . . ."

First India, then I call Cary again.

I let the phone ring eight times and listened to Cary's voice on the machine.

Then I dialed again, twice more.

Nothing.

Where the fuck are you, dude? I'm getting worried.

I thought about calling Setsuko, but she was crocheting in Aspen or whatever, so that wasn't going to work.

No answer at Mimi's, either.

I was even briefly tempted to call the cops, ask them to check the warehouse, but though I knew where it was, I had no idea about the actual street address.

And I would have sounded like a lunatic, probably.

I certainly felt like one.

A worried, worried lunatic.

I mean, what could I have said, "I had this weird dream, Officer, and I was just wondering if...?"

Even in Boulder, I doubted that line of reasoning could gain any traction.

Maybe *especially* in Boulder. Poor cops probably had volunteer psychics coming out their ears.

But I still couldn't stop feeling like something was really, really wrong. I tried to think the day through...I'd first called Cary around what, nine thirty that morning?

And I'd left a ton of messages.

I glanced at the clock in the kitchen: almost five, now.

Still light out, but that was a hell of a long bike ride, even for Cary.

And he was anally religious about checking his answering machine the minute he got home. I'd heard Dean teasing him about it.

Should I go by his apartment again, see if the truck is still there?

That would take an hour, though. At least.

I called his home number again. Waited until I heard the same old recording of him saying, "Hi, this is Cary...," before hanging up.

Winnie-the-Pooh had finished his musical number out in the living room.

I tried Mimi one more time. No luck.

I stepped out of the office and looked out the front windows, onto Mapleton.

The Galant was sitting across the street. Right where Dean had parked it, the day before he took off for Japan.

Wouldn't take an hour if I drove out to Cary's place.

And the keys were hanging on their little hook, just inside the front door.

I looked at the girls in their playpen and tried to talk some sense into myself.

Was this just dream-inspired paranoia, or was there a possibility Cary might actually be in trouble?

Maybe the New Age wiffleheads are getting to you, Madeline. Maybe you're soaking up idiocy by osmosis.

Yeah, in which case I would've driven for ten minutes—out to Cary's and back—for no real reason. Big fucking deal.

I mean, it wasn't like I didn't know *how* to drive... it was just a matter of paperwork.

And at the moment I didn't really care that I'd let my license lapse, back in New York.

I got the girls strapped into their car seats as quickly as I could, then climbed up behind the steering wheel myself.

Once I'd gotten the key into the ignition, I took a deep breath.

You used to own a Porsche, for fuck's sake. Step on the clutch and crank the thing up already.

So I was a little lead-footed on the gas pedal, so what. The engine roared to life like a pissed-off water buffalo.

"Here we go, girls," I said, slamming the gearshift into first and peeling out onto Mapleton.

Okay, so I left some rubber on the asphalt. German clutches were better engineered than Japanese ones.

"Wheee!" squealed India, from the backseat.

Hey, it was all coming back to me. Just like riding a bike—only with a far more satisfyingly selfish carbon footprint.

Way different from my Porsche, of course.

Center of gravity was a lot higher, as I found out the first time I took a corner on two wheels.

"Sorry about that," I said to my children.

Five minutes later, I was pulling up in front of Cary's building.

His truck was still parked out front, his bike was still gone, and he still didn't answer when I banged on the door.

This time, I'd remembered to bring a pen.

I wrote him a note and affixed it to his door frame, having also brought a thumbtack.

Dude, it read, *where the fuck are you? Been calling all day. You have me worried. Call me if you get this before I find you.*

Then I signed it.

And got back in the car. And didn't really consider going home to my house once I'd started the engine again.

I was already being totally illegal, right? So I figured I might as well drive out to the warehouse.

Just cruise past the place. Keep the doors locked the whole time.

Wouldn't get out of the thing, even if I saw something that worried me.

38

All I knew was that the warehouse was out past the industrial park where Ionix had its offices. In the blank stuff, the scrubby plains between Boulder and Longmont.

I ground the gears of the Mitsubishi and kept driving east. Not too fast, with the girls sitting behind me, but as fast as I maternally dared.

The trees started to thin out. I squeaked through a stoplight as it was just going yellow.

We were just past King Soopers when I saw the pillar of smoke.

I pulled the car up to the curb outside the entrance to the storage buildings.

Ionix wasn't the only business to keep shit out here,

but their logo was on the only building that was belching smoke and sparks out of its roof. Right up front.

There were four fire trucks and an ambulance beside it, parked all skewed like they'd shown up in a hurry. Which they had, of course.

A clump of guys was standing behind one of the trucks. Their faces and turnout coats were sooty and streaked. Nomex hoods under their helmets, respirators hanging loose around their necks.

First shift, tired out.

The building looked nothing like the one in my dream. It was all metal.

How the hell was it on fire, then?

I rolled down my window.

The wind shifted and I got a harsh full-face blast of sodden ash and that nasty sour fire-retardant smell, just like the place on Mapleton. I could hear the crackle of emergency radios.

Their voices were drowned out by a horrible creaking sound, right before this loud, sustained crash...the sound of beams colliding, maybe, or some big pile of weighty shit grinding and moaning as it collapsed in on itself.

Not the structure I was looking at, something inside it.

A second cloud of soot and sparks pillared up from behind the building's roofline.

The guys who'd been taking a break moved back toward the building.

Slow motion.

I rolled the window up, then opened my car door and got out. Closed it behind me so the girls wouldn't have to breathe any smoke.

Leave. Leave now. You shouldn't be here.

But I was frozen in place. Might as well have been duct-taped to the side of the Galant, for all the ability I had to actually act on that admonition to myself.

There was one guy up in the air on a ladder, lifted high above the truck it was attached to and shooting a jet of hose-water down into the roof below.

Someone had battered a loading-bay door open.

Another helmeted guy came out of it, looking for all the world like some World War I trench soldier, what with the respirator covering most of his face. Another guy had an arm over his shoulder. Limping.

A firefighter.

Don't be in there, Cary. Please God.

And then I was walking forward. Across the street.

A burly older guy in a white shirt and dark pants stepped forward to block me when I got near the trucks—both hands raised, his palms forward. "You can't be here, ma'am."

He was wearing a tie, too. Dark blue, same as his pants.

"Is Mimi Neff here?" I asked.

I didn't know what else to say. Already, the smoke was hurting my throat.

"Ma'am," he said, "you're going to have to leave."

Then I noticed a gold-bar name-tag thing, pinned to the left of the tie.

Chief Benjamin Davidian.

McNally's pal Benny?

"I'm a reporter," I said. "With the *Boulder New Times.*"

He stepped toward me, hands still up. "We've got a situation here, ma'am."

"I'm working with Jon McNally. Covering the arsons."

"Ma'am, be that as it may, I'm going to have to ask you to vacate the premises."

"You the guy McNally used to smoke-jump with? He told me to get my ass over here, make sure I talked to you first."

His hands dropped a little from the full-stop position.

"Benny, right?" I stuck out my hand. "I'm

Madeline Dare. I shadowed Mimi for an article last week, that house up on Mapleton."

He was listening. Taking me more seriously than I'd expected.

You sound more serious than you expected.

There was another cracking sound behind him, like a big tree snapping at the base, ready to fall. Benny turned to look, decided it was all right, then turned back toward me—suddenly all official around the mouth again.

"Ma'am..."

I was about to start babbling about lab results and accelerants and beers with Mimi, trying to sound all technical and impressive, when there was a long ripping sound and two far louder cracks.

Some guy behind us yelled, "Jesus Christ, Kevin...jump!" His voice loud and really scared.

Then half the long building caved in on itself, with dust and smoke and debris flying everywhere.

Benny threw his arms around me, tumbling us both to the pavement.

He'd knocked the wind out of me, but I realized he was curled over me, using his body to shield mine.

The crashing stopped, but the air was still thick and tough to see into.

Benny raised his head. "You okay?"

I coughed. "Yeah. *Yes.* Thank you."

He jumped up off me and gave me a quick once-over, like to make sure I didn't have a spike through my head or any other injuries masked by shock, then pulled me to my feet.

"Go home," he said.

"I have to talk to Mimi. Is she here?"

"On her way," he said.

"I have to wait."

I'd seen something, before the building caved. Something I was refusing to look at again. Over by the edge of the grass.

I had to tell Mimi about it. Only her. Not this guy.

I felt snot leaking out of my nose and wiped the back of my hand across it.

It came away black. I tried to breathe through my nose but my nose was having none of it.

"I have to talk to Mimi," I said again.

"Get back in your car. Drive to the end of this block," he said. "Where you came in from. Can you do that?"

"Yeah."

He looked at me funny. "You sure?"

I nodded. It made my head hurt.

"Quickly," he said. "And I want you to stay there."

I did what he'd told me, glancing back over my shoulder once to see him running full-tilt right back in toward the worst of it.

Now that he wasn't looking, I blew my nose into my fingers and flicked the snot on the grass.

Then I inhaled.

Yeah. The air reeked of gasoline.

The shakes set in the minute I'd reached the car. And then I started hacking up a bunch of nasty brown-black stuff I'd apparently inhaled.

Get the girls out of here.

The air started to clear just a bit. I could see Benny yelling into a radio now, standing at the driver's window of a red-and-white-painted Bronco with a seal on its door.

Mimi can wait. Get the hell out of here.

That's what half my brain thought, anyway.

The other half was apparently incapable of making me act on that suggestion.

I could hear more sirens starting up in the distance, louder and louder as they raced toward us all.

Another ambulance rushed in first.

Right behind it came Mimi's pickup.

I saw her eyes flash white, widening when she realized it was me standing next to my car, but she didn't stop.

She hit the truck's brakes and pulled up behind Benny's Bronco, jumping out of her truck's cab.

The ambulance guys ran past them, hauling a flat oval stretcher between them, tipped sideways like a surfboard.

The guy in front had something else tucked under his other arm. Might have been a neckboard.

Whoever Kevin was, his buddies were pros, and they weren't fucking around.

I'd wrapped my arms around my chest and was rocking, forward and back.

I realized I was talking to myself, muttering *not Cary, not Cary, not Cary* rapidly under my breath.

Over and over. A mantra.

But he was in there. I knew it for sure now.

And nobody was rushing to bring him out.

I got into the car and slammed the door behind me as quickly as I could, then started it up and drove well away from all the havoc.

"Mummie okay?" asked India, when I'd pulled over to the side of the road again.

"Yes, sweetie," I said, as calmly as I could.

Okay, but totally fucking stupid.

I knew Mimi would come back out and find me.

And that was a good thing.

Because Cary's bike had been lying on its side in front of the building. At the edge of the grass.

And this wasn't the serial-arsonist guy's MO. Whoever set this fire hadn't started it with acetone.

I had to wait until I could make sure Mimi knew that. Then I could take my children home.

I was far enough away now. So I got out of the car and sat down on the curb. I wanted her to be able to find me.

For some reason, I was sure she would.

It felt like I'd been sitting there thirty seconds. Or maybe a month. Time was rubbery.

My ass was numbly asleep on the cold concrete, but I was still rocking myself, forward and back, forward and back.

Getting dark now.

I felt a hand gripping my shoulder.

"Madeline, what the hell are you *doing* here?" Mimi's voice. "There's a fatality. We haven't even—"

"Cary," I said, cutting her off.

I kept rocking.

"Madeline?"

"His bike's out front. In the parking lot. I wanted you to know. And this was started with gasoline, Mimi. Not acetone. You can still smell it. McNally told me you could, even after they hit a place with water. He was right."

Mimi squatted down in front of me, got a grip on both my shoulders. "Look at me."

She made me stop rocking. I started shivering instead.

"You're in shock, Madeline."

"Yeah," I said. "No shit."

"We need to get you home."

The ambulance started up with a growl. It raced past us, sirens cranking up.

I tried to make my eyes focus on Mimi. "How's Kevin?"

I figured they wouldn't be going fast if he'd died, so it might be safe to ask.

"He's all right," she said. "Broken collarbone. Lucky as shit."

"Good. That's good."

"I'm going to get you a blanket, okay? And something to drink. You gonna be all right sitting here by yourself for just a minute?"

I nodded and started rocking again, arms tighter around my knees.

I saw her walk away. Couldn't really focus my eyes, or even shift what I was looking at. A line of trees. Nothing special about them.

When Mimi came back, she had an army blanket and a bottle of apple juice.

"I want you to drink this," she said. "You need a little sugar."

I drank down half of it and started coughing again. Hacked and spat on the sidewalk, once I'd gotten my breath back.

"Let's get you home," she said.

"I think I know who did this, Mimi."

"You drove here?" she asked. "I thought you couldn't drive?"

"*Listen* to me."

"Madeline, we have to leave."

"Mimi?" I started crying. "You have to look at Bittler for this."

"Just get back in your car," she said, grabbing me by the shoulders and turning me around. "Passenger side. I already cleared it with Benny. I'm going to drive you home now."

I didn't move, so she pushed me forward until I stumbled into movement, then walked behind me around to the other side of the car.

She leaned me against the back door, opened the front one for me.

"Jesus, Madeline," she said, looking into the backseat. "You brought your *children*?"

I was about to nod but instead I leaned forward and puked the apple juice back up, all over her shoes.

Mimi didn't say a word—just cradled me into the car and fastened my seat belt.

She used the blanket I was still wearing to wipe off my face.

So gently.

Then she shut my door, walking quickly around the front of the car.

The door on that side opened. She climbed up behind the wheel and started the engine.

India said, "Mimi!"

Parrish said, "Winnie-the-Pooh."

I couldn't stop crying, the whole drive home.

I tried really hard not to make too much noise, hoping I wouldn't scare my children.

When we parked in front of the house, I realized that I didn't even care anymore that Dean was away.

He couldn't have comforted me, not even if he'd been waiting for all of us on the front porch, arms opened wide to gather us in.

I didn't want my husband. Because this was all too awful.

I wanted my mom.

39

Mimi announced that she was staying over that night. She put the girls in the playpen. Then told me to go to bed.

"I have to make dinner for the girls," I said.

"I'll do it," she answered. "Don't worry about it, all right?"

I didn't even have the strength to feel guilty about burdening the poor woman with my life. I just thanked her.

Climbing the stairs was exhausting. It felt like it took three days.

I thought I wouldn't be able to sleep, but I was out before my head hit the pillow. Just too painful to be awake, I guess.

A long time later I woke up. Mimi was standing in the doorway of my bedroom, backlit.

"You awake?" she asked.

"Yeah." I sat up, suddenly terrified. "Are the girls okay?"

"They're fine."

I slumped forward. Relief wiping the will to sit up right out of my spine.

Tears started leaking down my face again.

"Hey there," said Mimi. "None of that."

She walked over and sat down on the edge of my bed.

"I'm so sorry. I don't know what I..." and then I couldn't even think of anything to say, after that.

"Listen," she said, as though I hadn't spoken. "I made them dinner. Some of the tortellini you had in the freezer. With apples. They were just fine with that. They're fast asleep now. Gave them a bath first, before I put them down."

I looked up at her.

She smoothed a lock of hair off my forehead.

"I'm sorry," she said. "I probably shouldn't have woken you up, but I thought I should tell you that your husband called. I explained what happened today."

"To Cary?"

I watched her nod.

"So I was right, then?" I asked.

"I'm so sorry, Madeline."

"Dean's not coming home early, though, is he?"

"He's going to try."

"Asshole," I said.

"He was devastated, Maddie. He wept on the phone."

"Won't change his ticket, though. Just watch."

"You should go back to sleep."

"Has anyone notified Cary's family? They live in Cincinnati."

"I'm sure they have," she said. "Don't worry about all that. Just lie back down and get some rest."

I did, but I cried for a long time first. The same words echoed all around inside my head, over and over again:

Terrible mother, terrible wife, terrible friend.

Mimi was feeding the girls breakfast downstairs in the kitchen by the time I woke up the next morning.

I felt a lot more clearheaded. Clearheaded enough to suffer the full weight of my own idiocy the day before: angst-ridden and self-recriminatory as shit.

What the hell had I been thinking, driving out to that warehouse with my *children* in the car?

Asshole.

I walked down the stairs and joined the breakfast party.

Mimi took one look at me and handed me a paper towel.

I blew my nose, wadded up the towel, and put it in the garbage can under the sink. Black snot, of course.

"Listen," I said, turning back toward her. "I am so grateful to you for last night. Everything you did…I was such an idiot, and you totally came to my rescue. I don't know how to *begin* to thank you."

"Drink some coffee," she said. "After that, don't worry about it."

I was tempted to burst into tears again, hearing that.

Mimi looked at her watch. "I have to take off in a few minutes. They need me down at the scene. Anyone I can call to help you out today?"

"Um," I said, "not really."

"That woman Setsuko?"

"She's on vacation. Skiing somewhere. And she should stay doing that. Bad enough she has to find out about Cary when she gets back here. They were pals."

"His parents should be out here by the end of the day."

Then she got quiet.

"What?" I asked.

"Someone else will want to talk with you. Today, as soon as possible. I can have them come here to the house."

"From your department?"

"Police," she said.

"So you guys think this is a homicide?"

"Yes. But that's all I can say, all right? It's not appropriate for me to discuss any further details with you."

"Of course," I said. "This is when it gets official. That's how it should be. I completely understand."

She looked relieved.

"But Mimi," I continued, "I still want to finish telling you what I started to say yesterday. Before I puked on you and everything."

"Okay."

"I think I know who was involved in this. A guy named Bittler. Cary worked under him at Ionix. Remember, the guy we were trying to avoid at the community meeting? There was a lot of weird crap going on in their office. Like, embezzlement. That's why Cary wanted to get into the warehouse—to follow up on stuff he suspected Bittler was doing. I told him not to go."

"That's why *Cary* wanted to get into the warehouse?"

"Yeah. And I guess he crowbarred the door open, after all. Bittler had the only keys to the place."

"He didn't," she said.

"Didn't what?"

"Crowbar anything open. Our guys had to bust in. It was locked up tight."

"But Cary was inside. How the hell did *he* get hold of Bittler's keys?"

"We don't know that he did," she said. "There weren't any keys on him."

"So he wasn't . . ." I stopped.

Couldn't bring myself to say, "burned to death."

But he couldn't have been, if they knew there weren't keys in his pockets, right? I mean, he had to have still had pockets.

I found incredible relief in that thought. But I didn't want to picture anything beyond it.

"He was dead before the fire started, Madeline," said Mimi. "He didn't suffer."

"How do you know?" I asked.

"We can't discuss this."

"Mimi, Bittler's the only one with keys. If Cary

didn't have them, that's another thing pointing to him. Who else could've locked him in?"

"Madeline," she said, "I *cannot* talk to you about this."

I looked down at the floor. "Okay."

"Would you like me to come back after work?"

"I want to say no, after everything you've done for me already. But it would be magnificent if you could."

"I'll swing by here around six thirty, then. Now finish that coffee."

"If you and I were lesbians, Mimi Neff," I said, paraphrasing my favorite-ever greeting card, "I'd move to Vermont with you so we could adopt Vietnamese orphans and open an organic bakery together. But since we're not, let's just celebrate the burgeoning splendor of this already magnificent friendship."

"You never know," she said. "Next incarnation— should we both come back as lesbians—I say we go in for the orphans and baked goods. Always liked Vermont, and I make a *killer* sourdough rye."

40

I held it together until I'd waved Mimi to her pickup from the front porch.

Then I walked back inside and started crying all over again.

I stayed just outside the kitchen doorway, leaning against the dining room wall out of sight so I wouldn't freak the girls out. Peeked in on them now and again, though, to make sure they still had waffles to chow on.

Then the phone rang.

I blew more black snot out of my nose, took a deep breath, and picked up in the office.

"Bunny? Are you all right?" Dean's voice, with no drunk colleagues clinking barware in the background this time.

Small mercies.

"No," I said, sliding down to the shag-rugged floor. "Not even fucking close."

"I'm so sorry," he said. "I wish I could be there with you."

"Get on a plane, then."

"I can't. Things are really complicated here."

"Fuck you, Dean Bauer."

"Bunny—"

"He was our *friend*. Cary was our friend, and you should be on your goddamn way home right now."

I heard my husband starting to cry, all those thousands of miles away.

Well, good. He should be crying.

Schmuck.

And then I heard someone knocking on my front door.

"I have to go," I said.

"Bunny, talk to me."

"I can't right now. I think there's a homicide detective at the front door. And the girls have finished their breakfast so I've got to get them out of their booster seats."

"I'll call you back, then."

"Sure," I said. "Why don't you *do* that."

I slammed the phone down and went to answer the door.

*   *   *

There were actually two people from homicide. A man and a woman. Young, tanned, fit. Both of them blond.

The woman was holding a bag of bagels from Moe's. Still warm, as I discovered when she smiled broadly and handed the bag to me.

I got the feeling they hadn't had a whole lot of practice with actual homicide investigations.

"Hi there," I said. "You guys are probably from Boulder PD, right?"

The guy badged me, then, blushing a little.

The chick stuck her hand out. "I'm Diane."

She was pretty, but just a teeny bit goofy-looking: mess of curly golden hair, wide-set blue eyes, big smile that brought out dimples in her cheeks and showcased a charming little gap between sparkling white front teeth.

Granted, goofiness probably had something to do with the fact that she was wearing Teva sandals on her very tanned little feet.

Not an unexpected fashion move in Boulder, but they did rather cancel out the professional intent of her prim blouse and beige pencil skirt. Or maybe she'd just nipped out of the office for a quick rappel down the Devil's Thumb. On her chai-soy-latte break.

She did seem a little bit out of breath.

I shifted the bag of warm bagels to my left arm and shook her hand.

"Madeline Dare," I said. "But I bet you guys knew that already."

Diane nodded, elbowing her partner guy. "Introduce yourself, Wes."

"I'm Wes," he said, blushing again as he stuck his own hand out toward me. "Nice to meet you."

He was a head taller than his partner. Just as blond, though. Just as blue-eyed.

"Nice to meet *you*, Wes." I shifted the bagels again so we could shake on it. "And I know that this is Boulder and we're all friendly here and stuff, but would you guys mind telling me your *last* names?"

Diane said, "Um, Bryant."

Wes said "Wyckoff."

"Thank you," I said. "I appreciate your sharing that information with me."

Then we all just stood there, on my front porch.

Both of them smiling at me, now. Dimples all around.

"So," I said. "You guys want to come inside? I have bagels."

I pointed at the Moe's bag, figuring they might need a visual aid.

Their corn-fed grins were undimmed, but they didn't laugh.

I would've gladly given my right arm to trade these guys for a couple of New York City cops—somebody smart and snarky, like my old pal Skwarecki from Queens.

This was going to be a very, very long morning. I could already tell.

I turned away from them and walked back inside my house. Hoping they'd realize they were supposed to follow along behind.

At several points during the interview that followed, I was sorely tempted to rip the notepad out of Wes's hands so I could just write down my answers in large block-capital letters.

It would've been so much faster than sitting there trying to look patient while he struggled to think up actual *questions* for me.

"Bittler," I said, for the third time. "B-I-T-T-L-E-R."

"Okay." He struggled to write that out on his pad.

I could've carved it into a block of marble more rapidly—with Diane's Teva and a toothbrush for hammer and chisel.

"*Two* t's," said Diane, looking over her partner's shoulder.

Dude, seriously?

We'd been at this for over an hour already.

I shoved half a bagel into my mouth. In lieu of shrieking.

My phone started ringing.

"Guys?" I said. "I have to get that. It's probably my husband, calling back from Tokyo."

The pair of them were still intent on Wes's note-pad progress, but Diane waved a hand at me without looking up.

I closed the office's French doors behind me and picked up the phone.

"Bunny?"

"Dean," I said. "Thank *God*. Look, I'm sorry I was such a bitch, before. So, *so* sorry."

"I'm sorry I'm not there with you. When things are so awful."

"They are," I said, closing my eyes. "Really awful."

I sucked in my breath and held it, not wanting to cry again. Just wanting to pretend he was standing next to me.

"I tried to change my flights home," he said. "As soon as I heard from Mimi last night. But they want an extra five hundred bucks, this late in the game. I just can't swing it."

I reached my hand up to my throat, then realized I wasn't wearing my pearls anymore. Couldn't remember when I'd taken them off.

When we got home from the business dinner?

Crap. I just hoped the clasp hadn't worn through the silk again. They could've fallen off anywhere.

And then I felt a bolt of shame rocket through me.

Really? Cary's dead and you're worried about your fucking jewelry, Madeline?

"Bunny? You still there?"

"Yeah," I said.

Still here. Still an undeserving asshole.

"Was it really cops at the door?" he asked.

"Yes," I said. "Not exactly rocket surgeons, either of them. They're making me miss the hell out of Skwarecki."

"How are the girls?"

I looked through the French doors' panes of glass, out toward the playpen. "India appears to be sending herself a letter in the Little Tikes plastic-garden-thingie's mailbox. Parrish is inspecting the rear wheels on a Tonka dump truck. Making sure they spin properly."

"I miss them," he said.

"I miss *you*," I replied.

He cleared his throat. "I've called the office. Cary's parents have planned a funeral. Wednesday afternoon."

I closed my eyes again, tempted to cross my fingers for luck. "You'll be home?"

"My plane gets into Denver around seven Tuesday night. I'll be back at the house as quickly as I can."

It was still only Sunday, I realized. Even though Saturday felt like it happened five years ago.

Longer.

Tuesday afternoon seemed so far away I couldn't imagine it actually ever happening. I'd probably turn eighty before Monday deigned to show up.

"Do you think I should talk with the cops while they're there?" asked Dean.

"Totally useless," I said. "They make Inspector Clouseau look like a goddamn genius. And that's *if* Clouseau had been an illiterate Department of Motor Vehicles employee with a lifelong fondness for airplane glue."

Dean groaned.

"Yeah," I said. "Exactly. But you need to talk to *somebody* about Bittler. I'm not getting the vibe that anyone's taking me seriously on that score. They might listen to you."

"I could call your friend Mimi."

"That would be great."

"And what should I be telling her about Bittler, exactly?"

"Everything Cary thought he was up to."

I related what I could remember about everything Cary himself had told me the night of the neighborhood meeting: missing spares, fucked-up invoices, how he'd wanted to get into the warehouse. Bittler having the only set of new keys.

"And Mimi said Cary was locked into the place," I said, "with no keys on him. He hadn't broken in. Someone had to have been there with him. And who else but Bittler, right? If he had the only keys."

"Jesus," said Dean.

"Just tell Mimi. Tell whomever you can … people at work. They have to at least look him *over* then, right?"

"Give me Mimi's number," he said.

I did. Home and work. "Call her now, okay? Before you do anything else."

"I will."

We said our good-byes and hung up.

I couldn't face the idea of more time in the living room with Tweedle-Dumb and Tweedle-Outright-Fucking-Idiot, so I called the main number at the *New Times*, instead, and asked if McNally happened to be in the office.

Sure, it was just after noon on a Sunday, but he was a newspaper guy. And we're all pretty damn weird in the journo business.

"Sure thing," said the chick who answered. "I'll put you right through."

There was classical music playing while she had me on hold. Some burbly Mozartian concerto.

India was bending the plastic flowers in her Little Tikes white picket fence. Parrish was still checking the alignment of her Tonka tires by spinning them around, repeatedly.

Gender-neutral, my girl. I felt good about that.

And I also felt pretty damn sure the Officers Tweedle weren't going to make shit for headway on Cary's behalf.

I knew if I stopped to let the full heft and weight of his death sink in—the *fact* of it—my resulting grief would be paralytic, literally. Full stop.

And I couldn't succumb to that. I had to keep functioning. Until Dean came home, at the very least.

I had to keep it together—cook and change diapers and play "Itsy Bitsy Spider." Tuck my girls in at night and get up with them in the morning.

If I squandered an ounce of momentum now, there was no fucking way I could get it back.

So don't think, do. Gird your goddamn loins already.

The only way to keep myself from falling apart over losing Cary was to concentrate on figuring out how and why he'd been killed.

Mozart cut out mid-burble.

"McNally," said McNally. "Who's this?"

"Madeline," I replied.

"What's up with you, this fine Sunday?"

"There's been another fire."

"I heard," he said. Serious, now.

"Friend of mine died in it."

"Shit. I'm so sorry, Madeline."

"I need your help."

"You got it. Where and when?"

"My house, as soon as you can get away."

"You're on Mapleton?"

"At Nineteenth. House with the Christmas crap still up, all over the porch."

"House number's right here on your résumé," he said. "You need me armed?"

I could practically hear the grin in his voice—like I'd just picked him first for my kickball team. But he wasn't exactly kidding, either.

"No," I said. "Or at least not yet. But I'd really dig it if you could get these *dopey* fucking cops out of my living room."

"Names?"

"Wes Wyckoff and Diane Bryant."

McNally snickered.

"Piece of cake," he said. "Be there in ten."

He made it in seven.

41

I'm not exactly clear on how McNally managed to clear the cops out of my house so quickly. One minute he was standing in the living room doorway, grinning at Wes and Diane, the next he had them out on the front porch, an arm draped across each of their backs.

A couple of words at a time drifted back into the house, barely audible.

His tone was familiar, reassuring. I heard him say, "grieving," and "keeping her chin up, for her little girls' sake," and, finally, "anything you need, anything at all...day or night."

By which point they were waving good-bye from my front walk, grins still plastered across their goofy faces, each of them gripping a copy of his business card as though they'd just scored a Golden Ticket from the hand of Willy Wonka himself, for chrissake.

He didn't leave the porch until they were driving away in their unmarked sedan.

"*Damn*," I said when he sauntered back into the living room. "That was like watching somebody take down a couple of particularly dim-witted calves at a high-end rodeo. Zip-zip, all four hooves lassoed and then you just yank it tight and tip 'em right over."

"Rope-a-dope," said McNally. "Good thing they're stupid."

I collapsed onto my sofa. "And, as my farmboy-genius husband would say, they're going to be about as much use as tits on a bull, aren't they?"

"Wes and Diane?" he asked, dropping into an armchair. " 'Tits on a bull' garners them entirely too much credit."

"Well, that's just fucking great. My friend's dead, Mimi won't talk to me about it, and the cops they send over have about as much intellectual gravitas as inflatable Bozo punching dolls."

"Pretty much the size of it," McNally agreed.

"So what the hell am I supposed to do now?"

"You're a *journalist*, Madeline. You're supposed to go out and investigate."

"I'm a *restaurant* critic, McNally. With toddlers."

"And yet you seem to have a disturbing familiarity with arson, plastic explosives, and the Radio Shack parts one might require to successfully blow up a helicopter. From a remote location."

"*Au contraire, mon brave.* I once tried to get a kid who knew how to do all that to read *I Know Why the Caged Bird Sings* and write a term paper about it. A task at which I failed, by the way, in rather spectacular fashion. And I'd hightailed it out of my job at that school before said kid had stolen the requisite C-4, much less duct-taped it to the fucking helicopter."

McNally grinned. "That so?"

"Yes. That's exactly so."

"You seem pretty calm about it."

"It was a shitty job at a shitty school and the guy who died was an evil asshole. Not that I condone murder."

McNally cracked another grin in my direction. "All the same, you strike me as a resourceful woman."

"Good thing, too. Since I'm going to be single-momming it with a couple of one-year-olds through Tuesday, the day after which I've gotta show up at a funeral. It's going to be a goddamn miracle of resourcefulness if I can even find a *babysitter* by then."

"I've got a niece," he said. "Junior at CU. Good head on her shoulders. She charges ten bucks an hour, and I happen to know she'll be free this Wednesday afternoon."

"How?"

"Because we had an appointment to go rock-climbing from noon to five, but I'm about to call and tell her she's getting stood up."

"You, McNally, are a prince among men." I pointed toward the office French doors. "Phone's right through there. Tell your niece she gets twelve an hour: hardship pay for watching twins."

He flashed me the high sign, walking off to dial.

"After that," I called out toward his retreating back, "you can help me nail the guy who killed my pal Cary."

He was through the office doors already, but his voice carried back toward the living room, loud and clear: "I'm a *doctor*, Jim, not a magician."

I shook my head.

You're a journalist, McNally, and I need you to kick some investigative ass.

It was noon, by the kitchen clock. Time to check diapers and make quesadillas.

"Hey there, Susannah," McNally was saying. "This is your uncle Jon-o. Listen, sweetie, I need to hit you up for a big, big favor…"

42

The girls were fed and napping upstairs, and McNally was riding shotgun as I typed up my neighborhood-arson-meeting piece at the desk in Dean's home office.

" 'Cajoled' isn't really a great verb, there," he said, pointing at my computer screen.

"Backseat writers are a woeful pain in the ass, McNally. Anybody ever cajole you *that*?"

He said it happened on a daily basis, then got down to business and read off everything relevant Buzz Rainer had said at the meeting, before grilling me on Mimi's profiling comments.

After that, I showed him the map I'd plotted the arsons on, back in the laundry room.

"Okay," he said, taking my chair at the computer desk for himself and opening up a new Word file, "now give me the straight shit on this Bittler guy. Everything you can remember Cary saying about him."

So I did.

He could type almost as fast as I talked, but his spelling was for shit.

"Your spelling's for shit, McNally," I said.

"So you'll fix it. This is just the frame. The starting point."

"Pretty much everything I have resembling facts, so far," I said. "But you know more about this kind of shit than I do."

"How so?"

"Well, for one thing, I've never been a firefighter. Jumping out of planes or otherwise. Even that first phone chat I heard you having with your pal Benny, you were way more studied up on the particulars than I'll ever be."

"How?"

"Accelerants, progression of the typical arsonist's narrative arc, et cetera, et cetera. Let's trade chairs. You talk, I'll type."

I could hear the girls coming back to consciousness upstairs.

"Mimi's going to swing by around six thirty," I said. "Want to stay for that? We could double-team her."

"Can't," he said, checking his watch. "Gotta hit the road, soonest."

"So what should I do next?"

"Save this file. Let it roll around in your head for a while. Trying to feel out where the gaps are. I promise I'll do the same."

"Got any more time free, between now and Tuesday?"

"Not really. I'm following a story. Legwork kind of thing."

"Bummer," I said.

"I'll keep in touch and bring Susannah over on Wednesday afternoon, though. Introduce you guys."

"That would be great."

"Leave me a voice mail at the office. Let me know what time you'll need her here, all right?"

"Absolutely." Parrish lit into a true wail upstairs. "I gotta go do the mom thing."

McNally snapped me a crisp salute. "Better you than me."

Mimi showed up at six thirty on the dot, with a pizza and some beer.

She chatted generally while I took two slices and

ripped them bite-sized for Parrish and India, but once we'd adjourned to the living room I started asking her about where things stood, investigation-wise, before we'd even sunk our teeth into our own triangles of cheesy splendor.

"Madeline," she said, lowering hers from her mouth, "I just can't discuss it with you. All I can say is that we're working our asses off. And that's the best we can do—having you mixed up in it wouldn't help."

I was chewing already, so I swallowed. "Just *promise* me you guys're investigating. Because the cops here are morons. Seriously."

"That's not true."

"Bullshit," I said. "My *kids* could run a better homicide investigation than the idiots who showed up here to question me."

She started laughing.

"Yeah, see?" I said. "And you *totally* know it, too."

"Officially, I shouldn't comment," she said.

"Fine. And of course I'm being really rude, especially since you brought dinner. I'll lay off you until dessert, anyway."

"There's dessert?"

"Um," I said, "not exactly. Unless you're a fan of Life cereal and banana slices."

"I'll pass. But I appreciate the thought."

We were quiet then, while we ate.

And then I thought about Cary, again. It hit me hard again. A rogue wave.

I'd been trying to fill up the day with talk, errands, other people. Anything to hold back the enormity of what had happened. What I should've done, or shouldn't have done...

The pizza in my hand had suddenly lost all savor. I put it down on the coffee table. Atop one of the paper towels I'd grabbed for us to use as napkins.

"You okay?" asked Mimi.

"No."

She nodded. "Grief..."

We looked at each other, then away.

I didn't say anything. Didn't have to.

"Try to finish that," she said, pointing at my half-eaten slice.

"In a minute."

"Okay."

Mimi had finished her own, but she didn't reach for another.

We sat there for another couple of minutes, just quiet. Companionable. Sad.

"Have you eaten *anything* today?" she asked.

I pointed at the paper towel in front of me. "Half

a slice of pizza. There were bagels at one point, but I can't remember if I ate one."

She got to her feet and walked to the kitchen, returning with a large glass of milk.

I drank it.

"I *know* you can't tell me anything about the investigation—" I said.

Mimi cut me off. "I met with Cary's parents this afternoon. At the Boulderado."

"Oh, *Mimi*."

"Benny came with me."

My eyes started leaking tears. "I'm sure that meant a great deal to them."

I should've called them, myself. I just couldn't face that. Not yet.

"They're lovely people," she said.

The tears backed up into my nose.

"My husband and I lost a child," she said. "My stepson Chris. He was fifteen."

My throat hurt even more, hearing that. "I'm so sorry."

We were quiet for another moment.

I would've held her hand if she'd been sitting next to me.

"It gets...easier," she said. "Never *easy*, but survivable, eventually. Takes a long time to get to that

point, though. And to see people, knowing that…
how it feels at first, how much longer it's going to
keep hurting them that badly, before it even *begins*
to dull…?"

I looked at the girls, my eyes fully leaking.

"You can't believe what it feels like to *have* a
child before it happens, can you?" she asked. "I
don't think anyone could explain how deep it goes."

"It's like someone ripping your most essential
organs out of your body and putting them into the
world," I said, "outside the protection of your body.
Totally vulnerable."

And you love them so much—you're horrified
and entranced and besotted with it. To the extent
that it's like walking around without any skin on.
And I mean walking through the scariest meat-
packing district in the universe with zombie hook-
ers throwing disease-crusted syringes at you and it's
three in the morning and you're *hung over* and skin-
less, just bleeding and feeling every last thing—the
slightest breeze, the gorgeousness of light spill-
ing all golden through trees in the late afternoon,
the ache of loss more profound than loss has ever
been—with no goddamn protection from *any* of it.

They're blood of your blood, bone of your bone,
and the most beautiful, terrifyingly lovely things
you've ever beheld, ever tasted, ever caught the per-

fume of. Lapidary and sublime. And at any moment they could wander out into the street, or be hit by a comet. Or feel sadness and pain. And you can't stop that. You can't protect them from *any* of it: UV rays or *E. coli* or bone cancer or runaway trains or just plain heartbreak.

I was feeling all that, but couldn't have put it into words right then, so instead I blew my nose and looked at Mimi and said, "The risk of it—being a parent—fucking *kills* me. And at the same time nothing's ever made me happier. It goes to eleven."

"Hostages to fortune," she said.

I grabbed her paper towel and blotted my eyes. "Is *that* what that means?"

"Francis Bacon: 'He that hath wife and children hath given hostages to fortune; for they are impediments to great enterprises, either of virtue or mischief.'"

"'Impediments' my ass," I said. "I mean, she that hath a *husband*..."

I stopped speaking, appalled with myself.

Mimi was trying not to smile. Failing.

Then she looked at my face.

I must've been wearing one hell of an expression—guilt and grief over Cary's death, pissed-offness at myself for once again lapsing into the comfort of snark and complaint when there were so many bigger, worse things in the world than my whiny, self-absorbed little list of petty domestic grievances.

The amusement that had been warming her features dropped away. She came over and sat down beside me, wrapping me in her arms.

I snuffled into her shoulder. "Mimi? It's just…I want to *do* something. I want to help…and there's nothing I can do, and even if there was I shouldn't because of the girls. And is this my fault? *Jesus*…"

She shushed me, and patted me on the back, and didn't seem at all worried that I was getting snot on her shirt.

"Look," she said, gripping my shoulders gently and making me sit up straight once I'd calmed down a little. "I know how much Cary mattered to you. And *you* have to know I'm going to do everything I can to find out what happened, but I really, really can't talk to you about that as it progresses, all right?"

"No, it's not all right. But there's not a damn thing I can do about it, is there? So I'll just have to abide by it. Respect the way you need to do this. Trust you. And trusting *anyone* is fucking hard for me, for more reasons than I could elucidate in a single twenty-four-hour period."

"I understand that."

I swiped an already sodden paper towel across my nostrils. "Has Dean called you yet?" I asked.

"He may have. I haven't been near a phone all day. I'll talk to him as soon as I can."

She helped me get the girls ready for bed, after that, telling me I should get some sleep myself while I could.

I agreed. "But I'm afraid I'm just going to lie there in the dark telling myself what an asshole I am. Which isn't really conducive to rest."

"Try anyway."

"Okay."

"I have to go," she said.

"I know. Thank you for staying last night. And for bringing dinner. You're a godsend."

I walked her out to the front porch. "I just want you to remember that Cary was someone's child, Mimi, and my friend. His parents don't even *have* a hostage anymore. Fortune got him. And fortune's going to be nailing them now, for as long as they last."

She nodded. Very grave. Then she hugged me.

"You know this," I said. "And *I* know I don't have to say it all out loud to you, but I just need to say it anyway, okay? I need to hear myself say all of it, right now."

"I understand. It's something you have to honor. And I'm listening."

"What you do matters a great deal, Mimi. Not just to me. That's all. And I admire the hell out of you for doing it."

"Good night, Madeline," she said, stepping off my porch and into the darkness.

"Good luck," I called after her.

I spent the next three days trying to do what McNally had suggested: rolling everything I knew around in my head, poking at the morass of it to find the gaps.

It was like sticking the tip of my tongue into a hideously painful broken tooth over and over again until I'd done it so often, my tongue started bleeding, too.

It hurt like a bitch. And I wasn't getting anywhere. But I couldn't really stop, so at least I had the consolation of thinking there might be a point to it.

McNally had said so, after all.

And he seemed like a guy who knew things.

Not like I could touch base with him. He was running around town researching *something*, and we kept leaving each other voice mails in the meantime.

I tried to leave Mimi alone, telling myself that I needed to concentrate on being a mother instead of investigating anything, that I'd already caused enough trouble, and that, furthermore, I should wait to see if there was anything safe and matronly I could help out with once Dean had returned home.

I busied myself with taking the girls on outings: to Pearl Street to play in the sand pit with the big rocks in it, for generic sunny walks around our neighborhood in the red wagon, and even, God help me, to the annoying Mom-and-Toddler group up at the community center.

The discussion topic that week was either Rolfing or Transcendental Meditation. I wasn't exactly paying attention.

And, okay, I spent a lot of hours staring at my map of Boulder with all the pins stuck in it. A lot. Trying to see if there was something, *anything* to be gleaned from it.

Plus which I told myself I *wasn't* actively scrutinizing every white male person between the ages of roughly twenty and forty who looked like he might be lacking in self-esteem and/or communication skills and/or could possibly have a bit of a drinking problem whom I happened to pass on the sidewalk, whenever I left the house.

Which would be a big fat lie, of course, but

"scrutinizing" seemed like a relatively harmless activity so what the hell.

McNally very kindly had the *New Times*'s accounting department cut me a check for my first two articles and another to reimburse me for the actual meals, so I was okay for money again. I even dragged the girls over to Mustard's Last Stand for Chicago-style hot dogs one night, and wrote a totally lame review of the place.

I mean, "Chicago-style" my Manhattan-born-and-bred ass. Give me an infinitely superior sidewalk-cart Nathan's with sauerkraut any day.

So, okay, I was bored out of my mind. Except when I started thinking about Cary, and then I just cried.

Dean wasn't home yet. McNally was out of reach. Mimi couldn't talk to me about anything that actually mattered.

And my best friend in this town was dead.

43

Cary's family didn't have a memorial service for him, it was a funeral. With a closed casket.

But it was beautiful. In a small old chapel with lovely stained glass, a dark beamed ceiling, and smooth white plaster that made the walls seem soft as comfort.

The altar was surrounded by white lilies—dozens and dozens—and they perfumed everything. Sweet and poignant and just fucking heartrending, all at once.

There was a large framed color photograph of Cary on a gold easel beside the dark-wood casket. Strange-looking... cheesy blue background, maybe a little airbrushed? It was like a high-school yearbook picture, only of a grown-up.

I kept trying to figure out who'd taken it and why—he was wearing a jacket and tie, but his hair was really different. Blow-dried, maybe. And his smile radiated discomfort.

I wanted an image that seemed more like *him*... standing on our front porch drinking coffee with his bike helmet under his arm, maybe, or helping Dean flip burgers on the Weber. Just... *laughing*, for God's sake.

I couldn't look and I couldn't *not* look.

Dean cleared his throat. We were on the aisle in the fourth pew, left of the altar.

He'd gotten in late the night before and promptly fallen asleep on our sofa with his briefcase balanced upright in his lap, pummeled comatose by jet lag and twelve hours of coach-seat tall-guy torture.

Parrish had woken up twice with night terrors, and I'd let him sleep.

Now he and I looked as though Satan-worshipping elves had spent the entire night working us over with veal mallets—especially around the eyes.

The kneelers were the kind I remembered from the church Mom took us to sporadically when we were kids.

Thanksgiving and Easter, mostly, because she liked the hymns: "We Gather Together to Ask the

Lord's Blessing," and that *a-a-a-a-a-lei-loo-oo-jah* one.

At least that's the way I still spelled it in my head—despite being pretty sure even Episcopalians would've hesitated to commit to that many hyphens in a single word, whether or not it was phonetically accurate. Which my version totally was.

Okay, so my mind was bouncing all over the place—before my dear late friend's funeral had even *started*—which made me feel like a deeply shitty person.

I'd had a lot of practice with that feeling lately.

I looked down at the kneelers, again. Little oval cushions, maybe ten inches high, upholstered in velvet that had probably debuted in a deep, rich shade of burgundy: the old Hearty Gallo, lugged down to beach bonfires by the seamed loop set into each bottle's neck—weight of the entire gallon depending from your single, overtaxed finger.

Okay, the velvet was probably meant to echo the color of communion wine. I just missed the Gallo, and that beach at night. All the grown-ups arrayed around the fire, sipping from paper cups.

Focus, Madeline.

I pulled my kneeler out, slid forward off the wooden pew's satiny edge. Sank down to my knees.

Assume the position: hands clasped on the railing, eyes shut.

It was uncomfortable immediately despite the kneeler, which I suppose was the point.

Penance.

I did the Lord's Prayer, not out loud.

Tried to remember the Nicene Creed from communion class.

One God, the father almighty, maker of heaven and earth and all things visible and invisible.

Um...

God of God, light of light, very God of very God...

I look for the resurrection of the dead, and the life of the world to come.

And really, why the hell not?

But that was all of it I could remember.

I could have reached for *The Book of Common Prayer*, but felt like that would be cheating.

I pushed myself up until my ass was level with the pew. Slid backward onto it.

The woman seated directly in front of us whispered loudly to her companion that Cary's best high school friend had flown in from Boston.

"He's going to play something," she said, and I heard her program crinkle.

I examined my own but couldn't see whom she was referring to.

An organist took his seat and began playing Bach.

Not our age, not Cary's friend.

Dean nudged me gently with his elbow.

I looked at him, wondering why, then saw Setsuko standing in the aisle beside us.

I scootched over.

Dean scootched over.

She took the aisle seat beside him.

Then the real thing started, and the three of us wept nonstop for more than an hour.

The priest talked. Friends. Family.

Then there was a bit of a lull.

A guy walked up to the altar, stepped onto the dais.

Ah, the friend.

Tall, around the same height Cary had been. Thinner, though, with paler hair.

He turned around, facing us but not looking at anyone, just gazing over our heads.

Someone handed him a black case. Old and battered, gray at the corners.

He squatted down, resting it on the floor, flipping three silver latches open, then raising its lid.

He stood up, light glancing off the length of gold he now held in both hands.

A trumpet.

There was utter quiet.

One cough from the back, echoing the way noise will in a high room with stone floors—fleeting and watery.

The guy took a deep breath, raising the instrument to his mouth.

I can't tell you exactly what he played, over the next ten minutes.

It started as "Taps," but then shifted upward—just after the note a singer would've raised his voice on, at the end of "from the sky…"—but leaving that right away for something light and silvery I'd never heard before.

Liquid.

Translucent.

And then part of Gounod's "Ave Maria," the beautiful one.

And then on into that sweet, sweet bit of Largo from Bach's Piano Concerto Number Five, which I'd first heard as a kid in *Slaughterhouse-Five* when the Tralfamadorians come down shimmering out of the stars to take Billy Pilgrim and his dog Spot away.

So the version I had in my head was Glenn Gould, with someone else doing a little pizzicato in the background.

Cary's friend just floated through the piano line

of it…soft, breathtakingly sad…and then suddenly it wasn't that Largo at *all* anymore.

I couldn't put my finger on the new melody, though I knew I'd heard it…Sousa, maybe—though mournful—but then it was gone.

On to the next, again familiar.

This one he stayed with.

"*Oh*," I said, not loudly, right when I knew.

Dean leaned so his lips brushed my ear. "What?"

I just shook my head.

I couldn't talk anymore.

It wasn't really profound, what he was playing. Simple—but he made the notes float, like you were hearing them from a very long way away.

Across a lake, maybe, near the end of the day.

A song I'd first heard the Ink Spots do, on a very old scratchy record of Mom's that she'd managed to keep intact since boarding school in 1957—though, as she'd often told me, "it was old even then."

A song that had always reached deep into my head, with its sadness and hope: "We'll Meet Again."

Jesus.

I knew the words by heart, thinking through them as Cary's friend sent the melody soaring through the chapel's old rafters…

Won't you please say hello to the folks that I know, tell 'em I won't be long…

Fuck.

I couldn't help it, I sobbed, biting the edge of my fist to try shutting myself up ... which I failed at pretty much immediately.

Because wouldn't it be the best possible thing, if it all really *did* turn out like that?

To think everyone really *is* waiting for you—for all of us—that each beloved person we have to lose has only gone on ahead to prepare the way, to let them all know you're coming, too, soon enough:

All we've done forgiven, all our sadness explained, all happiness triumphant.

All of us released to float up. Light as air, clear as water, sweet as the notes of that trumpet.

Oh, how I wanted that.

For Cary, for me ... everyone.

I saw Setsuko leaning forward, trying to catch my eye from behind Dean's shoulder.

I looked over at her and she handed me Kleenex.

And then the melody slowed down, down, down ...

"Taps" again, the ending of it.

Then he stopped, and it seemed absolutely still for a moment.

A void of sound, but not of feeling.

Not empty, just quiet.

But it wasn't quiet, not really.

Everyone was crying. The whole place.

Dean sobbed beside me.

Setsuko was sniffling—demurely, of course.

Cary's parents had collapsed into each other in the front row, his mother quivering, his father's shoulders quaking in hard, long spasms of grief.

A man directly behind me just gave in and let go, the noise breaking out of him so deep he could have been some huge, ancient animal, lowing in pain.

The last of its kind.

Then the overhead lamps were dimmed, slowly, until there was nothing but candlelight, and the lilies' perfume, and all of us crying out, our voices in unison literally sounding the very depths of what had been lost.

A hundred people.

No, more than that.

Family, old friends from across the country. Every last person Cary had worked with, here.

And that made me draw in my breath—so sharply it whistled backward through my teeth.

Here. The person who did this is right here...

I reached for Dean's hand, gripped it hard enough that he turned to look at me.

I didn't *want* to think about Bittler. Not now.

I wanted to think about Cary. To sink into the beauty of everything being done in his honor.

He deserved that from me.

But it was over.

Lights came up from behind the rows of pews: illumination to beckon us out, pass us onward and back into the world.

People stood, started moving slowly up the crowded aisle. Not a single person making the journey alone.

They passed in twos and threes...halting, leaning against one another.

Broken.

Dean and I were lying in bed later that night. Not doing anything, but not sleeping. On our backs.

We both had our knees up, touching lightly, rocking slowly back and forth in a tender rhythm.

It had taken me another two hours to stop crying after we got home.

Now I was spent.

Dean reached for my hand, tucked his fingers through mine.

"Bunny?"

"Mmm?"

"There's something I want to ask you."

I inhaled too fast again, the air whistling.

Nothing bad, please. I don't have anything left.

"Okay," I said, squinting my eyes shut, tight enough to hurt.

"I've been offered a job."

I exhaled. Our knees rocked.

"A good one. A pretty decent promotion, actually."

His voice was too tentative.

There's a catch...

"It's a lot more money."

I waited.

"Thirty grand for a moving bonus."

Ah, there it is.

"Where?"

"Massachusetts," he said. "Watertown."

Well, okay...

"Do you have to decide right now?" I asked.

"Soon, probably."

I thought of all the places I'd lived since Dean and I first met: Williamstown, Syracuse, Pittsfield, Manhattan...

It was exhausting, just making the list in my head. And that wasn't even counting the places I'd lived *before* Dean: Manhattan, Oyster Bay, Honolulu, Carmel, Dobbs Ferry, Bronxville, Dublin, Centre Island.

We hadn't even been in Boulder for six months

yet. And if I said yes, we'd be packing up and starting from scratch again.

Ellis's mother, Glenn, always used to say, "Three moves is as good as a fire." By that reckoning, how many fires had I racked up already?

And what exactly would you miss about the place, Madeline—all those MEAN PEOPLE SUCK *bumper stickers? The triathletes? The psychic academy?*

"When would it start?" I asked.

"Not right away. Probably June, maybe later than that. Before the end of summer, though."

"We could live in Cambridge," I said.

"Wherever you want," said Dean.

And just like that, I was okay with the whole idea.

I knew people in Boston. I even had family there: Aunt Julie and Uncle Bill and their kids. We wouldn't have to start from scratch.

The girls could go to a proper school. Someplace where they wouldn't require me to show up with vegan crap when it was my turn for snack day.

Maybe we could *buy* a house.

Something cozy, and old, with nothing orange anywhere. And if there happened to be any fucking shag carpeting, I could rip the shit out.

Shred it into confetti and throw it from the windows. Have a goddamn party.

"Cambridge borders on Watertown," I said. "You might have a shorter commute to your office than you do from here to Ionix."

Dean put our hands on top of our knees. "That would be really good."

"I think you should take the job. But it would be deeply amazing if we could use some of that moving bonus to hire professional packers."

He laughed, squeezing my hand tighter.

We needed this, Dean and I.

We needed the chance to keep things good—to sustain the fresh spring blades of sweetness we'd rediscovered in one another over the last week, even in the heart of all this tragedy.

Someplace new, untarnished.

Someplace that wouldn't make me cry, the way I had been for days now—every time I thought of Cary.

And, let's be fucking honest, every time you think about yourself, Madeline.

PART IV

Let's face it. We're undone by each other. And if we're not, we're missing something. If this seems so clearly the case with grief, it is only because it was already the case with desire. One does not always stay intact.

—Judith Butler, *Undoing Gender*

44

A week had passed since Cary's service, and I was still aching.

I needed to talk to a friend. Just spill my guts.

It wasn't as though I didn't have friends. I had dozens of them, all across the country. And lots of them were people I could've just unloaded all of this shit on, without the need for any chipper I'm-holding-up-all-right-despite-everything small talk.

But no one I'd tried calling was home: Ellis, my sister Pagan, my pal Sophia, my mother, Aunt Julie...just more voice mails to leave. And it was getting a little late to be calling people on the East Coast: close to eight o'clock here meant tennish in New York and Boston.

Who in California—Muffy? Katy? They'd just be sitting down to dinner in San Francisco.

I briefly flirted with the idea of calling my first stepdad on Oahu, something I did every other year or so, but that was guaranteed to be a train-wreck. He always told me the same stories about growing up on the South Side of Chicago in the Depression and working for Edward R. Murrow after the Marine Corps, and why the world would be a better place if we'd elected McGovern in '72. That part was fine, and I even found some comfort in the sheer repetition of the anecdotes, but then he'd start bad-mouthing my mother and I didn't want to listen to that. Plus it was exhausting to hear someone else's monologue when you wanted to talk about sad shit that was happening in your own life, and he wasn't the kind of guy who'd ever think to ask me what was going on with me.

And by the time I'd run through all those options, I didn't trust myself to hold up my end of a conversation without just starting to cry and not being able to explain to the poor person on the other end of the line why I was even crying.

I looked out the window at darkened Boulder. The girls were fed, bathed, and bedded down, but Dean was still at the office.

I turned on the TV: *Roseanne* was a rerun and I

couldn't stand *Frasier* or *Home Improvement*. *The CBS Tuesday Night Movie* was *The Dead Pool*, but I didn't need any more inspiration to go all Dirty Harry on Bittler, or anyone else.

I tried Fox and decided *Iron Eagle III* looked like irredeemable shit before I'd watched a full thirty seconds, despite Lou Gossett. I gave up and turned it off altogether.

An hour to go before my weekly hit of homesick–New Yorker Sipowicz bonding on *NYPD Blue*. Maybe Dean would come home by then and we could both watch it.

I considered writing a letter or two in the meantime, then remembered Ellis giving me shit about how it was time I tried using email.

If the stuff actually worked, I might hear back from her the same night—better than leaving her yet another plaintively whiny voice mail.

Fuck it, might as well try out this virtual-communication shit.

I sat down at the big desk in Dean's office, booting up our black Acer PC.

Sure, I'd toddled online once or twice, but to me computers were still strictly for word processing—especially now that I had articles to write again, like an actual human.

I read through the handbook and tried

connecting, leaning in close to the Acer's tower when it started beeping rapidly through a phone number.

I got a dial tone and then two busy signals in a row.

I coaxed it along in my very best HAL voice. *"I'm sorry, Dave. I'm afraid I can't do that..."*

The thing finally broke through: static-fuzz squawks ending in a metallic space-age wail.

Dean had shown me how to get onto CompuServe once or twice, scrawling his ID and password on a Post-it note for me. It had been stuck to the bottom of the screen for a long time.

Then the glue gave out and I'd stuck it somewhere for safekeeping.

In a book?

I closed my eyes, trying to remember.

The Joy of Cooking. Bingo.

I went into the kitchen and grabbed it out of a cupboard.

Yeah, there it was—little slip of yellow sticking up, marking the page for a beef stew I'd never actually made.

I typed in "DeanBauer" and his password: "big-angst."

It still took me ten minutes of noodling around

before I ended up at what looked like the screen for emails.

There was a list of subject lines going down the page. Mostly things referencing filters and spares, or model numbers of the various water-quality-testing scientific instruments he was the salesman for.

There were a few I figured had to come from this Saudi customer he'd been talking about recently, just because the syntax was so bizarrely amusing for business correspondence: "Wonderful you," "Hello!" and "So soon already we two will join in New Orleans."

I was so bored, and the body copy promised to be equally entertaining, something like the liner notes for a bootleg Bob Dylan cassette I'd once almost bought on a Hong Kong sidewalk on which the initial track's title was "Bowling in the Wind."

So, I pointed the cursor at "Wonderful You" and double-clicked.

The opening line read, "Oh my sugar dearest…"

The closing, "From your best fluffy kitten, Set-suko."

Bracketed between was the bitch's gushing thank-you note to my husband for their first-ever fuck. "Now you have taught me how to love, and this first of times with you has been like no other time, no other man. All of my dreams of what it could be, only so much sweeter, so much better."

It was dated March 9, the morning after my birthday. Which meant they'd been fucking for the very first time the night before, which pretty much explained why Dean hadn't bothered calling home to wish me any happy returns of the day.

That wasn't the end of it. I kept reading—not everything, just skipping randomly forward.

That hideous email, then the ones before it, then the ones after.

What had *really* been going on in my marriage since we'd moved here, with me so naively oblivious.

The last message was Dean's thank-you note to Setsuko. For taking him out to dinner with her father.

In Tokyo.

The three of them had dined on *toro* and Kobe beef at what was apparently a very elegant restaurant.

"Ski-trip vacation" my ass. The skanky bitch had flown to Japan so she could ball my husband's sorry brains out on her home turf.

*   *   *

Most transitions in anyone's life happen gradually. You can look back and see all the tiny little increments leading up to whatever it is that's going to shift into something different.

And then there are things that happen at one specific instant, huge and irrevocably sudden as your car doing a 360 into the parkway median after you hit a patch of black ice, when a split second before all you worried about was remembering to buy eggs and milk at the little market on your way home.

I stared at the computer screen, at that email, and watched everything I thought was my life writhing like that old Tacoma Narrows Bridge, the entire span undulating to bits for the delectation of newsreel cameras.

Steel and concrete aren't supposed to do that. Rows of streetlights are not supposed to whip and saw like buoys marking the progress of gale-force surf.

This wasn't a knife through my heart, this was full-body evisceration by the fucking Benihana dinner show—flying cleavers and all.

I ran from the room exactly the way that psychic guy had run from me, straight for the downstairs bathroom, and puked up what felt like everything in my being: the crusts of the quesadillas I'd made for the girls' dinner, hope and faith and trust, all of it, right down to the last acid mouthful of yolk-yellow bile.

I stayed there in the dark for another five minutes, wrapped around the toilet's chilly curves, my head heavy on my forearm. Water frothed into the cistern until the float rose to the top, then it was all quiet but for my breath and the metallic tinkling of icy snowfall outside, making everything white and soft and uniform.

I didn't want to get up. I just wanted to stay there forever, static—a body at rest, no expectations, no bullshit, no death, no pain.

I wanted my mom. I wanted my life back, the way it had been fifteen minutes earlier. I wanted to hit a giant fast-forward button and get through all the crap sure to come because it was all going to suck so hugely I didn't want to *begin* even imagining it.

I got to my feet, wobbly, and walked back to the laundry room desk to call Dean's direct line at the office.

When he picked up, I said, "You need to come home right now."

"I can't, Bunny. I still have a ton of work to do."

Those words hung between us for a long moment.

"I just read Setsuko's emails, Dean. And yours back to her."

Silence, then. I could hear the clock on his desk ticking. "Bunny—"

"Get your ass home," I said. "Right goddamn *now*."

Getting home would take him at least twenty minutes, so while I waited I read the rest of the electronic love notes. First all of Setsuko's to him, then his to her.

He'd written her the night after I'd taken him to the dentist for a root canal four weeks ago. I'd had to help him upstairs to bed because he was so unsteady on his feet from the anesthesia.

I remembered how heavy his arm had been, across my shoulders, as I pulled him up each step. I'd tucked him in, brought him a cup of tea from downstairs, smoothed his hair back from his forehead gently until I thought he'd fallen safely asleep.

"I spent the whole afternoon in bed," he'd written to her that night, "gliding along on opiate wings, thinking of nothing but how beautiful and sweet and perfect you are. How much I wanted to be with you, then and there. Kissing every inch of your silken belly."

Silken. Belly.

Those words Dean's fist, splitting my flesh starburst-ragged, smashing through the vulnerable skin-muscle-organs exposed just beneath the apex of my sternum's gothic arch and straight on back to my spine.

The slight force of a sob was enough to topple me forward, cheek against my knees, arms reaching tight around my legs.

I could never match Setsuko's perfection. She was exotic, a long-limbed Weston nude draped graceful across the snowy pasture of some expensive hotel's bed linen.

Excruciating detail: soft hank of my husband's wheat-blond hair falling forward, soft against her skin as the tip of his tongue limned her golden curves, her concavities.

I stood up and walked slowly through the dining room.

I had always been less lightning rod for entropy than child of diaspora—translucent and porous, eminently discardable.

I curled up in the dark on our sofa, watching yellow headlights slow-dance across the ceiling.

A car pulled up out front, some time afterward.

Its engine coughed out and a tinny door-slam echoed through the night. The rhythm of my husband's footsteps coming up our snowy front walk was reluctant, defeated.

Pure delusion on my part, having held so much as the slenderest belief that this marriage could sustain my fragile purchase on thin air.

In truth I'd crashed out of the sky a good twenty years before Dean and I first met.

I could still hear my escaping father's wing-strokes, his steady cadence unperturbed as I shot headlong toward the wine-dark Icarian Sea, trailing feathers and wax.

"Bunny?" Dean stepped softly into the darkened living room.

He's been crying.

"Here," I said from the sofa, still on my side, curled fetal. "Come sit?"

He lowered himself to the floor, resting a hand on the cushion's edge beside my head. "I'm so sorry."

Kissing every inch of your silken belly.

The perfumed concubine—burnished, cosseted, flawless.

I couldn't stand my own exhausted belly in the mirror: the baby-slack skin, stretched and stretched by the girls until it had been crosshatched permanently pink.

I closed my eyes. "How long?"

"The whole—" His voice caught.

I held my breath.

He covered his face with his hands. "Before we even left New York. Just...talking on the phone. We knew."

And of course only that first "we" meant Dean and me.

I remembered Cary calling me from the office on Valentine's Day, saying Dean was crushed because I'd winced when he kissed me that morning. The girls had been up all night in shifts. I'd shrugged him off, bitching, so tired my skin hurt.

And Cary had been so gentle with me on the phone, so patient: "You really need to call him, okay? I'm serious."

He'd known. He'd tried to protect me that morning and it made me miss him more than ever.

And that's what lay behind his declaration to me in the car, the day Dean had been such a pig at lunch. Cary hadn't been railing against that specific incident, Dean's little tantrum...he'd taken up arms on my behalf because he knew the whole of it, the ocean of betrayal I hadn't yet known I was drowning in.

He'd made Dean read my article that afternoon,

confronted him about who-knows-what else, stood up for me—even though I'd begged him not to.

And it had worked. What seemed like our new beginning, Dean's and mine, had started that night.

Tears started leaking down my face again. "Dean?"

"What, Bunny?" His voice so soft, his fingertips brushing so lightly against my hair.

"Is this why you want the job in Boston?"

He dropped his head. "Yeah."

I unfurled my legs and reached for him, pulling him onto the sofa beside me.

We curled up in each other's arms.

I felt his mouth against my ear. "I'm so sorry."

"I'm so glad you didn't leave us," I whispered back.

I had no idea what else to say. It was all I could think of, at that moment.

He was still here, with me and the girls. He wanted to leave Colorado, which meant leaving Setsuko. He'd already put the end of things with her in motion.

Even though he'd had dinner with her father. The three of them, laughing and drinking, treating themselves to whatever they wanted. And my husband had had the gall to call me from the fucking restaurant so he could crow about how great the Kobe beef was. The same day Cary was killed.

The images I couldn't help but conjure forth ripped me open, laid me bare and ugly and cold. Do you agree to meet the father of the woman you're about to abandon? Do you write a fucking thank-you note, telling her what a marvelous fucking time you had?

He hasn't left you. Not yet.

Was his recent kindness nothing more than the death throes of my husband's sense of duty? Not to a lover, but to the ruined, shabby vessel who'd borne his children? I was not the beloved, just the obligation to which he considered himself beholden.

I pulled myself up off the sofa and ran for the bathroom, sickened by the image of myself as I imagined he saw me.

There was still so much bile in my soul, so much acid. Maybe that's all I had *ever* been made of. Maybe that's why no one had ever wanted to stay. Dad through Dean—every stepfather, then every lover I'd had myself between the bookending pair of them: father-and-husband.

What did you expect? You've never been worth sticking around for, Madeline, and you never will be.

*   *   *

Dean fell asleep easily in our bed.

I lay awake, trying to cleanse my mind of his dalliances with Setsuko. Tried instead to think of us, to cast back through our years together for some evidence this outcome *wasn't* inevitable, or at least hadn't always been.

When I think back to that night, now—many years later—I wonder if a woman who thought *anything* of herself would have shared his bed that night.

Even though I know the answer: *No fucking way.*

But at the time I was as terrified that he'd slip away from me as I was repulsed by the depth of his unkindness.

I wanted my best friend back. But he was lost somewhere in the body of this person who'd just about finished me off, on top of everything else.

I stared up at the ceiling, watching tree-branch shadows shift, then grow still.

I tried to remember what it felt like, before this. At the beginning.

And all I could recall was that it had just felt like sanity, at the start—compared with the way my parents lived.

Now, as a parent myself, I could see that *they'd*

been absolute children. Married when they were ten years younger than I was that night: people who'd never been prepared for the world they'd actually have to inhabit, even before the ground dropped out from under their feet in the late sixties.

When I met Dean he just seemed solid, dependable, kind. No game-playing, no jerking my heart around.

He met my father and sister on our third date: a Dare family gathering Dad had driven east to attend.

We ended up sitting on the bed in the back of my father's van—me and Pagan, Dad and Dean—smoking some wicked sinsemilla of Dad's and getting so fucking stoned we were all pretty much paralyzed.

Then Dad whipped out *another* joint and said, "Okay, that was Brand X, and now you have to smoke some of this Brand Y, because it's the antidote," and meanwhile his seven surviving siblings were doing their various Brahmin-Lockjaw-Social-Register insanity dances around the place.

But Dean just rolled with it, that whole long weekend. He observed, he took us in with gentle but wry humor, he shared some fine insights about the whole spectacle with me—but most of all, he had my back.

I had a fine, tall, upstanding young man as my ally. For the first time ever, I'd achieved gravity within my own paternal family. A foothold. *Meaning.*

I had shown up with someone who commanded their respect. Which meant they had to rethink *me.* They couldn't exclude me from the clan's constellation, couldn't write me off as poor relation, abandoned child, unwanted daughter, un-dowried exemplar of the chattel gender.

It had always seemed to me that my family was like some too-closely-bred line of show dogs, neurasthenic and plagued with iron-poor blood, a tribe composed entirely of Northern-Puritan Tennessee Williams characters with double the crazy and none of the sultry charm.

Then along came this young strapping guy with the vitality of a line on the upswing. And I hoped he was someone who wouldn't leave me broke with kids and no protection by the side of the road somewhere—because I knew full well that in that situation I wouldn't have a shred of my mom's surprisingly feral toughness; that in her shoes I'd flame out entirely.

She'd had three kids in total with her first two husbands, then taken in a pal of ours as a foster child. No alimony, no child support after I'd turned eight, but she'd kept a roof over our heads and food on the table and gotten all four of us into college.

Dean twitched in his sleep, beside me. Falling through some dream.

I thought about the first time he'd come to see me in Williamstown. I'd been crashing on Ellis's dorm room floor since just after Christmas, that year, but it was spring break and she was in LA and the college locked up all the buildings over vacations.

A barroom pal of ours had paid four weeks' rent on an unfurnished room in this wretched boardinghouse for old drunk men, across the street from the Women's Exchange thrift store on the scariest street in the entire Berkshires, but he couldn't stand it after two nights and offered it up to me.

I didn't have a phone, and I was working for a construction crew—sanding Sheetrock all day in these condos on the edge of town. Four bucks an hour.

Dean called me on the condo's office phone Friday morning, saying he planned to leave East Syracuse on his Harley around one. We'd figured it would take him four hours to reach me, but there was a blizzard.

The crew's boss knew how much I'd been looking forward to Dean's visit all week, and he felt awful for me, sure there was no way a guy on a motorcycle could make it through that weather in early March.

So the boss told me he'd buy me a lobster dinner to cheer me up. He was a very sweet older man, avuncular (though he was also the coke wholesaler for half the county, driving in big counts from the Cape every other week).

I thanked him and said I'd take him up on it if Dean didn't show, but that I had to go back to my scuzzy room with the single bare bulb hanging from its ceiling just in case my beau managed to slog through.

So I went back to the boardinghouse and sat on my single mattress on the floor and waited.

The room was tall, its hideous wallpaper browned and peeling. The only furniture in it was six wire milk crates I'd stolen from Price Chopper to use as a bureau, an old silk-lined leather makeup case with a mirror inside its lid, and the aforementioned mattress.

No one in their right mind would dare piss in the shared bathroom down the hall, much less look behind its shower stall's rancid curtain.

The whole place smelled sharply of mildew, raw bourbon, and the two-weeks-abandoned fried egg shriveling on a tin plate just outside my door, in the communal kitchenette's sink.

I'd bought a vanilla-scented Air Wick to combat the stench, and to this day the slightest whiff of that fakey-sweet fragrance makes me break out in a pulp-novel death-row-inmate sweat.

I spent a lot of time thinking about my prospects as I waited, staring at the bare bulb's entirely too noose-like shadow on the wall across from me.

I was twenty-two years old, had left college three credits shy of graduation, and wasn't welcome in my mother's boyfriend's waterfront nine-acre estate on the Gold Coast of Long Island, or the VW camper in which my father had slept for the last thirteen years in the wild brown canyons north of Malibu.

Other than the mattress and the milk crates, I owned somebody's father's discarded tweed overcoat, a shitload of secondhand books, some crappy clothes, a rusting orange 1976 Volkswagen Rabbit, and your basic cheap seat at the lip of the abyss.

I'd failed at everything, even school, and now I was going to work at minimum-wage jobs forever.

But Dean did slog through that storm. It took him nine hours. He was soaked through to the skin, shaking from cold, blue-lipped and starting to get feverish.

I peeled his frigid sodden clothes off, layer by layer: motorcycle boots, quilted Carhartt coveralls, flannel-lined jeans, two insulated plaid work shirts, long underwear, and three pairs of white socks.

I toweled him off and made him get under the covers of my pallet on the floor, hung his clothes carefully over the spitting radiator, and climbed into bed beside him to twine my legs and arms tight as I could around his trembling body.

And so that night in Williamstown I also had Dean, to whom I mattered enough that nine hours of fishtailing through snowy, sleeting darkness had proved no obstacle.

Maybe I'd survived all the crazy and things were going to turn out okay, you know?

We didn't have a grand unsettling passion but something even better: A union we both took pride in. The commencement of our actual lives.

I heard a car drive slowly by out on Mapleton Street. One of the girls cooed down the hall, but settled back into quiet.

Dean turned over again in his sleep, murmuring something I was terrified to hear. Setsuko's name? A paean to her loveliness? To her lips around his cock?

I wanted to kill him—beat him and kick him and break his teeth and his bones and then twist his head around on his neck until I'd finished him, until every last sinew of the man who'd fathered my children was shredded and useless and suitably punished.

And I wanted to beg his forgiveness for every fault I'd ever had. Promise I could make myself perfect, that I'd never ask for anything again, never *need* another thing from him.

I wanted to do anything it took—*anything*—to keep for my daughters the loving father they deserved. So worth it, sacrificing myself utterly on a maternal-suttee pyre to ensure they'd never have to grow up broken and damaged and bereft and so unbearably goddamn *sad*...never have to feel the enormity of suffering by which I was being consumed in that moment.

Never have to become what *I* was.

And oh, *God*, I wanted Dean to save me, still.

I drew my knees up to my chest and hugged them tight, trying to hold the pieces of myself together—aligned, at least, if not intact.

45

I had thirty seconds of grace when I woke up the next morning—the tiniest moment of not-remembering before the golem of pain climbed back on, smashing its full weight into my chest repeatedly while it choked me, laughing its golem-y ass off.

I was being sodomized by my own life.

And not the fun kind of sodomy, either.

I wondered if actually opening my eyes might improve things, so I tried it.

Rumpled absence where Dean had been, cold to the touch.

For all I knew he was downstairs on the computer, telling Setsuko what a drag I was, the pair of them plotting out how to ditch me for their next session of hot monkey love.

Which for some reason engendered in me less anger at my faithless husband than a sudden all-consuming white-hot desire to whack his insipid strumpet as hard as I could full in the simpering, prissy, prettily golden fucking face with the flat of a heavy shovel.

Repeatedly.

Afterward I'd make Dean look, gripping his head from behind so he couldn't shy away.

"Go ahead," I'd whisper, tracing his ear's delicate rim with the tip of my tongue, hot and slick. "Try fucking her *now.*"

Hey, a girl can dream.

And the skanky bitch deserved it.

Not least for having convinced me to leave her alone in my house, watching over my children.

I found Dean downstairs in the kitchen. He was just standing backlit at the window, looking out. The girls were still asleep in their cribs.

I couldn't step over the threshold, couldn't muster the will to move another inch forward.

Maybe I'd fall down, right there in the door frame. Maybe I'd disintegrate, every numb atom of my being whirling away into some welcome void, nothing left but the fistful of salt grains and ashes that had once been my tiny black heart.

They'd sift slowly to the floor—spirals of glitter and smoke, serendipity tossed from Charon's decks at departure—making a tiny, negligible pile that was worthless as I had been.

I choked on that thought, some willful noise trying to fight its way out of my throat.

Dean turned around and started walking toward me without a word. He took me in his arms, fingers of his left hand snaking up into the locks of hair at the nape of my neck so he could press my cheek to his chest. Tenderly.

I could hear his heartbeat. *Feel* it.

I closed my eyes again and wept, trying with all my strength to keep from making a sound, to keep from betraying myself with the smallest hint of motion, or of breath.

"Shhhh, Bunny," he whispered. "Shhhhhhhh."

"I don't know how to do this…," I said, "survive it. I *can't*. I don't know what to do and it all just hurts so much. Too much."

"You don't have to *know* anything," he said, kissing the top of my head. "You don't have to *do* anything. Not a single thing. It's all right. It's over. We're all right."

I shook my head, slight range of movement

between the broad plain of his hand, the solid shield of his chest. "You don't—"

"What?" he asked, lips brushing the top of my head again. The part in my hair.

"Love me."

"Don't believe that. Don't think it."

"Not—"

He waited, and when I couldn't say anything more, asked, "Not *what*?"

"Like her," I said. "Not the way you love *her*."

Dean bent his knees, just a little. "Put your arms around my neck."

"No."

He lifted them himself, pressing them to curve around his neck one at a time, so gently.

"Open your legs," he whispered. "Just a little."

I did.

He cupped his hands under my ass and lifted me, no effort at all.

"Wrap them around my waist," he said.

I did.

"Tighter," he said. "Tilt your pelvis up."

I shook my head against his neck.

"Yes," he said. "I want to feel you."

So I did.

"Cross your ankles behind my back," he said. "Tight."

I did.

"Like that," he said. "Just like that."

And he carried me *just like that* across the next two rooms.

When he reached the sofa, he lowered himself down. Slowly, not letting me go, until my ass was resting on the middle cushion and he was down on his knees before me.

He bent forward until my back touched the pillows behind me, then he took my arms down from around his neck.

"You are the most honorable woman I have ever known," he said.

I looked up into his eyes.

"You are my wife. You are the mother of our beautiful daughters."

I waited.

"That means so much to me," he said. "It means the world."

I looked down at our clasped hands.

"The most courageous woman. The most admirable."

I wriggled against him, just a little bit.

"I'm awed by your strength, and your kindness."

Tell me I'm pretty.

"When I look at you, Bunny—"

Tell me I get you hard.

"I see a woman I don't deserve."

I shut my eyes.

It was like listening to a total stranger describe the Statue of fucking Liberty. Some bronze paragon in a goddamn toga, seen from the deck of the Staten Island Ferry.

Neither his lover, nor beloved—merely the embodiment of some principle he liked to imagine himself upholding, or, better yet, *defending*.

Because that's what decent men did.

And Dean was still utterly convinced he was a decent man, so this was an occasion to feel really, *really* good about himself.

For being so fucking decent.

"I am absolutely dedicated to our marriage," he continued. "With all my heart."

Tell me I'm better in bed than she is.

"I'm dedicated to our family—"

Tell me she's not hotter, and tighter, and wetter.

"I'm dedicated to the girls—"

Tell me you never think of her when you're fucking me, because I'm the best you've ever had—so good there's no room for anyone else in your head.

"To our future—"

Tell me she could never get you off the way I do. That you love my mouth and my tits and my ass. That

you love how I feel when you're sunk all the way in.
That you can't wait to taste me again.

"I will never again do anything to jeopardize what we have. It's too precious. I admire you too much."

We'd been in the same position for what, five minutes now? He'd carried me across the entire house with all my weight bearing down on the juncture of my pussy and his belly.

And the point of contact had moved lower on him when he'd laid me down on the sofa: the full length of his cock now pressed against the core of me.

Soft.

So limp one might think he possessed no genitals at all.

I twitched again. A bit of grind.

Nothing.

I looked up into his eyes.

He'd started to fucking cry.

"Everything Setsuko loved about me—"

Loves.

"Every single *thing* was something I'd learned from you. Something you taught me. The way I dress—"

He choked on that, couldn't finish voicing the thought.

Tell me you think I'm pretty.

Go ahead, lie.

I deserve that much.

"What was I supposed to do?" he said, sobbing. "A beautiful woman in her twenties fell in love with me…what was I supposed to *do*?"

I'm only thirty-goddamn-two.

I shoved him away from me, sitting straight up.

"What were you supposed to *do*?" I hissed.

He covered his face with his hands.

"You were *supposed* to keep your dick in your pants, Dean. Bring it home to your goddamn wife unbesmirched by the slime in your trollop's malicious, *conniving* little cunt."

I shoved him away from me.

His back hit the edge of the coffee table, wrenching it across the carpet.

It was made of solid cherry, my uncle Hunt's wedding present to us both.

My uncle had built it himself: planed its planks smooth, joined them seamlessly, rubbed beeswax into the grain until it glowed, warm and red.

Inset at its center was a bronze plaque that had once graced the brick wall encircling the lushness of my grandparents' no-longer-extant rose garden.

Dean and I had been married there. Standing on a pathway of bricks my great-great-grandfather had made out of Centre Island clay. Surrounded by a hundred friends.

I'd been the tenth generation to live there. The last.

"I'm sorry," my husband said. "I'm so *sorry*."

He sank down in front of me, ass dropping to rest on his heels.

He covered his face once more.

Penitent. Sobbing.

"You were supposed to be *kind*," I said, yanking his hands down. "*That's* what you were supposed to do, you worthless piece of shit."

"Bunny—" He couldn't even look at me.

"*That's* what you were supposed to do," I said.

I got to my feet.

Left him there.

Went upstairs to gather our daughters in my arms.

46

Bunny—"

I was back downstairs and Dean had followed me into the kitchen.

"It's over," he said. "I've ended it. Everything."

"When would *that* have been, Dean?" I said. "While the two of you were having dinner with her father in Tokyo, yukking it the day Cary fucking *died*?"

I lowered Parrish and India to the floor. Got up. Turned around to face him.

He went pale.

"Or maybe it was last night," I said, "when you had so much *work* to do at the office?"

He didn't answer that.

"Tell me, Dean. Was she sitting on your lap

when I called, or did you have her bent over your desk with her little pink panties yanked down?"

He turned red, then.

"Or maybe she was kneeling on the floor in front of you, sucking you off with that prissy little mouth."

"I'd never do that . . . I never *did*."

"Never did *what*, Dean? Let her blow you? Give me a fucking break."

"I made a point of not *ever* taking time away from you and the girls to be with her. Not once. Setsuko understood."

"How very thoughtful of you both," I said. "How *touching*."

He stood there, staring at me.

"*What?*" I said.

"I have to go to work."

"Yeah, I bet you do. I just *bet*."

"Bunny, it's over."

I crossed my arms.

"I ended it the morning of Cary's funeral," he said. "When I took the girls out in the wagon. I asked her to meet me at Pearl Street. By the sand pit they like to play in."

I thought I might puke again. "You took our *daughters*—"

"So she'd know I meant it. So she wouldn't try to—"

So she wouldn't try to fuck you.

Because you wouldn't have turned her down.

He dropped his head. "I wanted to show her *why*. That I was serious. Make her remember what was most important to me. What *mattered* more to me than she did, than she ever could. Parrish and India—"

Not me. Never me.

"Bunny," he said, sidling up to me. "Don't cry. *Please* don't cry . . . it's killing me—"

"You can't even—"

"What?"

I just looked at him, so empty. So goddamn sad.

"What, Bunny? Tell me. Tell me anything you want to say."

"You can't even *lie*, right now?"

"I'm not lying."

And then I wasn't crying anymore. "You can't pretend you ended it because *I* mattered to you, even a little?"

"Oh, my God, that's *not* what I—"

"You couldn't have tried to make me believe for one second that *I* crossed your mind at all, in any of this?"

"Bunny, of *course* you—"

"Too late," I said. "Too fucking late."

"That's not true. That's not how I feel about you."

"You've told me *exactly* how you feel about me: I'm kind and courageous and admirable. I'm the mother of your children. I'm the fucking Statue of Liberty, and you're the goddamn huddled masses, yearning to breathe free."

"You're more than that."

"More than *what*, Dean?"

"Bunny...the way I feel about you."

"I know what you *don't* feel about me. Shall I tot *that* up for you?"

He swallowed.

"You consider me neither young nor beautiful," I said, ticking down two fingers in turn. "You do not spend afternoons in bed drifting along...oh, gee...how did you put it? Something about opiate wings, 'thinking of nothing but how beautiful and sweet and perfect you are'? And you certainly don't yearn to 'kiss every inch of my silken belly.' Does that about sum it up?"

"Don't do this," he said.

"Do what, Dean? Let you know that I'm *perfectly* cognizant of how little you care for me?"

"Bunny—"

"Do you remember the last time you told me I looked pretty, Dean?"

He hung his head.

"Because I do," I said. "It was two years ago."

"Jesus, Bunny—"

"Want me to tell you the exact day, and where we were? Because I remember that, too."

"Don't be ridiculous. Of course you're pretty, you shouldn't need me to tell you—"

"Go to your office," I said. "You're not doing either of us a lick of good here."

He got on his knees. "Bunny, what can I do?"

"Christ, Dean. You could start with making a goddamn *effort*. A little lip service, at the very least."

"I don't understand. I don't know what you *want*."

"What if the roles were reversed, here, Dean?"

"How do you mean?"

"Really? You need me to fucking *explain* it to you?"

"Please," he said. "Help me out. Tell me what I can do."

"What would you want to hear if you found out I'd been fucking some hot younger guy?"

His mouth got tight.

"Sneaking around behind your back," I said. "Exchanging filthy secret emails and phone calls. Meeting up with him whenever you're out of town. Plotting how to get away from you, pull the wool over your eyes, steal time for the pair of us to lavish on balling each other raw... What would you want me to say, right now, if you'd had to read *my* emails about what he did to me, what I'd done to him?"

He didn't say a word.

"Let's say he's better at it—better than you ever were, even when you *did* bother. And he *loves* knowing that he's fucking your wife, behind your back. Making a fool of you gets him off. Gets us *both* off."

Dean's face went cold and he turned his head away from me.

"And let's say I spend all day, *every* day, thinking about how I'm going to get more of that. Where he's going to take me next...*how*. What I'm going to do to him. How much *better* it's going to be than when I have to throw you a mercy fuck, back home."

Lick it up, you piece of shit. Every word.

"I'm thinking about him when I cook you dinner, Dean, and when I ask you how your day was, and when I straighten your tie. But you have no goddamn idea, because you're so goddamn stupid and trusting. You can't imagine me doing that, *any* of it. And then you find out. Everything. Every last detail."

His jaw was clenched.

"You think that can't happen, Dean? You think it *hasn't*, already?"

"Bunny, I don't—"

"You don't *know*. And you never would, not unless I wanted you to. Because I'm better at secrets than you are, Dean. Trust me, I kick your sorry ass in that department. Always have."

"What are you trying to say?"

"I'm telling you what you just told me you wanted to *know*, Dean. What you should be doing, right now, to make this up to me. Think about everything I've said, you fucking asshole."

Now I was pissing him off.

"Then think about what you'd want me to say to *you*," I said, "once you'd found out. After I'd ripped away everything you thought you could trust in this marriage. After I'd made you feel like nothing. Like shit. After I told you I'd broken it off with him for the sake of the *children*, dragging them along when we met in public so I wouldn't be tempted to fuck him again, right on the spot. Only I *would* be tempted. Damn *right* I would. Wet for it. Hungry and aching."

He flared his nostrils.

"What would you want me to tell *you*, Dean, to make it go down easier. What lies would cushion the blow? Fake you out so I could keep on fucking him every chance I got—because *I* wouldn't give it up. Wouldn't be able to settle for *you*, afterward."

"I'd want you to tell me you love me. I love *you*, Bunny."

"You're full of shit, Dean. You want to make it up to me? Go steal those papers Cary was looking at, the ones that probably got him killed. Make yourself goddamn useful for a change."

"You can't be serious," he said. "Of *course* I love you. You have to believe that."

"No I don't, actually. I am not required to believe another shabby, lukewarm word that comes out of your thin-lipped, self-satisfied, and parsimonious little mouth. Not now, not *ever*."

"It's true. I love you."

"Fuck you, Dean. And fuck the candy-ass low-rent betrayal of a wagon train you rode in on."

I started walking out of the kitchen.

"Bunny!"

"Up the ass," I said, loud enough so he'd be sure to hear me without my having to turn back and look at him. "Up the ass with a goddamn *chain saw*."

The only answer to that was the back door, slamming.

Good.

47

I got the girls out of their seats and put them in the playpen.

It was eight in the morning, seven in California. I sat down in the kitchen doorway and called my mother.

I didn't even wait for her to say hello, just said, "Mom?" and started weeping.

"Madeline, what's happened?"

I gulped down a raggedy breath. "Um, Dean's been fucking his secretary? Since we moved to Boulder?"

I heard her breath catch. "That *asshole*."

"Yeah."

"I'm so sorry. Oh, you poor *thing*."

I couldn't really speak. It was all I could do not

to get snot on the phone. I swiped my shirtsleeve across my nose. Then I got all hiccupy, trying to breathe.

"Oh, Madeline..."

"I just...I don't..."

"Shhhh," she said. "Just take a breath. It's okay."

And then I mewled, "Mummie? This...is so... *awful*..."

"Do you want me to come there?"

Yes. Instantly. Put me to bed and bring me soup and toast.

"I don't...," I said. "Not right now. But maybe in a little bit? I have no idea what I'm doing."

"You let me know. I can come. Anytime."

"Thank you."

And we were quiet for a minute. Just breathing together.

Well, okay, she breathed, I was all weepy and shit.

Finally I said, "Mom?"

"What?"

"Is it ever going to feel okay again?"

"Jesus," she said. "I just want to *kick* him."

"I love you. And I would love to have you kick him. And I should go. At least grab some toilet paper and blow my nose."

"Call me again whenever you want."

"Okay," I said.

And we hung up.

I tried lying down in the playpen with the girls but I just kept crying and I worried my utter self-loathing would somehow leach into the air and taint them or something, so I checked their diapers and called Ellis.

"Hey," I said when she picked up, "are you sitting down?"

"I can if you want me to. What's up?"

"Dean's having an affair."

"That loathsome, ungrateful, unworthy, uncouth, hideously repulsive piece of *shit*," she said. "Who's he fucking? Want me to shoot him? Want me to shoot *her*?"

"Exactly. His secretary. Yes, and yes," I said. "Not necessarily in that order."

"What the fuck is *wrong* with him?"

"What's wrong with *me*?" I said, and started crying again.

"Oh, sweetie, no no no no *no*. You are not allowed to think anything about this at *all* except that your husband deserves to die a lingering death. Preferably of something venereal and incredibly painful, involving weeping abscesses and the pissing of acridly painful blood. Except not something he could possibly infect you with, of course, and then the bitch he's fucking should have her twat fall out in front of lots and *lots* of people before it crawls away into a storm drain and gets swept out to sea. That *asshole*."

I sniffed, loading my other cuff up with snot. "That's just what Mom said."

"Deserves to die a lingering death or the thing about the storm drain?"

"Actually, she just said, 'that *asshole*.' She wants to kick him. And fly here."

"Excellent. You should let her do both."

"Not today," I said. "Today I just want to feel sorry for myself and loll around and get snot on everything."

"Don't be an idiot," she said. "Free babysitting. Naptime. Someone to glare at your repugnant shit-for-brains husband so you don't have to."

"Tempting," I said.

"I repeat: Don't be an idiot. Call her back, tell her to get on a plane."

"I'd have to clean."

"Make Dean do it. That *asshole*."

"I just...I feel like I don't have any skin left. And I feel so *ugly*."

"Shut the fuck up," she said. "You're gorgeous. Like I-*hate*-you-for-being-so-fucking-gorgeous gorgeous."

"Ellis?"

"What?"

"She's, like, twenty…and Japanese and shit. And a neat freak. And I let her *babysit*."

"Oh, *ewwww*. What was he, taken over by some giant alien pod creature? Fucking a twenty-year-old *neat* freak? That's just embarrassing. For *him*. I'm disappointed in our friend Dean. I thought he'd picked up some taste from you, at the very least. That *asshole*."

"And she probably gives way…better…*head* than me," I said, suddenly all sobby again.

"Dude, no fucking *way*. Categorically."

"Yeah, right, like you'd have any idea."

"Actually, I've heard reports. And even the, um, *French* judge gave you a ten."

"No shit?"

"None," she said. "You were the talk of campus."

"You have just really, really cheered me up."

"Hey, what are friends for?"

"Telling you you give decent head, apparently."

"Oh, *shit*," she said.

"What?"

"Perry just ran over the neighbor's cat with his Big Wheel."

"Harsh," I said.

I heard a wincing intake of breath, then an "*Oooo…*"

"Don't tell me," I said. "He backed over it, just to make sure?"

"Exactly."

"I'll let you go. You totally rock."

"Not as much as you. I'll call you later..."

And with that, she was gone.

I picked myself up off the floor, looked in the bathroom mirror, and decided to put ice cubes on my eyes.

My husband still sucked, but my women had made me feel better.

Much better.

The phone rang.

It was Ellis.

"Listen," she said. "There's nothing wrong with you a shot of bourbon and a smoking hot seventeen-year-old lifeguard named Bruno can't fix."

"Sven," I said.

"I keep forgetting you like 'em blond..."

"Damn straight. Surfer boys, from way back. Dumber the better."

"I think stupid's pretty much the only flavor they come in, Madeline."

"You'd be surprised. Those boys come all *kinds* of ways."

"Atta girl," she said.

I was about to ask her if the neighbor's cat had survived, but she'd hung up on me.

Time for Parrish and India to have a little nap.

They actually went to sleep, which surprised me, considering how little we'd actually done that morning.

I thought about going to sleep myself, then put on makeup instead.

And then I called Mimi at work.

"My husband is fucking his secretary," I said, the minute she picked up.

No preamble, no salutation.

"How can I help?" she asked.

"Give me something to do. Something that *matters*."

At which point I was tempted to fucking cry again. Which just pissed me off.

"God*damn* it," I said, pinching the bridge of my nose. "I am so sick of crying."

"You're going to survive this," she said. "I promise you."

"Whether I want to or not."

She laughed at that. "I'm going to call you back in about an hour. I have to think a few things over—about what I could use your help with."

"And we're still pretending not to know each other?"

"Yes," she said. "That part holds a hundred percent."

"So this is going to be remote, then. Clandestine."

"Goddamn right," she said. "I'm going to *make* you survive, if it's the last thing I do."

"Awesome. I always wanted to be a spy chick when I grew up."

"Go drink some bourbon, Harriet," she said. "First step to getting your mojo back."

I'd just replaced the phone in its cradle when the front doorbell rang.

I glanced out the living room windows. There was a florist's van, parked out front—FTD's Hermes logo danced across its side panel.

I stepped into the hallway and opened the front door.

"Delivery for Madeline Dare?"

Young guy. Blond. *Delicious.*

I considered asking whether he'd join me for a glass of bourbon. Upstairs.

When he'd left I stuck my face into the bouquet and inhaled. Not much fragrance, but of course I read the card.

You are beautiful. You matter more to me than anything, or anyone, ever could. I love you.
　　　　　　　　　　　—Intrepid Spouse

A start.

I dialed the main number at his office.

Setsuko answered, of course. "Ionix. Good morning, how may I help you?"

"Good morning to *you*, Setsuko."

Sharp little intake of breath, on her end of the line.

"I'd like to speak to my husband, please," I said. "To thank him for the beautiful, beautiful roses he just had delivered."

Silence, on her end.

"So thoughtful, don't you think?" I asked. "He knows the red ones have always been my favorite—and three *dozen* of them, isn't that sweet? I'm hoping he'll come home for lunch, so I can thank him properly. I think he'd enjoy that, don't *you*, Setsuko?"

Silence.

I listened to her breathe.

Shallow little puffs, like she was trying not to cry.

I waited, twining the phone cord around the base of my fingers—tighter and tighter until they turned white and felt all sparkly, wishing I had the cord wrapped around her swan-like fucking neck instead.

"Are you all right, Setsuko? You sound a little…

upset. I certainly hope you're being treated well at work?"

"Please hold," she said.

And, oh . . . that little catch in her voice was gorgeous. So very, very sweet.

"This is Dean Bauer."

"They're beautiful," I said. "And what you wrote is lovely."

"I'm glad you think so."

"Come home for lunch?"

Just the briefest hesitation. "Of course, Bunny. I'd love to."

I still had time to take the girls to the child care center and get back before Mimi was due to call, if I hauled serious ass.

I didn't particularly want to try seducing their father while Parrish and India looked on from the playpen.

48

The phone was ringing as I was hauling ass back up onto the porch, breathless from racing the wagon uphill and running back down again without it.

I slammed the front door wide open and sprinted inside, diving for the phone, snatching up the receiver. "Hello?"

"Madeline, I was about to give up," said Mimi.

"Sorry," I said. "I just ran the girls up to this babysitting place. Dean's coming home for lunch."

"Good for you," she laughed.

"What's the good word, *chère* Mimi? I take it you've thought of a task for me?"

"Yes, grasshopper."

"Do tell…pretend to let Bittler stalk me, until

he steps onto the mat of native grasses I've craftily woven to camouflage a pit full of punji sticks?"

"I wouldn't recommend that," she said.

"Oh, come on, I bet I'd be *excellent* at getting stalked. And weaving grass mats."

"I need to see that paperwork. The stuff your friend Cary was looking into."

"What a coincidence," I said. "I asked Dean to make Xeroxes only this morning. With any luck he'll bring them home for lunch as a peace offering."

"Tell him to be careful. Maybe he should do it after hours."

"I will, if he hasn't managed it already. But I thought you were planning on a warrant, official channels and everything?"

"It's tricky. We don't want to tip anyone off just yet. This would be unofficial, just help me to dial things in a little."

"How am I going to get them to you? Meet under the old clock at midnight, I'll be the man smoking two cigarettes?"

"We'll figure something out. Give me a call this afternoon, let me know what's what, all right?"

"Bet your sweet ass," I said, hanging up.

I raced upstairs and brushed my teeth, then primped a little. Lipstick, a little perfume, different earrings.

What to wear?

A short skirt. Sheer black stockings, what the hell. Shoes with a little toe cleavage: black satin Ferragamo pumps with narrow straps cutting diagonally across my insteps, each fastened with a tiny rhinestone button.

Pointy toes, slender three-inch heels.

Ridiculous for Boulder, especially midday.

Hmmm...what else? Shirt unbuttoned to show a little *actual* cleavage.

Didn't bother with underwear. Ahem.

Then I went downstairs and made a little plate of food: pâté, raspberries, some chèvre.

Brought it to the coffee table, put it down next to the roses.

And then I sat down on the sofa to wait.

The smell of the food was really strong. I realized I hadn't eaten anything since lunch the day before.

I sure as hell wasn't hungry *now*.

I sat there for maybe ten minutes, nervous as hell.

Finally, I heard the doorknob rattle, out in the front hall.

I got up and walked toward the sound, just as Dean was letting himself in.

"Bunny," he said, putting his briefcase down on a little bench. "You look so pretty."

I stood on my tiptoes, reaching my arms up around his neck.

He kissed me, then buried his face in my neck. "And you smell good, too."

"Not nearly as good as you do," I said, unbuttoning his shirt.

He laughed. "What do I smell like?"

"Like yourself," I said, pulling his shirttails free and starting on his belt buckle. "Delicious."

Twenty minutes later, I was straddling Dean's lap on the sofa, my own shirt unbuttoned all the way, his off completely.

"I'm sorry," he said.

"What can I do?" I leaned in until my lips brushed his ear. "Anything. Tell me."

"It's not..."

"What?" I whispered.

"You're doing everything right," he said. "I *want* to. You have no idea how much."

Actually, I had a pretty damn clear idea.

I was skin-to-skin with the applause meter, after all. Which appeared to be taking the afternoon off, utterly unimpressed with the home-team talent.

"I'm sorry," he said again. "I just feel so..."

"What?"

"Guilty. Horrible. About everything."

I climbed off his lap, trying to make the exit graceful.

I moved all the way to the end of the sofa. Leaned back, closed my eyes.

"Bunny..." He scooted over toward me, ran one finger down the black lace edge of my bra, to the little bow at the center.

He bit my earlobe.

"Just stop." I shoved his hand away.

"What?"

Tears pricked at my eyes. Chunky little crystals of salt.

"*What*, Bunny?"

"This is just...embarrassing." I started buttoning my shirt.

He looked down at his dysfunctional lap. "Don't go. Please."

"Where the hell would I go? I'm a fucking house-wife. This is my fucking house. *You* should go."

"What are you *talking* about?"

"Dean, Jesus. I feel like a fucking *idiot*."

He reached for my hand, tried to pull me back down. "Bunny—"

"*Please* don't touch me."

"Why not?"

"*Because I feel like a fucking idiot*, Dean."

"Why?"

I started to goddamn cry again. "*Why*? Why do you think?"

"I have no idea."

I yanked my hand away. "Because I'm *dressed* like an idiot, all tarty and shit in thigh-highs and lipstick, and my husband can't get it up. Which would obviously be because *I'm* not the one he wants to be fucking. *That's* why. Clear enough now, or do you need flash cards?"

I kicked off my stupid shoes and ran upstairs.

I hadn't thought I could feel any worse than I did the night before, or even that morning.

Wrong. Again.

I lay down across our ill-omened bed on my stomach, burying my face in a pillow so I wouldn't make any noise.

Stupid, stupid Madeline. Won't Setsuko laugh when Dean tells her all about this…what a perfumed clown I'd made of myself, and how grotesque he'd found the pitiful spectacle.

"Bunny?" I felt him sit down on the edge of the bed.

I pulled the duvet over my legs, turned my head away from him without looking up. "Please go away."

"Why?"

"Please. Just give me some time alone."

"I don't want to," he said, rubbing my back. "I want to be with you."

"I don't want you here."

"Why not?"

"Because I've just humiliated myself. Because it hurts too much."

"You didn't," he said, leaning down to kiss the back of my neck.

"Don't."

"Don't what? Don't do this?" He kissed me again.

"Just leave. Go back to your little girlfriend. You can have a good laugh about me, at the office. I'm sure she'd love that."

He lay down beside me, started playing with a piece of my hair. "It's not like that. It was never like that."

"What *was* it like, then? I bet you never had trouble getting it up with Set-goddamn-suko."

"Bunny, *Jesus*." I felt him lean closer, kiss the side of my head.

I started crying again.

"Look," he said. "She's not..."

"Not *what*?"

"She's, like, about as interesting as a gum-cracking hairstylist. There's nothing to talk about.

Never was. She's not beautiful—not striking, like you. She's just kind of...*fluffy*. Insipid."

"And yet you had no trouble fucking her."

"I don't *want* her. I want you. I was sick of it. I'm glad the whole sorry little episode is over. *I'm* embarrassed, and I goddamn well should be. And what just happened downstairs is that my *dick* is embarrassed, which *it* goddamn well should be. *That's* why I couldn't get it up."

He kissed my hair again.

I tried to stop crying.

For one thing, because my father used to yell at me for *not* crying. He was into Primal Therapy and all that seventies shit, and believed profoundly that people who didn't immediately express every little inkling of pain or sorrow or whatever that they'd *ever* experienced were kowtowing to The Man or something. He always seemed to be bitching to me and my sister Pagan about how we needed to "have our feelings" whenever we'd visited him as kids.

Not having feelings has never been my problem. My feelings were a giant pain in the ass, frankly. I'd've been perfectly happy just to dump them in a locker in some dank Midwestern bus terminal and walk the fuck away.

So maybe my not wanting to cry was some last

vestige of adolescent rebellion. But I really believed that it was more my way of fighting against just being borne out to sea on my emotions like they were a fucking lethal riptide.

Plus crying never meant catharsis to me. Whatever sucked enough to have made you weep in the first place didn't exactly go away once you'd worked yourself up into a snot-nosed, puffy-eyed woundball over it.

It always *still* sucked, only now you looked like shit into the bargain.

"Look at me," Dean said.

"No."

"Why not?"

"Because my eyes are all swollen and I probably have mascara down to my fucking chin."

"I'll lick it off."

"Like hell you will."

He cupped his hand around my far shoulder, trying to make me turn over.

"Stop," I said.

"No."

I felt him sit up, reach across me with both hands. I tensed up but he flipped me anyway.

"Please," I said.

He took a corner of the duvet and licked it, then

started cleaning my face with the little nub of fabric, gently as a cat.

"This is silly," I said.

"No, it's not."

He rubbed a little harder at one spot on my cheek. "There. All finished. Now you're perfect."

The duvet corner was streaked with black.

"I brought that little plate of food up," he said. "You should eat something. It looks delicious."

"Not hungry."

"I'll feed you," he said.

49

No more," I said. "Please. I'm really not hungry."

He popped a raspberry into my mouth, then ran his thumb against the corner of my lips.

"Cheese," he said, licking it off.

"Don't you have to go back to work?"

"Probably. Eventually."

"We could use the paycheck, you know. I'm not making any money with this writing shit."

"I have another job already, remember?"

"Oh," I said. "Right."

"By the way, what happened to our children?"

"Sold them to a passing circus. I'm sure they'll be much happier. All that fresh air. Elephants. Ferris wheels."

"Really, Bunny. Where are they?"

"At the child care center, up Mapleton."

"Why don't I go pick them up? I brought the car home."

"Can you throw the wagon in the back? I left it up there."

"Absolutely. Why don't you sleep a little, until I get back."

"That sounds like a really, *really* good plan."

He got up from the bed, put his shoes back on.

"Oh," he said. "I brought you home a present."

"What?"

He leaned down to kiss me again. On the mouth this time. "It's a surprise. I'll show you when I get back."

"It's at least another month until Mother's Day."

"I know," he said. "But what have I done for you lately?"

"Excellent point. Hurry back."

I punched the pillows up into a downy cloud and laid my head down, closing my eyes.

Gum-cracking hairstylist . . . Fluffy. Insipid.

I was out like a light, but with a trace of a smile.

I could feel the happy, even in my sleep.

Dean woke me up a couple of hours later by climbing onto the bed with the girls. Giggling and cooing—all three of them.

"Ready for your present?" he asked.

"That's a rhetorical question, right?"

"I'll be right back."

I sat up against the window, that trace of smile still on my face. Bigger, now.

I heard him jog down the stairs, then back up.

"Close your eyes, Bunny," he said, before he came back into the bedroom.

"Okay."

I could feel a gentle shift of weight as he put something on top of the duvet, right at the center of my lap.

"You can open them now," he said, very, very pleased with himself.

So I did, expecting to look down and see a little velvet jewelry box. Black, probably.

That wasn't it. Not at all.

There was just a pile of papers. Xeroxes, with streaky toner.

"Um, what is this?" I asked, trying not to sound disappointed.

"Cary's paperwork. You told me to make you copies of everything this morning, remember?"

"You're such a romantic," I said. "Thank you."

Three dozen roses already today. Lighten up, Madeline.

"Go back to work, Intrepid Spouse," I said. "I can take it from here."

He leaned down to kiss me, whispering, "Why don't you take off your stockings and that little skirt, leave them folded up right here under the pillows? I'm thinking they deserve an encore later."

"I've always heard the secret to a kick-ass opening night is a deeply crappy dress rehearsal. Wonder if there's any truth to that?"

"Bet we can have a pretty damn good time finding out," he said, insinuating his fingers slyly between my stocking-sheathed knees. "I can think of *several* things I'd like to open, starting right about here."

"Mmmmm," I said.

He pulled his hand out, then tapped my knee. "Break a leg."

I called Mimi, back in my jeans again.

When she picked up, I said, "I have zee papers, old maaaan."

"What the hell are you talking about, Madeline?"

"Cheech and Chong routine. Totally classic."

"Cheech and *who*?"

"I'll buy you the tape," I said.

"You mentioned something about papers?"

"Thirty-two pages of hot piping fresh Xerox with your name on them. So to speak."

"How should we arrange a transfer?"

"For chrissake, why don't you just park in the alley behind our backyard? Come into the kitchen through the back door."

She sighed, not happy with the idea.

"After dark," she said. "Sun sets tonight around six thirty. Let's say seven."

50

Dean came home so close to five I wondered if he'd commuted in a time machine with Sherman and Mr. Peabody.

"I haven't seen you home this early since you were unemployed, in Pittsfield."

"Seemed like a good day for it. Wouldn't want you to think I'm, ah, *malingering* or anything otherwise untoward."

"Thank you," I said, reaching up to kiss him.

I poured him a glass of wine and started puttering around with dinner for Parrish and India. "Mimi's supposed to drop by around seven."

He pursed his lips. "Is that a good idea?"

"She's going to park in the alley, come in the back door."

"I don't know—"

"Drink your wine. I want to give her the Xeroxes."

"Want some more pâté?"

"Not quite hungry yet, but thank you for offering."

He was still looking down into his glass, swirling the wine around a little. Hadn't tasted it yet.

"It's that kind you like," I said. "Vendange."

Not a vintage to write home about or anything, but the bottles were big and we could afford them. Better than Hearty Burgundy, but what wasn't, really?

I still preferred beer, though I was trying to become a wine person. Kind of.

Well, okay, it was a totally half-ass effort. The kind of thing I resolved to do on New Year's Eve, then promptly blew off.

What can I say? I was abused with cheap Liebfraumilch as a child. Mom liked it, she said, because it tasted like lychee nuts.

Maybe I'd drink *only* wine for Lent this year. If I hadn't missed it already. I tended to do that with Lent.

"Do you know when Easter is?" I asked Dean.

"April sixteenth, why?"

"I might try drinking wine instead of beer for Lent. Try being more of a grown-up."

"It's totally fine if you want to drink beer," he said. "Grown-ups drink beer all the time."

"Later, maybe. When Mimi comes by."

"Should I give the girls a bath, a little Spa Dad?"

"*Before* they eat?"

He laughed. "Right. Might as well get the broccoli off, too."

"Not to mention the melted cheese. Quesadillas tonight."

"Think they're hungry now?"

"Why don't you go hang in the playpen with them. Run 'em around a little and build up their appetites."

He kissed the top of my head again.

"Do you ever get bored of being so tall?" I asked.

"Never," he said, grinning back at me as he skipped out into the dining room.

I lit a burner under the skillet and got some tortillas out of the icebox.

Dean was apparently playing "tickle monster." I could already hear the girls shrieking with glee.

I sat cross-legged on top of the toilet, lid down, while Dean finished up with the girls in the tub.

"Time for a little conditioning treatment, my darlings," he said, breaking out the Suave.

"I'm going to start calling you Serge," I said. "You're a little too good at this."

"I can do you next, Bunny—"

"We shall see."

"Petunia," he said to Parrish, "here comes the fun part..."

He rubbed a big sploodge of conditioner into her scalp, then got out a wide-toothed comb and started working it gently through her tangled hair, from the ends up. He was so gentle she barely noticed she was getting knots combed out.

Then it was India's turn. "Ready to go, Puppy? Tilt your head back a little."

She stared up at him—beatific—eyes wide in utter adoration.

"You're so pretty," he said. "Look at your beautiful little face. You're destined to break hearts, sweetness."

That's what it should be like for little girls. Just like that.

"Time to comb you out, and then we rinse," he said.

He didn't get a drop of water in their eyes.

"Time to get out, Thing One and Thing Two," he said, shaking out a big bathsheet.

He lifted India onto it, wrapped her up snug as a bug. Then it was Parrish's turn.

When they both looked like fat white caterpillars, or maybe Q-tips, the phone rang.

"Why don't you get that," I said. "I've got diapers and pajamas. I can finish up in here."

"Thank you, Bunny," he said, standing up and drying his hands.

He walked out through the dining room, into the office.

I got the girls into their diapers first. Then the pajamas.

I finished by ruffling their hair up with a towel, then kissing them both loudly on each cheek.

"There you go, now you're *gorgeous*—the pair of you."

I tickled India's belly through the soft fleece of her footie pajamas. Pale blue, with cows and moons all over, then put her down into the playpen with her sister.

Parrish had her plastic truck upside down again, ignoring both of us. She was very intent on spinning one of the tires. I stood up and turned toward the office, where Dean was still on the phone.

I wanted him to come upstairs with me and help put the girls to bed, happy to wait until he was finished with this call.

Then he made a heart-wrenchingly terrible noise, and I rushed toward the office doors to see what was wrong.

He was crying, with his free hand over his eyes. "Don't *say* that. Please."

I watched him hunch forward over the desk.

What the hell?

"Dean?"

He didn't hear me over the sound of his own ragged breathing.

"No," he said.

Then "No," again.

Then another "Please," the word wrenched out of his throat like it had razor blades all over it.

"You have to *promise* me."

I felt really, really cold, all of a sudden.

I was about to reach out to him, put my hands on his back.

"Setsuko," he said, sobbing, "I can't do that. You *know* I can't. We've talked about this. You *know* why."

I dropped my hands. Colder still.

"Just, *don't*—"

He listened for a while, hand over his eyes again.

"All right," he said finally. "All right. I'll come over. Promise me you won't do anything until I get there."

He listened again. "*No . . . promise me. Right now.*"

I hugged my arms around my chest. Tight.

"Yes," he said. "Yes . . . in twenty minutes. And you won't do anything until I get there? I have your word? All right then."

He put the phone down.

"No fucking *way* are you going over to that woman's house, Dean."

He turned around, eyes wide. Hadn't realized I was standing behind him.

"Bunny," he said.

"Bunny *nothing*. No fucking way."

"She's threatening to kill herself."

Give me a goddamn break.

"Seppuku, I hope?"

"This isn't a joke."

"Dean, it's the oldest trick in the book. Mistress Histrionics One Oh One. She's full of shit."

"I don't think so."

"Of *course* you don't. You're a guy. That's why this kind of manipulation works."

"I have to go there, make sure she's okay."

"Give me your car keys," I said, holding out my hand.

"What are you going to do, *hide* them from me?"

"No, you fucktard. I'm going to drive over there

and talk her down myself. Least I can do for the poor bitch."

"That's crazy."

"It's so *not* crazy, you should be kissing my feet right now."

"Bunny, she's expecting *me*."

"Damn right, she is. And she's going to act all freaked out and fluttery and fucking delicate, telling you how she can't live without you over and over again until she gets you in bed. And meanwhile I'm going to be sitting here all fucking night *knowing* exactly what's going on. No fucking way in the *world* is that happening, Intrepid Spouse."

"Bunny, that doesn't make any—"

"It makes perfect sense. Because you know what's going to happen when she opens her goddamn door and she sees *me* standing there, instead of you?"

He didn't respond.

"She's going to stop crying pretty damn fast. Probably before I even step over the threshold. Because I'm a chick, and she's going to know I'm hip to *exactly* what she's doing. Because I am, and she's full of crap. And if she can get you over there by pulling this little number once, she's going to do it over and over again. Until even *you* figure out it's a crock of shit, Dean. So let's just skip that whole

Ring Cycle, shall we? Give me the fucking car keys. And tell me where she lives."

I held my hand out again. "*Now*, Dean."

"You don't have a driver's license, Bunny. You can't drive."

I didn't think this was a good time to mention that I'd already driven the stupid car.

Especially considering how that turned out.

I thought of Cary, then. For the first time in a while.

God, how awful this had all been. I missed him right now, so very much.

And then I lifted my chin.

"I used to own a Porsche, Dean. I know perfectly fucking well how to drive a car."

He gave me the keys.

"What time is it?" I asked.

"Six forty-five."

"Mimi's going to be here in fifteen minutes. Give her the papers. Ask her if she wants a beer. I'll be home in an hour."

"This is a *really* bad idea."

"No. You fucking Setsuko was a really bad idea. *This* is the only way to remedy the inevitable ramifications of that initial piece of idiocy on your part."

"Bunny—"

"And you might want to remember this moment,

the next time you're tempted to trot your dick out in a bed that's not ours... Think on it a *very* long time."

"What will you do if it turns out she's serious?"

"Slap her."

He closed his eyes.

"Look, Dean—I wouldn't give a shit, frankly, except that I don't need *you* haunted by your poor little mistress's tragic death for the rest of our fucking marriage. So I'll make sure she *doesn't* off herself."

He looked totally defeated.

"Where does she live?" I asked.

"Creek Gardens Apartments."

"Which is where?"

"Twenty-ninth Street. On the left before you hit Arapahoe. Apartment Four-G, around the back."

"Write it down for me."

He did. "If you see the Denny's, you've gone too far."

Perfect.

"Her car will be in front of the door," he said.

"And what exactly does she drive? A fuzzy-pink-angora Yugo?"

"Honda Civic. Hatchback."

"Color?"

"Powder blue. With a vanity plate."

"Which says what, exactly?"

He coughed. "K-I-T-T-E-N-1."

"*Kitten One?*"

He nodded.

I shook my head. "Men will fuck *anything*, won't they?"

He held out the note with her address on it. "If you're going to do this, you should go."

I grabbed the thing and shoved it into my front pocket. "Mimi's going to knock on the kitchen door. Don't forget."

51

Okay, so I had to turn around in the Denny's parking lot. But that actually worked out, since Twenty-ninth Street had a planted divider down its middle separating the two lanes. I would've had to do a U-ey anyway. Better there than Arapahoe.

And I was liking the Galant even more. Still not a Porsche, of course, but it had decent pickup and a nice butch growl to it. Kind of like driving a filing cabinet.

I pulled in behind the back of the building. Blue shingles and lumpy white stucco, in that really odious sixties-Mansard format.

I parked right next to KITTEN1.

Gag, gag, gag.

Her windows were lined with vertical blinds, tiny slivers of light shining through.

I rang the bell, happy there wasn't a little view-hole lens in the slab door. She'd think I was Dean and open right up.

There you go, twitching the blinds open—and here's the Galant, right out front.

I heard a chain being pulled out of its clasp, then the click of a deadbolt.

"Oh my dearest...," she sobbed. But of course stopped short when she realized it was me.

Yeah, bitch stopped crying immediately. Surprise, sur-fucking-prise.

She squinted at me. Tough little face, when she wasn't happy about something. And *boy* was she not happy about finding me on her doorstep.

She was wearing a mint-green satin bathrobe, over something slinky. Full makeup. No bra. And her hair was perfectly curled.

"Suicidal" my ass.

She seemed to resent my dismissive take on her tits and gripped the robe closed with her free hand. Way up high on her neck.

"Why are *you* here?" she said. "Where's Dean?"

"He's busy taking care of our children," I said, shrugging. "Aren't you going to invite me in?"

She didn't want to, but she took two steps back and opened the door wider.

"Please," she said, ducking her head a little.

"*Tayo agay detekoy*," I replied, under my breath.

Her face got kind of squinchy. "I beg your pardon?"

I coughed into my hand, stepping over the threshold. "I'm probably coming down with a little something."

There was a row of shoes just inside the doorway, and looking at them, I had a whole lot of simultaneous epiphany shit happen in my head.

First: I had a choice whether or not to take off my shoes here. Respect her culture, the sanctity of her household aesthetic—or, literally, walk all over it.

Second: Although she didn't know it yet, I'd already won this battle. My husband had not only told her he was breaking off the affair, he'd taken concrete steps to keep himself—and *all* of us, me and the girls as much as Setsuko—geographically separated from any temptation to resume it.

He'd gone out and found himself a distant job, and he'd done so even before I knew there was something to break off. Which meant a lot, as far as I was concerned. And I had an inkling she didn't know about the cross-country-move part of the equation, yet.

Third: Or maybe she did, and *that* was the impetus behind her obviously bullshit suicide threat. Either way, this was a desperate gambit on her part. You sure as shit don't threaten to off yourself over a guy if you believe you're securely ensconced in his affections.

You don't have many strategic options if the threat doesn't work, in the chess of the heart.

I mean, sure, you can actually go *through* with it, but that's not exactly a ticket to requited love.

So, fourth: There was the row of fucking shoes, still. And much as I wanted to deck the skanky-slag-bitch-ho-creepy-nemesis-suckbag trollop, then and there—I knew in my tiny black heart of hearts that it would fuck with her *way* worse if I just niced her around the goddamn mulberry bush, instead.

Like, get all totally patronizingly chilly and correct and to-the-manor-born and brimming-with-*sympathy*-for-you-my-poor-dear Grace fucking Kelly ice princess (but of course thoroughly evil under what we'd *both* know was the paper-thin patina of my faux-compassion and devastatingly Zen-Debutante-*wah* charm) on her sorry-jilted-insipid-woebegone ass.

Because, hey, in those rare moments—of which this happens to be one—that I am actually suffused with my own mojo, said mojo is a goddamn exquisitely luminous vanquishing June-14-1940 Panzerkorps of offhand casual superiority. So you might want to lie down and make like the Champs-Élysées, bitch, as I prefer my triumphal invasion boulevards straight, flat, and tree-lined.

Which is to say that I kicked off my sneakers and squatted down to align them neatly at the end of her existing row.

"Thank you," she said.

Standing up, I smiled at her. "I used to live in Hawaii. When I was little. Removing one's shoes at the front door was the custom there, as well, and I certainly wouldn't want to be impolite or disrespectful in your house. That's not at all why I'm here tonight."

Setsuko and I allowed my unspoken *comma, you cunt* coda to hang in the air for a moment.

"Please," she said, "come into the living room. We'll sit down."

Dude, you so wanted to bow right then. And I so would have bowed deeper.

"Thank you for agreeing to talk with me, Setsuko. I appreciate it very much. I know this wasn't what you were expecting, but I thought it might be better for everyone if the two of us were to have a conversation."

"Yes," she said. "Would you like a drink? Wine cooler, or soda?"

"I'm fine, thank you. But do please get something for yourself if you'd like."

We were in the living room proper now. Big cream-colored leather furniture, the kind with pillows for arms. Sofa, love seat, one chair. Cheap repro Louis-the-Umpteenth side and coffee tables. Two fat pink lamps with swoopy flowers splashed across their pleated shades.

She'd hung a framed poster over the gas-powered fireplace's ersatz-white-brick mantel: waterfall, out of focus, with some kind of poem written over it in loose white script.

On the wall to my left was one of a couple walking along a sunset beach. More poetry. Fifty bucks it was Kahlil Gibran.

G-g-g-gag.

Her crochet bag sat up straight at the end of the sofa. And she was apparently a fan of light jazz. It was all rather reminiscent of the waiting area at a nail salon. Complete with tabletop fountain.

"Please," she said, motioning to the love seat, "sit."

I did, and she took a seat across from me. Knees primly together, holding the neck of her robe closed.

I coughed into my hand again. "Setsuko, I know that you care very much about Dean. You and I *both* do, of course—I hope you won't think it indelicate of me to say so."

She bobbed her head, conceding me that.

"And I'm very *sorry* for you, the way things turned out. I know you must be sad. And I imagine you didn't set *out* to be in this situation."

She looked down at her lap.

"My goodness," I said. "People fall in love with one another. They just *do*. We don't get to choose when that happens, or with *whom* it happens. Believe me—I understand that, I really do. I don't blame you for what occurred, all right?"

Like hell.

She looked up at me, curious now.

"It's just..." I didn't quite know how to phrase the next part.

Don't want to chew the scenery, but perhaps just a touch of hand-wringing? Mmmm, perfect: making sure my engagement ring twinkles, catching the light.

"Oh, *Setsuko*"—*poignant catch in my voice*—"Dean told me what you said to him on the phone tonight. And I'm"—*pause for effect, thoughtful*—"so very sorry that you're in this much pain. My heart goes *out* to you, you poor thing. I mean that most sincerely."

And, okay, at that moment I kind of *did* mean it, too.

I mean, I was rather fond of Dean myself.

And only by the grace of *whomever* had I managed not to fuck anybody married, during the course my own long history of round-heeledness. More because the husbands in question had been mensch-ier than my own than because it hadn't ever occurred to me.

Especially when I was in my teens.

I mean, *hello*—daddy issues? all-girl boarding school? Please. I would've flipped up my kilt and balled the bejesus out of any dick-bearing dorm parent willing to hold still for longer than a goddamn heartbeat.

And I bet they all knew it, too.

Had to admire their restraint, in retrospect—though it pissed me right off at the time.

"Setsuko," I continued, "I don't know how to say this, exactly...You're a very beautiful young woman. And I can tell that you're kind. I *know* you're smart...Can I just be blunt here? I don't know how else to do this."

"Yes. Please go ahead."

"Don't kill yourself, okay? This is going to be a tiny piece of your life. You are lovely, and I actually envy you quite a bit."

She didn't believe that.

The little table fountain was annoying. They always made me feel like I had to pee.

"*Everything* is ahead of you," I said. "Your whole life. Everyone else you're going to know, meet, *love*. This part is not important."

"It feels important. To me."

"Of course it does. I'm not trying to say you *don't* feel this, and very deeply. I'm just sorry that you have to feel hurt. I *am* sorry about that, please believe me. I know what it feels like. And I'm very sad, too. We're in love with the same man—how could I not understand what you're feeling? He's caused us both a great deal of pain. And he cares about us both. I know *that*."

She didn't say anything, mulling all of it over.

I sat there listening to the stupid fountain.

Oh, for chrissake.

"Setsuko, I'm embarrassed to ask you this, but may I please use your bathroom?"

"Of course," she said, rising to her feet.

"Down the hallway," she said, swaying gracefully in front of me. Small steps, long legs.

I followed her past the kitchenette, then she stepped aside and gestured down the hallway's white-carpeted length.

"It's the door on the right," she said. "The light switch is outside."

"Thank you," I said, walking past her.

There was a samurai sword set hanging on the wall. I wondered if she was as tacky in her native decorative taste as in her sorry attempts at the expatriate version.

Probably.

I admit I was expecting pink accessories in Setsuko's powder room. I hated the term "powder room," but for this it was fitting.

There wasn't anything pink, though. She'd gone for lavender: toilet seat cover, bath rug, towels. Even her toothbrush in its silvery holder.

I turned the water on before sitting, not particularly keen on her hearing me piss.

Then stood up to wash my hands, after flushing.

And, okay, I spat on her candy-ass purple toothbrush, hoping I really *was* coming down with something. I swear that was my only petty moment.

I mean, hey, I could've wiped my ass with it, but I exercised restraint.

I also didn't bother looking into the mirror above the sink, just opened the door softly and stepped back out into her thickly carpeted hallway.

You couldn't see into the living room, really, from where I was now standing.

All I could hear was the tinkle of that fucking fountain.

I turned off the bathroom light, but didn't move forward.

The door across from me was open. I hadn't noticed that on my way into the bathroom.

Across the threshold I could see that her bed had an elaborate brass headboard, the soft light of a table lamp beside it playing along its golden curves.

I tried closing my eyes, but that didn't get rid of the image of Dean and Setsuko rolling around on those sheets, in ecstasy.

God, Madeline, just leave already. She's not going to off herself, your work here is done, so get in your fucking car and drive home.

I didn't, though. I felt like I was being pulled into that bedroom by a tractor beam, half its magnetism composed of my self-loathing, half of morbid fascination.

Lots of pink in the room's color scheme: pink rug, pink lamp shade, pink quilt folded at the foot of the bed. But the lavender had spilled across the hall from the bathroom, as well.

The white bureau's drawers were lavender, as was the skirt hiding the legs of a mirrored dressing table.

There was even a lavender set of shelves, hung on the wall to the left of the mirror.

One of those little tree things on it, the kind that you hang earrings off of.

Hers were arranged by size. Next to that was a little lucky cat statuette with its paw up.

I walked toward the large oval mirror, dropping my gaze to all the perfume bottles arrayed on the dressing table's surface so I didn't have to look again at the photograph Setsuko had stuck in the mirror's frame.

Dean held her aloft in his arms like a new bride. Setsuko's toes were pointed and the two of them laughed at the camera.

There was snow on the ground and you could see the Flatirons. Three bikes, one of them Cary's, leaned against a stone wall beside them.

No, Cary would never have told me about my husband and Setsuko. He'd tried to be a good friend to all three of us, keeping our various secrets.

Her perfume was all cheap drugstore crap. In the front row there was a bunch of Avon and then a bottle of White Diamonds, "body mist" aerosol knockoffs of Giorgio and Obsession, even some Love's Baby Soft stuff I hadn't seen since middle school.

Beside these was a wide, shallow bowl.

Pretty, thick-walled, and heavy, in a beautiful rich streaky green: malachite. The kind of catchall you might use for loose change, cufflinks, maybe a stray paper clip.

This one held three objects.

My grandmother's string of pearls lay clumped in a heap on top. Setsuko must have stolen them from me when she babysat my daughters.

I picked them up carefully and put them on, making sure the clasp was solidly fastened before I slid it around to the back of my neck.

Now there were only two things lying in the bowl: the four-leaf clover charm I'd given Cary and Bittler's Playboy Bunny key ring.

Those I didn't touch.

I raised my eyes once more to the big dressing-table mirror.

Setsuko was now reflected in its surface, standing in the doorway behind me.

She was holding a rather large kitchen carving knife.

I guess the samurai sword on her hallway wall was papier-mâché.

52

I stood there empty-handed, and Setsuko was still behind me with a big-ass knife.

"So," I said, "you must've been fucking Bittler, too."

Well, okay, *that* pissed her off.

But she didn't answer. More important, she didn't move. Which was why I'd said it.

I needed a little time to consider my options.

I didn't turn around, but I kept talking.

"I mean, no point killing Cary just because he was going to tell me you were screwing my *husband*, right?"

Not that I was seeing anything on the dressing table worth a shit for self-defense, but still.

"You would've *liked* that," I said. "Get me all

pissed off, make Dean step up to the plate once and for all—because you still think he'd choose you over me and our kids."

"He loves me."

"He thinks you're boring," I said.

Bittler knew she'd been fucking Dean, of course. That's why he'd asked me if she was inside my house, the day he wrecked his bike on the Creek Path.

Fine piece of tail, that Setsuko.

In the end, Cary must have taken my side.

Maybe he hadn't liked the idea of Setsuko alone with my children, maybe he didn't like the way Dean treated me that day in the restaurant. I doubted I'd ever find out.

Cary planned to come clean with Dean about Setsuko and Bittler, though, and he must have told her so. That's why she killed him.

But she still believed Dean would abandon me, just as long as he never found out about that particular detail.

Too bad I'd quit smoking. If I'd had a lighter on me, I could've gone all *Live and Let Die* Roger Moore on her ass and made an aerosol-can flamethrower out of her fakey-fake "Obsession."

Because she sure as shit didn't want me leaving here alive.

Too bad she hadn't left, say, a shotgun leaning

conveniently against the end of her bed. I could've used one, right about then.

Think, Madeline.

Okay, so there was also a round box of dusting powder on the table. Which was perfectly useless unless of course I suddenly remembered some secret recipe for making tear gas out of it. Or pulled a magic wand out of my ass and bibbety-bobbety-booed myself up a sparkly fairy-godmother grenade.

Although it did cheer me up to think that after Setsuko hacked me to death, Dean would *probably* figure out she'd done it, and not be in any hurry to propose to her afterward.

My husband was a philandering asshole, but he wasn't particularly slow on the uptake—despite his patently execrable taste in side-pussy.

Fuck it, I was going to have to try *talking* my way out of this.

And that seemed like the dumbest plan ever. But it was all I had.

I would've tried it, too, if she hadn't charged me with the knife instead.

So instead of chatting I grabbed the malachite bowl and whipped around fast, pitching it at her face with everything I had.

I've always had a mean arm, for a chick, and I at least grazed the side of her head.

She was off balance now, but she was still coming toward me.

I waited until she was close and then ducked, which was a good thing, because she missed me with the fucking carving knife on her first swing.

Not, unfortunately, the second.

53

On the bright side, Setsuko only got a light slice in, across my left forearm. Not enough to disable me or anything, but plenty to wake me the fuck up.

Unfortunately for her, I dove past her and toward the bedroom door while she was slashing me.

I was now looking down the hallway with my eye on her entry foyer. From which I really, really hoped to escape into the parking lot.

Setsuko was right on my heels but I did my level best to follow the advice of Satchel Paige: "Don't look back, something might be gaining on you."

Like, say, a knife-wielding psycho. Who was screaming all kinds of crazy shit while she chased me, by the way.

Not that I had any idea what she was saying.

Probably a good thing: It didn't sound like she was shrieking anything very complimentary.

And then she must have taken another swing at me, because I felt this nasty sting in the middle of my left shoulder blade.

Not deep, again—lucky me. I was still moving fast, still pumping my arms just as hard, but she'd gotten a taste. And it fucking *hurt*, too.

It also meant she was close enough that if I stopped to open the front door, she'd take me out before I turned the handle.

So when I was almost there, I faked left away from the door and launched myself airborne over Setsuko's appallingly ugly love seat.

Hadn't hurdled since I ran track in sixth grade, but I'd been damn good at it back then and the instinct hadn't deserted me.

Didn't think, just kicked my right leg straight out in front of me, snapped my trailing knee up high and sideways, and cleared that mofo like a goddamn springbok, I shit you not.

Thank you, Title Nine.

Okay, so I almost did a face-plant into the brick fireplace mantel, but I got my hands up in time and bounced myself into a 180 turn—in time to watch Setsuko hip-check the love seat, hard.

Probably good she didn't try to jump it, what

with the big-ass bloody knife in her hand and everything.

Maybe not good for *me*, exactly—because, hey, I would've been more than happy to see her go splat and impale herself—but she might just as easily have cartwheeled over the damn thing all akimbo and shanked me, flailing, on her way down.

And that love seat sure as shit slowed her down for a few precious seconds. Caught her right at the pelvis, and the momentum snapped her torso forward.

Too much to hope, that a stop that sudden would break her grip on the damn knife and bring it clattering perfectly to rest at my feet.

But it did wrench a big "*oof*" out of her, and she sliced open a leather cushion as she fought to regain her balance.

Better it than me.

She was up again now, and even more pissed off.

But I'd used the downtime to equip myself with a brass fire poker and matching long-handled ash shovel from the andiron set she'd put conveniently next to the fireplace.

Purely decorative objects, since it was a gas fire, but awfully handy for me. And way more lethal than talcum powder, too, if I played my cards right.

"Wouldn't worry about any damage to the furniture," I said. "It was already so fucking ugly."

"Now it's ruined, like yours. But my house is still cleaner."

I mean, seriously, she wanted to insult my *housekeeping* at this point? Fuck prolonging this bullshit. I wanted her dead.

She started edging around the love seat. "That's why Dean wants to be with *me*."

"Dean's *bored* with you, you stupid cunt. We're moving to Boston. He got himself a job there *before* I found out you two were fucking. Not to mention before he found out you killed Cary, or were doing the nasty with Bittler. Which knowledge is not exactly going to improve his opinion of you."

"You're not going to tell him. Because you're going to be *dead*."

"Oh, for fuck's sake, Setsuko. Now you're boring *me*."

She was around the corner of the love seat now, coming toward me slowly.

"Dean doesn't love you," she said. "He loves *me*."

She lunged at me, but I parried with the shovel and managed to get a good whack in with the poker. Right across the side of her rib cage.

Made her wince.

"He also thinks you're tacky," I said. "And not tremendously bright."

I swung at her, but didn't get another lick in.

"I mean, really, sweetie," I said, taking a step back, poker up in front of me, "he didn't even want to *fuck* you anymore. We laughed about it."

"I'm a better wife for him. Better than you."

I took another step back. A big one. "Why, because you're so bereft of wit and imagination that you actually *enjoy* cleaning?"

She took another slice at me. I jumped back, right up against the wall.

That made her smile.

I smiled back. "My husband likes smart, articulate women, Setsuko. You don't happen to be either."

"I am going to kill you," she said. "And Dean will be happy. Because he wants to be with me. He calls me his sweet little kitten."

She came at me low, making me swing with the shovel, but it was a feint and I fell for it.

She tried to slash that arm, but missed.

"Big fucking deal," I said, dancing out of range. "He calls me Bunny—which, although it is nowhere near as grotesquely insipid as 'kitten,' has always struck me as an idiotic endearment."

She lunged again but I whacked her with the poker.

I tried to nail her with the shovel, too, but I was bleeding a lot now. Which kind of messed with my grip.

She tipped it right out of my hand with the fucking knife. I heard it hit the carpet with a dull clang, but didn't make the mistake of looking.

Not good.

"I am going to kill you," she said.

She went for my right arm this time. Sliced my sleeve near the elbow, but no other damage. And I sure as shit didn't let go of the poker.

I was breathing hard now, and she wasn't.

And I was losing blood. Which she also wasn't.

"Your children deserve a better mother," she said.

I didn't look down at it, but my left arm was seriously wet. I could feel a steady line of warm liquid running down my palm and onto the floor.

Not just dripping. Worse than that.

Kind of pouring, actually. I mean, not arterial spray or anything, but, like, I could actually hear the drops landing on her already-wet carpet.

"Dean knows it," she said. "So do you."

I was a little dizzy, but didn't feel cold yet. That was good.

And then I thought: *Fuck, the bitch is waiting me out. She knows I'm getting weaker.*

She nodded, as though I'd just spoken those words aloud. "Parrish and India won't remember you. And I'll be a *better* mother."

I don't fucking think so.

Setsuko telegraphed her next move, raising the knife up to her shoulder in what had to be slow motion.

Really? We're gloating now?

"Oh, Setsuko!" I cried out. "I'm so sorry! I'm *bleeding* all over your pretty white *carpet*!"

She dropped her eyes to my bloody left arm.

Which was indeed leaking rather profoundly onto her tacky albino wall-to-wall, but still, stopping to look? Right up there with falling for the old, "Look at my thumb. *Gee*, you're dumb."

I walloped her across the face with my poker, really fucking hard.

Right under the cheekbone.

Hard enough to break her teeth.

I heard them crack and splinter. And I have to say it was rather a *pleasant* sound, considering.

"Ha," I said. "Made you look."

And then I hit her again. Same cheek, only harder.

She was still standing, though.

So I swung low and hard into her left kneecap, then snaked my foot around the back of that same knee and hooked it forward.

She went down screaming.

That sounded pretty damn good, too.

54

I had Setsuko down on the floor now. But she was still kind of armed and everything.

Which didn't seem prudent.

So I put my left foot on her throat and proceeded to whack her across the hand with the poker until she let go of the knife.

I stepped a little harder on her windpipe when I leaned down to pick it up.

Just in case.

Oh, poor *thing*—I kind of leaned my weight on that left foot, getting up. With her throat all under it and everything.

And, okay, after I was standing again and holding her sword instead of the poker, I gave her another good lean on the windpipe.

Not, like, hard enough to break the hyoid bones or anything. Just hard enough to make her start crying.

I mean, you'd think having a bunch of her teeth knocked out would've achieved that worthy goal already, but it hadn't.

And besides which, she totally fucking deserved it.

Because you do *not* mess with me, when it comes to my daughters.

I will hurt you.

I will inflict serious damage on your dumb, sorry ass.

Especially if you murder a friend of mine, and *double* especially when you've been fucking my husband.

"You fucking *killed* Cary?" I said. "What the hell is wrong with you?"

"He was going to *tell*," she said, kind of mushily, what with her mouth all full of blood and teeth.

"Dean was right," I said. "You're really stupid."

She looked like she wanted to bite me.

So I pressed my foot down on her throat with a little more conviction.

"Go ahead, spit them out."

She mumbled something, kind of garbled.

"Your teeth, you dumb bitch," I said. "Because you *really* don't want to choke on them, the next time I hit you."

Not a happy Setsuko...poor baby.

"Go ahead, spit," I said. "I already bled on your carpet."

So she spat out her teeth, which took a couple of tries.

And when she was finished, I grabbed her by the hair, lifted her head, and punched as hard as I could at the corner of her jaw, trying to get the mandible to slap against her cranial nerve.

I had to punch her again before she lost consciousness.

"Jesus, you're an *idiot*," I said. "It's kind of astonishing, actually."

Yeah, so much for that not-being-a-bitch thing. Again.

But she'd killed a really nice man. So she could keep fucking my husband. And steal my children.

I waited there for another minute, making sure she wasn't going to move.

Then I leaned down.

Still breathing, *check*.

Not in any hurry to get up, *check*.

Okay, time to call Dean, back home.

I went into her kitchen and grabbed a nice fat bunch of fluffy clean tea towels, with which I applied pressure to my bleeding arm.

Then I picked up her phone and dialed.

55

Dean picked up on the first ring. "Bunny?"

"This is she," I said.

"Are you all right? What's going on?"

"Well, your girlfriend is kind of unconscious on her living room floor, and there's a lot of blood on the carpet. Most of it mine. Also, I knocked about half her teeth out. With a fire poker."

"What the *hell*—"

"You should probably call an ambulance and give them Setsuko's address, but not until after you send Mimi over here for me. My arm's going to need stitches where your little side dish slashed me with a carving knife."

"Bunny, slow down...what the hell happened, how did this start?"

"Setsuko killed Cary, Dean. And tonight she tried to kill me."

"*What?*"

"Well it turns out she was also fucking Bittler, and Cary was going to tell you. Setsuko didn't think that would be convenient."

"Oh, my God."

"Apparently, she is also under the impression that she would be a far better wife and mother than I am. And that you would be entirely on board with her killing me so she could prove it."

"Are you all right?"

"About fucking time you asked. I'm bleeding. Send Mimi over, then call nine-one-one. I'm going to hang up. I'd like to sit down for a while."

"Bunny, wait..."

I kind of slid down the kitchen wall. "You have *incredibly* shitty taste in girlfriends. This one's a fucking *nightmare*. Total psychopath. With absolutely no taste."

"Bunny..."

"Just send Mimi. Stay home with the girls. I'm going to hang up now. I might need both hands free, if the dumb cunt wakes up."

I didn't really want to stand up again, but I had to, to hang up.

And then I figured I might as well do something about that fucking fountain.

So I lurched into the living room and tried to figure out how to unplug it.

Since that would've required crawling around on the floor, I just pushed it off the table instead.

Then I sat down for real in the love seat.

Her furniture was hideous, but kind of comfortable—like Marshmallow Fluff, only not sticky.

I had a pretty good view of Setsuko from there, too.

She wasn't going anywhere. No big deal, neither was I.

Mimi got there first, which was definitely a good thing.

All I had to say was, "Bittler didn't kill Cary. Setsuko did. And came after me."

After she'd made sure Setsuko wasn't going to imminently die or anything, I led her into the bedroom and showed her the shamrock I'd given Cary, which I picked up off the floor and put in my pocket, then pointed out the keys.

"Those are Bittler's," I said. "He dropped them on the floor when he was drunk at a business dinner a while back. I doubt a Playboy Bunny is a really popular key-ring motif here in Boulder."

I didn't touch them, even though for all I knew my fingerprints were still on them from Alice's Restaurant.

"Tell me why this is important," said Mimi.

"The key to the warehouse that burned down is going to be on it. Which is how Setsuko got into the place with Cary, and how she locked up after she killed him there."

"How'd she get Bittler's keys in the first place?"

"Well, she was fucking him. So she probably just stole them from his bedside table or something. Maybe he'll remember when they went missing."

"She was fucking Bittler *and* Dean?"

"Apparently."

"Why?"

"Maybe she wanted to cover her bets for getting her visa renewed, how the fuck would I know? Ask *her* when she wakes up."

"I'll let the cops do that."

We walked back out to the living room and Mimi made me sit down again.

The ambulance came, then two fire trucks, then a couple of cop cars.

When they'd taken Setsuko out on a gurney, Mimi told me she'd drive me to the hospital.

She took care of the cops, making sure I didn't get arrested just at the moment or anything, although she had to promise them she'd bring me down to the station for a statement the minute my arm had been stitched up. My shoulder blade wasn't a big deal, apparently, though it sure as hell hurt like it was.

Sometimes it's good to have a police force that doesn't really know how to deal with investigating a homicide.

"So," I said to Mimi, "you're going to make sure the cops don't fuck up and pin this on *me*, right? I mean, I'm willing to admit I kicked Setsuko's ass, but that was in self-defense and the skanky bitch deserved it."

"I don't know, Madeline," she said. "What have you done for me lately?"

We were sitting on the tacky condo's front steps while a young firefighter/EMT guy Novocained my arm and then put a nice fat bandage on it to keep me from bleeding all over Mimi's car on the way to the hospital.

"That should do you," he said, running a final strip of tape gently around my wrist. "Just make sure you get someone good for the stitches. Hold out for a plastic surgeon."

"I will, thank you."

He looked up at Mimi. "Sure you don't want me to run you both down there, Meems?"

"Thanks, Jerry," she said, "but then I'd have to come back for my car. And Madeline's tough."

"Yeah," he said, looking wide-eyed into the blood-spattered living room behind us. "I guess so."

"Ready?" she asked, standing up.

I was still kind of shaky, so she pulled my good arm across her shoulders.

Jerry looked uncomfortable, like he was about to insist I make the trip lying down in the back of the paramedic rig, but in the end he didn't say a word.

Smart man.

I made Mimi stop for a minute in the parking lot so I could throw the shamrock down a storm drain.

"Really?" she asked.

"It was hideous," I said. "And *nobody* needs more luck like that. Not even Setsuko."

56

It took almost two hours before we got my arm stitched up. Probably would've taken longer if I hadn't been with Mimi, but she knew some people in the ER and made them deal with me.

I didn't really care, since my arm didn't hurt that much and it wasn't bleeding so badly anymore. And she made sure I got to lie down in a little curtained cubicle while I waited.

"You're going to be up a long time," she said. "Might as well sleep while you can."

"I really have to go down to the police station? Couldn't they just send someone here?"

"You hit a woman in the face with a fire poker, Madeline. This is going to be formal."

"Self-defense," I said. "I mean, hello, she'd

already murdered someone. And she was trying to stab me to death."

"All of which you're going to have to explain to the cops. They're not going to take my word for it."

Of course she was right. If we'd been in New York, I'd be handcuffed to the side of the bed I was lying on already, with a couple of uniforms glaring at me.

"Fine," I said. "Know any good lawyers?"

"Yeah."

"Want to go call one and let me sleep?"

"Sure," she said.

I was out before she'd pulled the curtain back.

The lawyer was a young guy named Art Selby. He was waiting for us at the cop station in cargo pants and a Moe's Bagels T-shirt with his curly black hair all rumpled, but he knew his shit.

They wouldn't let Mimi be in the interview room with us, of course. Someone took her statement outside.

I was exhausted by this point, but grateful for two things: First, they had really good coffee. Second, I wasn't being interviewed by either of the two idiots who'd showed up at my house the day after Cary died.

I got Wilson, a nice grizzled old guy who probably

lived out in Longmont and actually knew what he was doing.

Why he was on duty at three in the morning was beyond me, but maybe they'd woken him up, too. Arson and love triangles and murder and that kind of stuff not being your run-of-the-mill crimes in Boulder.

It took a while to give my statement since Selby kept interrupting, which was fine with me. It was boring and the only part that mattered was a discussion of what I was going to be charged with.

"We're looking at a charge of second-degree assault here," said Wilson. "If not first-degree."

Selby shook his head. "Give me a break."

Wilson looked all serious. "Reckless cause of bodily injury with a deadly weapon. COV."

"COV?" I asked.

"Crime of violence," explained Selby. "Absolute *horse* manure. This is third-degree assault, if that. First offense, mitigating circumstances, *and* self-defense."

"Your client hit the woman in the head with a fire poker and took half her teeth out. Broke her cheekbone. Lucky she didn't lose an eye."

Should've aimed higher.

"Are you going to put me in jail?" I asked.

"Of course not," said Selby.

"Maybe," said Wilson.

"Look, I just want to lie down." I said. "I'm really starting not to care whether it's at home or behind bars or whatever. I could go to sleep right on this table, with all the lights on. You want to put me in jail, go ahead. Just don't make me sit here for the rest of the night."

Selby got all incensed on my behalf. "Ms. Dare's lost a *serious* amount of blood tonight."

I held up my arm. "Seventeen stitches. Plus she stabbed me in the shoulder blade. I'd show you that bandage, too, but I'd have to take my shirt off."

"Wilson, let her go home," said Selby. "We can come back in the morning. She's not going anywhere. She's got little ones at home. Twin girls."

"Please," I said, trying to look all sweet and non-threateningly maternal for a change.

Wilson was weakening.

"Better yet," I said, "come to my house. I'll make my husband go out for bagels."

Hey, I'd seen Wilson checking out Selby's T-shirt from Moe's. The man was as tired as I was, not to mention hungry. And this wasn't a doughnut kind of town.

"Fine," Wilson said. "Ten o'clock."

Sometimes, you really gotta love small-town police forces.

Mimi drove me home. Selby had ridden his bike.

*   *   *

Four weeks later, Mimi and I were sitting in my living room.

The whole assault thing had been straightened out pretty quickly. No charges.

Setsuko hadn't made bail so I didn't have to worry about running into her shopping at King Soopers or Wild Oats.

I'd gotten the stitches out, and the scar probably wouldn't be all that noticeable once the redness had faded.

Dean's face still wrinkled up with concern whenever I pushed my sleeve back.

Or maybe guilt. Hard to say.

I promised I'd fly back out from Massachusetts if they needed me to testify, but nobody thought that would be necessary in any kind of a hurry.

Nice to have Mimi vouching for me, though. And McNally and I had done a hell of a job on that final article for the *New Times*, if I do say so myself.

They'd caught the first arsonist, in the meantime.

Turned out it was a homeless guy. History of fire-setting, pretty delusional.

He'd come in from Seattle. Wanted there for arson, too.

Bittler got fired, which was pretty great. He hadn't exactly been embezzling, but he hadn't been exactly on top of the financial stuff, either. And maybe the bosses had finally figured out what a little shit he was, generally.

Dean and I were working hard at patching things up.

At the very least, I had a feeling he wouldn't be tempted to fuck around on me again. Not for a long, long time, anyway.

And as my mother always said, you have the best shot with your first husband. Especially if you have kids together.

"You always run the risk of marrying the same person again anyway," she said. "I've certainly done that once or twice. Can't say I recommend it."

Dean was trying to be nicer to me. Not always succeeding, but the effort was commendable and it's not like we were getting more sleep, what with having twins.

He still couldn't get it up, either. But I really did believe at this point that it was because he was ashamed of himself, so it didn't seem quite so insulting.

Also, I'd lost twenty pounds in the last month. Shockingly horrible life events aren't conducive to having much of an appetite, as it turns out.

But I looked damn good.

And I had my mojo back in spades.

*   *   *

I had my driver's license now. Dean still had about six weeks' worth of work to finish at Ionix. And I told him he could clean the fucking house himself, considering—once the packers were through with everything.

I packed some clothes and some Cheese Nips, loaded the girls into the Galant, and started east without my husband.

Mom thought I was nuts, but I said we'd be staying in motels and eating at Denny's or whatever turned up. That seemed like a perfectly fine vacation to me—no cooking, and somebody else doing the dishes the whole way.

As for Boulder, I sure as shit wasn't going to miss it.

PART V

Fall 1995
Hamilton and Cambridge, Massachusetts

It is elsewhere, elsewhere, the neighbor-
  hood you seek.
The neighborhood you long for,
  where the gentle trolley—ding, ding—
    passes
through, where the adults are kind
and, better, sane,
that neighborhood is gone, no, never
existed, though it should have
and had a chance once...
        —Thomas Lux, "The Neighborhood
                of Make-Believe"

57

Listen, Bunny?" Dean's voice sounded wretched, on the phone. He was still in Boulder.

I'd found us a house, or most of one—the upper two floors of a staunch old Edwardian place out on leafy Huron Avenue, in the western part of Cambridge. We were waiting to close on the place, no more renting.

It was toast-colored clapboard surrounded by boxwood hedges and old roses, a jumble of beautiful little rooms painted dark green and pale coral and butter yellow and icy Gustavian blue. There were chair rails and linen closets and proper old wooden floors and banisters without a spot of orange Formica or carpeting anywhere.

There was an upper porch and a corner dining

room that felt like a tree house for grown-ups—two sides of it tall casement windows and two covered in French wallpaper, set at the height of the lushest, greenest boughs on the block.

While we waited, the girls and I were staying with my aunt Julie and uncle Bill in verdant Hamilton, on the North Shore.

Aunt Julie had made me a vodka tonic and steered me out onto their screen porch with the telephone when Dean called that night, waving me toward a beautiful old chintz-covered chaise longue and closing the porch's French doors discreetly behind her as she went back inside.

"Bunny?"

"I'm here," I said, watching three fireflies glide and swoop above the tall grass at the lawn's far edge.

"Ellis called tonight. From Cincinnati."

Not more about Setsuko, then. I didn't have to come back for the trial yet.

I hadn't realized I'd been holding my breath.

I let it out all at once, soothed by the brassy purr of crickets, out in the woods. The night air was still and hot, heavy with the promise of an impending thunderstorm.

"Are you all right?" I asked. "You sound exhausted."

Sad. Heartbroken.

"They saw this documentary on PBS last night. Ellis and Seamus."

"And she called you?"

Of course she had, she didn't know the number here.

"She was…," he said. "She started crying."

I sat up straight in the dark. "Is she okay? Are Perry and Hadley okay?"

"They're all fine."

I could barely hear him. "Dean?"

"The documentary," he said. "It was about kids with autism."

"*Why* would Ellis—"

"She said that all the kids were like Parrish. She started to freak out, watching it, and then Seamus turned to her halfway through the show and said 'You have to call Maddie.'"

"What the fuck does that even *mean*, 'they're all like Parrish'? That's such bullshit. Parrish was running around Julie and Bill's house all day today yelling 'Winnie-the-Pooh!' at the top of her lungs and laughing her ass off. She's *fine*."

"Of *course* she's fine," said Dean, sounding relieved.

"Jesus. This is ridiculous. It's just that Ellis is a hypochondriac, you know?"

"Absolutely."

"I mean, since *college*...," I said. "She's always having an allergic reaction to something or whatever. Usually when the dinner party's boring and she wants to leave early. Strawberries. Sushi. But what the *fuck*? Like, where does this shit even come from, you know? I've never understood it. Munchausen's or something."

"That's what *I* said."

"You told Ellis she had Munchausen's? Seriously?"

I knew the exact smile that'd be playing across his mouth in response to that. "Of course not, she's your friend. She's *our* friend. I just...I don't know. Told her Parrish is fine and she was overreacting."

"What'd she say to that?"

"She made me promise we'd check it out. And to call you. Not necessarily in that order."

"Sure. No biggie. The HMO stuff's all set up. I'll make an appointment. Both girls should get a checkup anyway. And then I'll call her back and tell her she's getting a little nutty about stuff like this."

"She means well," he said. "I mean, even if it's nuts, it's nice of her to be concerned, right?"

"Of course it is. But it's also crazy."

"She wants you to call. Do you have her number?"

"Yeah," I said. "But I'm going to bed soon. This is crazy. I'll call her in the morning."

"I miss you and the girls," he said.

Not necessarily in that order.

"We miss you. Are you getting everything wrapped up out there?"

"The house is spotless," he said. "The packers and moving truck came this morning, said they'd be in Cambridge in about three days. I've swabbed the whole place down so we'll get the deposit back, no problem."

"Play any Wagner?"

That made him laugh. In our first tiny apartment back in Syracuse, Dean used to blast "Ride of the Valkyries" on my piece-of-shit old tape deck whenever he mopped the kitchen floor.

"Where are you going to sleep?"

"I've got a couple of blankets in the living room, on the lovely orange shag. Bachelor heaven."

"Don't go getting any ideas," I said, trying to sound light.

"Of course not, Bunny."

Slightly easier to believe now that that fucking bitch Setsuko's in county lockup, bail denied.

"I love you," said my husband.

And maybe I'll believe that again, too, someday.

"Love *you*," I said.

"Kiss the girls for me?"

"Of course."

We hung up and I exchanged the phone for my cocktail, taking a cool bittersweet swallow of quinined vodka.

The night sky flashed purplish white: first zig-zag of lightning from out beyond the marsh.

I counted *one thousand six, one thousand...* before the thunder started rolling toward me across the heat-stilled acres of cattails and brine, kettledrums leading into some doom-riddled Beethoven finale.

The fireflies winked out with the first fat drops of rain. One more bright flash with an instantaneous crack-and-bang and then the rain rushed earthward full-tilt, hot and wet and soothing.

I set my glass down on one of Julie's delicate little side tables and clenched both fists, aching to pound the rest of Setsuko's pearly teeth down her swan-like throat.

Skanky cunt.

My HMO's wait for a new-patient pediatrician appointment was nine weeks, so I settled for one with a nurse practitioner two days later. I'd picked the office complex closest to our new house, which was an hour's drive from Aunt Julie's.

As we headed into the crush of Boston-driver morning insanity on Route 128 some butthead in a Camaro cut me off, and then traffic stopped altogether.

The Camaro pulled forward, and we were finally going slowly enough that I could read the sticker on its rear bumper:

NICE PEOPLE SWALLOW.

I hadn't laughed that hard in a year, at least. Maybe five.

The windows were down and the sound of me laughing frightened a dozen crows into the air, flapping and cawing in panic, swirling upward like a chunky whirlwind of soot.

I'd picked out our new health insurance plan, and to tell the truth I'd probably done a crappy job of it. Dean's new employer had mailed us jewel-toned pocket folders from three Boston HMOs, crammed with medical marketing fluff: large type, catchy bullet points, and big color photos of beaming, fit, and strategically ethnic catalog models. The fine-print stuff that actually mattered was tucked in behind on forgettable onionskin, extensively foot-noted, and utterly impenetrable.

Figuring it would've been impossible to figure out which of these three meds-keteers was apt to screw clients over the worst until after one of us had thoughtlessly lost a leg to a passing express train or come down with a bad case of leukemia, I crossed my fingers and signed us up with Harvard Pilgrim.

Fuck it, if I ever needed chemo, maybe I could show them Great-Grandmother Fabyan's Society of *Mayflower* Descendants certificate and ask for a discount.

Their Watertown medical center had a big parking lot with several hundred cars already jammed into it. Having forgotten the stroller Aunt Julie had found me at a garage sale back in Hamilton, I hoisted Parrish and India to my hips and started slogging across the acres of shimmering asphalt.

Pediatrics was on the fourth floor, and I was breathing hard by the time I deposited the girls next to a pile of plastic trucks and locomotives on the alphabet-carpeted waiting room floor. One of the ladies behind the chest-high reception counter took my name and co-pay before handing me a clipboard thick with triplicate forms and a ballpoint pen to which someone had affixed a large plastic daisy as an anti-theft device.

I kept a weather eye on the girls and attacked the blur of waivers, disclaimers, medical histories, state lead-testing requirements, vaccine schedules, and who-the-fuck-knows-what-Faustian-else for the next twenty minutes, stopping only to shake the cramps out of my hand.

I handed the forms back in and joined the girls on the floor for another half hour past our scheduled appointment.

Parrish had her thumb in her mouth and a plastic dump truck upside down in her lap so she could spin its front wheels with her free hand. India had unearthed one of those Fisher-Price wheel-of-fortune things that make different animal noises when you pulled the plastic cord.

After its ninetieth "moo," I was thinking this plaything would make a deeply satisfying skeet-shooting target, but India was loving it and talking right along with the voice inside, so I gritted my teeth and let her keep cranking it up.

Twenty minutes later, a young nurse took us back to the exam rooms.

Another fifteen minutes later, the nurse practitioner walked in.

She was wearing big glasses with Life Saver–green frames, white clogs, and fuchsia scrubs with black-and-white cartoon cats and dogs on them. She flipped through the paperwork, reading the girls' heights and weights aloud.

"Fraternal twins?" she asked.

"Yes," I said, gently stopping India from bunching up the exam-table paper with her fists, telling the nurse each girl's name.

"Full term?" she asked.

"Three days past the due date," I said, knowing the drill. "India was Baby A—seven pounds. Parrish was six pounds, nine ounces. Vaginal birth, no complications. Good Apgar scores. Up to date on their vaccines."

She smiled, jotting on her clipboard. "And you just moved here from Colorado? I hear it's pretty out there." Local chick—no r's in her "heres" or "theres."

"Couple of weeks ago. It's nice to be back on a coast."

"Massachusetts requires that all toddlers get a blood test for lead, okay?"

I winced, hating the idea of needles in my daughters' chubby little biceps. "Okay, I guess."

"We'll send you down to the lab for that. Any other concerns?"

I took a deep breath. "Well, Parrish's godmother Ellis saw some documentary on PBS a couple of nights after we stayed with her on our way east, and now she thinks Parrish might be autistic. I read up on it in a bookstore yesterday and to tell you the truth, the symptoms sounded more like me than either of my kids, but I told her I'd check it out."

The woman looked up at me, smirking with a little shake of her head. "Trust me. If your kid's not sitting in a corner spinning plates, you have nothing to worry about."

I was starting to like her. Maybe she could call Ellis for me, deflate the hypochondria a little.

"For the first year," I said, "Parrish hit all her developmental milestones before India did—rolling over, sitting up, standing. Our pediatrician back in New York got me all worked up about that. Now India's pulling ahead a little. I figure maybe twins take turns."

She nodded. "Kids do things at their own speed, in their own time. I get moms in here who have conniptions if they can't tick everything off on a monthly checklist in some parenting book. You've got the right attitude."

I thanked her.

"I mean it," she said. "Half the women in here, I just want to tell them to relax, you know? Ninety percent of good parenting is patience. I get the feeling you've mastered that part of the job."

"I don't know if it's patience so much as exhaustion, most days."

She grabbed another form from a brown-plastic display thing screwed to the wall next to the cotton-ball-and-tongue-depressor cabinet, handing it to me along with her pen and clipboard. "Fill this out for Parrish, all right? You can tell your friend you covered all your due diligence. Any kind of screening starts with communication, at this age. Meanwhile I'll get started with Miss India, here."

I sat on a chair with Parrish and the clipboard balanced on my lap.

The form had a list of ten questions beneath the heading "Speech and Language Milestones, 18–24 Months," with checkboxes for "yes" and "no."

The first few questions seemed silly, starting with *Do you know when your child is happy and when your child is upset?* Well, duh.

But toward the middle of the form I had to think harder.

Does your child point to objects?

India was patting the animals printed on the nurse's shirt, saying "Dog! Cat!" Parrish leaned into my shoulder, thumb still in her mouth as she hummed a little tune to herself.

About how many different words does your child use meaningfully that you recognize (such as baba for bottle; gaggie for doggie)?

I looked up at the nurse again. "This might be kind of a dumb question," I said, "but what does it mean when they ask about words your child uses 'meaningfully.' Parrish uses a lot of words and phrases, but sometimes it's like she just enjoys saying them, not like it's for any particular purpose."

The woman smiled at me, nodding. "It's probably a good idea to make a note of that on the back of the form, okay? Just describe the kinds of things she says, give them an idea."

She picked India up from the exam table. "All done, sweetie."

I carried Parrish over to her, taking my seat again with India in my lap.

"Hi, Mummie," she said, patting my cheeks with her hands.

"Hi, sweetheart," I replied, kissing the top of her head.

The form's next question made me grip the pen harder, my left arm tightening around India's waist.

When you call your child's name, does he/she respond by looking or turning toward you?

I checked the "no" box.

Does your child pretend to play with toys (for example, feed a stuffed animal, put a doll to sleep, put an animal figure in a vehicle)?

I thought about how the girls had just played in the waiting room, India interacting with the available toys, Parrish quietly spinning another upside-down truck's wheels as it lay in her lap.

Another "no."

Does your child follow simple commands without gestures?

I put the pen down.

Seven no's.

The nurse pressed her stethoscope to Parrish's bare chest and my daughter let loose a peal of laughter, kicking her bare heels with delight against the exam table's vinyl-upholstered front panel.

"Is that ticklish?" said the nurse, smiling along with her.

"Ticklish!" cooed Parrish, kicking her feet again.

Nothing to worry about. Nothing at all.

"Beautiful, healthy girls," said the nurse, when she'd finished up.

I gave her the clipboard back and thanked her.

She glanced down at the questionnaire at the top of the pile. "They'll call you at the front desk with paperwork you'll need for the blood test in a few minutes. And to make appointments for the girls' next checkups."

"Okay," I said.

She tapped a finger against the edge of the papers. "Let's make you one with speech and language, too."

I must have blanched because she put a reassuring hand on my shoulder the moment she looked up.

"It's just routine, honey," she said, "and I think Parrish is absolutely fine, all right? Kids develop at their own pace—like we were talking about. But they'll want to take a look whenever you answer 'no' to more than three of these questions. It's a precaution, that's all ... test her hearing, things like that. I'll see if I can get you in this week. Then you can call your friend, tell her everything's checked out."

I nodded.

"She's gonna be just fine, I promise. And you can tell your friend that autism's incredibly rare. Less than one case in fifteen thousand births. Then *Rain Man* comes out, right? Another thing for the nervous moms to obsess over. But we've *never* had an autistic child in this practice. I've been here twenty years, and I've seen just about everything else."

"Okay," I said, incredibly relieved.

"You've got two terrific kids here, and you're doing a great job with them. I don't want you to worry about this. You look exhausted, and Lord knows twins will run you ragged. Not to mention you just moved here, right?"

"I drove across with the girls, from Colorado," I said.

Her eyes went wide. "Alone?"

I shrugged. "Yeah."

"Now, *that* takes guts."

"My husband still has some work to finish up out there. He's due in tomorrow night."

"My Teddy ever tried making me drive our kids cross-country without him, back in the day? He'd *still* be sleeping in the garage."

"Actually it was kind of fun," I said. "I blew bubbles for the girls to chase around on rest-stop lawns every couple of hours. *And* I didn't have to do any dishes, which was totally awesome. The only bummer was when we got to Kansas City late at night during an undertakers' convention. Wasn't a motel room for miles—I had to drive all the way to Leavenworth."

She laughed. "See? You're one tough cookie."

India decided this was the perfect moment to trot out her new favorite sentence: "Mummie farted!"

I bit my lip, trying not to encourage her by laughing.

"That India's gonna be *trouble*," said the nurse, shaking her head as she stifled a grin of her own.

58

Sometimes, the worst possible shit in life unfolds slowly, inexorably. And I think maybe that's harder to take than sudden disaster—tornadoes, car crashes, spontaneous combustion. That kind of stuff, it slaps you into fight-or-flight instantly. You can't even think about it. You're just there and you have to dive in, no questions asked. You make it or you don't.

The slow tragedies, though...suffering that inches forward just outside your line of sight, one appalling grain at a time, until it's too late? You look back and can't believe you didn't know, didn't appreciate the last precious, unsullied time while it was building all around you, eating away at the walls and the floorboards and your very marrow.

The most awful thing that's ever happened to me

took a month. Well, it was happening even before that month. The month was how long it took for the experts to weigh it and poke and pry and type up the reports.

First the nurse practitioner. Then an audiologist, who passed me on to a speech pathologist in the office next door.

That prompted a diagnostic panel, two weeks later: eight clinicians, a playroom with a one-way mirror, signing release forms so they could video-tape the session.

Me and Parrish in that little room for two hours, people coming in and out. Colored blocks. Different toys. Tests. Questions. Play-Doh.

All of them trying to get her to look up, engage, speak.

Parrish did cheerfully utter what had lately become her two favorite phrases: "Happy Birthday!" and "Winnie-the-Pooh!"

Apropos of nothing in particular. Giggling. Not really looking at any of us.

And still, I didn't know.

None of it scared me, and it fucking well should have.

After the little white room there was a big beige one. A round table, lots of chairs.

We all sat down. I had Parrish on my lap.

And they didn't say anything, not at first.

Or look me in the eye.

I smiled. "So?"

The woman directly across from me put down her clipboard. Dark-haired, nice-looking. Maybe ten years older than me. Child psychiatrist.

"Madeline," she said, leaning forward so her lab coat bunched up a little, hands clasped on the table in front of her.

She looked up at me.

"Yes?"

"Parrish is a wonderful little girl," she said. "Gorgeous. Very sweet. And you're wonderful *with* her."

"Thank you," I said.

"It's... We've agreed on a diagnosis."

"Okay." I rubbed Parrish's belly, jiggled her a little on my knees.

"This is what we classify as PDD-NOS," the woman said.

I waited.

She smiled at me just a little, her eyes crinkling up. "That stands for 'Pervasive Developmental Disorder, Not Otherwise Specified.'"

I nodded. "Um, okay... I don't know what that means."

"It's relatively recent terminology, actually," she

said. "Describing a newly recognized, well, subtype of an existing disorder."

"Of which disorder?"

I still didn't get it, that her next word would be the poleax, whistling down toward the back of my neck.

Sharp enough to slice clean through a sheet of paper, a column of bone.

One word to cleave my life in two: before/after. Ignorance/devastation.

"Autism," she said.

It was twilight out, when I carried Parrish up the stairs to our new place. Everything soft outside, purple.

Dean was on the sofa in the living room, watching India play on the floor.

I stopped in the kitchen doorway, Parrish quiet, straddling my hip.

How the fuck do I even begin?

He looked up at me. His eyes were red, the lids swollen and puffy. He inhaled a ragged breath and I watched tears slide down his cheeks.

I walked over to the sofa, sat down beside him.

He knows already. Okay.

He reached for Parrish, pulled her over onto his lap, pressed her head against his chest. He rubbed her back and she started sucking her thumb, relaxing into him.

"Bunny?" he said.

I took his nearest hand, twined our fingers together.

His breath caught in his throat again.

"Shhhh," I said. "It's okay. We're going to get through this."

He shook his head. "Setsuko hung herself last night."

I took my hand back, then got to my feet and reached for Parrish.

"Please tell me the bitch is actually *dead*," I said.

Parrish wrapped her legs around my waist, laid her head to rest against my collarbone.

Dean slumped forward, and then he had the gall to *sob*.

"For fuck's sake," I said. "Tell me she got *that* right, at the very least. The suspense is killing me."

He didn't say anything, just nodded.

"Excellent," I said. "*Outstanding.*"

Dean looked up at me, haggard.

"Oh, please," I said. "You expect me to feel *sorry* for her?"

He didn't answer that. Didn't ask how it had gone with all the doctors that day.

More tears.

I shrugged. "News flash: *Madame Butterfly* had a happy ending."

I turned away from him, lowered Parrish gently to the floor beside India. Stood up again.

"Bunny—"

"Tell you what," I said. "I'm going to go to the kitchen. Pour myself a beer. So I don't fucking punch you in the face right now."

He had the grace to blanch, I'll give him that.

I got my beer—last bottle in the icebox. Popped the top off. Carried it back into the living room.

Dean's head was bowed, hanging low and slack from his shoulders. A bull resigned to the coup de grâce, one he richly deserved.

I took the chair farthest away from him. Put my feet up on the coffee table.

The beer was good. Cold and bitter.

"Ask me how my day was, Dean," I said. "You haven't remembered to do that in a while."

His lips got all tight. Pissy looking.

I actually laughed at that, surprising myself. It made my throat hurt.

"Jesus Christ," I said. "You worthless sack of *shit*."

He crossed his arms across his splayed knees, brought his forehead down to rest on them.

"She killed *Cary*. She tried to kill *me*."

Our daughter has autism.

"I know," he said, voice muffled by his sleeve.

"You know nothing, Dean."

Then something else occurred to me.

"So who told you?" I asked.

"Who told me what?"

"Who told you she was dead. You obviously didn't know when I left this afternoon or you would've started sniveling *then*. So someone called you here, *at our house, while you were taking care of India*."

He closed his eyes.

They snapped open again when I grabbed him by the chin and yanked his head around so he was facing me. "Answer me, you *asshole*. Who called to tell you?"

"Her father."

"That bitch's *father* had our home number?"

He couldn't look at me.

"Did *she*?"

No answer.

"Had you been talking to *her*, too? Taking collect calls from jail?"

"Bunny, it was my fault. All of it. Everything that happened. Because I was selfish, because I didn't allow myself to think it could hurt anyone. All the damage. To you. To Cary..." His voice broke.

"You're damn right it was your fault," I said.

And then I hawked up everything I had and spat it into his face.

"She tried to fucking *kill* me. Dean. She tried to fucking *hack* me to death with a fucking knife so she could steal *my* children. She told me she'd be a better mother than me, and that they'd love her more, and that they wouldn't remember me because they would be too young when she killed me."

He wept. I'll give him that.

"And you know what else she told me?" I asked.

No answer, of course.

"She told me she'd be a better wife. That you loved her more than you loved me."

I hadn't told him any of that, back in Boulder. I'd been too afraid to discover he believed it, too.

"That's not true," he said. "For God's sake—"

"Fuck you, Dean Bauer. I'm a better wife, but Setsuko was *exactly* the wife you deserve."

"Bunny—"

"Because you're still in *love* with her. Even though she tried to kill the mother of your children, and even though she's fucking dead."

I stood up.

"Let me tell you how *my* day was, Dean. Not that you care."

His head dropped again.

"Our daughter Parrish was diagnosed with

autism this afternoon," I said. "*That's* how my fucking day was. And I hope you rot in hell."

Dean fell to his knees, bellowing like he'd been gored through the heart.

As well he should.

He wrapped his long arms tight around my thighs, pulling me close so he could bury his face in my belly.

I grabbed a fistful of hair and yanked his head back.

"Get off me," I said.

"Bunny. *Please.*"

I let go of his hair, but only after he'd dropped his arms.

"Do not *touch* me," I said. "Do not say another fucking *word* to me, you worthless, revolting sack of shit."

I walked away, squatting down with the girls.

They were unfazed. Happy.

India said, "Love, Mummie."

Parrish added, "Happy birthday."

I was back again, fully in the right-there, the right-then.

Alive. Brimming. Grateful—to my beloved dead—to all those I'd lost, whom I could feel around me, right then.

Thank you for this.

For my daughters.
For what I have left: sweetness and light.
It's enough. More than enough.
More than I deserve.
Let me be brave enough to merit it.
Thank you.

Sweetness and light: what my father used to call me.

Words I had wanted to redeem, ever after.

I rose to my feet.

"Make our children something to eat," I said, not looking back at Dean. "Give them a bath. You love them so much more than you've ever loved me, and they both need you right now."

Two hours later India was sleeping, tucked into her crib.

I sat on the girls' bedroom floor in the dark, cross-legged, stroking Parrish's fair hair as she dozed in my lap.

The exquisite oval of her face was silver-gilt in the moonlight, touched with the palest blue. Mouth parted slightly, long lashes curving dark against her cheeks.

Even in her beautiful sleep, a tide I could not stem was bearing my daughter ceaselessly away: out of my arms, out of herself, out of the world.

She looked like her father, she looked like me.

She looked like everything I'd ever wanted. Everything I'd ever had to lose.

Hostage to fortune.

I didn't know it yet, not that night: how much I *still* had to lose, and that I would never, ever again have a moment of unadulterated joy.

I could have survived Setsuko. I could have learned to be happy again, even with Dean. We might even have come out of it stronger, he and I. Learned to care about each other more tenderly, around the broken places.

But the woman I had been did not survive losing my second-born daughter, although she is still very much alive as I write this, these many years later.

Long before the diagnosis, she was being spirited away. I hadn't known it.

I will always *always* despise myself for that. For every moment of her that I squandered.

Everything since has been underscored by that heartbreak. All gains tempered by the dull impasto of that loss, and all light dimmed.

I would learn, quickly, that Setsuko meant nothing by comparison. Dean's faithlessness even less.

I'm so glad I didn't have to know all of it, that night: how very much sorrow I had yet to wade through. How much deeper into that ugly water I'd be forced to walk.

Until it was over my head, by fathoms and fathoms.

As it remains, and always will.

You do become accustomed to that, though not easily. Mimi was right.

But I couldn't have borne having to comprehend *any* of what was yet to come, that night. Let alone all of it.

She was right about that, too.

Everyone's past is filled with pain enough. We don't need to see what's yet to be endured.

I leaned down in the darkness, brushing my lips across Parrish's, basking in the soft, sweet exhalation of her breath.

Like clover, like honey, like summer.

Fireflies. Innocence. Racing and tumbling barefoot across wide green lawns while the grown-ups watch over us, luminous in the porch light; shimmering and elegant, behind the screens.

Of course they're there. We don't have to look, sure they'll keep us safe forever.

A blessing, not knowing all that we must lose. All that will be sacrificed.

I gave Parrish another kiss.

My darling girl.

My changeling.

ACKNOWLEDGMENTS

This novel took far longer to write than I intended. Some excruciating stuff happened during the years it took me to finish it: my father committed suicide, I got divorced, and I moved from one coast of the country to another.

I am tremendously grateful for the grace, patience, and wisdom of my stellar agent Amy Rennert and my two magnificent editors at Grand Central Publishing, Celia Johnson and Emily Griffin. (Les Pockell, you too. We all miss you.)

My daughter Grace is just an entirely amazing person and friend. Also, she is *really* funny. मैं तुम्हें मेरी सुंदर बेटी से प्यार

Without the heroic members of my writing group—Madeleine Butler, Karen Catalona, Daisy

James, Sharon Johnson, Kirsten Saxton, and emeriti Charles King and Karen Murphy—this book would not exist, and neither would any claim to sanity I might have left.

Kelly Davidian very kindly vetted the fire stuff for me. She is awesome. I'm sure I've still made mistakes, but she did the very best she could to keep me from looking like a total idiot.

Candace Andrews and Rae Helmsworth and Andi Shechter and Ariel Zeitlin (alphabetically) were kind, thoughtful, and encouraging about this work. As they are about everything. I am damn lucky to have them as my pals.

I am also deeply thankful to my fellow bloggers and backbloggers at Murderati and The Lipstick Chronicles, because you all made me feel like I had "home" with me no matter where I was actually living.

There are many, many people who did yeoman work helping to maintain my mental equilibrium over the past three years. If you made me laugh or listened to me weep (on the phone or in person or by email) when the shit was hitting the fan and throughout the aftermath, you know who you are and I hope you know I seriously love you for it. That goes triple for you, Mom.

Riegert...dude, you rock.

And lastly, as promised, I'd very much like to thank Evyn Goldstein, the really cool kid I sat next to on the plane to Vancouver last summer, for making me laugh even though I didn't get any sleep the night before. I hope you and your family had a really, *really* great time in China.

ABOUT THE AUTHOR

CORNELIA READ grew up in New York, California, and Hawaii. A reformed debutante who currently lives in New York City, she is the author of three previous books: *A Field of Darkness, The Crazy School,* and *Invisible Boy.* To learn more about the author, you can visit her website at CorneliaRead .com.